FOOTSTEPS IN AMBER

Kalianne VanDusen

ISBN: (Paperback) 979-8-9998840-0-8
ISBN: (ebook) 979-8-9998840-1-5

Cover art by Diletta De Santis
www.artstation.com/didies

A Patchwork Printing book

First edition: 2025

To my partner and best friend, Shadow,
who read every chapter as it was finished.
To the friends who supported me
through this whole tumultuous adventure,
Eric and Matthew
To Anya, without whom I would still be on the fifth re-write,
and Sorecco's song wouldn't exist.

I love you all.

And to everyone else who answered my questions
and helped me through this,
Thank you.

CHAPTER ONE

Arrival in Natari

Tzedef watched the gap between the pair of massive cliffs with calm anticipation. It had been a long journey east from Fernil to the Permani Isles, the furthest west point of the continent of Malfeir, and soon it would all be worth it.

Footsteps on the deck approached him as the tide pushed the ship closer to the entrance to the harbor and, he was sure, closer to his goal.

"Sir," the footsteps stopped, and Tzedef glanced down at the halfling who had spoken. "We're getting ready to head into port. If you could wait in your cabin, someone'll call for you when we're proper settled, yeah?"

"Aye." Tzedef said, his voice a basso rumble as he nodded. "I'll get out of your way. I merely wished to get a look at the isle."

"Of course, Master Healer." The halfling nodded and glanced disinterestedly landward before turning expectant eyes back on him.

Tzedef sighed silently, took one more long look at the massive ballistas perched on the peak of each cliff and turned, heading back to his cabin.

The cabin he'd rented was a tiny thing, and in his opinion he had spent far too much of the last few months inside it. Still, it couldn't be helped; the trip across the Serlin Sea had been plagued with unseasonable weather, so he'd needed to stay out of the way as much as possible.

The captain and crew had handled themselves admirably through the odd storms, but Tzedef's services as a medic and healer had still been requested a few times. He'd done what he could to the best of his ability, as was outlined in the contract that dictated the terms of his passage, and the sailors had seemed grateful to have their hurts and illnesses mended.

His cabin was dimly lit by a crystal he didn't dare touch, embedded in one of the overhead beams, but it was bright enough that his vision didn't shift to the shades of grey of his night vision. A mercy that he'd been more than glad of many times. As nice as it was, seeing at night, Tzedef still enjoyed color, and had no wish to lose that ability.

It was an irrational fear; he had never heard any credible reports of people losing their color sight from too long spent in darkness, but it was still a small, private dread.

With a soft sigh, Tzedef settled on the bunk that was attached to the wall and closed his eyes, easily falling into a light meditation as he contemplated what steps he would need to take when he reached land properly. Hecate had told him what to look for, and given him a general direction, but the details were up to him, and *something* about the approaching island was niggling at the back of his mind. Hopefully, with a bit of concentration, he'd be able to pinpoint what it was.

"Master Healer?" The voice, coupled with a soft knock at the door, brought him back to awareness.

Tzedef twitched, opening his gleaming red eyes to blink at the door. "Yes?"

"We've docked now." It was one of the sea elves; identical triplets that prided themselves on their ability to confuse others as to which was whom. They had delighted in performing increasingly ridiculous stunts, attempting to get reactions from him until Inral, the quartermaster, had put her taloned foot down.

"Thank you." Tzedef climbed to his feet, his tail sliding under the bunk and sweeping his bag out from underneath it. A moment's work retrieved his mace, the weapon that had served him on the battlefields at the edges of the Evernight, from the sea chest at the end of the bed and when he opened the door, it was to find that the sea elf was already gone. Eager, no doubt, to finish her duties so that she might take as much advantage of her shore leave as possible. Still, being left on his own was no difficulty, and so Tzedef headed up onto the deck.

The early evening air was cool against his scales, with the faint bite of autumn promising that winter was well on its way. But Tzedef didn't have a chance to enjoy the fresh air, because 'fresh' was hardly the word one would use to describe the air at the docks. Instead, the reek of fish guts, seaweed, and gull droppings lay thick in the air, and Tzedef's muzzle wrinkled at the stink.

"Welcome to Yunxing!" Captain Teralia, a middle-aged rabbitfolk with long ears and grey-brown fur called across the deck, waving him over. "It looks like we made it in time for the harvest festival!"

"Marvelous." Tzedef said dryly as he approached, and she laughed at him.

"Don't be so dour. Everybody likes festivals!"

"Festivals are fine." Tzedef agreed absently, surveying the harborfront from his vantage on deck. "It is the crowds I'm not overly fond of."

The harborfront was thick with all manner of beings, and the docks themselves were swarming with sailors, loading and unloading and shouting this way and that until it all blended into an indecipherable cacophony of industry. Up close, the port was a seething mass of life that ebbed and flowed in much the same way as the sea he'd just crossed, and, much like that sea, it would swallow him whole if he were unwary.

"Thank you for your services." He turned politely toward Captain Teralia, and she waved him off with an easy smile.

"You paid well enough, and filled your end of our contract besides. I wouldn't mind takin' you on again, if you find what you're lookin' for before we head back across."

He turned his attention back to her fully. "And when would that be?"

"Sometime next spring. With how bad the storms were, I don't wanna risk another trip across the Serlin this year. Still, Yunxing isn't our last stop. We're headin' for Tyona after a bit of a restock, and we'll spend the winter there. If you want passage to the mainland, we can do that. Just give it… mmmm, a week? Week and a half?" She shrugged and glanced up at him. "If you want passage, check back in a day or two and I'll have a better idea of how long the resupply'll take."

Tzedef nodded slowly, thinking. A week wouldn't be long enough for him to canvas the entire island, but with a festival on there would likely be bards from every island in the Permani chain, all gathered to make what coin they could. If anyone would know anything about an ambered castle, it would be the bards.

"Very well. I shall return in a day or three and let you know if I'll be needing the cabin again."

"Great!" she chirped, and reached up to clap him on the back. "Sounds like a plan. Was there anythin' else you needed before we start the unloadin'?"

Tzedef grimaced internally at the overly familiar woman, but kept his expression mild as he shook his head. "No, thank you, unless you are familiar with any inns in the area?"

Teralia paused, wincing. "Yeah? But also no. See," she hurried to explain, "it's the harvest festival. I can give you a couple of names, but like as not they're gonna be full up."

This time, his grimace was entirely external.

"Wonderful. I'll take those names regardless, if you please; I may as well have somewhere to start looking."

"Sure." She nodded easily, and rattled off the names of three inns, all of which she promised were within twenty minutes of the harbor. Tzedef nodded along as she spoke, then thanked her and bade her farewell before heading down the gangplank.

Being down on the dock was worse than looking at it from the deck of the ship. People crowded, and bumped, and pushed, and shoved; jostling each other back and forth until one couldn't walk in a straight line but instead had to take a meandering path through the crowd. At nearly seven feet tall, with the muscles gained from wielding his mace and wrestling recalcitrant patients into place, Tzedef was lucky that his bulk made it easier for him to plow his way towards the gates.

The crowd followed him up through the gates and past the guards easily enough, then spread out and thinned as people peeled off to go their separate ways. Previous experience had taught him that allowing himself to look lost, particularly in a port city, was a surefire way of inviting trouble, so he glanced around quickly to orient himself against Captain Teralia's directions and a moment's thought had him following the part of the crowd that headed left. Absently, Tzedef reached up to rub at his amulet. A Wheel of Hecate that he had commissioned several years ago, it was a piece of silver about an inch and a half across that hung from his neck on a leather cord, and it was precious to him.

The gesture wasn't new; he'd fallen into the habit

during the last year or so of the war between Tremaine and Yaelin, when more and more often he'd found himself needing the care and comfort of his goddess. She hadn't answered in any way that he could directly contribute to her, but the act itself had granted him a measure of calm and clarity that he had sorely needed. Now, all he needed was a touch of guidance. A hint of where to go that would best help him meet his goals.

Unbidden, his feet turned the next corner, and soon enough Tzedef found himself lost in a maze of twisting streets. By the time he reached a street lit mostly by red lanterns and red crystals, the last vestiges of evening light were just fading. People of all races were wandering the street, some dressed as provocatively as possible, while others were dressed in the more muted garb of travelers and sailors; clothes that wouldn't show dirt or stains easily, and were hard wearing. Still others wore the bright colors and fancy dress of festival goers, and perfumes and incense hung heavy in the air, covering but not disguising the scent of the harbor not far away.

Tzedef stopped, resisting the urge to sigh heavily. Of all the places to just happen to wander to, the red light district was not first on his list of places to find lodging.

"Your sense of humor needs work, my lady." He murmured under his breath, and eyed the nearest door contemplatively. On the one hand, he had no interest in the wares that were peddled at such establishments. On the other, even with a festival on, it was likely that there would be rooms available, albeit at much higher prices than most inns would charge. If he explained that he simply wished for a room for the night, and not companionship, then —

The thought cut off as a nearby catling approached him, dressed only in a complicated array of delicate silver chains, scarves, and veils that served to accentuate his impeccably groomed smoke-grey fur and seductive smile.

"Lookin' for some company, handsome?"

Tzedef shook his head. "No, thank you. I am searching for lodgings. Could you perhaps give me directions to somewhere I could spend the night?"

The catling grimaced sympathetically. "I would, but Ma'am'll get on me if I'm not workin'. You sure I can't tempt you?"

Tzedef shook his head again. "Thank you, but no."

"Right, well…" The catling glanced over his shoulder toward the buildings on the other side of the street, then looked back at him again. "If you follow this street back south a ways, and turn right when you hit the cobbler's shop, that street'll lead you to the more respectable parts o' town. There'll be inns and things there."

Tzedef nodded slowly. "South, and right when I find the cobbler's shop. How will I know the cobbler's shop?"

"'S got a boot shaped sign out front, an' it smells o' leather." The catling replied promptly, and Tzedef nodded again, fishing in his belt pouch for a couple of copper coins which he passed along. Sharp teeth gleamed in the low light as he beamed at Tzedef, then turned and sauntered off, his long, fluffy tail swaying in his wake.

He should have simply followed Captain Teralia's

directions to begin with, Tzedef sighed to himself as he turned around and began heading south.

"THIEF!" The woman's shriek from behind him made him jump, then pause and turn to look.

Sure enough, there was a person bolting down the street; a half-orc, judging from the smaller stature, greyish skin, and heavy tusks. He wore simple, rough cut clothing, and didn't *seem* to have anything in his hands that could have been stolen, but—

A woman, presumably the woman who'd screamed, came darting out of an alleyway behind the half-orc, frantically trying to set her clothing to rights as she scrambled to chase the man.

Ah. That would explain it, then.

"Thief!" she shouted again, her wooden sandals clattering against the cobblestones, and several of the workers moved to converge on him, but he put on a burst of speed that left them in the dust.

Tzedef was now the only thing between the presumed thief and freedom.

He sighed, stepped into the man's path, and braced himself.

Getting hit directly in the sternum by two hundred pounds of well-muscled half-orc running flat out was not Tzedef's idea of a good time, but he'd braced himself well enough that his own mass was able to absorb the impact, and he caught the man's shoulders.

"Hello, friend." Tzedef said mildly.

The half-orc froze. Just for a moment, but it was

long enough for the woman to catch up, and an even dozen of the other streetwalkers to gather in an unhappy circle around them.

"Lemme go!" He snarled, shoving away from Tzedef who, obligingly, let go, only to watch with an arched eye-ridge as the half-orc fell over from the force of his own shove.

"Fuck!"

Several people snickered as the half-orc scrambled to his feet, and his cheeks darkened with embarrassment.

"Fucker! What's yer *problem*!?"

Tzedef shrugged. "I have no problem. These fine people, on the other hand, seem to have a bone to pick with you."

"Yer gonna listen to *whores*?" The incredulity in his voice was so thick that Tzedef resisted rolling his eyes with an effort of will.

"I am going to listen to people who *provide a service*, about someone whom, it seems, has taken advantage of them."

"I'll fucking say." The catling from before said, shouldering his way through the crowd with a scowl on his face. "What, Rugar, you got blacklisted from so many brothels you decided to start trying your luck with the streetwalkers?"

"Shaddup!" The half-orc, Rugar, apparently, snarled, and half turned to face the catling while still trying to keep Tzedef in view. "I en't got blacklisted from shit!"

"Liar!" someone sang mockingly, "*I* heard that you

treated poor Kayala so bad that she's still abed! And *then* you had the utter *gall* to try to walk out without flashing so much as a cop for the back half-payment!"

The catling's tail flirted from one side to the other, his amber eyes bright with irritation. "And Kayala's not the only one, either. *My* Ma'am blacklisted you two weeks ago, and I know that Ma'am Shirly and Ma'am Cesca blacklisted you just after. In fact," he glanced around, "I don't think there's a single brothel in the district that *hasn't* blacklisted you at this point. And if you're just gonna pull the same shit with the streetwalkers, then I say we just finish what the madams started."

"Oh yeah?" Rugar laughed, "What're you gonna do, shithead? What're *any* of you gonna do about it?"

"All in favor of banning this asshole from the district entirely?" The catling's voice rang out clearly over the crowd, and there was a resounding *'Aye!'* from not only the small crowd surrounding Rugar and Tzedef, but from people standing in doorways or hanging out windows up and down the street.

He smirked, the expression very much at home on his muzzle, and cocked one hip, making the silver chains around his waist jingle softly. "Well then. Sounds like it's unanimous. Time for you to go, little man."

"You an' *what feckin' army*?"

Tzedef, having watched and listened to the whole situation with slowly growing amusement, went to step forward and volunteer his services to 'escort' Rugar out of the district, only to be cut off by the woman who'd initially been chasing the half-orc stepping forward and shoving him backwards. Judging from the gobsmacked expression on his face as he stumbled back, Rugar hadn't been expecting either the shove, or to actually be *moved* by it.

"Me." she said, and shoved him again as hard as she could as the crowd parted behind him.

"Bitch!" Rugar snarled, and swung at her.

Tzedef's hand caught his wrist before it could make contact with the woman.

"And that," he said mildly, "is enough of *that*, I think."

One flurry of movement later, Tzedef had Rugar's arm twisted around and bent behind his back as he howled obscenities.

"Miss." Tzedef nodded to the woman who'd shoved Rugar, then tilted his head towards his captive. "I believe he owes you something?"

"Damn straight he do." She said sharply, and stepped forward, rifling through his pockets and dodging his flailing other hand with careless aplomb until she found his coin purse; only then did she dance backwards, out of reach.

Tzedef watched as her face soured at the thinness of the purse, and when she opened it and poured out three silver coins and a scant handful of copper, it darkened further.

"You *bastard*!"

And back she came, aiming a kick at Rugar's balls.

Tzedef tugged him just slightly out of the way, and

the kick landed on his inner thigh instead, making him swear even more vociferously.

"He is restrained." Tzedef explained patiently when the woman glared at him about it. "Unless you wish me to release him so that it might be a more fair fight...?"

"Tch..." she scoffed, and turned towards the opening in the crowd. "Fine. Bastard's gettin' off *lucky*. Fuckin' *three sil... Asshole...* Come on. Bring 'im this way."

Tzedef cocked his head, curious despite himself, and maneuvered Rugar in front of himself before propelling him down the street after the woman.

She led him down the street, back towards where the red lanterns stopped abruptly, and paused on the red light side of a line of bricks in the street that were a different color than the surrounding cobblestones.

"Shove 'im on that side." She said, waving, and Tzedef arched one eye-ridge, but did as he was told, pushing the man over the line of bricks.

"You can let 'im go, now."

Tzedef blinked, but did so, and Rugar wrenched himself out of Tzedef's hands as soon as his grip loosened, then whirled on his heel to lunge at the woman, a snarl on his face.

She didn't flinch, and Rugar slammed into the air directly in front of her with a faint crunch of breaking bone.

Curtains in the upstairs of nearby buildings flickered as the half orc howled in pain, staggering backwards and clutching his mouth with both hands.

"Me tooth! Me tooth! You bitch you broke me fuckin' *tooth*!"

"She did no such thing." Tzedef said, irritation bleeding into his tone. Honestly. Fresh off the boat, and he stumbled into *this* ridiculousness. All he wanted was an inn and a *bed*. "One might call it just punishment from the gods, though attributing your own stupidity to the gods may well be considered unbearable insult. What did you think would happen, when she made no move to defend herself?"

"Shut the fuck up!" Rugar roared, and swung at Tzedef, then *howled* in pain as his fist crumpled against thin air. "You bastard! I'll show you! You gon' *regret* this!"

But the effect of the threat was somewhat ruined by his watering eyes and his stumbling steps backwards.

"Mmm." Tzedef hummed, his tail flicking with silent irritation. "I'm sure."

"You watch y'fuckin' *back*!" Rugar snarled, then turned and hurried away down the empty street, cradling his broken hand gingerly.

Tzedef watched him go, then sighed and turned to look properly at the woman next to him.

She wasn't bad looking, for a human. Golden brown skin glowed warm and healthy in the light of the nearest crystal lamp, and dark hair shone sleek and clean. Dark brown eyes watched him warily, but a spark of intelligence and hidden good humor softened them.

"Do you need healing?" He asked, "From what the others said, he has not been particularly kind to any of his past acquaintances. If you do, I can do that for you, if you like."

She frowned. "Yer a priest, then? Or a cleric? From one of th' other islands?"

Tzedef nodded. "A cleric, yes, as well as a medic, but not from one of the other islands. I hail from Yaelin, in Fernil. You might say that healing is something of a specialty."

"How much?"

Tzedef arched an eye ridge and considered her for a long moment. "How much would you ordinarily pay a healer, here?"

"Five sil." She said cautiously, and Tzedef nodded slowly. It wasn't the least he'd ever been paid for a healing, and...

"Three sil, and you help me find lodgings for the night."

"An' if that takes all night?" She demands, offended. "I gots money t'make! Rent that needs paid!"

Tzedef grimaced and conceded the point. "Very well. Assist me at least with information on which inns in the area are affordable, and which are there simply to cheat travelers of their coin, and we shall call it even."

"There ain't gon' be room at th' inns, now." She warned him. "With th' festival on an' all. Natari's packed with people from th' smaller islands, same as every year."

He sighed, reaching up to knuckle the spot between his eyes, hoping to stave off a burgeoning headache, and the woman watched him for a long moment.

"Right. Yes. I was warned. More the fool am I for not

simply staying on the ship…"

"Tell ya what." She said abruptly. "I'll take ya to th' temples. Ya c'n get a bunk there, most like, an' if ya can't…" She hesitated, looking uncertain. "How serious's yer god about oaths 'n such?"

Tzedef blinked at the non sequitur. "Fairly so? Hecate is not a trickster goddess, or a goddess of thieves or the like. Why?"

"Swear t'yer goddess that ya won't bring no hurts t' me an' mine, an', if there's no room at th' temples, ya c'n come'n kip at my place for th' night."

He stared at her.

"What?" she asked defensively, shifting uncomfortably, "I ain't think yer a bad sort, ya helped me run off that fecker, after all, but I gots t'be sure, yanno? I ain't stupid."

"No." He shook his head. "That is not at all what I was thinking. I just… that is uncommonly generous of you."

She scoffs. "Not hardly. I'll still be wantin' that oath, after all, if th' temples're full."

"Very well." Tzedef nodded, then stretched out his hand. "I'll need to touch you, for the healing."

The woman's hesitation was barely perceptible, and then her hand slid into his, warm flesh to cool scales, and he reached up to touch his amulet.

"Lady Hecate, guardian of gates, grant me the light of healing that I might soothe wounds and ease pain."

Saffron light flared mutedly between their palms,

and the woman startled, jerking in his grasp before relaxing abruptly.

"Oh, that's so much better!" She sighed, and graced him with a small, genuine smile. "Thank you."

Tzedef inclined his head, taking his hand back and lowering the other from his amulet.

"It was no trouble."

"It was a trouble t'me, an' ya fixed it, so take th' thanks." She retorted, then started past him, crossing the line of bricks and heading south. "C'mon, th' temples're this way. I'm called Chase, by th' way. 'Snice t'meet ya."

"Tzedef." He introduced himself, and followed, his long legs eating up the distance and letting him keep pace with Chase as she trotted down narrow streets, and dark alleys overhung with layers of the massive seashells that every building he'd seen seemed to be roofed with.

"Gotta go this way." Chase explained, leading him down yet another too-narrow alleyway. "Else we'll get all caught up in festival shit, yanno? Ya c'n go explorin' on yer own once ya got yer stuff stowed safe at a temple."

"Is there a problem with pickpockets, then? Or thieves?" Tzedef inquired, and Chase snorted.

"For sure, 'smuch as there is in any bigger city, right? An' with th' crowds so thick'n all, ya can't tell if someone's tryna squeeze past'r get inta yer pack. Festival time's busy as shit in Natari."

"Right." Tzedef sighed, and resigned himself to trying to find information in the midst of what seemed to be a festival on par with some of the larger celebrations back

17

in Yaelin.

CHAPTER TWO

Chase and Sorecco

The temples of Natari were not like any temples that Tzedef had seen before. Instead of being made of marble, metals, and granite, they were made of wood and plaster, with wide, swooping roofs tiled in the same over-sized shells as the rest of the buildings he'd seen in the city.

Chase paused in front of one, turning to eye him speculatively. "Yanno, 'm not sure where ya should go. Ya look like dragonfolk, but ya gots ears like a demonkin, and them eyes, t'boot. So I guess it's up t'you. Which side of yer family are ya best pleased with?"

Tzedef stilled. "I fail to see what that has to do with anything."

Chase gave him a pitying look. "Ya really are fresh off th' boat, aintcha? Yer in th' Permani Isles. Not yer mainland whatever. We ain't do big gods. We gots small gods. Family gods. Live by th' words of our ancestors an' all that. Our temples're fer th' people what ain't got space or kin to set up fer a home shrine. So. Which side d'ya like

19

the best?"

He grimaced and shook his head. "I have no family. No ancestors to claim, and none to claim me save for my goddess."

Tzedef frowned. "Will that be a problem?"

"Noooo?" she pulled the word out uncertainly, "It shouldn't, I don't think…"

Chase shook herself, and shrugged carelessly at him. "No idea! Still, ya gotta pick one an' try, so ya might as well get on with it."

She paused, glanced between the two temples and lowered her voice. "If ya asked me, I'd go with th' demonkin. Dragons're one stuffy lot, an' sweet bones if they don't get uppity if ya ain't just so!"

"I see." he said, and considered the two temples for a moment. Everything he knew about dragons aligned with what Chase had said. Granted, everything he knew about proper dragons and not just the dragonfolk that were their halfbreed offspring came from his father; a powerful, arrogant, white dragon who had not allowed age to instill in him anything so mundane as manners. At least, not manners that applied to anyone below a certain status, either mundane or magical.

"So the demonic temple is more lax?" Tzedef asked, and Chase shrugged again.

"Eh, lax, mebbe. Acceptin's more like th' right word, though. There's plenny of kindsa demons an' devils after all, an' it ain't do to be fightin' with family. Or mebbe family. Could be family?"

She frowned, then waved that train of thought away. "Anyroad, y'might as well try 'em. Bones'n'ash, try 'em both! I'll wait fer a bit, an' if they kick ya out on yer tail then I'll have that oath from ya an' we c'n head back t'my place."

Tzedef nodded absently, then looked over at the temple Chase had indicated was dedicated to demonic ancestors.

The plaster walls were just as white as those of the draconic temple, but the evenly spaced wooden pillars in the walls were heavily carved in intricate detail. Every carving depicted a different breed of demon or devil, and some had small amounts of paint on them; splashes of color that stood out against the dark, weather-worn wood. Even the front doors were painted and carved. Not with any one demon or devil, but with a stylized map of the hells themselves; twelve concentric rings of mazes that blurred and shifted under his eyes until he drew closer.

Only the innermost three rings hadn't cleared of the blurring effect by the time he reached the doors, and to his surprise they opened to his touch, letting him step inside and glance around.

The building opened up just inside the doors, turning into a large, wide open room that was lit with scattered stands of light crystals, all glowing with a soft yellow-white light. Here and there, large, ornate standing screens of painted silk or woven wicker sectioned off parts of the room, providing little oases of privacy for those who desired it. Incense smoke drifted through the air and tickled his nose, the light scent of sweet berries mixing with the darker, earthier scents of cedar and sandalwood.

The doors closed silently behind him, but he barely noticed, too caught up in tallying up the multitude of statues and symbols that littered the room, and the demonkin that were praying at them. He recognized some small few of the effigies; symbols of devils that he had learned as a child were hereditary enemies of his family or statuettes of demons that his tutors had dismissed as, ultimately, subservient to his bloodline.

Not, they had been certain to impress on him, that he had any right to claim that bloodline. Tzedef scoffed internally and glanced away from the praying and meditating demonkin, only to jump and make an aborted grab for his mace when he noticed the short, butter-yellow, young demonkin woman standing next to him, watching him with amused blue eyes.

One slender hand came up to hide her twitching lips, and Tzedef sighed, forcing himself to relax.

It took her a moment to regain control of herself, but when she lowered her hand, her face was as serene as a statue's.

"Welcome." Her voice was quiet and wispy, barely there in some ways, which, Tzedef assumed, was perfect for someone who likely spent a great deal of time trying not to disturb people at prayer.

"Thank you." He said politely, then, not willing to make unwarranted assumptions, "Are you a member of this priesthood, perchance?"

"I have that honor, yes." Her smile was still serene,

but no less genuine for it. "Is there something I can help you with?"

"Yes." Tzedef nodded. "I have been informed that, since the local inns are full, I should seek lodging here. If it helps, I am a cleric of some small ability; I can assist with any healings that your temple might need to provide."

The smile fell off her face and the amusement in her eyes vanished, replaced by a kind of icy detachment that confused him.

"I see." Her voice was still wispy and quiet, but there was a coldness there now that hadn't been there before. "Unfortunately, all of our spare rooms are full. We have no space to take in more travelers."

"I see." Tzedef echoed, searching the woman's face for some clue as to what he'd done to get this sort of reception. Obviously, he'd done something wrong, but try as he might, he couldn't figure out what. "Very well… thank you for your time."

He bowed very slightly, then turned to go, his ears flicking at the uncomfortable feeling of eyes boring into the back of his head.

Chase was leaning against the low, rocky wall that separated the temple grounds from the street, examining her fingernails in the light of a nearby crystal lamp. It was one of dozens that lit the streets of Natari, and now that it was full night, they cast their light brightly. Tzedef headed down the path toward Chase, still puzzling over what possibly could have gone wrong in such a brief exchange.

"No dice?" she asked sympathetically as he drew

near, and Tzedef shook his head.

"No. And it seems as though I offended the priestess I spoke to in some manner, though I can't imagine how."

Chase cocked her head, curious, and Tzedef relayed the conversation to her.

"That's... weird." she frowned. "I don't... I ain't know why they'd be full. Ya even said ya could help with healings an' such?"

"Yes."

"Then why...?"

Chase's eyes widened, and she clapped a hand to her face, groaning quietly. "Oh for mother's sake."

Tzedef watched her, curious about what she'd just realized.

"Yer a healer." She said, muffled behind her hand. "A cleric. From th' mainland. I'm an idiot, an' they're assholes."

One eye ridge arched as Chase pushed away from the stone wall and turned away from the temples. "C'mon. There ain't no point in checkin' with the dragonkin temple. Not with ya bein' from the mainland an' all."

Now thoroughly bewildered, Tzedef followed her away from the temples.

"What does my being a cleric have to do with anything? Or being from the mainland?"

"It's a thing." She said dismissively. "Stupid, 'swhat it is, but them mainland temples do keep sendin' more'n more priests over t' tell us that we're hurtin' our ancestors, worshippin' 'em. Not surprised it's made th' temples cold t' outsider clerics."

Tzedef blinked, then frowned, trying to parse Chase's broken Common.

"Do you mean to tell me that there are temples on the mainland that disagree with your local practices? And they actively send priests over to try to 'correct' this?" His voice was incredulous, and Chase nodded, not looking back at him as she led him back toward the harbor — away from the center of the city and the festival.

"How has that not incited a war?!" Tzedef demanded, and Chase laughed.

"So far it's stayin' mostly between th' temples, but our lot're bein' pretty loud about how if th' mainlanders start anything, then they'll be the ones to finish it. Th' ancestors're all for it, too, so it's not like we'd be pushovers."

Tzedef blinked. "Just how powerful are your ancestors, then, if they feel they can stand up to the power of a fully realized god? You said that they were small gods."

Chase flashed him a grin over her shoulder. "Well, yeah. But how many families d'ya think live in the entire Permani Isles?"

Tzedef's eyes widened, and he almost missed a step before catching himself.

Yes, he could see that. He could see that very well, actually. It would be like ants against a deer. It didn't matter how much bigger the deer was; as long as the ants kept coming, it would die eventually. And even if it escaped, it would be wounded. In pain. And wary against trying the same thing again.

Chase made a satisfied sound, apparently taking his silence as sign enough that he had made the connections she'd implied, then stopped and turned to look at him properly.

"Right. I'll take that oath, now, 'fore we go any further. 'Less ya decided t' head back t' th' ship ya came in on?"

Tzedef considered that for a bare moment, then shook his head. As reassuring as the water lapping against the hull had become over the last few months, he had no intention of staying practically on top of the stench of the harbor. Nor was he in the mood to deal with rowdy sailors celebrating getting paid.

"No, if the offer to retire to your home is still open, then I will gladly take you up on it. What sort of oath do you require?"

"Swear that no harm'll come t' me an' mine from yer hand, while under our roof." Chase directed him, and Tzedef nodded slowly.

It was an easy enough oath to make. He had, after all, no intention of harming Chase or anyone else she might live with, so long as he wasn't attacked first, and he made sure to include that caveat in the impromptu oath he swore to Hecate.

The saffron light that glinted around his fist where he held his amulet sealed the oath, and Chase relaxed when she saw it.

"Great. Okay, c'mon."

"Just like that?" Tzedef checked, and Chase cocked her head.

"What else were ya 'specting?"

"Perhaps another oath not to steal from you? Or at least a demand for a promise along those lines?"

Chase snorted, grinning crookedly as she shook her head. "Nope. No need. M'brother'll make sure ya don't take nothin'. Not that there's much t' take."

Tzedef blinked, and rapidly reevaluated everything he'd learned about Chase in the short time he'd known her. He'd thought that, when she'd said 'me and mine' and implied that there were more people in the home, that she had been speaking about a child. It had made the oath seem more than reasonable. To find out that she had, instead, been speaking about a brother...

He reached up and knuckled the spot between his eyes, resisting the urge to call himself five kinds of idiot.

"What?" She asked, crossing her arms and cocking one hip. "Got somethin' against men or sommat?"

"No." Tzedef sighed. "Not at all. Just reminding myself of the consequences of jumping to conclusions."

At least this time it hadn't been about anything important.

Chase raised a questioning eyebrow at him, but didn't actually ask. Instead, she turned and headed at right angles away from the direction she'd been initially leading him.

"Right, so th' flat's this way. We live down by th'

docks. Not the best area, but we get on alright. There's even a bakery sorta nearby!"

Tzedef grimaced internally. He'd been hoping to avoid the scent of the harbor by taking Chase up on her offer. Instead, it seemed he'd doomed himself to a fishy, briny, gull-filled stay, regardless. At least he wouldn't be needing to put up with the revelry of the sailors in close quarters.

"So here's th' deal," Chase said briskly, trotting back toward where Tzedef could see the bay between the buildings with her wooden sandals raising a racket against the cobblestone street. "Me brother ain't know I'm a whore, an' I wanna keep it that way. I used t' apprentice at th' bakery an' as far as he knows, I still does."

"I see."

"Sos I ain't want t' hear that ya told him shit, okay?" she glanced back to pin him with a severe look, and Tzedef nodded.

"It is none of my business what you have or have not told your brother. I will not disabuse him as to your profession."

Chase nodded, satisfied with that, then turned sharply and ducked into a gap between two buildings that was created in such a way that, from the angle they had been approaching, it was nearly impossible to see.

"I'd take ya in th' front way," she said over her shoulder as Tzedef stopped, staring in dismay. "but th' front door ain't work. Th' lock's jammed shut, so we ain't got in that way in over a year."

"Miss Chase…" He said, slightly helplessly, and she paused, turning to look at him fully.

"What's wro—oh."

She stared for a moment, then palmed her face and, from what he could see, smothered a grin.

"Yer gonna hafta turn sideways and come the best ya can."

"Can the front door not be Mended?" He asked, taking off his bag and shield and turning sideways with a resigned sigh. It was lucky, he supposed, that he wasn't in his armor, or the scraping would have been unbearable. "Surely there's someone for hire that would be willing to do so?"

She snorted. "I ain't know that kinda magic, an' the feckers 'round here'll charge more t' fix it 'cause they know I'm a whore. Ain't worth the trouble when th' back door works just 's well."

"Ah." He considered that for a moment, then resolved to at least take a look at the lock himself, if he could. He had no knowledge of locksmithing, but if it was something that a simple application of oil might fix, then he could assist Chase in that way. It would be an appropriate payment for allowing him to spend the night, if nothing else.

Chase paused in front of a small, green painted door and fished around in the front of her dress for a moment before pulling out a small brass key and opening the door with it. "Sorecco, I'm back!"

"Casey?"

Someone moved in the dark interior of the flat, and Tzedef followed Chase inside, ducking under the doorframe with a quiet grunt.

The movement stilled as Tzedef blinked, letting his night vision adjust to the unlit gloom- darkness, after so long on the decently lit streets.

"Who's with you?"

"This here's Tzedef." Chase said easily, and glanced back at him. "Tzedef, this's me brother, Sorecco. 'Recco, there was a uh… problem, with a customer at the bakery, an' Mister Tzedef helped us out. He's just in onna ship, an' Master Jespar said I could go fer a little while t' help him get settled an' such. But th' temples said they're full up when I took him 'round, an' you know what the inns're like 'round festival time, so I said he could kip in my bed fer th' night."

The figure in the dark resolved itself into a tall young man with sleek, dark hair that was pulled neatly back into a long braid. He looked like Chase. He didn't look happy.

"Really, Casey? Are you sure that's a good idea?"

"It'll only be fer th' night!" Chase defended herself, and Tzedef nodded again.

"Yes. I fully intend to go out and find alternate lodging in the morning. I have no wish to impose, or cause problems for anyone."

Dark eyes flitted over to Tzedef, but didn't quite meet his as the man thought for a long moment, then nodded reluctantly.

"I guess that's fine, then. A newcomer sleeping out on the streets would do no-one any good."

Tzedef wasn't sure if he should be offended by that or not. On the one hand, it would be nice to have a… reasonably safe place to sleep for the night. On the other, he wasn't so helpless that he wouldn't last a single night sleeping in a park or doorway.

"Thanks, 'Recco." Chase sighed, relaxing. "Truly, thanks. Now, I gotta get back afore Master Jespar gets too angry. I'll be late home, too. Gotta make up th' lost time, so don't wait up, mmkay?"

"Right." Sorecco sighed, and Chase turned and slipped past Tzedef out the door, pulling it shut behind her and blocking out even the bit of light that had filtered down the alley from the street.

Tzedef waited.

Sorecco stood there.

The door slammed back open, making them both jump.

"And for ancestor's sake, light the crystal!" Chase cried, exasperated but fond, and she didn't wait for an answer before closing the door again.

This time Tzedef could hear, faintly, her footsteps retreating down the alley, back the way they'd come.

Sorecco sighed.

"Well, welcome to our home I guess."

CHAPTER THREE

Information Exchange

Tzedef watched as Sorecco stepped over to the table just to the left of the door and fumbled around on its surface, looking for something.

It was an odd dichotomy. On the one hand, the man moved through the space confidently, avoiding the chair in front of the table with ease, and not bothering to give Tzedef himself a wide berth. It gave the impression that Sorecco was gifted with some sort of night vision, as were many of the kin of Chaelu. On the other hand, watching his fingertips glide along the table's surface and carefully examine anything they ran across, gave the exact opposite impression; that he was just as blind in the dark as any other human would be.

"Ah." Sorecco made a soft, triumphant sound as his fingers ran into, then across, a rough, unpolished lump of crystal, about the size of an apple.

A split second later, the crystal started to glow, the light weak and watery, and casting odd shadows from where there were inclusions that hadn't been worked out of the stone. It wasn't much light, but it was enough to negate Tzedef's night vision, and he blinked as colors came back.

Sorecco, it turned out, had dark brown hair and pale brown eyes that didn't quite meet his when he straightened up.

"There." He said with a huff. "Light. Presumably. Now."

He turned toward Tzedef and crossed his arms.

"Tell me you aren't one of my sister's 'clients'."

Tzedef stared at him.

"What?"

"Clients." Sorecco said impatiently. "Customers, Johns, Fares, Janes, Temledi, evwynali, ysli—" He cut himself off, and Tzedef blinked at the rather impolite Human words before Sorecco reverted to Common. "You know what I mean! Tell me my sister didn't just bring a client home with her!"

"No?" Tzedef tried, and then, when Sorecco bristled, shook himself and tried again. "No. I am not one of Miss Chase's clients. She was not lying when she said there was a problem with a customer, and I stepped in to assist her in sorting it out."

Sorecco sighed wearily and turned away, heading across the room to where a large reed screen was set up, sectioning off one small area from the rest of the flat.

"Casey sleeps over here."

Tzedef followed, silently observing the flat as he went.

It was small and neat; a single room that was relatively uncluttered, but full of things nevertheless. There were small trinkets that cluttered the built in shelves along one wall, and various clothes draped across and over the small amount of furniture, and a spinning wheel arranged neatly in front of what Tzedef was sure was a window, for all that the curtains were shut tight.

"Her's is that one." Sorecco informed him, pointing at the bed that was crammed into the corner. "So. That problem you stepped in to sort out. How bad was it?"

Tzedef paused, then turned to look at the young man, his expression considering.

"Do you truly wish to know?"

Sorecco looked uncertain, and Tzedef sighed, sliding his bag off his back and turning to sit on the indicated bed. "She required a small amount of healing, which I provided. I will not tell you the cause, or any details about what required healing. It is not your business. The man was driven off, and I do not believe he will seek her out again."

Sorecco dropped to sit on his own bed, a thoughtful look on his face.

But all he said was, "You're a healer?"

"A cleric." Tzedef nodded, and Sorecco's head cocked slightly to one side.

"Really? Casey mentioned that you just came in on a ship. Are you from the mainland? Or one of the other islands?"

"The mainland." Tzedef confirmed. "But not Malfeir.

I hail from Fernil."

Sorecco's face cleared. "I see. And you told the temples you were a cleric, and suddenly they were 'full'?"

Tzedef's face twisted. "Indeed. Miss Chase explained everything to me once she realized her mistake. Are there really clerics that come from the mainland to try to change your people's ways?"

Sorecco snorted. "Oh yeah. The worst ones worship some death goddess or something? I don't know. I'm not usually around the temples when they show up."

"The Dark Lady?" Tzedef asked, thoroughly bemused, and Sorecco snapped and pointed in his direction.

"That's the one, yeah. Sometimes they'll even come into the taverns and interrupt the bards." He sounded genuinely irritated about that. "Makes it nearly impossible to learn anything when they're around."

Tzedef cocked his head, curious. "Are you an apprentice bard, then?"

"No." He said flatly, his voice bitter. "None of the bards on this island have teaching beads, and they won't teach anyone anything other than the very basics because they don't want to get censured by the Colleges. Which, I get that, I really do, but it makes it damn hard to learn. I have to figure everything out myself, by ear."

"But you know the basics." Tzedef pointed out. "And a thorough grounding in the basics is often more important than any other skill or technique one can learn."

"Oh sure." Sorecco snorted. "The basics. Here, let

me light a fire with my fingertips. Let me call a small breeze. Let me sing you some of the songs we use to teach the children, or recite a ballad that everyone has heard six thousand times."

Tzedef hummed softly. A quiet, sympathetic sound. He'd had no such experience, really. Most of his learning had been through tutors while he still lived with the Lord and Lady, or on the job once he'd entered the army. In both cases, there had been people there to guide him through what he needed to know. The only time he'd had to rely on his own instincts and ideas to teach himself had been after he'd become a devotee of Hecate.

After all, most priests and clerics tended to avoid getting caught up in wars. If there was no indication that the gods either approved or disapproved of a mortal conflict, then the conflict wouldn't become one between followers of different tenets.

"Anyway," Sorecco said with a grimace, "those're my problems, and I don't need to go dumping them all on someone I've just met. You have my apologies, Mister Tzedef."

"It was nothing you need to apologize for. I can understand the frustration of being denied something that ought to be easily obtainable."

He snorted. "'Something that ought to be easily obtainable.' That's certainly one way to put it. I'm not sure it's correct, but it's certainly one way. Anyway, that's beside the point. You said you're from Fernil? What brings you all the way across the Serlin Sea?"

"A request from my goddess." Tzedef said, leaning back on his hands and looking up at the whitewashed ceiling. "I am to seek out and learn something called 'Candle Magic'. The only thing she has been able to tell me is that it can be found somewhere known as the 'Ambered Castle'." He glanced down at Sorecco. "I don't suppose you have heard of any such place?"

Sorecco frowned, thinking hard, then slowly shook his head. "I don't think so, no. Not that I can recall, at least. Still, I only know what I know from listening to the bards that come around Natari. With the festival on, there'll be bards from all over Yunxing Island, and the other islands to boot. There might even some from the mainland, but I sort of doubt that. The celebration on Hauli Island is bigger, so they usually get most of the mainland folks."

"I see." Tzedef said thoughtfully. "Well, I will be heading out in the morning to search for other lodging. I may as well question any bards I come across whilst I do so."

"That's probably your best bet." Sorecco agreed, and stood up, heading back around the screen. "Have you eaten yet, Mister Tzedef?"

"Just Tzedef is fine. And no, not yet. I was planning on eating at whichever inn I ended up staying at, except..."

"Except there's nowhere for you to stay." Sorecco said dryly, "and Casey dragged you here without checking to see if you'd eaten, didn't she."

"Indeed." Tzedef agreed, equally dry, then shrugged and stood, moving his bag to the floor at the end of the bed as he followed Sorecco. With it there, it was neatly out of the way but still easily accessible. "Not that it truly matters. I have some rations in my pack, and I have some coin. With the festival on, there is likely no end to the food stalls and vendors available."

"Don't bother." Sorecco snorted, stepping around the small counter that separated the 'kitchen' area from the rest of the flat and reaching out to test the air above the cook stove. "I still need to eat as well, and there's no point in you going out for something if I'm already going to cook. It's just going to be fish, and maybe some baked squash or something, but it should at least be filling."

"Very well." Tzedef agreed, and sank into one of the chairs at the little table, watching with interest as Sorecco moved with practiced ease around the tiny kitchen.

He could see that the stove was dark, and, from the small, disgusted noise that Sorecco made, it wasn't giving off any heat at all, so Tzedef watched quietly, curious to see how the blind man would handle it.

The answer, it seemed was just like anyone else, albeit with a bit more fumbling involved as he opened the stove, grabbed a couple of pieces of wood from the bucket to the side, and settled them across the bars above the ashes from previous fires. Still, Tzedef didn't see any striker, and Sorecco hadn't bothered with kindling, so lighting it was going to be—

Tzedef almost missed the sharp gesture Sorecco made, but he didn't miss the snap of his fingers. Nor did he miss the sudden crackle of the flames that dropped from Sorecco's hand and landed on the wood, flickering for a moment before settling and beginning to burn merrily.

Magic. Of course. It shouldn't be a surprise. Lighting a stove fire was a simple task, and required very little training, and Sorecco had just mentioned making small fires. Still, the fact that he had done it without an incantation… that spoke of long hours of practice and a keenly honed will. It was impressive, and Tzedef was duly impressed.

Sorecco bustled around the little kitchen, pulling out cookware and ingredients, and before long a pair of fish were sizzling away in a pan on the stove.

"Oh for the love of ancient mothers— Why can't you ever put anything back when you're done with it?" Sorecco grumbled, arm buried up to his elbow in one of the cabinets above the counter.

Tzedef craned his neck slightly, and caught a glimpse of a small horde of jars, all in different shapes and sizes, each of which Sorecco was pushing to the side as his fingers fluttered over them.

"Is there a problem?" He asked, and Sorecco paused, grimacing.

"Only in that my sister forgets to put things away when she's in a hurry. Do you see a small jar, about this big, with a round bottom anywhere?" He gestured with his hands, indicating a bottle about three inches tall, with a bulbous bottom. "It should be about half full of salt."

Tzedef blinked, then glanced around, scanning for the jar in question until something at his elbow caught his eye.

A little clay jar, about three inches tall, with a bulbous bottom and a little fitted lid.

"Is this it?" He asked, picking it up and lifting the lid to peer inside.

Sure enough, inside it was half full of white crystals that Tzedef assumed was probably salt.

"Give it here?" Sorecco asked, and Tzedef handed it over for Sorecco to inspect.

"Yeah, that's it." He sounded relieved as he moved back over to the stove. "Thanks. I'm sure I would have thought to check the table eventually, but not before the fish burned, probably."

A pinch of salt was sprinkled over the pan, and then Sorecco firmly put the jar into the cupboard where it apparently belonged, as if telling the jar itself to stay put.

The rest of the meal came together relatively quickly, and before long, the scent of fried fish and toasted bread filled the air.

Neither man spoke as Sorecco cooked; Tzedef content to simply watch, and Sorecco apparently preoccupied with his own thoughts. Nevertheless, it was a comfortable silence that lasted until some quality of the sizzle of the fish changed, and Sorecco flipped both fish out of the pan and onto waiting plates.

"Now." He said, holding one plate out in Tzedef's general direction and settling at the table with the other once Tzedef had taken it. "I've well and truly interrogated you, and, as they say, turnabout's fair play, so. If you've got questions, go ahead and ask. I won't be offended."

Tzedef paused. That was a rather open ended offer, especially for a relative stranger. Still, there was something that Sorecco had said earlier that was nagging at him.

"You mentioned that none of the local bards have teaching beads. What exactly does that mean? Are they not allowed to teach in general? Or are there specifics that they cannot pass on?"

"No, see, I was born blind, so healing spells won't work. I—" Sorecco paused, looking taken aback. "Wait."

Tzedef blinked. That was not remotely the answer to anything he'd asked.

Sorecco cocked his head. "You didn't ask why I'm still blind."

"Correct." Tzedef replied, rather bemused. "It is none of my business."

"Huh." Sorecco said, sounding even more bemused than Tzedef felt. "That's a first. Usually that's one of the first things out of people's mouths. Either that or something along the lines of 'you're just doing it for attention'. Anyway, nevermind that. You asked about the bards and their beads?"

"Yes." Tzedef nodded, and Sorecco settled in happily to explain.

CHAPTER FOUR

Searching for Lodging

The conversation meandered a bit after that, from the bardic colleges in Yaelin and Vraka, to the instrument trade on Yunxing, then to the festival that was currently going on.

By the time Sorecco had finished explaining the basis behind the festival, Tzedef was stifling yawns.

"But you're tired," Sorecco said abruptly, "and here I am, yapping away when you could be in bed. Sorry about that."

Tzedef waved him off, then grimaced. "It is no trouble. The conversation was interesting."

"Still." Sorecco said, and stood. "I'll clear the table. Casey'll get the dishes tomorrow morning. Feel free to use the privy- it's outside and to the left, the door with the water sigil carved on it."

"My thanks for that, and for the meal." Tzedef nodded, and stood as well.

By the time he was done taking care of the

necessities, Sorecco was seated at the spinning wheel, a basket full of wool at his feet.

Tzedef blinked. He'd thought that Chase... But as he watched, Sorecco found the end of the thread that was on the wheel, unwound it from its place, and started to spin.

"I'm going to stay up for a while longer." He informed Tzedef. "Go ahead and put out the crystal if you want. I don't need it."

"Very well." Tzedef nodded, glanced down at the table, and reached over to place a finger on the crystal.

Nothing happened.

Tzedef sighed softly, took his finger away, then put it back.

This time the light winked out as quickly as though it was a snuffed candle, and Tzedef blinked as his vision returned to shades of grey.

Chase's bed was surprisingly comfortable, and the blankets warmed quickly when he wrapped them around himself. Despite that, however, sleep came with difficulty. The soft whirring and occasional clacking of the spinning wheel would lull him to sleep, only for him to jolt back to wakefulness as people passed by on the street, laughing and talking at volumes that bespoke spectacular levels of drunkenness, and behind all that was the odd, uncomfortable little niggle that had been bothering him on the ship.

All in all, he'd gotten very little rest by the time the

back door creaked softly open and Chase slipped inside, closing it quietly again behind herself. The spinning wheel stopped, and that alone was enough to rouse Tzedef again, if only enough to listen.

"Kelisra." Sorecco's voice was very, very quiet as he welcomed his sister home.

"Tak." Chase murmured a soft thanks as weak, watery light bloomed behind the screen that separated the beds from the rest of the room.

A chair scraped on the floor and Chase sighed heavily.

Sorecco was silent for a long moment, and Tzedef floundered his way more fully towards wakefulness as the siblings spoke in quiet Human.

"Chasli nen ka balae." Sorecco bitched gently, and Tzedef wracked his brain for the translation. Something about the salt?

The thinking woke him up enough that, even with his limited Human, he could mostly parse the rest of the conversation. Anything he couldn't fully understand, he could cudgel his sleep-muddled brain into guessing about, and the more he woke up, the more he understood.

"Sorry Kolby…" Her voice was a tired murmur, and another chair scraped the floor before footsteps crossed the room, the floor creaking softly.

"Sorecco." He said, and Tzedef could hear the wince in Chase's voice when she spoke again.

"Sorry. I forgot."

There was a long pause, and then she asked, very

hesitantly, "does it really bother you that much?"

Chase sounded almost mournful and Sorecco sighed.

"Kinda, yeah. Whoever heard of a bard named Kolby?"

"You could be the first." Chase offered, a smile in her voice. "Kolby the Great. Or, or maybe they'd call you something like Kolby Silvertongue. Kolby of the Thousand Instruments!"

"Shut up." Sorecco grumbled, but there was no heat in his words. "Seriously, Kolby is a stupid name for a bard. I like Sorecco. It's got weight to it. It flows."

"If you say so." Chase sighed, and Sorecco huffed.

"I do."

"Fine. Sorecco. I'll remember."

The silence that fell lasted so long that Tzedef had almost fallen completely back to sleep, only to jolt awake when Chase spoke again.

"How was our new friend? He swore to his goddess he wouldn't hurt you, but…"

"Nah, he was fine." Sorecco said easily. "We chatted for a bit. He seems like a pretty easy-going guy. A little uptight, I guess, but polite. He didn't even ask about my eyes. Said it wasn't his business."

Chase made a soft, surprised noise. "Really? He didn't? I was almost sure that he'd at least offer. He healed me up quick as."

"Yeah, no. He didn't even mention it. Just asked me a bunch of questions about the bards around here, and the festival."

"Huh. Weird."

"Yeah."

Again, silence fell.

"He seems like a good enough guy, though. He didn't mention your job at all." Sorecco said eventually. "Didn't seem to care about it, either. I wouldn't mind him staying until the end of the festival, if he can't find somewhere else."

"Really?"

"Yeah. I'm surprised. Usually the men you bring home are all puffed up and self-righteous to tell me so I can 'protect your virtue' or whatever."

Chase snorted, and Tzedef frowned. So it had been a test, then. That was sly of them. Part of him was a bit irritated about it, but the rest of him acknowledged that he had no real right to be bothered. It was a good way to get someone's measure, at the least, and he was staying in their home.

"Virtue's a myth made up by people in power to control the masses."

"I know." Sorecco sighed wearily.

"So's 'honor'." Chase added, and Sorecco sighed again, even more long-sufferingly.

"I *know*... Anyway. Tzedef. Staying longer. Thoughts?"

"Sure. Means we'd need to share a bed, but it's not like we've never done that before, so I don't mind." She agreed, then groaned softly. "I'm exhausted, I need to sleep."

"Did you eat?"

"Yeah. I had a cheese roll and some grilled veggies from one of the vendors before she closed up."

"Good. I'll sleep in a bit, but I need to work some more on this yarn. Old Lady Halven is getting impatient; she was down here three times yesterday, harassing me about it."

"That old harpy…" Chase growled softly. "One day I think I'd like to *feed* her the yarn she's so obsessed with."

"She's still my best customer," Sorecco said, slightly reprovingly, "and you *know* not many people will buy from someone not guild certified."

"Yeah…" Chase sighed, and a chair scraped again.

The light behind the screen shifted, and Tzedef, realizing what was happening, promptly rolled over to face the wall.

Her footsteps faltered for a moment, then, when he made no further movements, Chase came around the screen and put the crystal down on the small table between the beds.

There were a few moments of rummaging, the sound of cloth shifting, then being tossed somewhere, and then the light from the crystal went out and darkness enveloped the small flat again.

The floor creaked as Sorecco headed back over to the spinning wheel and, just after the whirring restarted, Chase spoke again.

"Sorecco?"

"Hmm?"

"Will you sing to me?"

"He's sleeping." Sorecco pointed out softly, and Chase made a small, disappointed sound.

"True, but... you don't have to sing loud."

Sorecco sighed quietly, the sound more fond than exasperated. "Okay. If you insist."

Chase made a pleased humming sound and Sorecco picked up the tone, humming along and sliding quietly down the scale until the hum turned into words.

"When waves are gold and sunlight greets/
The line where sea and sky must meet/
Where sailors drift and halt their race/
To join in twilight's soft embrace/
We look and see our siblings high/
Scattered brightly through the sky.

They call us one by one to sleep/
To join them in their darkness deep/
And one by one we children retire/
To dream the world as they desire."

His voice was calm. A mellow, soothing baritone that slid quietly through the air. The song was unfamiliar, but the cadence wasn't. It was a lullaby. A children's song, and Chase sighed happily as blankets shifted on the bed opposite Tzedef.

Slowly, Tzedef too, relaxed, letting the quiet song work its magic on him just as much as it did on Chase.

He didn't notice when the tide of sleep pulled him under again, this time for the rest of the night.

Tzedef woke to sunlight streaming through the window next to the spinning wheel; the thin curtains that covered it doing almost nothing to block the light. He grumbled softly to himself, squinting, then sighed and sat up. The wooden floor was cool under his feet, but the wall, where his tail pressed against it, was warmed by the morning sun, and the contrast was a nice one.

Sorecco was still asleep, curled into a ball that left most of the bed free, though there was no sign of Chase in the small bedroom alcove. Wondering if she'd already left to go to work, Tzedef stood and stretched, his tail sweeping his boots out from under the bed so that he could stoop and grab them, then wander out from behind the screen.

To his surprise, Chase was sitting at the small table, already dressed in practical trousers and a loose, green, long sleeved shirt, with a pen in one hand and a small, battered book on the table in front of her.

"You rise early." He observed, then winced when Chase nearly jumped out of her skin, flinging the pen across the room.

"Feckin' *bone dust*! Ya walk like a cat! Make some noise, will ya!?"

Tzedef bit back a smile. "My sincerest apologies. I did not intend to startle you."

Chase scowled and stood, slipping the little book into her pocket and going to retrieve her pen.

"Ain't natural, someone yer size walkin' that quiet." She grumbled, "Feckin' Lost…"

Tzedef blinked, but remained silent until she straightened back up and turned to look at him.

"Well then. Yer up. G'mornin'. What's yer plan fer the day?"

"Good morning. I was…" Something occurred to him. "I was going to simply leave to attempt to find alternate lodging, but I just realized that I have just spent a great deal of time on a ship, where bathing and washing facilities were at the bare minimum. Please tell me there is a public bathhouse and a reasonably priced laundry somewhere nearby."

Chase blinked at him, looking utterly nonplussed. "What's a laundry?"

His heart sank. Were public laundries not a thing in Permani?

"It's a place? One takes their soiled clothing and linens there? They wash it for you…?" Tzedef's voice trailed off as he spotted Chase's twitching lips, and he sighed.

"You know exactly what I'm talking about, don't you."

She burst out laughing. "Yeah, but the look on your face! 'What's a laundry?' Ancestors above, that was *priceless*!"

He sighed again, and waited until her laughter died down. "Yes, you got me. A fitting vengeance for me startling you, I suppose, but the question stands."

"Yeah, there is." Chase nodded, wiping away tears of mirth, "Gemori's place is the best laundry on this side of the harbor, and there's a bathhouse not far from there, too. Gemori does regular and magical washings, so if you're in a hurry it's about half again the cost of the regular washing."

She glanced at the window, then shrugged. "I can whip us up a breakfast, an' ya can go when yer done. Both of 'em should be pretty empty this time o' day."

Tzedef blinked. "Are you sure? I wouldn't wish to put you out at all, and Sorecco very graciously gave me dinner last night. It wouldn't be a bother to simply get something from a vendor."

Chase waved him off. "Don't worry 'bout it. I ain't mind. Oh, and, if ya don't find somewhere t'day, then me and 'Recco don't mind ya stayin' another night or two, as ya need."

"…Your kindness is admirable…" Tzedef said slowly, trying to pick his words carefully, "But while you and your brother's hospitality is most appreciated, I have no desire to put you out of your own bed without any form of recompense."

She snorts, but her eyes take on a calculating gleam.

"If it's that big a deal t'ya, then we can call it six cop a night, with meals included. That's a better deal'n you'll get at a proper inn, which's only fair, since you'll be sharin' a room of sorts with me and 'Recco."

Tzedef cocked his head, thinking about it, and nodded slowly. "That seems fair enough. Very well, I accept. In the event that I find no other suitable lodging, I will return here to stay."

"Good." Chase nodded firmly, and stuck her hand out to shake. "It's a deal, then."

They shook on it, and Chase grinned up at him, then turned towards the kitchen. "Great. Now you sit down and let me do us up some brekkie."

Obediently, Tzedef sat at the table and put his boots on, watching as Chase poked around the kitchen. She rummaged through the cupboards and cold box until she had a decent amount of ingredients laid out on the counter, then stood there, frowning at them.

"Ya got any allergies?"

The question surprised him, but he shook his head. "No. None that I'm aware of."

"Lucky jerk." Chase said amiably. "I can't do potatoes. They make me throat itch, an' the healer said if I kept doin' 'em then it might make me throat close up altogether. 'S fuckin' rude is what that is. 'Taters is nice."

"Yes, I can see how that would be irritating." Tzedef mused, "Potatoes keep quite a while. Not being able to eat them must limit your diet annoyingly."

"Eh," She shrugged. "It ain't too bad. I know a guy, he's dead on allergic t' wheat. No bread. No ales. Nothin'."

Tzedef winced sympathetically. "Now that is an inconvenient allergy."

Chase nodded absently, tucking a couple of ingredients back into the cold cupboard. "I dunno if I'd be able t' keep to it, honestly. I might probably've just died instead. But he seems t' manage well enough so... each their own, I guess."

Tzedef nodded, then glanced over toward the screened off part of the flat as Sorecco groaned and shifted around.

"Mornin' ya Arlith. Finally awake?"

"Shaddup…" Sorecco grumbled back. "'M not an arlith. I didn't get to sleep for ages. Pretty sure I heard Forst next door moving around before I went to bed."

Chase winced. "Ouch. Ain't he usually up with the sun?"

"Supposedly." Sorecco sighed, and there was some faint shuffling around before he came wandering out from behind the screen in dark brown trousers, braid disheveled, with a dark blue shirt in his hand. "Does this match? It's the red one, right?"

"Blue." Chase told him. "I know you can tell the difference between linen and cotton."

"Shaddup." Sorecco said again, with no heat at all in his voice. "I'm tired. Sue me. Does it at least match?"

"Yeah, you're fine." Chase said airily. "D'ya want toad inna hole for food?"

"Sounds good." Sorecco said, voice muffled as he pulled the shirt over his head. "Is Mister Tzedef still here?"

"I am." Tzedef said, and Sorecco nodded.

"Good. G'morning, by the by. Sleep well?"

"Well enough." Tzedef agreed.

"Good." Sorecco said again, and stepped over to the table, searching for the other chair before dropping heavily into it and letting his head hang over the back with a groan. "Remind me to tell Old Lady Halven that her lack of planning doesn't mean I'm going to act like it's an emergency when she realizes that she's supposed to make three sweaters before winter and the harvest festival's on. She's known about the cursed things since early spring. She could have put in her order at any point between then and now, but no, she had to put it off until the last possible minute, and now she's riding me about it like *I'm* the bottleneck here."

"To be fair," Chase said reasonably as she buttered thick slices of bread on both sides, "you *are* making the yarn she's got to use for them. That is a bottleneck."

"Well, yes," Sorecco admitted, "but that doesn't mean she couldn't have put in her order earlier."

"Fair enough." Chase agreed. "You could tell her that you're only able to spin enough for one at the moment, and she should go see what the Guild has on offer."

Sorecco made a face. "Ugh… I probably should, shouldn't I."

"Probably."

"*Ugh.*"

The siblings fell silent, and Tzedef, with nothing to say, was content to let the silence linger. Instead, he watched as Chase cut a hole in the center of each piece of bread, then laid them into the hot pan on the stove and cracked an egg into each hole.

Soon enough, the smell of frying bread and egg filled the little flat, and not long after that plates with a couple of eggy pieces of bread each were placed in front of Sorecco and Tzedef.

"Alright!" Chase declared, returning to the stove to make up her own, "Eat up, boyos! We've shit t' do today!"

CHAPTER FIVE

Cleanliness is Next to...

Breakfast ended up being a swift affair and, once they'd all finished eating, Chase gave Tzedef directions to the laundry and the bathhouse.

"They're near the red lights." She said. "But not on 'em. Gemori gets a lotta business from 'em, though, so its a good place for 'em. Most o' the highfalutin folks from further inta the city don't bother comin' down here."

"And you said that this Gemori runs the… laundry?" Tzedef checked, and Chase nodded.

"Yup. She's quick as anythin', too."

"Wonderful." Tzedef said fervently. Now that he'd remembered that his clothes hadn't seen the inside of a laundry in months, his scales itched with the feeling of filth, real and imagined.

"You good, then?" She inquired, and Tzedef nodded, lifting his pack and shield.

"Yes. Thank you for the directions, the bed, and the meal. They were all appreciated."

"Y'welcome." Chase said, and grinned up at him. "Now dontcha go forgettin' our deal, yeah? If ya can't find a place t' stay, then come on back here, okay?"

"I will remember." Tzedef inclined his head. "Rest assured, should I find no lodging I shall return."

"Good." She nodded, and Tzedef turned and squeezed his way out the back door, edging down the alleyway until he could step out onto the street proper with a relieved sigh.

"Move!" The squawking, cracked voice of an old woman made Tzedef look down. The white and gray feathers, bright yellow beak, and rheumy yellow eyes of an elderly gull birdfolk glared up at him.

Tzedef blinked, but stepped to the side and the woman hobbled past him, banging his shins with her walking stick as she passed.

"Good for nothin' layabout young people not even up until near to noon and barely managin' to keep 'emselves fed!" Her voice grated on his ears like a fork on ceramic, and Tzedef peered after her as she wobbled down the tiny alley and stopped in front of Chase and Sorecco's door.

"BOY!" The squawk was now a shriek. "Boy you'd best have my yarn done!"

Nope.

That was not something Tzedef had any interest in getting involved with, and he turned sharply away, barely catching the door slamming open and Chase appearing in the doorway.

"Hello Missus Halven, how are you this morning? Sorecco and I are fine, thank you for asking…"

Her voice faded into the general city noise as Tzedef strode down the street, and slowly, the tension in his shoulders relaxed.

He knew how to handle superior officers shouting at him. He knew how to handle the jeers of his enemies.

Civilians?

Those were a different kettle of fish entirely.

Gemori turned out to be one of the incredibly rare sapient arthropods; a nearly human-sized isopod with a green and black patterned carapace.

"You want it all how quickly?" She asked, clicking softly as she looked over the small pile of clothing that Tzedef had emptied from his pack onto the counter.

"Ideally today." He admitted, "But if that is not possible—"

"Oh no, that I can do." She interrupted him. "But it will cost."

"I was told half again as much for a magical cleaning?" Tzedef said, and Gemori's upper half bobbed forward. A nod, as best the isopod could manage.

"Yes. Or double for a rush."

Tzedef hid a reflexive grimace, and fought back the urge to start haggling. Double to cut in line wasn't actually all that bad. He'd had to deal with worse from military suppliers in the past; compared to the merchants that would charge double or triple as a matter of course, this was positively generous.

"Very well, a rush then, if you please."

"Good." Gemori said, sounding satisfied. "Come back in an hour. Clean and dry everything will be. Or wait here; I care not. You will pay when things are done."

Tzedef nodded again and turned to leave, only to pause and glance over his shoulder when Gemori clicked her mouthparts pointedly.

"Your chit." She said simply, holding out a small wooden disk.

His tail cringed, curling the way he wouldn't allow his shoulders to, and Tzedef spun back around to take it.

"My thanks."

She bobbed again, and said nothing as Tzedef headed for the door and stepped out of the warm, humid building.

The crisp breeze off the harbor, heavy with the scent of rotting seaweed and fish, made Tzedef's nose wrinkle, and he drew his cloak around himself a little more firmly as a shiver worked its way down his spine in protest of the sudden temperature change.

At this point, there was nothing more he wanted in the world than a hot bath, and so, keeping Chase's directions in mind, off he set to find just that.

Over an hour later, Tzedef emerged from the bathhouse in a cloud of scented steam.

There had been a multitude of soaps to wash away the dust and salt and grime of ship-life, and, for only a moderately extortionate price, scented oils to make his scales supple and smooth. Soft cloths had been provided as well, and between the oils and the cloths Tzedef had polished his white scales until they gleamed.

Out of everything he'd disliked about being in the military, and there honestly wasn't that much, the lack of proper bathing facilities was his second most beloathed factor. (The war, of course, was the first.)

Tzedef despised being dirty. He hated the feeling of dirt on his scales, and loathed the grimy, gritty feeling of dirty scales rubbing against each other. It was the tangible equivalent of nails on a chalkboard, to him, and even just thinking about the sensation put his teeth on edge.

The fact that he'd had to put his dirty clothes back on had, for a brief moment, had him seriously considering returning to Gemori's laundry wrapped in nothing but a towel. The memory of the chill breeze off the harbor had put a solid halt to that idea, and, shuddering, Tzedef had reluctantly dressed himself again.

Taking the bath *before* his clothing had been washed was a stupid idea, he reluctantly admitted to himself. It would have been better to simply wait the hour or two for his laundry and *then* bathe, but he'd been too eager to get clean; too impatient to feel like himself again, and he'd made a stupid mistake.

It left him with a conundrum: to change or not once he'd retrieved his clothing from Gemori, but one glance at the sun's location in the sky dissuaded him. He'd spent enough time on himself. Now it was time to find somewhere to stay while he was on the island or else he'd be returning to Chase and Sorecco's home without having accomplished anything.

A long, low growl interrupted his thoughts, and Tzedef blinked.

Finding something to eat was, apparently, also on the agenda.

Backpack full once again, and shield hooked comfortingly over it, Tzedef retraced his steps back towards Chase and Sorecco's home. Chase had implied that the main festival was nearer the city's center, and so, Tzedef reasoned, if he wanted to find any inns, he would simply need to head away from the harbor.

Sure enough, the further he got from the harbor the more the people on the streets wore light, gauzy, floaty clothing instead of the sturdier, thicker clothing of those nearest the harbor. So too, could he hear the sounds of music and revelry, gradually growing louder as he drew closer, and smell the scents of cooking food and mulled wine in the air.

It was a cacophony- an overwhelming assault on his senses, and Tzedef had to pause once in the shadow of a building to brace himself before continuing out and onto one of the main streets of the city of Natari.

The street was as different from the streets around the harbor as night and day. Where the others were simple and undecorated, lined with crafter's businesses and homes, this street was bedecked in lanterns and banners, with cloths hung between buildings to provide shade for the festival goers on the street below. Farm stalls were everywhere, each boasting piles of fresh fruits and veg, or cuts of meat kept fresh by chilling runes carved into the crates and barrels they'd arrived in. Here was a stall selling honeys and various preserves. There was a stall selling fresh roasted nuts, and through it all, wending this way and that in an inexorable tide, were the people.

Tzedef took a deep breath, braced himself again, and stepped into the crowd.

To his surprise, he wasn't swept up in the throng. No one bumped into him, or jostled him. Instead, it was as if he were simply a large stone in a stream. The crowd parted before him, and closed behind him, all with a kind of absent-minded politeness that was almost more baffling than anything he'd experienced to date. Still, he wasn't one to look a gift horse in the mouth, and so he followed the crowd, all the while searching for anything that might indicate an inn.

A wooden sign hanging from a building with a bright blue door caught his attention, and the carved image of a tankard and a bed made his ears perk a little. That was just what he was looking for, and so he altered his course, winding diagonally through the throng until he reached the door. A turn of a brass knob, polished bright by hundreds of hands, admitted him into the relative quiet of the inn's main room.

It was a blessed, blessed relief.

Although it was between what might be typically considered meal times, there were patrons scattered here and there, seated at tables in ones or twos, or perched on barstools at the bar, drinking and idly chatting with the firbolg behind the counter. Food and drink were on equal display, and Tzedef's eyes flicked over the gathered customers as he made his way to the bar, cataloging and assessing, just in case.

Tzedef's footsteps stuttered minutely when he noticed Rugar sitting in a corner and sullenly nursing a pint of something dark, one hand splinted and wrapped in bandages. Hopefully Tzedef would be able to complete his business and be gone before the other noticed him.

"'Ey!" The firbolg behind the bar grinned at him as he approached, and Tzedef dipped his head in a polite nod. "Welcome! You 'ere for a meal?"

"N—" His stomach cut him off with another long, low, growl. "Yes, please. Whatever is on offer. As well, I was hoping to find accommodations. Have you any rooms available?"

The firbolg grimaced, and their face turned apologetic as they turned to pull down a bowl and started ladling out a decent helping of a thick chowder from a cauldron near the fire. "Sorry, sir. We're flat full, an' a couple of rooms're doubled up, even. It's the same up and down the main roads, everyone's packed t' th' gills. People want easy access to the festival, see? But there's a few smaller places around town. Less known, y'know? They might 'ave rooms, but mosta them don't 'ave dining attached, y'know? You'll 'ave to fend for y'self for food."

They placed the bowl of chowder down in front of him with a flourish, then cocked their head questioningly and jerked their thumb over their shoulder at the casks along the wall.

"Yes." Tzedef answered the unasked question. "Something light, if you please. And I do not mind needing to sort my meals out myself. It is a minor inconvenience, all things considered."

"Great!" They said, and their tail swayed, pleased, as they turned to pull a mug of a pale, golden ale.

"Well then. The closest place to 'ere is called The Waggin' Dog, an it can be a right bitch t' find, so listen close."

Tzedef listened closely as the firbolg gave him directions, first to that inn, then, as he ate and drank, to no less than half a dozen others, all scattered throughout the city.

"If you go in that order, you should 'ave to backtrack much at all." They said firmly. "An' 'onestly, I don't truly recommend much o' any of 'em. The last two, for sure, are right shitholes. But if y' need a place to stay..."

They spread their hands, and shrugged, and Tzedef privately resolved that, no matter if they *should* have rooms available, if the rooms were truly as bad as the firbolg was making out, then he would simply return to Chase and Sorecco's flat.

"You have my thanks." He said, and pushed his empty bowl back in the firbolg's direction. "And my compliments. The meal was excellent."

They brightened. "Yeah? Gramma'll be right pleased to 'ear that. She does all the cookin' 'round 'ere."

"Oh? Well then please, give her my compliments."

"Give 'em 'er yourself!" The firbolg retorted

genially, and half turned toward a curtained doorway that was seemingly wedged between casks. "Oi! Gramma! You got a fan!"

Something chattered behind the curtain, and the niggle that Tzedef had been resolutely ignoring came back in full force, shoving itself to the front of his brain just as a brightly painted skull poked out from behind the curtain.

Tzedef stared.

Pale blue light glimmering in otherwise empty eye sockets stared back.

"Ah…" He started then cleared his throat as the firbolg grinned gleefully, mischief in their eyes.

"The meal was delicious." Tzedef managed. "Thank you."

The pale blue glow brightened slightly, and the skull's jawbone clattered softly before withdrawing back behind the curtain.

"Well that's just made her day." The firbolg said casually, and Tzedef sighed.

"Glad to have been of service."

The firbolg sniggered, then cracked, breaking into raucous laughter that made some of the other patrons look up, roll their eyes, and return to their meals, drinks, or conversations.

When Tzedef finally left, it was a silver lighter, and with plenty to think about.

Necromancy of *some* sort was, apparently, completely legal in Permani, or at the very least, on Yunxing Island. This was unusual, and, if he were completely honest, something that interested him quite a bit. It would be nice to take some time to study the why and how of the necromancy of this island nation. But even as the thought crossed his mind, Tzedef reluctantly put it to the side.

Hecate had requested his assistance in finding the Ambered Castle. He would be a poor cleric should he put his own desires above those of his goddess.

Perhaps when he had finished this quest, he would have time to return, and study it...

Movement at the corner of his eye, purposeful and coming directly toward him, made his shoulders stiffen, but Tzedef didn't turn to look. Instead, he stopped suddenly, his attention seemingly caught by the odd looking fruits in the stall next to him. The movement kept coming, cutting through the crowd with purpose.

Tzedef's hand dropped to where his mace was hanging from its loop on his belt, and the rodiamo woman behind the crates looked alarmed, her fluffy dormouse tail twitching.

Tzedef caught her eye, shook his head minutely, and waited.

He didn't have to wait long, and he didn't let the outstretched hand land on his shoulder before spinning around and glancing his stalker up and down quickly, assessing him.

It was Rugar.

Because of course it was.

Judging from the smell wafting off of him, he was

spectacularly drunk.

Because of *course* he was.

CHAPTER SIX

A Festival Affray

"Ya owe me *money*!"

One scaled eye-ridge arched incredulously. "I do not think so, sirrah."

"Bollocks!" the other shouted, and Tzedef's eyes narrowed. "Ya owe me fer me hand, an' me feckin' *tooth*!"

The tusk, Tzedef noted, was back in place, properly affixed and looking just as healthy as the one on the opposite side.

"I wouldn'ta had t'pay fer healing fer my hand if ya hadn'ta butted in, sos the way I sees it, ya can either pay up, or I kin take it outta yer *hide*!"

Tzedef sighed, and straightened up to his full height, taking a step forward and looming over the man in much the same way the half orc had attempted to loom over him the night before.

People were already stopping, forming a semi-circle around their little altercation; drawn to watch by morbid curiosity.

"You attempted to steal from a prostitute." Tzedef said, taking another step forward and crowding the half-orc backwards, away from the fruit stall.

The people on that side of the circle shuffled backwards, not willing to risk getting involved.

"Not only did that action result in her injury, but it forced *me* to get involved." Tzedef's voice was flat as he took another step forward. "Your coin was forfeit the moment you attempted not to pay for services you recieved."

"Bitch wasn't worth what I paid fer her!" the half-orc snarled, taking another step back, out of Tzedef's shadow. "

"The value of the prostitute's service is not in question here." Tzedef retorted calmly, "The value of your personality, on the other hand… well. I'd say it leaves much to be desired, but that implies that there is anything there to base a personality on."

On the list of ways that Tzedef had seen fights started, that was, he thought, rather tame. Still, the half-orc snarled again and lunged for him, eyes alight with rage.

As drunk as the half-orc was, it only took Tzedef stepping smartly to one side and leaving his foot outstretched to put him on the ground, measuring his length on the cobblestones face first.

"Ya dust-boned fecker!" The half-orc howled, rolling over and clutching his mouth.

Tzedef arched his eye-ridge again, and the other joined it when the half-orc pulled his hand away from his mouth to reveal that, once again, one tusk had broken in his fall.

The same tusk, actually. How many times had that tusk been broken, to leave it so fragile?

He was almost impressed when the half-orc rolled to his feet.

He was considerably less impressed when the other man brandished a short knife at him, his hold inexpert and his stance sloppy.

"I really do not think this will be as productive as you hope." Tzedef said mildly, and the half-orc sneered at him.

"What, ya think yer *better*'n me!?"

"Sirrah," Tzedef said patiently, "I do not have to *think* so when you provide ample evidence at every turn."

Snorts and chuckles whispered through the crowd surrounding them both, and the half-orc's face darkened thunderously.

Tzedef kept his eyes on him, watching his center of mass. If the half-orc was going to do anythi—

He lunged, aiming to stab Tzedef in the gut, and Tzedef stepped into the movement, sliding past the knife and putting one foot between the half-orc's. His momentum carried him over Tzedef's hip, and Tzedef helped the half-orc over with one hand at the back of his neck and the other on the wrist of the hand holding the knife.

The half-orc hit the ground flat on his back and wheezed as the air was forced from his lungs, gaping like a landed fish.

Tzedef stooped, and plucked the knife out of the

half-orc's nerveless fingers, inspecting it carefully as he stood back up.

It was actually fairly decent quality, but poorly cared for and dulled. Tzedef hummed softly, letting it dangle carelessly.

"I wouldn't do that." He advised as the half-orc, still wheezing, tried to sit up. "You are outclassed, and I now have not only my weapon, but your own."

The half-orc didn't listen, and, after a moment of watching him struggle to both breathe and sit up, Tzedef shrugged, and turned around. The crowd melted away in front of him and, without a backwards glance, Tzedef walked away.

Hopefully that would be the end of that, but he sincerely doubted it. Still, he was relatively certain that he could handle anything the half-orc might dish out, and he had other, more important things to think about at the moment. Like finding a suitable inn.

This it turned out, was just as difficult as everyone had made it out to be. One after the other, Tzedef was turned away from the inns on the list the firbolg had given him. Some of the innkeepers were truly apologetic. Others were entirely unsympathetic. To his surprise, however, the last inn *did* have a room available. For the only slightly exorbitant price of four silver a night.

When Tzedef poked his head into the room, however, the scent of rat piss and mold made his muzzle wrinkle.

The bedbugs he found along the seam of the mattress sealed the deal.

He would rather sleep on the ship than in *this*.

So, moderately irritated with having wasted most of a day on something that multiple people had told him was likely pointless, Tzedef wound his way back through the city to the harbor, and down onto the ship he'd sailed in on.

Only to find out that both Captain Teralia and Inral were away. Predictably, the overly officious, rulebound yeoman refused to rent him a cabin without their leave, and so it was a throughly disgruntled Tzedef that squeezed his way back down the alley and knocked slightly too hard on the semi-familiar door.

A beat passed.

Two.

Tzedef knocked again, and the door flew open to reveal Sorecco, disheveled and exasperated.

"Missus Halven, it takes *time* to spin yarn of the quality you wish for. Time that you are *wasting* by continually harassing me to hurry up. If you are in such dire need, then I truly suggest going to one of the guild shops and simply buying your yarn there."

Tzedef blinked.

"I will keep that in mind," he said after a long moment of silence.

Sorecco's eyes widened and blood rose in his cheeks. "Ancestors take me now… Mister Tzedef, welcome back. I am *so sorry*, I didn't realize it was you and not Old Lady Halven…"

"Somehow, I gathered that." Tzedef said mildly, and watched with a small, private amusement as Sorecco colored further.

"Yeah, well…" He said, flustered, and stepped back out of the doorway to gesture Tzedef inside. "I take it you had no luck, then?"

"Technically, there was a room in the last inn I was directed to." Tzedef admitted, stepping over the threshold and out of the way. "However, with the price so severely outweighing the quality of the room, I thought it was a better option to simply take advantage of the deal I negotiated with Miss Chase."

"Ah." Sorecco nodded sagely, closing the door with a thud, then moving back toward his spinning wheel. "That bad, huh."

"Very much so." Tzedef agreed, following him across the room to tuck his pack and shield next to the end of the bed he'd used the night before. "I do not *know* that the rat piss caused the mold, but it certainly did not help."

Sorecco froze, then shuddered delicately.

"That's disgusting."

"I agree."

Silence fell, comfortable in the evening light that filtered through the windows, and Tzedef let it hang, perfectly content to listen to the quiet whirring of the spinning wheel.

Something jiggled his memory just the right way, "Oh,"

Sorecco hummed questioningly from his wheel.

73

"I just recalled, I wished to look at your front door's lock."

The whirring paused. "You did? Why?"

"To see if it might be repaired."

"Oh." Sorecco said, nonplussed. "Um…"

Tzedef glanced over at him, one ear flicking. "Do you mind?"

Sorecco startled, "No! By all means, if you think you can fix it, then please, feel free! It's not like you can make it any worse."

"Oh you would be surprised." Tzedef snorted, and his smile was crooked when he stood up and went over to the front door.

He had to move a few things out of the way, most notably a basket full of dark gray fluff that threatened to blow away just from the breeze of his moving it, but soon enough the floor in front of the door was clear, and he knelt down in front of it.

He was lucky, he concluded, that his night vision made things like the dark interior of the lock trivial to deal with. There was no need to futz with a candle, or try to get a light stone to work properly. All he needed to do was look and, occasionally, probe at the interior with a small stick or needle or bit of wire.

None of which he had.

Hmm… that was a difficulty he hadn't expected.

Tzedef glanced around then reached for his pack and started rummaging around through it, searching for anything that might be thin and long enough to poke into the lock itself.

Nothing but the needle in his medkit, and that was too delicate for this kind of work.

He huffed, and tossed the pack back toward the end of the bed.

"Sorecco?"

"Hmm?"

Sorecco turned his face toward Tzedef, his hands and feet not pausing as the spinning wheel whirred and whirred.

"Do you have something long and thin, perchance? A stick of some sort, or a bit of wire?"

Sorecco's head tipped slightly to one side as he thought. "Would a knitting needle work?"

"Possibly," Tzedef said, and pushed himself to his feet. "Do you have one?"

"There's a jar of them on the bookcase behind me." Sorecco replied, then frowned. "Or at least, that's where they're supposed to be. They're Casey's, though, so who can tell."

Tzedef hummed a soft acknowledgment and looked past the spinning wheel and the man running it smoothly, to the shelves behind him.

He hadn't paid much mind to the shelves before; there'd been no need, and it had honestly felt a bit too much like unnecessary snooping. Now however, he looked, and what he saw was informative.

A few books. Very little dust. Skeins of spun yarn, as yet undyed but neatly wound all the same. A couple of small statuettes, clumsily made and painted with bright colors.

A tiny shrine that looked like it could, if it needed to, fold up and be moved easily, with a small scrap of cloth and two hard sweets in front of it.

And indeed, after a moment's search, there was a jar stuffed full of knitting needles of all sizes.

"I see it." He reported, and Sorecco nodded, satisfied.

"Good. Then you can use one of those, if you like. Just try not to break it, if you would."

"Of course," Tzedef nodded, and made his way past Sorecco to extract one of the thinnest wooden needles from its prison before returning to the floor in front of the door.

His eyes almost crossed as he focused on the small keyhole and slipped the slender wooden stick inside, probing gently at the pins.

None of them budged.

Frowning, he probed harder, working entirely by feel as he slipped the needle deeper into the lock and pressed around until he found something he was almost positive should move.

It didn't.

Frowning even more deeply now, Tzedef withdrew the knitting needle and examined the end, then stood and turned toward the small kitchen.

It was the work of a moment to run one white-scaled hand under the tap and get it wet, and when he returned to the door it was easy to trickle a few drops of water into the lock.

"What are you doing?" Sorecco asked curiously, and Tzedef responded as he shook the remaining water off his hand and dried it on the hem of his shirt.

"None of the pins would move when I pressed on them, and the interior mechanism seems locked in place. I didn't see any signs of rust on the knitting needle when I withdrew it, which leads me to believe that some other method of fusing the lock was used. If it was glue, then the water will loosen it a bit and cause it to smell. If it was a spell, then the water won't do anything."

"A spell?" Sorecco echoed, and the spinning wheel stopped. "Or glue? Do you think someone messed with our lock on *purpose*?"

"It is possible, yes. Probable even, though I do not see what purpose that would serve."

Sorecco sighed quietly, the sound weary. "Who knows. It could be as simple as someone wanting to mess with the whore and her crippled brother."

Tzedef blinked at him and waited for any further explanation, then silently called himself an idiot and made a questioning noise.

Sorecco shrugged. "People are stupid. There's no real way to know who, if someone did it, or why. We just get to live with it."

"I see," Tzedef said with a small frown, and he did, to a point. People were always derisive of differences, regardless of the fact that, with so many different kindred in the world, there were *always* going to be differences. It was ridiculous to deride and disparage others for something as silly as *profession* when there were actual threats in the world. If people would put *half* the energy they spent on ridiculous bigotries into making the world a better place instead, then—

A whiff of fish jolted Tzedef out of his thoughts, and he blinked, then leaned towards the lock, sniffing again.

"I was correct," he announced. "It was glue."

"Oh great," Sorecco sighed, "so we're just never getting that clean, then."

Tzedef's eye-ridge arched. "Not so. A minor cleaning cantrip will do for this in essentially no time. Do you know one?"

"Of course not. And there's no one around here I could ask, either. Our neighbors tolerate us, but we're not really at the point of favors between friends."

Tzedef considered that for a moment, then grimaced. "There is… Another way. You have a decent grasp of magic, if you're casting fire spells without speaking. I know the theory of a cleaning cantrip. Would you care to attempt to learn?"

"Yes!" Sorecco yelped, sitting bolt upright. "Ahem… I mean, please, if you wouldn't mind. I'd love to learn."

"Excellent." Tzedef shifted, moving a bit away from the door so that there was enough room for another person between himself and the door. "Come over here, in front of the door, and kneel down. We'll practice you on the lock itself."

"And if I screw up and make it worse?" Sorecco

asked dryly, but stood up and came over anyway.

"Then nothing will have changed." Tzedef said calmly. "You already haven't had use of this door in, as Miss Chase put it, 'ages'; this will simply be more of the same."

"Fair point." Sorecco admitted, his hand sliding across the well sanded wood of the door, a good six inches above where the knob would be.

"Lower." Tzedef told him, and Sorecco hummed an acknowledgment and slid his hand lower, bumping the wrought iron knob, then grasping it and lowering himself into a kneel.

"Alright, I'm here. Now what?"

"May I touch you? It would be the easiest way for me to demonstrate the needed gestures."

"Sure." Sorecco shrugged, and Tzedef shuffled around until he was behind the man, leaning forward slightly to grasp his wrists and move his hands until they were on level with the lock.

"Which hand is dominant?"

"My left."

"Very well, then you're going to want to circle the fingers and thumb of your right hand, like so... good. Now arrange your left hand like this. Index finger pointed like so."

Careful prodding adjusted Sorecco's fingers into the correct configuration, and he guided Sorecco through the small, swooping motions required for the casting of the spell.

"You will need to ensure that you touch what it is you wish to be cleaned, as the spell releases." Tzedef informed him, letting go, and Sorecco nodded, a frown of concentration drawing dark eyebrows together.

Over and over, Sorecco practiced the movements, and at first, Tzedef needed to stop him and step in, guiding him again through the motion as smoothly as he could. But Sorecco proved to be a quick study, and truly, this was a cantrip. A spell for children to learn to determine what, if any, real aptitude they had for magic. It was made to be as simple as possible. There were other cleaning spells out there, more in depth and complex, like the one that Gemori had likely used on his clothing, but Tzedef didn't know any of those. This would suffice for such a small thing.

"So..." Sorecco said slowly, going through the motions again as Tzedef watched with a critical eye. "If you know the theory, the movements, and the incantation, why don't you just cast the spell?"

Ah.

There it was.

The five hundred plat question that he'd been hoping Sorecco wouldn't ask.

"I cannot." Tzedef said, his voice quiet.

Not ashamed.

Never ashamed.

"You can't?" Sorecco's surprise was expected, but the soft "huh," and total lack of follow up questions wasn't.

This must, Tzedef thought to himself bemusedly, be how Sorecco had felt the evening before when he hadn't asked about his blindness.

It was a refreshing change from disbelief and the derision that followed on most finding out about his disability.

After all, even newborns held some measure of innate power.

But every drop of Tzedef's came from his goddess.

In the place where the well of magic that should beat in his chest like a second heart should be?

There was nothing.

There had always been nothing.

"Right," Sorecco said, nodding firmly as he completed the gesture for the fifth time without Tzedef needing to correct him. "I think I've got it, now. What's the incantation?"

Tzedef huffed a soft laugh. "You will appreciate this, I think. Remember, this is a spell for children so the incantation is easy to remember and say; all it is, is 'clean'."

Sorecco stilled, then groaned and buried his face in his hands. "You're joking."

"Not in the slightest."

"'Clean?' *Seriously*??"

"Absolutely."

"That's the stupidest thing I've ever heard."

Tzedef's head cocked. "Is it really?"

"Well, no," Sorecco admitted, "*that* prize probably goes to the woman who, during one of the last big storms, climbed up to the top of the lighthouse and started screaming at the Storm Queen."

Tzedef's eyes widened. "Someone *what*??"

"Yeah," Sorecco snorted, grinning crookedly. "That was pretty much everyone else's reaction, too. Along with being generally amazed that she survived the fall when the wind picked her up off the observation deck and threw her a good extra two hundred feet in the air."

"How on *Chaelu*—" Tzedef cut himself off, shaking his head. "Nevermind. There will always be fools, and fools will always have Persis' blessing."

Sorecco cocked his head, "Who?"

"Persis." Tzeded repeated. "He is a god local to my home country, with the domains of Fools, Ignorance, Misinformation, and Luck. "

There was a long moment of silence as Sorecco digested that tidbit.

"Why 'Misinformation', and not 'Lies'?"

"Let us finish the door, and I will explain as best I can."

"Oh right!" Sorecco exclaimed, "The door! I'm sorry! I forgot what we were doing!"

Tzedef's quiet chuckle took both of them by surprise, and after a moment Sorecco grinned sheepishly.

"Sorry," he said again, and turned back to the door, sliding his hand over it until he'd relocated the knob and lock again.

Then he did something that Tzedef wasn't expecting at all.

Instead of moving his hand away and performing the gesture the way Tzedef had shown him, Sorecco kept his fingers pressed to the lock, then made most of the gesture with his free hand.

"Clean!" He commanded, and Tzedef opened his mouth to say something, only to close it silently as the fishy scent from the lock grew stronger, then faded away entirely.

That...

That was *exceptional* talent.

"Well done." He said instead, and Sorecco leaned forward, sniffing.

"It got stronger though, did I wreck it? I know I did it wrong, but you said I needed to touch the lock and I wasn't sure I'd be able to land on the lock for sure if I did it right, so I just thought maybe if I did it like this then—"

"Peace, friend," Tzedef interrupted Sorecco's increasingly worried rambling. "It worked. You did well."

"It did?" Sorecco perked up, "Really?"

Tzedef nodded. "As far as I can tell, yes. Of course, there's one way to tell for certain..."

"Oh!" Sorecco bolted to his feet. "Right! The key! Hang on, lemme just..."

Tzedef watched as Sorecco swept across the flat, narrowly avoiding the things that Tzedef had had to move out of the way of the door, to go rummage through a drawer in the kitchen.

"I have a copy of the key so I can lock up whenever I go out, but it's been so long I just tossed it in here, I think..." He frowned, and rummaged a bit more, then brightened and held up a key. "Ha! Here it is! Probably."

He came back with a bounce in his step, and Tzedef

pushed himself to his feet, then stepped out of the way.

It only took a moment for Sorecco to find the lock again, and the key slipped in easily. A moment of jiggling, and it turned, and Sorecco whooped happily, then yanked the door open.

Tzedef's ears flattened themselves to his skull as the hinges shrieked in protest, and Sorecco's jaw dropped, a pained look on his face.

"Ow…"

"Those very definitely want oil." Tzedef said, entirely unnecessarily, and Sorecco nodded fervently. "You'll want to oil the lock as well. That spell might be small, but it *is* thorough. It wouldn't do to have the lock jam due to lack of lubrication."

"Right." Sorecco agreed, and the hinges screamed as he shut the door again. "That can wait until Casey gets home. In the meantime, are you hungry?"

"A bite wouldn't go amiss." Tzedef admitted.

"Then I'll get dinner started." Sorecco said, and went off to do just that.

CHAPTER SEVEN

A Mountain Full of Dwarves

The hinges were duly oiled the next morning, and Chase was delighted by the fact that the front door was now free to be used; thanking Tzedef profusely, and then, when he deferred and said that Sorecco had fixed it in truth, dropping a kiss on her brother's cheek with a wide, pleased grin.

"So yer staying?" She checked, and Tzedef nodded.

"Yes. It seems that everyone was correct. There truly are no rooms in Natari at the moment."

"Well then." Chase said, propping her fists on her hips, "You might as well know the truth. I hate using that accent more than I have to, so there."

Tzedef blinked at her. "Then why do it?"

She shrugged. "Habit. Anyway, hi. M'name's Casey. It's nice to properly meet you."

Casey held out one hand, and, bemused, Tzedef reached out and shook it.

"Great," she said briskly, "now. We've already

reached an agreement about you staying here, so that's that, but I want you to let us know if you need anything else, alright? Directions, more food, whatever. We'll do our best to help out, if we can."

Tzedef considered her for a moment, then nodded slowly. "Very well, but I will expect the same from you. Should you need assistance, or should my presence put too large a strain on you, then I will endeavor to remedy the situation."

Casey squinted at him for a moment, then nodded sharply.

Tzedef nodded back, and that, it seemed, was that.

The next two days passed easily. There were morning conversations with Casey, and evening conversations with Sorecco, and check-ins with Captain Teralia to find out when exactly the ship would be departing, and in between all that Tzedef dogged the footsteps of the local bards, hunting them down one by one and asking them about the Ambered Castle. All for naught, as it turned out, because of the few who recognized the name, only one had any information to give him.

"Iss inna mountain!" The cervid woman proclaimed, swaying drunkenly in her seat, "Onna mainl'nd. Bu' good luck gettin' in. I heard, I heard," She leaned forward, beckoning Tzedef closer and dropping her voice to a 'quiet' hiss.

Which was only slightly lower than her normal speaking tone had been, before she'd started drinking.

"I heard," she said again, "tha' th' Amber Castle is got a... a thingy 'round it."

"A... thingy." Tzedef repeated, and sighed inwardly. He should have remembered that cervids had notoriously low tolerance for alcohol. But beer and ale worked well to soothe the voices of those prone to talking, and made them friendly, besides.

She nodded, apparently satisfied that he'd understood what she meant, and beamed at him.

"What sort of 'thingy'?" Tzedef prodded, and she leaned back.

"Nobody knows." She said, obviously aiming for mysterious but landing firmly in obnoxiously smug instead. "Th' dwarves... they keep it secret, y'know? Iss speshul. Preshus. Way th' guy what tol' me 'bout it said, they don' let nobody even touch it."

She scowled suddenly, and knocked back the last of her ale in one long draught before slamming the mug back down on the table. "Cheatin' bassard conned me outta my bes' flute with a marked deck! Bassard!"

Tzedef stifled a sigh, and sat back in his chair, only half-listening to the woman in front of him as she went off on a tangent about cheaters and flutes. The rest of him was busy mulling over the information he'd just gotten.

The Ambered Castle definitely existed. He'd known that to begin with- Hecate wouldn't have sent him on a wild goose chase- but it was good to have outside confirmation.

It was surrounded by something. A shield of some sort? A barrier? Perhaps an actual, physical wall of some kind? He set that aside for the moment. Without more information it was pointless to speculate.

It was inside a mountain, somewhere on Malfeir. He'd known the last part, obviously, but the inside a mountain part was news to him, and somewhat alarming news at that. There were quite a few mountains on the continent, after all, and if he had to search *all* of them then Hecate was going to be waiting quite a while for her Candle Magic.

However, the next bit of information narrowed that down. It had something to do with dwarves. Or rather, dwarves were keeping it, somehow, and preventing access to it. Possibly even they had created the 'thingy' around the Ambered Castle, and were maintaining it.

That might complicate things, if it were true.

So. He was looking for a mountain, with dwarves.

Yes, that narrowed things down nicely.

Not.

Tzedef waited until he found a gap in the cervid bard's rambling, then excused himself politely and made for the door of the tavern, still rolling the new information over in his mind.

The evening air was crisp, and thick with the smells from different food stalls, and, as Tzedef made his way back to Casey and Sorecco's home, one scent in particular caught his attention- spiced and sweet and meaty.

He couldn't help himself. One stop later, and he had a piping hot package of meats and fruits and vegetables, all skewered on sticks and grilled. It would be a nice little surprise for Sorecco and Casey; a small gift for the pair that had shown him nothing but kindness.

Tzedef was nearly bowled over by an ursine as he turned the corner onto the correct street, and he had to make a quick step to the side to avoid running directly into the elf next to them. Neither so much as broke stride, much less stopped to apologize, and Tzedef frowned, making note of their neat clothing and the round, dark blue patches each had sewn to their upper sleeve.

It was an oddity, but one pair of assholes was not going to be enough to ruin the relatively good mood that the skewers had put him in.

Knocking on the front door, Tzedef waited until he heard Sorecco call for him to enter before opening it and slipping inside, pulling the door closed behind himself with his tail and heading straight for the kitchen.

"I have returned."

"Welcome back, Tzedef." Sorecco said, and he sounded so distracted that Tzedef paused and turned to peer at him.

Sorecco, usually neatly dressed and carefully groomed, was in disarray. His hair was mussed, his clothes rumpled and twisted, and... Tzedef peered closely, there was a bruise beginning to blossom on his cheek, right above the bone.

"Sorecco?" He couldn't keep the concern out of his voice. "Are you all right?"

"What?" Sorecco turned toward him, and Tzedef frowned at the way his hands were twitching, almost like he wanted to wring them, but wouldn't let himself.

"Are you all right?"

"What?" He said again, and frowned, "Yes, of course, I'm fine. Why wouldn't I be?"

"You…" Tzedef hesitated. He'd kept from prying too far into their lives, content to keep to a kind of live and let live policy, but this was… concerning. "You have a bruise. On your cheek."

One hand came up to touch the injury, and Sorecco flinched.

"I fell." He said shortly, straightening out his clothes with rough tugs. "Tripped over my own damn feet and hit the wall on the way down. I'm fine."

"Ah." Tzedef blinked at that, but kept his peace. He supposed that was one of the hazards of being alone all day as a blind man; sometimes injuries happened. Still, it wasn't in his nature to allow a friend to remain hurt if he could help it, so, "would you like healing?"

"It's a *bruise*." Sorecco sounded incredulous. "Not a fractured skull. I'll be fine in a day or three. Don't waste your magic on such a small thing, Tzedef."

"Fair enough."

It was his choice, after all, and far be it from Tzedef to force a healing on someone who didn't want one. "I brought food."

Sorecco turned, then sniffed the air lightly. "Lamb?"

"And grilled fruit and vegetables." Tzedef agreed. "On sticks."

"Kebabs!" Sorecco lit up, "I love those, but they're

only really sold during the festivals. How many did you get?"

"Four for each of us." Tzedef headed for the table and put down the greasy package of food, opening up the packet and pulling out four of the kebabs. Those got handed over to Sorecco, and Tzedef removed his own from the package before re-wrapping it, the better to keep the remainders fresh for Casey.

"So," Sorecco said as he sat down to eat, "Did you find anything today?"

"Actually, yes." Tzedef nibbled at a piece of onion, lightly charred, and considered the flavour. "There was a cervid who'd heard something of the Ambered Castle. Apparently it lies in a mountain somewhere on the mainland, where it is guarded by dwarves."

"Helpful." Sorecco said, dryly sarcastic, and Tzedef huffed his agreement.

"It would be more helpful if I knew how many dwarven settlements there are on Malfeir. I know in Fernil there are only three worth speaking of."

"I've heard of two, offhand," Sorecco offered, "Though there's probably more."

"Do you know anything about either of them?" Tzedef asked, and considered a piece of vegetable with a dark green skin and paler green flesh before cautiously tasting it.

Sorecco hummed thoughtfully around a mouthful and, after a moment's chewing, swallowed hard. "A little. I've heard that the Lorinn Mountain range is actually entirely hollowed out and the dwarves have massive cities in there. Whole countries, practically. It's probably complete garbage, of course. It's a *mountain range*. Where would you even put what got dug out of it?"

"Perhaps the legends of dwarves eating stone is true?" Tzedef suggested, and smiled quietly to himself at Sorecco's outraged scoff.

"Complete bullshit. Utter nonsense. There's no possible way that that would work. Besides, it would still end up being *literal mountains of shit*. Where would they *put* it all?"

"Drop it into the sea?" Tzedef suggested, thoroughly enjoying winding Sorecco up.

"Oh yes," Sorecco scoffed again, with a badly stifled grin playing about his mouth. "I'm sure the local mer population would have *absolutely* let them get away with that. There's no possible way that would go wrong. Not to mention the fact that getting it there in the *first* place would be a job and a half."

Tzedef chuckled, soft and low, and Sorecco paused, head cocked curiously.

"Not that, then." Tzedef conceded, and took another bite. "What about the other? The second settlement?"

"That one I know less about. Not a lot of folks from Reyfil mountain come down this far south. I've heard that they tend to be pretty reclusive, though, so if you're looking for something that's being guarded by dwarves and it's there, you're probably in for a bit of a rough time."

Tzedef's muzzle wrinkled. "Lovely... Ah, on

another note entirely, is there perhaps a gang of some sort around Natari?"

Sorecco paused, taken aback. "A gang? Not that I'm aware of, why? Did something happen?"

"In a way," Tzedef said, and explained about the ursine and the elf in their matching clothing and identical patches. "It's odd. That is behavior I would expect more from the guard, or soldiers, or others accustomed to some measure of violence, but their clothes were quite fine."

"Weird." Sorecco said with forced casualness, and Tzedef looked at him sharply, taking in the slight tremble of the other man's hands before he pressed them against the table and stood. "I don't know of any gangs in the city like that, no, and we don't typically have soldiers move through Natari, either."

Tzedef hummed thoughtfully, and watched as Sorecco paced over to the kitchen sink and started running the basin full of water, leaving behind half of his last kebab.

"Sorecco?"

"I'm full. Help yourself to the last of it, if you like, or leave it for Casey. She'll eat it."

"Very well..." Tzedef agreed slowly. That hadn't been what he'd been about to ask, though.

But apparently Sorecco wasn't in a speaking mood anymore, and it was dark enough that Tzedef's vision was all in shades of grey again.

Carefully, he tucked the half eaten kebab back into the package, and left that on the table as he stood, then stretched.

"I think I shall sleep." He said after a long silence, broken only by the sound of Sorecco scrubbing industriously at the dishes from that morning.

"Alright." Sorecco said, and though he was obviously trying to sound normal, there was a certain tightness in his voice that wasn't usually present. "Sleep well, then, Tzedef."

"Goodnight."

Tzedef frowned, going back over the interaction as he readied himself for sleep. Still, nothing he could point to that he'd said would have made such a reaction reasonable. In the end, he had to conclude that it was something about the two that had nearly run him down that had triggered Sorecco's sudden change in mood.

That, coupled with Sorecco's disheveled appearance when Tzedef had gotten back, painted a potentially unpleasant picture. But who would shake down a blind man, and why? What was the purpose? It wasn't as though Casey and Sorecco were particularly well off, though they weren't destitute, either...

It wasn't until the front door opened, then shut softly and the lock clicked to, that Tzedef realized he'd been worrying at this train of thought for a lot longer than he'd meant to, and Casey had come home.

"Welcome home." Sorecco said softly, the sharp syllables of the human language softened by his attempts to keep his voice low.

"Thanks," Casey said wearily, then sighed. A

moment later, Tzedef heard soft sniffing. "Do I smell lamb?" She sounded quietly delighted, and Sorecco made a noise of assent from the table.

"Tzedef brought back kebabs." Sorecco said, and he sounded mostly normal, to Tzedef's ear. Nevertheless, Casey paused.

"What's wrong?"

"Eat first, then I'll tell you."

"Kol— Sorecco, what happened?"

"Nothing that can't wait. Eat your food, Casey. I know you're hungry."

There was a long pause, then Casey moved across the room and sat at the table, lighting the crystal with a softly murmured word.

For a few minutes, there was nothing but the quiet sounds of eating and soft, happy sounds from Chase, then the last stick clattered gently against the others, and Casey sighed.

"All right, I'm done. Tell me. What happened?"

Sorecco hesitated for a brief moment, then sighed as well. "The Weaver's Guild paid me a visit today."

There was a sharp inhale.

"Okay…" Casey said hesitantly. "That's… unusual. Who was it? Not the entire guild, obviously so…?"

"The enforcers." Sorecco bit out. "Apparently word's gotten out about my little side business. They *politely* requested that I stop selling the yarn I spin."

"Oh."

"Casey," This time his voice trembled, "They're

fining me for damages to the guild's reputation. They said, if I can't pay, I can sign on to the guild. There's a contract. They left it with me."

"Damages to the guild's—!" Casey's voice went high with disbelief, "Who the hells do they think they are? The Governor?! They can't just *fine* you!"

"Shhh!" Sorecco hissed, "You'll wake him!"

Casey subsided, and, after a moment of silence in which Tzedef kept his breathing slow and even, spoke again.

"How did they find out?"

"I don't know," Sorecco said miserably, "Hells, maybe old lady Halven told them or something, I don't know, Casey, I really don't. I've been *careful*, I swear I have!"

"No, hush, it's okay. I believe you. No, I do, really. I just…" Casey sighed exhaustedly. "You said they left a contract? Let me see it."

There was the rustle of paper, then silence, and eventually Casey spoke again, her voice utterly incredulous. "Kolby *what the fuck*?"

"What? What does it say?"

"Kolby, this is a fucking *indentured servitude* contract!"

"*What*!?" Sorecco's voice cracked.

"It's worse than that, actually." She said, simmering with rage, "You won't get paid anything, they don't take any responsibility for your well being, housing, or food, anything you make is the property of the guild to use or sell as they please… This isn't even indentured servitude! This is fucking criminal!"

"Fuck." Sorecco breathed, and took a deep, shuddering breath. "Fuck, Casey… I can't sign that contract."

"You won't have to." Casey was firm. "I promise, you don't have to sign this contract. We'll figure something out. Maybe if I take this to the guard, they'll—"

"Do absolutely nothing about it." Sorecco said quietly, his voice tight. "I'm breaking guild law. It's well within their rights to demand that I at least repay them for some of their potential lost income."

There was a long moment of silence.

"Well shit."

"Yeah."

Casey sighed, and there was a soft thump of something hitting the table. Her hand, perhaps. "Maybe I can take out a loan, or maybe they'll let us pay it back a little at a time. I'll go talk to them tomorrow and sort it all out. I promise, Kolby, everything'll be fine."

"You're sure? I… I can go and talk to them. It's my fault. I should be the one to take care of it."

"It's fine. I don't mind. Just… give me tomorrow, or maybe until the day after, and I'll get this sorted out. It'll be fine."

"Okay." Sorecco's voice was quiet, and for a very long moment, neither of them said anything. Then Sorecco took a deep, shuddering breath and let it out slowly, the sound faintly wet.

"C'mon," Casey said kindly, "we should sleep."
"Yeah, okay."

The next night, Casey didn't come home.

CHAPTER EIGHT

A Well Timed Gift

Sorecco putting on his boots and muttering quietly
to himself woke Tzedef when it was still dark enough that
his vision was painted in shades of grey, and, for a moment,
Tzedef contemplated rolling over and going back to sleep.
But there was a note of genuine worry in Sorecco's voice
that pricked at his brain and woke him as quickly as an
alarm horn being sounded.

"Sorecco?" His voice was a thick, sleep-laden rasp,
and Sorecco stilled. "What is wrong?"

"Casey isn't home yet. I'm going to go out and look
for her."

"What?" Tzedef blinked, then sat up. Sure enough,
Casey was nowhere to be seen in the small flat.

"What time is it?"

"Don't know." Sorecco said shortly. "Hours past
when she'd normally be home, though. I know that much."

Tzedef stood and stepped over to the window,
pulling aside the curtain enough to peer out. Outside, the

faint greyish light of predawn lit the eastern sky, and he frowned.

Sorecco was right. This was *well* past when she had returned the last few days.

"Nearly dawn." He informed Sorecco, who swore and started tugging at his boots again. "Sorecco."

"What?" Sorecco snapped, and Tzedef blinked, then shook it off.

"Do you want help looking?"

Sorecco paused. "You'd do that? Help?"

"Of course I would." Tzedef said, a trifle insulted. "The two of you have been nothing but kind to me. It would be ungracious to the extreme not to assist in the event that something has happened."

"Right…" Sorecco said slowly, obviously finding that somewhat hard to believe. Still, after a moment he nodded sharply. "Okay. Sure. That'd be great, actually. We'll be able to cover more ground that way. I'll take the area around the weaver's guild, since she said she was going there at some point. Can you look around the red light district?"

Tzedef nodded, paused, called himself an idiot, and spoke. "Yes, I can do that, easily. When shall we meet back here?"

"In an hour, or whenever one of us finds her." Sorecco said firmly, and stood, reaching for the walking stick propped against the wall next to the back door. He slid one hand up to the top, where a bundle of cloth was wrapped around something, and started to unwind it to reveal a bell. It was small and silver, with a pure chime that rang clearly whenever the stick moved, and now when Sorecco moved around the flat to get to the front door, there was a measure of surety to his step that Tzedef hadn't even realized had been missing.

"Alright." Sorecco said, his voice grim, "I'm going now. I'll see you in an hour."

"Very well." Tzedef nodded.

The door opened. Closed. And Tzedef was alone.

He dressed quickly, forgoing proper trousers in favour of his soft, brown sleeping trous and just throwing a shirt and his cloak on to stave off the morning chill. He hesitated for a brief moment over his mace and shield, then shook his head, shoved his feet into his boots, and slipped out of the flat himself.

The red light district, Sorecco had said, and Tzedef, now more familiar with Natari's streets, wound his way unerringly in that direction.

Up and down the streets of the red light district he searched, even going so far as to venture down the myriad alleyways that branched off the main street, and he found nothing save for various clients staggering their way out of various buildings. The few workers he managed to question said that they'd seen her, yes, but the night had been slow, so she'd left early.

One man pointed him towards the docks.

"If it's slow here, sometimes the sailors are a better crowd." He said casually, and Tzedef nodded, passed him a couple of copper as thanks, then turned and headed straight for the docks.

The docks themselves, once one was past the gate that controlled access to and from them, were actually not all that large. The docks as an area, however, were quite large indeed, with warehouses in neat rows in the center of the area, where anyone attempting to break into one would be plainly visible.

That, at least, was the idea of the first round of warehouses.

Trade, however, had grown since then, and with it came higher demand for storage space, and specialty storage spaces for rare, unique, or particularly hard to acquire merchandise. So more warehouses were built, and then more, and soon enough the warehouses were packed all the way up to the wall surrounding the docks. With hidey holes and odd passages around and between the warehouses, it was the perfect place for smugglers. Or someone looking for private place to tryst.

Hopefully Casey had just found a particularly amorous client, and would be fine. Hopefully she would have already finished up, and she would be at home when he returned. Hopef—

A spark flickered at the edge of his awareness, and Tzedef swore, and turned, orienting on it as best he could before taking off at a speed that his large size belied.

It was guttering.

Flickering.

Fading, and Tzedef cursed again and reached up to

his neck, pulling free his amulet and clutching it tightly as he ran.

"Tzedef!" Casey waved at him from the end of one alley, down the road he'd just turned onto. "Tzedef hurry! I'm over here!"

The phrasing was odd, but not so odd that it distracted him from the dying ember in his mind, and he nodded to her sharply as he turned into the alley. She was dirty, and her clothes were in disarray, but she wasn't injured; he'd apologize for his rudeness later.

Someone lay in the middle of the alley, clothes torn and dirty, one arm bent at an awkward angle, face bruised, breathing shallow.

Even so, Tzedef recognized her as he fell to his knees at her side.

She'd just spoken to him, after all.

The ember guttered, and Tzedef gritted his teeth. Questions could come later.

Casey needed healing right now.

The words for a prayer to spare the dying tumbled from his mouth hurriedly, the plea having more meaning than he usually put into it. More fervor than he'd felt since he'd lost the last of his true comrades in arms.

But it worked.

Her chest rose, and fell, and rose again as her breathing steadied; growing stronger even as the ember in his mind brightened until it became a steady flame, then faded out of his awareness.

She was no longer on the cusp between life and

death.

Casey would live.

"Am I okay?" Casey asked, leaning over his shoulder anxiously. "I tried and tried, but I couldn't get me to wake up, and I can't go very far from myself, and I was a little afraid to try to move me."

"I don't know." Tzedef said tersely, the presence at his back making the scales at the back of his neck prickle with unease. "If you will stand to the side, I will check."

Casey obediently backed up a few paces, and stood, bouncing nervously on her toes as Tzedef carefully straightened the limbs of the Casey on the ground. He grimaced at the feel of the broken arm, but straightened it as well.

It was lucky for him that Casey didn't seem to be predisposed to tears. He wasn't good with weeping, and he'd been told more than once that his bedside manner was atrocious. It wasn't something he'd cultivated on purpose, but his brusque attitude and intolerance of stupidity had left him with a reputation for having a stick somewhere unmentionable.

He, on the other hand, didn't see what the purpose was in going out and doing stupid things that invariably ended up with one or more of the participants in the medical hall. Or tent. It was a waste of his time, and, the greater sin in his eyes, a waste of medical supplies that were often in short supply while on campaign. It *irritated* him.

Still, despite his terrible bedside manner, Tzedef's

hands were as gentle as they could be when he palpated her stomach to check for internal bleeding, and he tried to keep his touch as soft as he could as he checked her face and skull for damage.

"Broken cheekbone," He muttered to himself, quietly furious as he cataloged Chase's injuries. "And a fractured skull. Which means definitely a concussion."

It was a common misconception that healing magic did what it did without any input at all from the caster. That things would be fixed as the body intended for them to heal. But Tzedef had been told, long ago, that this was, in fact, false. Healing magic worked based on what the caster knew of the body and how it worked.

To that end, Tzedef had done everything he could to learn as many mundane healing techniques as possible, and even gone so far as to attend several lectures at the Yaelin Healing Halls during his down time. He'd been incredibly fortunate that one such lecture he'd attended had included a dissection of a recently deceased human male, and he'd made copious notes and drawings that day, and pored over them endlessly.

Granted, there were differences between the races, and Tzedef knew that well, which is why some small, ghoulish part of him had been almost glad when the war had kicked off again in truth.

His superiors had been glad to allow him access to the enemy dead once he'd promised that they'd see results in his treatment of his comrades. And they had. The potency of his healing magic had increased drastically once it no longer had to fill in so many gaps in his knowledge, and Tzedef had been able to heal more, and longer, than several of his lesser educated fellows.

All of his notes and anatomical sketches and written theories had been confiscated when he'd been discharged, but he still had what was in his head. They hadn't taken that from him.

"A fractured skull?" The Casey to one side said, her voice small. "That's bad, right? Am I going to die?"

"Not if I have anything to say about it." Tzedef muttered, concentrating hard. "Hecate from whom my power flows, stretch forth your light and guide this body toward rejuvenation. Cure what ails her, and restore what was broken to its most perfect form, I beseech you."

Saffron light, muted in intensity, suffused Chase's body for a moment then faded away, leaving behind only rapidly fading bruises.

Ever thorough, Tzedef checked her over again and, once satisfied that everything had returned to normal, he sat back on his heels and looked at the other Casey.

"So." He said. "Would you care to explain?"

"Well…" Casey said slowly, twisting her fingers in the front of her dress, "I'm not entirely sure I can."

"Start at the beginning, then." Tzedef said, as gently as he could manage. "How did this person come to look like you? With these injuries?"

"That's me." Casey said, "Of course I look like me. I'm me."

Tzedef blinked, then looked down at the still unconscious woman on the ground, then reached out and poked Casey in the arm.

Solid.

This isn't a case of the soul having gone wandering, then, which meant there were two other possible explanations.

"What is your name?"

"Casey." Casey said, and Tzedef sighed. The likelihood of this being a shifter was low, which meant...

"I think this is my Gift." Casey said quietly, and Tzedef nodded.

"Very well. Congratulations on awakening your Gift. Now. What. *Happened*?"

Casey's story turned out to be relatively short.

Things had been slow in the red light area, so she'd come down to the docks in search of clients. And then she'd run into Rugar, who'd grabbed her.

"I screamed, obviously," She said matter-of-factly, "but he covered my mouth, dragged me back here, and started beating me. I thought..." She shivers, and hugs herself, her nonchalant manner dropping for a moment. "I thought I was gonna die."

"You have not." Tzedef said firmly. "Nor will you, while I can prevent it."

Casey nodded, still hugging herself, and Tzedef reached up, undid the clasp of his cloak, and offered it to her.

For a moment, it looked like she was going to refuse, then one trembling hand reached out and took it.

"Thanks." She murmured, wrapping it around her

shoulders.

"You are welcome." He replied, and waited a few moments before prodding her gently. "What happened next?"

"Me, I guess." She said, shrugging. "Suddenly I was there, and I started screaming for help as loud as I could, and trying to get him off me. I guess he wasn't expecting two of me, so he ran off. I tried to run and get help, but apparently there's a distance limit or something, because I could only go about halfway up the street you found me on."

"I see." Tzedef murmured, then sighed and reached down to gather the unconscious Casey into his arms, standing with a soft grunt. "Would you like to go to the guards for this?"

"No." Casey said sharply, then huffed bitterly. "Not like they'd do anything about it, anyway. All the evidence is gone, except a couple bruises, and those'll be gone in a day or three."

"I'm not apologizing." Tzedef said mildly, and Casey blinked at him.

"I never said you should. I was just bitching about the guards. And, honestly, truly, thank you. I would have died. Or... that me would have died? I don't know how this works, and honestly, I'm not keen on finding out what happens if one of me dies!"

"That is reasonable." Tzedef agreed, turning and heading towards the mouth of the alley, Casey on his heels. "And now is not the time to experiment, either. Sorecco was worried."

"Oh no…" Casey murmured, "Did he want to go out looking?"

"He did go out looking. He left before I did." Tzedef informed her mildly.

"Oh *no…*" she said, utterly dismayed. "He's going to be furious with me…"

Tzedef snorted. "Not likely. He'll be more likely to go to the guards himself."

Casey sucked air between her teeth, a sharp, concerned sound. "I hope not…"

Why, Tzedef almost wanted to ask, but kept the question firmly behind his teeth, focusing instead on getting the Caseys home.

It didn't take too long, but the sun was properly up by the time they stopped in front of the door to the flat.

Casey paused, and Tzedef stopped as well, unable to open the door with his arms full of her other self.

"Is something wrong?"

"Sorecco is going to be so mad." Casey fretted. "The only reason he was alright with my job was because it's actually pretty safe around here. Now that *this* happened…"

She sighs, then winces and looks guiltily up at Tzedef. "Right… I didn't tell you… Sorecco actually knows about my job…"

"Oddly enough, I had figured that out." Tzedef said dryly, and twisted his tongue around the sharp, unfamiliar syllables of Human. "And I sleep lightly."

Casey stared at him. "So you…"

"Heard you speaking of your test. Yes." He said, lapsing back into Common.

"And you aren't…?"

"Angry?" Tzedef shook his head. "No. It's perfectly reasonable to attempt to judge to trustworthiness of those you invite to stay at your home."

"Oh good." Casey sagged, relieved, and Tzedef cocked his head toward the door.

"I believe he will be more relieved that you are well than angry with you, however, if you wish to know for certain, there is one sure way to find out."

"There is?" Casey looked up at him, puzzled, and Tzedef arched one eye-ridge at her.

"Open the door and go inside." His voice was very, *very* dry, and Casey flushed.

"Oh, right. Yeah. Okay." And so saying, she opened the door and slipped inside.

Sorecco was sitting at the table, his staff leaning against the wall next to the back door, his knuckles white from how tightly he was gripping his own fingers.

"Tzedef? Is that you? Did you find her?"

"He found me." Casey assured him, and Sorecco leapt to his feet.

"Casey? Where've you been!? What happened? Are you okay?"

"I'm fine." Casey said, her voice trembling. "I'm okay. Tzedef found me. I'm okay."

"Casey?" Sorecco came over, hands questing until

Casey reached out and caught them, then pulled her brother into a hug.

"I'm okay." She said again, her voice shaking, and Tzedef carefully stepped around behind the pair, going over to the bed they'd been sharing and laying the still-unconscious Casey down.

Should he explain the situation? Or should he let Casey?

Before he could decide, Casey sniffled. Her breathing hitched. She buried her face in Sorecco's chest, and started to cry.

Tzedef sat, as quietly as he could, on the other bed. These were the tears he'd been dreading before, but now Sorecco was there to take care of them, shushing and soothing and trying to calm his sister, wiping away her tears even as bewilderment grew on his face.

Slowly, in bits and pieces, the story fell out of Casey's mouth, and Sorecco went from confused to furious as he listened.

Still, he didn't move, and Tzedef admired his vocal control, because even though the look on his face promised death to whoever had hurt his sister, his voice was still calm and soothing. As reassuring as he could possibly be.

"But- but Sorecco, I found my gift... I fou—" Casey was cut off by a soft groan from the Casey on the bed, and Sorecco stiffened.

"Who else is here?"

"That's the thing," Casey said, leaning away a little to look up at his face. "It's me. It's just that right now, there's two of me."

Sorecco was silent for a long moment. "Two of you?"

"Mmhm." Casey nodded.

"Oh *no*." The resigned words were sighed, but they made Casey laugh, her voice a little bit thick with tears still, but lighter.

The Casey on the bed mumbled something, and shifted, then thrashed and snapped awake, gasping for breath.

Tzedef watched as her eyes flicked from the bedside table, to himself, then down at the bed she was on before she sagged, relaxing abruptly.

"You found me?" She croaked, and Tzedef nodded. "What happened?"

"You had a fractured skull." The other Casey said.

"A fract—" the Casey on the bed sat bolt upright, then stopped, staring at herself with her mouth agape.

"Hi." She waved, and the Casey on the bed snapped her mouth shut.

"Who in the endless wheel are *you*!?"

CHAPTER NINE

Exit Via Ship

It took a decent while to explain Casey's presence to herself, and for a while she regarded her other self with no small amount of suspicion.

That lasted all the way up until the two of them brushed hands while one Casey was handing the other a cup of water, and abruptly there was only one Casey again.

"Oh." She said dumbly, then her eyes widened. "Ohhhh…"

"Are you well?" Tzedef asked, and Casey nodded.

"I think I get it now, at least a little. We have the same memories until we split apart, then we have separate memories, and when we recombine, we share the memories of when we were apart. That's… wow, that's amazing. The distance limit makes it not as useful as it could be, though… Not that I'm complaining!" She added hastily, "This is an incredible Gift!"

"Can you split apart again?" Sorecco wanted to know, "because if it only happens when you're in life threatening danger, that's not very useful, either."

Casey blinked, then winced. "Yeah, I'd rather not use it, if *that's* the trigger."

"Try, then." Tzedef suggested, scooting a little further away from her, just in case.

She nodded absently, already focusing hard enough that she looked mildly constipated. Tzedef privately resolved to never share that particular insight with her, and watched with interest. He'd never seen someone discovering their Gift before, or even tangentially participated in their exploration of its possibilities. This was new to him, and interesting enough that he could feel a sliver of Hecate's attention on the proceedings, at first mildly interested in whatever had had her cleric calling on her in such a hurry, and then curious about this new Gift.

There was a soft puff of displaced air, and a second Casey stood where the first Casey had been staring.

"It worked!" They chorused, and grinned at each other.

Then the experiments started in earnest, with Sorecco and Tzedef both throwing out ideas for her to test as they thought of them. It was a good distraction, and eventually there were three Caseys, around the flat, and Sorecco was perched on the bed with one of them.

"There isn't an original, or a copy." One of the Caseys was explaining from the kitchen table. "I'm *all* Casey, or at least, that's how it feels to me. It doesn't seem to matter how I recombine, either, every body is my real body."

"Though it is *really* weird hearing me talk about myself in a weird sort of plural," the Casey on the bed complained, and the third Casey, the one next to the window, shrugged.

"We could just go with 'we' and 'us'."

"That would be less odd to any passersby." Tzedef put in, and Sorecco snorted.

"Less confusing for me, too. At least when you talk about yourself in a proper plural, I'll know to expect a few of you."

"Fair," the Caseys chorused, and Sorecco flinched, then chuckled softly.

"That's going to take some getting used to."

"More getting used to than using your bell?" One Casey asked, curious, and Sorecco shrugged.

"Maybe, yeah. I mean, my Gift came pretty naturally to me, once we figured out what it was. Having *three* sisters nagging at me from all sides is..." He paused, a tiny smirk playing around his lips, "actually, maybe it *won't* be all that different."

"Hey!" The Caseys yelped, and the one leaning against him on the bed reached over, grabbed the pillow, and beat him in the stomach with it.

"Jerk!"

Sorecco's smirk turned into a full blown grin, and he fell back dramatically, laughing fit to burst as Casey kept beating him with the pillow.

"I'm not that bad!"

"You could be!" Sorecco argued between peals of

laughter, "How would you know? You've never heard yourself before, have you?"

"Shaddup!" Casey said, and moved from beating him with the pillow to trying to smother him with it.

Tzedef fought back the thrill of alarm that shot down his spine, making his scales prickle uneasily. Sorecco was still laughing, and Casey was grinning. This wasn't serious. They were playing.

Still… he waited until there was a momentary lull, and then, in the hopes of averting more sibling violence, spoke.

"I do not think I know Sorecco's Gift. Do you mind if I ask what it is?"

Casey paused, suddenly seeming to remember that Tzedef existed as her other two selves burst out laughing at the look on her face.

When the hilarity has died down a bit, and the Casey on the bed and Sorecco had sat back up, Sorecco started to explain.

"It's actually a pretty useless Gift," he started, and Tzedef blinked. That was certainly *one* way to start out. "It's because of how it works. Basically, if I hear or produce a pure tone, it gives me an idea of my surroundings. That's what the bell on my staff is for. The problem is that the tone *has* to be pure, which means if it gets muddied or muddled by other noises in the area, I don't get anything, or what I do get is garbled. The louder the surroundings, the less I get. Living here, I only really get much of an idea in the late evenings, early mornings, or the dead of night."

Tzedef blinked. "That sounds… inconvenient."

"Not usually." Sorecco said, shrugging, "It's just how it is. It's why I usually keep the bell bound. Having all the jumbles shoved in my head is annoying, and if it's that loud already, having the bell ringing just adds more pointless noise for me to try to sift through."

"I see…"

"So yeah," Sorecco continued, "basically useless. But at least I know what it is. Some people go nuts trying to figure theirs out."

"That is true." Tzedef agreed, and although the Casey by the window looked like she wanted to ask if Tzedef knew what his Gift was, she said nothing. Silence fell and lingered for a while; none of them willing to be the one to break it and bring back up the elephant in the room.

What was going to happen now?

Eventually the Casey on the bed sighed. "Can you two disappear for a while? I get the feeling this is going to be easier with only one of me around."

The two Caseys that were across the room traded glances, shrugged, and wandered back over to her. One touched her hand and vanished, while the other tugged gently on a lock of her hair before vanishing as well.

"Right," Casey sighed, and sat up from where she'd been leaning against Sorecco's side. "So I talked to the Weaver's Guild."

Sorecco stilled. "Oh?"

"They said it was pay them back, or sign the contract, or be prepared for things to get '*difficult*'. Their word exactly. We've got a week."

Sorecco paled.

"So." Casey said, faux cheerfully. "Which island would you like to move to?"

"What?!" Sorecco yelped, "Island!? *Move*?!?!"

"Yep. There's no way that the guild will just let this drop, even if we move to another city on Yunxing. A different island, on the other hand, we might be able to get away with. I've heard that Hauli island is nice."

"Except for the crazies who train *battle goats*." Sorecco retorted, scowling. "I'm sorry, but I'm not interested in living somewhere where goat fights are a recognized *sport*. Honestly, cock fighting is bad enough."

"Aww…" Casey sighed, disappointed, but with a small smile playing around her mouth. "No battle goats? I heard that it's a *really* lucrative business, training them and breeding them and all."

"Casey, *no*." Sorecco said, exasperated, "You don't know the first ancestors blessed *thing* about goats! Much less training them, breeding them, or caring for them in general!"

"I could learn!" Casey defended herself, but moved on quickly when Sorecco took a deep breath. "Okay, so not Hauli island. What about Mataka?"

"Too far south." Sorecco rejected the idea immediately. "The heat would be the death of both of us."

Casey rolled her eyes, now exasperated herself. "It's still north of Jelwynth."

"North of Jelwynth doesn't mean 'not basically

tropical'" Sorecco retorted. "If *you* want to deal with mosquitoes basically year-round, feel free, but I'm not going."

She paused, then shuddered. "Oh yeah. I forgot about the mosquitoes. Nevermind. What about... um..."

Something about the conversation niggled at Tzedef's mind. Something important. They were talking about moving, so...

"Why not move to the mainland?" The words were out of his mouth before he could stop them, and both Casey and Sorecco fell silent, each looking rather like he'd just hit them over the head with something quite heavy.

"The bardic college is there," he continued, now thinking it through a little more, "granted, from what you told me its quite a bit further inland, but it's a reasonable surety that the Weaver's Guild shan't follow you that far."

"The- the college?" Sorecco croaked, "I could... Casey, could we? Is that possible? Could we afford to move that far?"

Casey frowned thoughtfully, chewing on her lower lip. "It's... possible. I don't know how much an escort to Vraka from Tyona would cost, and that's a long way for just the two of us, but if we found a merchant caravan heading up that way, they might let us join..."

She trailed off into mumbling, thinking out loud, and Tzedef hummed to himself, weighing options for a long moment.

"Or I could escort you."

The mumbling stopped.

"What?" Sorecco asked blankly.

Tzedef sighed. "I could escort you. Yesterday I met someone who, although they had never heard of the Ambered Castle, recommended that I go to Vraka and request usage of the Bardic College's library. Apparently it is quite the attraction to researchers from all over, and may have more information than I have been able to gather here. So long as you do not mind a stop at the dwarven settlement in the Lorinn Mountains along the way, then I would welcome your company on the way to Vraka."

"What?" This time it was Casey.

Tzedef sighed again. "If it is my ability to keep you safe that that you are worried about, I can assure you that I am fairly confident in my ability to handle protecting the three of us on the journey."

"No!" Casey yelped, then waved her hands, shaking her head furiously, "I mean, yes! I mean, wait, just- just hang on a second. Just lemme-!"

She paused, taking a deep breath.

"I think what my beloved sister was about to say," Sorecco interrupted dryly, "Is that no, we weren't particularly worried about that. Never mind the fact that you are, from what she's said, massive, the mace and shield are hardly there for decoration, are they?"

"No." Tzedef confirmed, his muzzle twitching against a smile at the indignant look Casey was giving her brother.

"I was more just surprised you'd offer!" Casey interjected, "I mean, staying here aside, and saving my life aside, you still barely know us. Offering to escort us, that's sticking around for at least a month, isn't it?"

"Several," Tzedef agreed mildly, "if what I've seen on the maps I've looked at is correct, at the very least."

"Are you sure you're alright with that?"

"Yes." Tzedef said simply, then elaborated at Casey's unconvinced look. "I could do quite a lot worse in terms of traveling companions than a pair of clever siblings, one of whom can scout an area without leaving his spot, and the other of whom can take three watch rotations independently. Besides which, Sorecco learns quickly, and you yourself are likely good with people to an extent that I am very much not. Traveling together would allow us to cover each other's weaknesses when it comes to supplying ourselves, getting information, and then the very travel itself."

Sorecco frowned, confused. "What do you mean, about me scouting the area? That'd be a *touch* difficult…"

"Ordinarily, yes." Tzedef agreed, "but your Gift allows you to perceive around obstacles, as well as perceiving the obstacles themselves, correct?"

"Well, yeah." Sorecco admitted, "But I can't really *use* it unless it's really early morning, or very late at night. Any other time it's too noisy for me to get the kind of pure tones I need to get a good idea of the area around me. It jumbles it all up until it's so much noise I can barely think. I'm just glad it's not something that's always active, or I'd've gone mad years ago."

"But a country road is not a crowded city street."

Tzedef said simply, and watched as realization dawned on their faces.

"It'd be quiet." Sorecco breathed. "I'd be able to… it'd work. Casey, it would *work*!"

"There would still be some outside noise." Tzedef cautioned, "Contrary to how most city folk see it, the land outside of cities is not completely silent. But I do believe they would be sounds that would be easier to… filter out, so to speak."

"And you think he'd be able to use it well enough to scout?" Casey asked intently, and Tzedef shrugged.

"I believe it is worth attempting, but we will not know until he tries."

"Huh." Sorecco said thoughtfully, then shrugged. "Well, I'm fine with giving it a try. Casey?"

Casey nodded firmly. "Agreed. Assuming we can get passage to the mainland, we'll travel to Vraka with Tzedef."

The smile that lit Sorecco's face was brilliant, but Casey only gave him a moment to bask in the thought of going to the bardic college before she was all business.

"Alright. Now that that's settled, we've got a lot of stuff to do, and not a lot of time to do it in. We need to get passage on a ship, we need to get traveling supplies, and we need to pack everything we think we'll be able to take with us, and sell everything we can't."

"I can see if Captain Teralia has picked up other passengers," Tzedef offered. "I know there was a second cabin that was empty on my journey here."

"That'd be great." Casey flashed him a smile. "As for

packing... I think getting a couple of bottomless bags would be a good idea. We've never needed them before, but if we're going to be packing up our entire *lives*, then yeah. We need 'em."

Sorecco nodded. "That's probably for the best. It means we won't have to buy as much when we get to Vraka and find a place there."

"Exactly." Casey snapped her fingers, pointing at him. "So. While Tzedef goes and checks with Captain... Merlia?"

"Teralia."

"Captain Teralia," Casey corrected herself, "we'll go see about bags."

"That sounds like a reasonable plan." Tzedef nodded, and Casey clapped her hands.

"Alright! Let's do this!"

Tzedef nodded, and glanced out the window, judging the time from the slant of the sun.

It was still early enough, he thought. Captain Teralia or her first mate should be around.

He hoped.

He hated having to deal with the Yeoman. The dwarven man was stuffy, rulebound, inflexible, and had taken a thorough disliking to Tzedef for reasons he had never discerned.

"I will return once I have secured the three of us passage, then." He announced, and headed for the door before pausing. "Is there anything I should know before I do so?"

Both siblings paused, looking thoughtful.

"What kind of food does this ship of yours stock for trips like this?" Sorecco asked after a moment's thought. "I know things like rice and peas and stuff, but what about things like root vegetables?"

"Ah, yes." Tzedef blinked, "Miss Casey's trouble with potatoes. I do not think there should be any problems. It's mostly peas, salted meats, and biscuits." Tzedef said. "Along with whatever we might fish up on the way. Not the most varied of diets, but it suffices."

"Alright, then." Casey said, "Thank you, Tzedef."

Tzedef nodded, then glanced at Sorecco, who still looked thoughtful. "Was there something you needed, Sorecco?"

"Hmm?" Sorecco shook his head. "Actually, yes. Here."

He held out the second key to the front door, and Tzedef paused.

"You might as well take it," Sorecco said, "we're all going to be in and out randomly for the next while, and it's impractical to make you wait to be let in all the time, or keep one of us with you whenever you go out."

Tzedef hummed an acknowledgment. Sorecco had a point. "Very well, then. Thank you."

He took the key, tucked it into his pocket, and headed for the door.

It would be best to get this done as quickly as possible.

"Two more passengers?" Captain Teralia's nose twitched as she thought, "Sure, we've the room for them. There's the cabin just next door to yours still free, and we're still workin' on gettin' our supplies ordered and loaded, so it won't be too much trouble to add in enough to feed and water two more."

She peered up at him curiously, "Didn't take you for the type to find travelin' companions though. I thought you didn't like crowds?"

"I don't." Tzedef said, slightly stiffly, "But two is hardly a crowd."

She laughed, "Even on a ship this size, two is crowd enough."

Tzedef sighed softly, and something of his mood must have come across, because Teralia sobered.

"I can't give your friends the same deal I gave you." She cautioned, and Tzedef nodded.

"I had assumed as much. Quite aside from the fact that neither of them are healers, you will need to make money somehow to last out the winter months."

"Exactly." She nodded, satisfied that he understood, "Still, they'll be alright sharin' a cabin? It's a two week journey, and I don't want to find out four days in that they can't fuckin' stand each other."

"They are siblings, and share a small flat already." Tzedef informed her. "I believe two weeks in slightly closer quarters will be fine."

"Great." She clapped her hands once, "Then let 'em know it'll be four sil a day, and you're all to be here at the third hour four days from now, alright? I won't wait if you're late; I want to catch the tide out of the bay, and that'll be the best time for it."

"Understood." Tzedef said, and took his leave.

He took his time heading back, and by the time he got back to the flat, Casey and Sorecco were there, already bickering over what items to pack in which bag.

"Oh good, you're back." Sorecco said distractedly. "Here, hold this for me, will you? It keeps flopping over when I put it down…"

He handed Tzedef a medium sized, reasonably well made pack, and Tzedef immediately handed it back.

"What?" Sorecco asked, taking the bag back confusedly. "I just want you to hold it while I pack it."

"No, you do not." Tzedef said firmly. "This is a bottomless bag, correct? Bigger on the inside and weighs only a fraction of what a loaded pack would weigh?"

"Well, yeah." Sorecco said, exasperated, "How else would we pack all of our things up in two bags if they weren't?"

"Bottomless bags don't work for me." Tzedef said flatly.

Casey stared at him, and Sorecco's face took on a disbelieving cast.

"What?"

Tzedef sighed, then took the bag back from Sorecco. "Observe."

He flipped the top flap open to reveal a perfectly ordinary bag interior. The seams looked a little bit rough, but considering the fact that no one was supposed to ever be able to *see* those seams, it was perfectly acceptable.

"What the fuck?" Casey breathed, leaning over to peer into the bag. "'Recco, look. Here, stick your hand in here, this is insane!"

Sorecco fumbled around for a moment, and Casey caught his hand and guided it into the bag, letting him feel around at the sides and bottom as an increasingly disbelieving look grew on his face.

"What in the *hells*!? Tzedef, did you break my bag?!"

"No." Tzedef said flatly, "Remove your hand and I will demonstrate."

Sorecco did, and Tzedef flipped the bag shut again, then opened it again.

He was greeted with the interior of the bag again, and he sighed heavily.

"This is what I mean by they don't work for me."

Closed, open.

Bag again.

Closed, open, closed, open.

Bag again.

"It is… intermittent. Sometimes I can open a bottomless bag a hundred times in a row and get the expanded space. Other times, like now, I see only the bag as it was made before it was enchanted. It's useful, I suppose, in that I can access the normal confines of the bag to store things that others have no chance of accessing,"

Close, open.

And this time the interior of the bag was pitch dark, with no visible bottom or sides, and Tzedef made a satisfied sound.

"*There* it goes. Annoying little… anyway. The point is that it's very inconvenient for me if I ever need to access something in either side of the bag in a hurry, because I can never guarantee that I will get the proper result on the first try. I've learned it's far easier for me to simply limit what I carry to what will fit in a normal backpack."

"That's *weird*." Casey breathed, fascinated as Sorecco reached into the expanded space and felt around.

"That's impossible." Sorecco corrected her, "At least, it's impossible based on what I know about magic, which honestly isn't that much so maybe I should shut my mouth. Still, it's really weird."

"That's what I said," Casey said, a bit crossly, and Sorecco shrugged carelessly.

"So I was agreeing with you."

Casey scowled, but didn't reply, and Sorecco took his hand out of the bag, still looking mildly intrigued.

"Is it your Gift?" He asked, "Being able to turn bottomless bags off and on?"

Tzedef stiffened.

"No." His voice was curt. Almost sharp, and Sorecco paused, tilting his head curiously. When Tzedef spoke again, it was an effort to modulate his tone.

"I have no Gift. I have no magic save for that which my goddess grants me. Magic items in general do not work consistently for me. Even light crystals will fail intermittently when I hold them."

"Wow," Casey said, interrupting before Sorecco could ask the questions she could see written on his face, "that must make traveling a massive pain."

"It is inconvenient," Tzedef agreed, handing the bag back to Sorecco. "I must carry multiple canteens if I do not know where water sources are on my route, since a water stone may not work for me. I travel lightly by necessity, and I cannot always be assured of a warm fire at the end of a long day, should it have rained recently."

"Wow…" Sorecco said sympathetically, "That sounds like just about the worst."

"It is nowhere near as comfortable as I have seen other travelers be," Tzedef admitted, "but it is my life, and I will live with the hand I have been dealt. However, that means that, should the two of you wish to travel more comfortably, you will need to handle the majority of the magic item usage."

"That's fine." Casey said agreeably. "I've got some contacts that I can tap to get some magical items on the cheap. Fire starters for if we're too tired to light one ourselves, and water stones, and a light crystal for me. I'm assuming you have night vision of some kind?"

"I do, yes." Tzedef nodded, and Casey headed over to the bookcase and pulled down a small sheaf of heavily marked paper.

"I'll make a list of the things we need, and see how much of it I think I can get discounted."

"The ship I am scheduled to take to the mainland

will leave in four days." Tzedef informed the siblings, "Can you be ready in that time? Or should I attempt to find other passage for the three of us?"

Casey paused, glancing around the flat worriedly. "I *think* we can be all packed up? We'll have to leave most of the furniture here, anyway. It won't fit into the bags, but the spinning wheel can be taken apart, and almost everything else is small enough to fit, so… Four days? Yes, I think we can make that."

"Good." Tzedef said, "Now. Tell me how I may assist."

The next four days were a storm of packing and preparation. Quite aside from getting the flat put to rights, the siblings needed to get sturdy traveling clothes, bedrolls, and various other sundries that would make their lives on the road easier.

The two of them worried over every spent sil, and when she wasn't busy packing, Casey was out working long hours to ensure that when they arrived in Tyona they wouldn't be flat broke. Anything that they felt they could live without was taken to the market and sold, either to the junk dealer or to the pawn shop, all to add to their small stash of coin.

It wasn't easy; in fact, it was downright exhausting, but the three of them worked well together, and the siblings ended up completely packed and waiting around anxiously outside an echoingly empty flat just before they needed to leave on the fourth day.

"So you're finally leaving?" The voice was unfamiliar to Tzedef, but Casey turned with a weary smile to look at the long-faced elf that was striding down the street towards them.

"Yes, Lefwel, we're finally leaving. I have both keys here for you."

"You'd better." he said, but without any heat, as he came to a stop. Tzedef watched him with narrow eyes as he reached for the keys, but the elf gave no indication of antipathy as he took them and looked them over, then walked over to the door and stuck his head in to check the flat.

"I'm not paying you for the bed you left here." He said, his voice muffled, and Casey sighed long sufferingly.

"I wasn't expecting you to."

"Right." He said, pulling his head back out and fishing in his pocket for something, "Well, you've left the place in good enough condition, and it's clean, which is more than I expected, honestly, so here."

He tossed her a small pouch that clinked softly as it flew through the air, and Casey caught it handily. "What's this?"

"Half your initial deposit." He said gruffly, and turned to lock the door again. "So don't go saying I never did you no favors."

Casey gaped at him, and Sorecco made a strangled noise, then cleared his throat hard.

"Th-thank you!"

"Like I said," Lefwel said, "don't go saying I never

did you no favors. Now be off with you. Stop loitering on my doorstep like so much trash."

Tzedef bristled, but Casey caught his eye and shook her head slightly.

"Right. We're going. Thank you very much, Lefwel."

"Bah." He snorted, and waved them off, "I shoulda kept half *that*, for you lot making me get up this ancestor's damned early. Go on, get. Out of my sight, all of you."

Casey didn't waste any time at that, the threat of losing half of however much money was in the little pouch making her reach over and seize Sorecco's hand, tucking it into the crook of her elbow before starting off down the street.

Tzedef watched the elf for a moment longer, then turned and followed the siblings, willing to let it lie if they were.

CHAPTER TEN

Sailing and Schooling

Life on the ship was, in many ways, similar to Tzedef's stay in Natari; he woke early, with the ship's bell signaling the morning shift, ate with Casey in the galley with the sailors, and generally tended to his own business. The main difference between the flat in Natari and the ship was that Sorecco usually didn't end up eating with them all. Apparently the man got incredibly bad seasickness, something neither of the siblings had known, and Tzedef hadn't been aware was *possible* for a blind man.

Unfortunately, healing magic did nothing for seasickness, and so Tzedef was left with what only mundane remedies he knew of for sour stomachs.

It worked well enough most of the time that Sorecco could at least nibble on the hard crackers that the ship's cook kept on hand, and the sailors, rather than being derisive, were relatively kind to the man whenever he ended up leaning over the side of the ship again.

Once they were well out to sea, though, the

seasickness eased up and Sorecco returned to his usual quick-witted, charming self, leaving Tzedef at loose ends again.

With nothing better to do, he ended up watching as Casey and Sorecco rapidly assimilated into the crew, sketchbook in one hand, charcoal in the other.

It was a skill he'd been taught, growing up, and he'd honed and refined it during his stolen time at the Yaelin healing halls, and during the long stints when he'd had nothing really to do while on campaign. Now, as with the trip from Fernil, it helped to pass the time, and it earned him a couple of cop here and there, as members of the crew wanted this or that drawing, of themselves, each other, or just random happenings around the ship.

To his dismay, the book was rapidly filling up. The siblings, as objectively attractive as they were, made good subjects, and watching them interact with the crew had given him a chance to truly study the way they moved and carried themselves in the world. He'd spent hours putting those impressions down on paper, each time drawing closer and closer to truly capturing the life they exuded just as a matter of course.

It was while he was sketching one day, absently paying attention to the conversations around him as he worked to capture the way the sunlight glided off of Inral's dark, glossy feathers, that he heard it.

"-portation." Inral was saying casually to Casey, and Tzedef stilled, then forced himself to keep drawing, his attention firmly fixed on the two of them.

"It's a pretty neat little trick. Lets you get your hands on pretty much anything you can see, so long as it's not warded against." Inral said, leaning back against the rail of the ship, as casual as could be.

"Apportation?" Casey rolled the word around in her mouth, and Tzedef's blood ran cold. "That sounds useful! Could you teach me?"

Inral cocked her head, considering it. "Do you have something to trade?"

Casey hummed thoughtfully, tapping one finger on her lower lip. "I've got the recipe for a feather dye that one of the crowfolk back ho- back in Natari, uses? He swears by it. Says he doesn't even need to bleach his feathers or anything. It's simple as, too."

Inral perked up, "That good, ey? Alright then. Deal. I'll teach you, you teach me, and if you pick it up fast enough, I'll lend you a couple knives to practice with."

"Really?" Casey asked, and Inral nodded, making her break out into a wide grin. "Thanks!"

Tzedef was, on his stool, very carefully, very quietly, choking the life out of his urge to rush over and demand answers from Inral.

Apportation was the precursor to transposition.

Transposition was one of Yaelin's most closely guarded military secrets.

How in the Fourteen's halls of judgment did Inral know about it!?

The ship rolled slightly to the side, and Inral paused mid-word, glancing around as her feathers slowly fluffed up.

"Captain!" She called, and Captain Teralia, up at the wheel, frowned as the ship rolled the other way, as though something very, very large were moving under the ship quite close to the surface.

"I see him," She called back, sounding resigned. "Do we even have any more shark?"

"I'll go check."

Casey made a questioning noise as Inral pushed away from the railing, and Tzedef watched as the woman absently patted Casey's shoulder as she headed below deck.

The ship rolled again, and Teralia swore, then spun the wheel counter to the rolling.

"Brine!" The word was bellowed, and Tzedef abruptly became aware that almost all activity on deck had stopped, the sailors that had been talking with Sorecco shushing him gently. "Get up here and stop molesting my ship!"

Tzedef's heart nearly stopped as a massive, pitch-black tentacle lifted forty feet out of the water, curling and coiling on itself before laying so, so gently across the deck of the ship and over the other side.

Another tentacle slid over the railing from the opposite side, and one of the triplets yelped and dove out of its way as it curled its way across the deck to hang over the other railing.

The ship groaned, and sank a good two feet in the water as, out in front of it, a huge, dead white, humanoid torso rose out of the water, bringing with it the scent of deep-sea mud and fish.

It was male, most of Tzedef noted, while some small, interested part flipped to a clean page in the sketchbook. Or at least, it appeared to be as male as any bipedal mammal did, which, judging from the tentacles that were coiling lazily through the water and holding the ship steady, it might very well not be. It had eyes as red as his own, and long, white hair in a sopping, tangled braid, and was littered with jagged, ragged scars. Some that seemed distinctly sucker shaped.

"Get off my ship!" Teralia shouted, lashing the wheel in place and then storming down from the helm and across the deck to kick one of the tentacles in her way.

It was taller than she was.

"What?" The creature said, sounding hurt. The distinct undercurrent of amusement in its deep, resonant voice made that hurt much less real. "You wanted me up here. I'm up here. Make up your mind, lovely."

Captain Teralia snorted, sinking her stubby claws into the thick, rubbery flesh of the tentacle and clambering over it. The creature didn't seem to care in the slightest. "Lovely my entire ass! If you break my ship, you're paying for a new one!"

"Would you actually let me?" The creature, Brine, Tzedef supposed, asked, sounding interested.

"Yes," Teralia said shortly, and grunted as she hefted herself over the second tentacle. "But I'd be stuck on land the entire time they were building the damn thing."

Brine made a moue of distaste, and the ship creaked softly as the tentacles relaxed a little more.

"What are you doing here, anyway?" Teralia demanded, "I thought you'd've moved on by now. It's mating season down south, isn't it? The kraken aren't going to kill themselves."

"It is," Brine said easily, "and they won't, no. But you were running late this year."

Captain Teralia shot him a disbelieving look. "You stuck around an extra three weeks because I was running late?"

"Yes." Brine said bluntly, and adjusted the ship, turning it sideways and lowering his body until his face was level with the deck. "Why so disbelieving?"

Teralia frowned at him, one foot tapping gently against the deck. "I told you before. You're not to give up on your life for me."

Abruptly, Tzedef realized what was going on, and barely managed to keep from gaping. Forget the difference in kin between his own parents... This was something out of a tale.

"I'm not." Brine said calmly. "I'm wasting time I can afford to waste. I'm allowed to do that, am I not?"

"You are." She said reluctantly, and Brine smiled at her, long teeth almost impossibly sharp.

"Good. Now..." He sniffed softly, and glanced across the deck, obviously tallying up those present.

"You have new crew members?"

"Passengers," Teralia corrected him, "heading for

Tyona. Do *not* terrorize them."

"I wouldn't dream of it." Brine assured her, so blithely that Tzedef was almost positive the man had already come up with at least three ways to drive himself and his companions to distraction.

The door down below banged open, and Inral staggered up onto the deck with a massive barrel over her shoulder.

Brine, on spotting her, lit up. "Is that...?"

"Yes." Captain Teralia said, and for the first time, sounded fond. "That shark you like, from the Ansel Sea."

One hand, huge and clawed and webbed and scarred came up, and swooped towards Inral, dripping seawater all over the deck.

Inral only flinched a little as the barrel was plucked off her shoulder, and Tzedef gave her a respectful nod when she happened to glance his way. He wasn't sure he could have done that without severe distress in the general tail area.

Still, judging from what this 'Brine' was saying, and how Captain Teralia was reacting to him, this was something that happened at least on a yearly basis. Inral might very well be used to it by now.

Slowly, Tzedef forced himself to relax, and although part of his attention stayed on the massive mer-creature, now plucking pieces of shark the size of Tzedef's own head out of the barrel and eating them like one might eat jellied sweets, the rest of his attention was on the crew, Casey, and Sorecco.

Casey was, predictably, as pale as it was possible for her to get, staring with eyes so big they nearly swallowed her face.

Carefully, Tzedef closed his sketchbook and stepped over to her, holding firm when she frantically clutched at his arm.

"Tzedef." She whispered hoarsely. "Tzedef tell me I'm crazy. Tell me there's no possible way I'm seeing what I'm seeing."

"I cannot." Tzedef murmured softly. "There is, indeed, a… merfolk… the size of several large buildings wrapped around the ship."

Casey let out a bark of semi-hysterical laughter, shrill with fear, then choked herself into silence when Brine's red eyes slid her way.

The sly curl at the edge of his lips told Tzedef that the man knew exactly the effect he was having, and found it hilarious.

It was impossible to relax fully while those huge black tentacles were wrapped around the ship, but slowly, Tzedef's tension eased. If his suspicion was true, then Brine wouldn't do anything to bring harm to Captain Teralia's ship or crew, or, hopefully, her passengers.

And, Tzedef admitted to himself, even if Brine did decide to do something, there was very little that he himself could do about it, save die.

Eventually, Captain Teralia convinced Brine to get his tentacles off her ship, which bobbed back up with a protesting groan as the weight slid off either side. Still, he didn't seem inclined to go anywhere, and kept pace with the ship as Teralia reoriented them to face north-east again, and they got back underway.

Slowly, the crew got back to it as well, returning to their conversations or games or tasks, but more mutedly, no one willing to risk interrupting the conversation that was being held between the captain, now back at the wheel, and the massive man idly swimming alongside the ship.

"Hey," Inral said, coming back over with a backwards glance up at Captain Teralia, "you doing okay?"

"Fine!" Casey said, her voice far too high-pitched. She cleared her throat. "I'm fine… but um… *Who* is that?"

"That's Brine." Inral said, sounding fondly exasperated. "He's… kind of a common fixture around here. Or he tries to be. Captain refuses to let him follow us around, so it's more that he meets up with us a few times a year, when our path crosses the mer migration routes at the right times."

"How did he come to be so… large?" Tzedef inquired, casting his own glance up at where Captain Teralia was blatantly rolling her eyes at something the massive mer had said.

"Dunno." Inral said comfortably. "Captain knows, but she ain't sayin', and Brine ain't offered to tell, so I guess it's some sort of mer secret or something. Anyway," she turned back to Casey with purpose, "lessons. Might as well start now. If you can do it with him distracting you, then you'll be able to do it pretty much no matter what."

Tzedef wasn't fast enough to throttle his desire for

answers this time.

"How did you learn apportation?"

Inral shrugged casually, "Picked it up here and there. Came in handy more'n a few times, I'll tell you. Why? You wanna learn?"

"No, thank you." Tzedef said, and retreated back to his stool, mulling the non-answer over in his head.

He kept an ear on the proceedings, ready to intervene if it seemed as though Inral were teaching Casey incorrectly, but, to his mingled pleasure and dismay, the woman was a good, thorough, learned teacher. She spoke with an easy confidence in what she was saying, and nothing she said mis-matched anything Tzedef had heard the transpositioners talking about when they were schooling new recruits to their ranks.

But transpositioners weren't allowed to retire from the military. Once they signed up, they were in for life, and Yaelin kept strict control over where they went. All it would take was one deserter to side with an enemy, and Yaelin's military superiority would crumble. After that, they would be swallowed whole- a country too small to hold their own without tricks.

From what he knew, Inral had been working for Captain Teralia for years. If there had been a successful desertion by a transpositioner, it would have happened while Tzedef was still enlisted, and the uproar would have made sure that every active member knew about it, and knew who to keep their eyes open for.

So Inral couldn't have been a transpositioner.

Was she perhaps a spy from another country?

He dismissed that thought almost as soon as it came to him. That didn't make any sense at all. If she was from a different country, then Yaelin would already be crushed, and he doubted she would be here. No. The two most likely explanations were that she was either a deserter from Yaelin, or a retired soldier who, like himself, had listened in more than the commanding officers would have liked, had they known about it.

Either way, it wasn't any of his business, Tzedef concluded. He'd been removed from the Yaelin military, and exiled. Telling Yaelin about Inral now, after the war was already concluded, would do nothing but serve to ruin Inral's life.

Adding in a hint of shadow to the side of Brine's face in his book, Tzedef nodded, satisfied with his decision.

It wasn't as though he owed Yaelin anything, anyway.

Still, that night he had difficulties falling asleep, plagued by 'what if's and 'if only's. Thoughts that had no use, that he could do nothing about, and nothing to stop. So out on deck he went, heading for the prow to try to let the chill night air wash the bitterness from his mind.

He was only mildly surprised when Inral joined him a few minutes later.

"So." She said quietly, "Eks Company, huh?"

Tzedef glanced sideways at her, surprised, and she caught his look and laughed softly.

"What, you didn't think I'd bring it up? You've got

the company crest on your shield, man. I knew exactly what I was doing, offering to teach Casey that while you were in earshot."

"Why, though?" Tzedef asked, bewildered, and Inral laughed again, the sound a little mournful.

"Would you believe me if I said I don't know?"

"Not really." Tzedef said honestly, and Inral shrugged.

"It's the truth. I really don't know. All I know is that I heard the war with Tremaine was over, and then you showed up a couple months later, looking for passage, with that crest on your shield, and there were all those ridiculous rumors about how the war ended, and..." She huffed, then sighed and shook her head. "I don't know. Maybe I wanted someone to know. Maybe I wanted someone to talk to."

There was a moment's pause, and then she snorted on a laugh. "Halls, maybe I just wanted to hear the latest gossip, I don't know."

"You weren't a transpositioner," Tzedef said, and Inral took it as a question, shaking her head.

"No, not me. I've never been particularly good at magic. I can apport well enough, if the item is small enough and close enough, but actual transposition? Absolutely not."

"Then...?"

She cast him an amused look. "That'd be telling."

Tzedef rolled his eyes, but sighed and accepted the fact that the woman likely wouldn't be telling him much about herself.

"So," she said, a hint of eagerness in her voice, "go on, tell me. How'd the war *really* end?"

Tzedef's tail curled.

"What have you heard?" He asked very carefully, and Inral shrugged, turning to lean back against the railing, elbows propped up on it.

"Mostly rubbish, like I said. Stuff about the dead turning on Tremaine, or a devil lord turning up and tearing through the army by itself, or a curse from the Fourteen themselves... That one nearly got the dumbass spouting it tossed outta the pub. Everyone knows the Fourteen don't interfere in the world any longer."

Tzedef hummed an absent-minded agreement.

"Yes... if the Fourteen *were* to interfere, then it would likely be for something a great deal more important than a mere mortal war."

"But Eks Company..." Inral said, fluffing her feathers slightly, "You were on the front lines. You had to've seen or heard *something*."

"Not really." Tzedef lied. "It seemed to me as if the war was more heated than ever one day, and the next it was over."

"Awww..." Inral drooped, "damn. I was hoping to finally get a straight answer from someone who'd know."

"Apologies." Tzedef said, and hoped his voice didn't sound as terse as he felt. "As it was, I was a mere medic."

Inral hummed, then glanced sideways at him, her expression somehow sly. "See, that's what I don't get, actually. You're a cleric. Bound up with that goddess, what's her name?"

"Hecate." Tzedef said, his voice tight.

"Right, Hecate. That was it. But… ever since the War of Philosophies, it's been agreed by pretty much everyone that the gods, even the *small* gods, be kept *out* of mortal wars. So what was a cleric doing in the healing tents on the front lines?"

He kept his face straight, barely, but his tail curled again, and, judging from the knowing look in Inral's eyes, she'd noticed.

"Healing." He said shortly.

"Mmm…" Inral nodded slowly. "Hecate… what was her domain again? You mentioned before, but I've forgotten."

"Magic."

"*Magic*…" Inral nodded with an air of enlightenment. "Right. Magic, healing. Makes sense. And you're a quite good healer, too. You healed Benji's broken arm quick as. Takes a good working knowledge of the body, that. Or so I've heard."

Tzedef said nothing, and after a moment, Inral shrugged, then pushed away from the railing and stretched.

"Well, if you don't know, you don't know, and I've got no real reason to care. I'm long shot of them, and for all they know, I'm dead. I'd like to keep it that way. No sense raising suspicion, is there?"

Tzedef nodded. "No. Letting the dead lie is typically considered the best policy."

"It *is*, isn't it?" She asked rhetorically, and wandered back toward the helm.

He watched her return to her post and turned away.

Spy. The word made curses bubble in his throat, trapped behind gritted teeth.

She had to have been a spy.

And she knew, or guessed, far too much for his comfort.

But he knew, or could guess, enough to put *her* in a world of discomfort as well, and she was perceptive enough to know that.

He snorted, darkly amused.

Mutually assured destruction, then. Because that had worked out *so well* last time.

Water sloshed against the side of the ship, and Tzedef froze.

He'd forgotten about *Brine!*

Sure enough, the massive mer's head rose above the side of the ship, pale skin shining with damp in Ran's silver moonlight. Thankfully Haula wasn't up, or the orange moon would have made the man look as though he were either drenched in blood, or fire.

"So." Brine said conversationally, his voice low. "I take it you haven't spent a lot of time on the water."

"Not as such, no." Tzedef said around a knot in his throat, and Brine nodded.

"Yeah, so. Sound carries *really* well over water. Just so you know. You know, in case you need to have any other midnight heart to hearts."

"Right." Tzedef croaked, and Brine chuckled, the sound low and rolling, like distant thunder.

"Don't be so worried. Even if I *had* heard something incriminating, what do I care? Landdweller problems are for landdwellers to figure out. I worry about the seas."

"Captain Teralia implied as much." Tzedef said, then cleared his throat roughly and swallowed hard to try to get the knot out of it. "Something to do with killing kraken?"

"Mmhm." Brine hummed, looking a touch bored. "That *is* my job, among other things."

"Forgive me, but I don't know what a kraken is." Tzedef said, leaning on the railing as Brine sank a little bit down towards the water, getting more comfortable.

"Kraken are giant sea creatures. They don't have a uniform look- some of them look like massive squids, others can look like sea turtles but wrong, and others look like giant sea serpents, but, again, wrong. The one thing they've all got in common is a voracious appetite and the ability to eat just about anything but rocks and sand. Luckily, they only feed every few months, but when they do, it's devastating."

Tzedef blinked, one hand creeping up to run his fingers over his amulet. "And there are... many of these creatures?"

"Fewer than there were," Brine said, as easily as if commenting on the weather. "And once I head down south, there'll be fewer still. I won't be able to get them all, obviously, and some'll go on to lay their eggs places I won't find 'em, and in a while there'll be a whole crop of new little ones, and I'll have to thin them out again."

Tzedef blinked again. "That seems... extreme. Hunting something so fervently, I mean."

Brine shrugged. "I mean, it's my job. I guard the mer migration paths, and keep the kraken from thinning *our* number. I'm just a little more proactive than the last couple of Guardians have been, I guess."

"Guardians?" Tzedef asked, curious, and Brine blinked at him, his red eyes gleaming in Ran's light.

"Guardian of the Seas." He said after a long moment, "That's the official title, at least. More like 'Guardian of the Mers' with the way the elders from some of the clans go on about it, but it's my job, and I'll do it how *I* please. And *I* am pleased to keep the kraken away from landdweller ships as best I can, too."

"That is likely very much appreciated," Tzedef observed, and to his surprise, Brine snorted.

"Not hardly. If I do my job right, no one even knows I'm in the area. If I do my job wrong, then most of the landdwellers die. I've managed to save a few, but they usually end up thinking I'm another kraken, and it's more trouble than it's worth trying to convince them otherwise. Ehrli's the only one that actually *listened* once she woke up from being nearly drowned."

Tzedef blinked. "Ehrli?"

"Captain Teralia." Brine corrected himself with a wry twist to his lips, and Tzedef 'ahh'd softly.

"Speaking of," Brine surged upwards, sending water slopping over the deck and putting his face on level with

Tzedef. "I don't really *get* the whole dramatic, hidden past thing you've got going on, and I don't really *care* to get it. Landdwellers have so much drama it's too much of a pain to keep track of. But if anything from *your* past comes up to hurt Ehrli in the present? Or the future? *Stay on land.* Because I will find you, and I will make it *hurt*."

Sharp teeth flashed with each word, and Tzedef held carefully still.

"I understand." He murmured once Brine was done speaking. "I can assure you, no one from my past should be hunting me down. The conversation with Inral was simply a matter of things best left forgotten."

Brine watched him for a moment, then nodded firmly. "Good. Glad we understand each other, then."

He sank back towards the surface of the water, and his voice drifted back up towards Tzedef.

"We can talk more tomorrow, if you want. For now, I need to go hunting."

"Right." Tzedef nodded, though the massive mer couldn't see him, and when silence fell he waited until the sea had stopped slapping at the side of the ship quite so hard before letting out a long, wheezing breath.

Right.
Bed.
Sleep.
In that order.
Fuck tonight, with all it's intrigue.

CHAPTER ELEVEN

Tyona

The rest of the trip to Tyona went surprisingly smoothly. Tzedef was carefully polite when Brine greeted him the next morning, which emboldened both Casey and Sorecco to start chatting with him. Sorecco, in particular, was fascinated by the stories and songs of the merfolk that Brine guarded, and Brine, in turn, was happy to share them in return for new stories and songs from Sorecco.

Still, he left after a couple days, citing an urgent need to 'take care of' some kraken down in the Kaskin Sea, and Captain Teralia's mood noticeably soured with his absence.

Other than that, all proceeded as normal, with Inral teaching Casey more about apportation during her down times, and although Tzedef was on edge whenever she was around, Inral proceeded to treat him not one whit differently than she had before.

That was a skill Tzedef definitely envied, because he himself couldn't help but be more watchful around her;

more wary. The only saving grace was that Casey and Sorecco didn't seem to pick up on his unease.

By the time they sailed into port at Tyona, Tzedef was more than ready to be off the ship.

Ten minutes off the ship, and Tzedef was wondering wistfully if, perhaps, Captain Teralia might simply allow him to stay on as a member of her crew.

It was too loud. Too bright, and everyone wanted to *touch* him. If it wasn't people jostling his shoulders on the streets, it was merchants trying to catch his sleeves to get his attention. If it wasn't the merchants, then it was the ragamuffins that scuttled here and there through the crowds, all trying to pickpocket the best loot from unsuspecting tourists and travelers without being caught. Add on to that the fact that there was nearly always someone *directly behind him*, and Tzedef's already thin patience was near shreds.

Thankfully, they didn't actually need to stay in Tyona for longer than it would take to get a weather reading, regain their land-legs, let Sorecco recover a bit, and pick up some additional supplies. *What* would be bought was dependent on the weather reading, but Tzedef was almost positive that tarps would be needed.

Tzedef glanced over his shoulders at Casey and Sorecco, the latter of whom was staggering along with a distinctly greenish cast to his cheeks, hand in the crook of Casey's arm, bell wrapped tightly in cloth to silence it.

Coming into port had been particularly rough on the

poor man, with the waters choppy from a brisk wind blowing down from the north.

Tzedef had done what he could, but he'd used most of his ginger root on teas for Sorecco on the way out, and so Sorecco had had to ration what little there was left on the way in.

"So where are we going?" Casey asked, peering around curiously at the brightly painted buildings they were passing.

"According to the harbor master, there is an unaffiliated temple close to the east gate." Tzedef told her. "As a cleric, I, and any companions I am traveling with, may expect to receive at the very least a meal or two from them. At best, we may be given rooms and meals for the duration of our stay in Tyona."

"Really?" Casey blinked at him, surprised. "They'll do that for you, just because you're a cleric?"

"Yes." He said, and dropped back a little to walk alongside her instead of leading the small group. "There is a certain… fellowship among priests and clerics, even of differing gods, that we can rely on one another. Few other people can understand the strains that we are under, and so we lean on each other."

"I thought all the gods were rivals, though." Casey said, and Tzedef shrugged.

"If your parents argue, do you take a side? Or do you lean on your sibling?"

"Oh…" Casey said, sounding very thoughtful. "Yeah, that makes sense."

"Besides which," Tzedef continued, "just because they are rivals, does not mean they cannot work together, when needed. The Unaffiliated Temples prove that; they are all staffed with initiates or lower level priests from whatever temples may reside in the city or town."

"Oh." Casey said again, and looked around with renewed interest. "Okay, so that's what they do for priests and clerics. What's the point of them for everyone else?"

Tzedef huffed a quiet laugh. "The 'point of them' as you say, is to give those who worship small gods, or those gods without temples in the area, a place to go. Temples are not just places of worship- they are places of community. The poor come to be fed. The destitute come for alms, or work, or both. The ill or injured come for healing, and those who are well come to help, or to gather with others of like mind."

He frowned as, at the edge of his mind, in the direction they were heading, an ember flickered to life. And then a second, smaller one.

"We should hurry. I have the feeling that we will be needed."

"Really?" Sorecco asked, "Why? What's going on?"

"It is an ability granted by my goddess." Tzedef said tersely, picking up the pace and making Casey and Sorecco hurry to match his pace. "I will explain, but later."

Neither sibling responded, too busy trying to keep up to ask questions.

Custom, habit, and general good manners would have had Tzedef catching the attention of a passing initiate or priest once he entered temple grounds, and normally he would have.

This time, however, the embers were guttering dangerously low, and he beelined around the temple towards where he could feel them struggling for each new moment of life. He barely paused at the doorway, shucking his travel bag and shield, and tugging his cloak off to throw it over the pile.

"Casey. Sorecco. Stay here." He said, his voice sharp. "I will return. You will be safe. Ask an initiate if you need help."

And he turned on his heel and pushed his way through the door.

The sharp scent of herbs and potions, overlaid with the thick, cloying scent of blood hit his nose like a frying pan to the face, and for a moment he was back in the healing tent, shouting orders as he tried to hold someone's guts in place long enough to get a healing spell off.

He gritted his teeth and shook it off.

Not now. He couldn't afford it *now*.

Now, he had lives to save.

His ears perked, searching, then orienting on the direction where the most noise was coming from, and he took off down the hall.

The priests and initiates were surprised, when he burst into the room, but a few snapped words, and surprise turned into relief as they scattered and made way for him.

This was a fight Tzedef was familiar with. The camp followers had, occasionally, forgotten certain precautions and some had decided that the resultant pregnancies were wanted, and so Tzedef had delivered a fair few infants in his time in the military. This was no different than one of the more difficult births, and the part of him that wasn't busy saving two lives was utterly livid over the lack of care that had been shown. A healer should have been called *long* before they'd gotten to this point.

Eventually it was done, and both mother and child had fallen into an exhausted sleep.

Tzedef nodded at the two initiates that were cleaning everything up, accepted a towel from one of them to clean himself as best he could, and stepped out of the room.

The door clicked shut very, very quietly behind him.

"Where," Tzedef said, his voice perfectly, *furiously*, level as he looked at the young gnomish woman in front of him. "is the Head Priest? Where are your Shadows? *Why was no healer called?*"

"Lady Pelmin and the other healers were called out of the city to deal with a rockslide down the coast a day and a half ago." She said, her voice shaking slightly, though if it was from nerves or exhaustion, Tzedef couldn't tell. "All that was left was us Lights. We were trying to figure out which temple I could get to fastest to get help when you showed up."

"I see." Tzedef said, and took a deep breath, letting it out slowly. "Th—"

"You're a healer." The woman said, her hands twisting in front of her as she looked up at him. "We've got a packed infirmary. I know I've no right to ask, but…"

please… Some of them were hit in the head."

One hand clenched into a fist.

"Show me." He instructed, and resolved privately to have a very *thorough* conversation with this 'Lady Pelmin' as soon as she returned. Or at the very least leave her a scathing letter.

The woman in front of him sagged with relief and turned to lead the way.

They made a stop along the way to let Tzedef change into a robe that one of the other initiates handed the woman as they passed. The woman, who introduced herself tightly as Sorka, told him to leave his clothes in the room where he'd changed with a promise that they'd be cleaned and returned to him, and Tzedef extracted a promise from her that Casey and Sorecco would be looked after.

They reached the main infirmary, and Tzedef stared at the room where every bed was full, and pallets lay on the floor.

Part of him was horrified.

Was this how the temples treated those who came to them in supplication in Malfeir?

Was this *common*?

The other part of him, the part that faced the world, took a deep breath, gritted his teeth, rolled up his sleeves, and got to work.

"Bless your heart," The woman he'd been leaning over beamed at him, her wrinkled old face creased with a toothless smile as the saffron glow faded from where he'd been examining her previously broken ankle. "What a nice young man you are. Tell me, are you married?"

Tzedef's eyes widened, "Madam, I— You— That is —"

He paused, closed his eyes, and took a deep breath. "No, madam, nor do I have any interest in becoming so, though I thank you for your concern for my well being."

"Ahh…" She nodded sagely, and reached down to pat his hand. "Well then, if you ever change your mind you just stop on by my little tea house. My Margot's a good girl, and I'm sure the two of you would get along nicely."

"Thank you," He said again, gingerly moving his hand out of reach, "I'll be sure to do so if the mood ever strikes me. Can you stand? I'd like you to test your ankle, just to be sure nothing else needs work."

"Oh sure," The old woman swung her legs to the side and slid off the bed she'd been sitting on, moving carefully from one foot to the other as she tested to see if it would hold her weight. "Well that was quite well done of you! Look at this, it's like I never broke the darn thing in the first place!"

She did a small jig in place, then nearly fell over and Tzedef darted in to catch her, holding her by her shoulders until she was stable again.

"Missus Fernlach, that is how you broke your ankle in the first place. Perhaps you should refrain from such antics in the future?"

"Bah!" She scoffed, "The day I can't dance is the day they should put me in the ground, I say! Don't dance…

why, my dear old hubby would spin in his grave if I quit dancing!"

Tzedef blinked at her.

"Stop telling people I'm dead!" The aged, cracked voice from behind him made Tzedef turn just in time to see an old man hobble into the infirmary, scowling crankily. "You crazy old bat, I en't dead, and I en't going to *be* dead until long after you're in the ground!"

The woman beside Tzedef cackled happily, and hobbled over to the man, who reached out to tuck her under his arm, where she snuggled, pleased as punch.

"Rupert, this nice young man just fixed me up, good as new! Now we can go help out with Jessamine's barn raising!"

"Joy." He deadpanned, and cast Tzedef a look. "I don't suppose I could pay you to keep her in bed for the next week?"

That made her laugh even harder, and she reached over to pinch the man (who Tzedef assumed was her husband) gently. "Don't be like that, now! You know you'll have a good time, and Jessa's promised to make us your favorite beetroot pie!"

Now he looked interested. "Beetroot pie, you say? Why didn't anyone tell me that earlier?"

"They did, you silly old man! This is what happens when you get a thought in your head and stop listening to people! You miss things! Like your favorite pie!"

"Bah," He grumbled, "People should lead with the important things, I say. Let me know there'll be pie first, then tell me I have to work for it."

He paused, then shook his head. "Actually, just give me the pie. Why can't we do it that way, huh?"

"Because Jessa's seven months on, and needs a hand or five." His wife said tartly, and poked him in the ribs. "Come on now, you know you want a chance to see everyone, so quit grumping already!"

"You see what I got to deal with?" Rupert complained, "She'll be bossing me around when I've one foot in the grave, telling me that I'm doing it wrong!"

This did not seem to be an undesired outcome, based on the way he was comfortably leaning into his wife, and Tzedef kept his mouth shut as she laughed at Rupert again.

Instead, he tried to redirect the conversation. "Was there something you needed assistance with, Mister Fernlach?"

"Naw, no." He waved Tzedef off, " 'M just here to pick up Lily, here, and make sure we're all settled up. We'll get off your scales now, don't you worry boyo."

"Thank you again, young man." Lily beamed at him, "I feel ten years younger!"

Tzedef nodded politely, and watched as the two elderly humans turned and, wife still tucked under her husband's arm, walked out of the infirmary.

He 'watched', with the sense that wasn't quite sight, as the two flickering, guttering embers moved away from him, and eventually out of his range of perception.

She may have felt ten years younger, but he knew she

was on the cusp. If she had a year left in her, he would be surprised, and he was almost positive that her husband wouldn't be far behind.

But that wasn't his problem. They were quite old, after all, and seemed to have led full lives. Hecate would guide them home when it was time, and that was all there was to it.

Tzedef sighed and straightened up the bed that Missus Fernlach had been sitting on, then glanced around. The rest of the infirmary was empty save for the initiates who were even now cleaning up the remaining pallets from the floor.

"Thank you." Sorka's voice from directly behind him made Tzedef whirl on his heel, heart pounding.

His first three responses died quick deaths behind his teeth before he simply nodded.

"You are welcome," he said, "Is that everyone? You do not have a second infirmary also packed to the gills?"

Sorka shook her head. "No, that's it. Thank you. Truly."

"You're welcome," he said again. "Now explain to me exactly *how* this came to happen, so that I can adequately express my ire to a Head Priest that would leave her temple in such disarray, with not a single magical healer to assist the Lights in her charge."

Sorka winced. "Technically…" She started, and Tzedef's heart sank.

As it turned out, Head Priest Pelmin *had* left behind a healer. Her Second. A Shadow aligned priest of Meskli, the god of sailors.

"But she's about as reliable as a wet noodle." Sorka explained. "I don't know why Lady Pelmin left her behind, unless it was so that *she* didn't have to deal with her. She took off as soon as Lady Pelmin was gone, and no one's seen her since."

Tzedef's eyes narrowed. "That is unacceptable." He said, his voice crisp with anger. "To leave with a packed infirmary and—"

"It wasn't full when she left." Sorka interrupted, and Tzedef paused.

"Do you mean to tell me," he said slowly, "That all of those injuries came about in the last *day and a half*!?"

Sorka nodded, close-cut curls bobbing with the motion.

"How?!" Tzedef demanded, and Sorka winced again.

"Well... I'm not sure myself, but from what I've heard..." she trailed off, fidgeting nervously, and Tzedef's already fraying temper snapped.

"Spit it out!"

"The temple of the Storm Queen got smote during yesterday's storm. They said it got blown in half!" She said, all in a rush, and Tzedef frowned.

"There was no storm yesterday. I was on a ship heading this way; if there was a storm, we might very well have been blown off course."

"No," Sorka shook her head stubbornly. "There was a storm, really! But it was a weird one- nobody had any warning about it at all, not even the priests at the Storm

Queen's temple, and as soon as the temple was smote, it cleared up."

"That is…"

"It's weird, right?" She said, a little eagerly, "But anyway, a bunch of people were hurt, and since we're the closest temple, we got a lot of the injured. Us Lights, we were doing our best, but until you showed up, we didn't have a way of magicking anyone better, and when we tried to tell the people bringing them in that, they just ignored us!"

The indignation in her voice was clear, and Tzedef sighed, reaching up to massage the bridge of his muzzle.

An understaffed temple with no head priest and a Second who'd taken off the moment she'd felt able. Other temples that felt comfortable ignoring the words of one of their fellows, *regardless* of status. A god that had smote *her own temple.*

Marvelous.

He'd been in Malfeir for less than a day and already he was ready to head back to Fernil.

Or at the very least, return to the Permani Isles.

"I don't suppose…" Sorka said, her voice suddenly hesitant, "actually, wait, do you mind me asking what rank you are?"

"I am a cleric of the thirteenth hour of night, sworn to the small god Hecate." Tzedef replied, a sinking feeling in the pit of his stomach. If she was going to ask—

She made a muffled squeaking sound, her hands flying up to cover her mouth as she stared at him with big, round eyes.

"But I cannot stay for long. I am obligated to escort my companions to Vraka safely." He added, hoping to avoid the question he'd seen coming.

"No no!" She burst out, "No, I definitely don't want to impose, I was just- that is- I was only wondering if you might need supplies for your journey!"

The lie was an obvious one, but aside from arching an eye ridge at her, Tzedef let it slide. If his rank was going to keep her from asking him to stay and take charge of the temple until whenever this 'Lady Pelmin' returned, then he was going to keep his peace.

CHAPTER TWELVE

The Wheel of Fourteen

Getting Sorka to guide him to Casey and Sorecco was as simple as asking where they'd been put, though Sorka declared that another change of clothes was absolutely necessary.

So it was that Tzedef followed the gnomish woman into a dining hall where Sorecco and Casey sat at the end of one of a series of long trestle tables, all of their things piled up on the floor at the end.

Casey spotted him first, and said something to Sorecco in a low voice that had him twisting around on the bench, his head cocked. Tzedef sighed softly; all of that, and now he had to explain himself, too.

Neither of the siblings said anything as he stepped over the bench and dropped to sit next to Sorecco with a weary sigh.

Apparently his instruction to care for the siblings had been taken seriously, because Sorecco had a still steaming cup in front of him that smelled strongly of ginger, and there was a small stack of dirtied dishes at the end of the table, just waiting to be taken back to the kitchen.

"Do you need anything, Lord Tzedef?" Sorka asked, and Tzedef winced, his ears flattening.

"Please do not call me that." He said, a trifle stiffly, and Sorka paused, looking puzzled.

"I- okay? Are you sure?"

"Very sure." Tzedef said firmly, and glanced at her. "A cup of something hot would be appreciated."

"Yessir." She bobbed a slight bow and trotted over towards where the kitchen opened up into the hall.

Casey had the good grace to wait until Sorka was most likely out of earshot before turning to him with raised eyebrows.

"*Lord* Tzedef?"

"It's ceremonial." Tzedef sighed again, and dropped his face into his hands, scrubbing at his eyes.

"For what ceremony?" Sorecco asked, interested, and Tzedef stifled a soft groan.

"Can we get to the part where I apologize for leaving you so abruptly in a strange place and ignore this, please?"

"Apology accepted," Casey said briskly, "but also, no. Strange place, strange titles... If we're traveling with nobility, then I'd like to know. Also, what happened to your clothes?"

"They're being cleaned, and no, it's nothing like that." Tzedef grumbled, then sighed a third time and lifted his head to look at Casey and Sorecco, both of whom looked curious. "It's… internal, I suppose you could say. A way of establishing who is in charge, in various situations where there might be multiple priests or clerics in the same place, at the same time, for the same purpose."

"So… it is nobility, then? But just for religious people?" Casey wondered, and Tzedef's muzzle wrinkled.

"No." He thought about it for a moment, and then, more reluctantly, "In a way, yes."

"How does it work?" Sorecco asked, "Are there tests? Quests? Challenges?"

Tzedef snorted. "No. It's nothing like that. It's simply a matter of what rank your god decides you are. Typically, the longer one serves ones god, the higher rank that person becomes."

"And the ranks are… what? Duke and earl and baron and that sort of thing?"

"*Gods* no!" Tzedef said disdainfully. "Quite aside from the fact that the mortal nobility would take issue with it, it would be quite as confusing to anyone not a priest or cleric, just as it was for you. No, our ranks are the ranks of hours. Just as there are twenty-eight hours in one day, divided equally into fourteen day hours and fourteen night hours, so too are there fourteen Light ranks, and fourteen Shadow ranks."

Casey looked at him blankly as Sorka came back over a steaming mug and, to his surprise, an equally steaming bowl.

"Here." She said, setting them down in front of him. "Eat, too. I know you probably aren't hungry from channeling that much divinity, but you still need to eat."

Tzedef grimaced, but nodded, acknowledging her point even as his stomach rolled at the scent of the rich beef stew. "Thank you."

"You're welcome. Let me know if you need anything else, okay?"

Sorka went to leave, but Casey, as sharp-eyed as ever, spoke up.

"You should stay."

"I'm sorry?" Sorka asked, startled.

"You should stay." Casey said again. "Get something for you to eat too, then come and sit. Take a break. You look dead on your feet."

Sorka wavered, hesitating, and Tzedef took a moment to look her over, catching the waxy cast to her skin and the shadows under her eyes.

"I can make it an official request, if you like." He said mildly, "If I need to eat, then you most certainly do as well."

"No, don't…" She sighed, "Alright, if you don't mind me joining you, then I will. Give me a moment."

Casey nodded, satisfied, and Tzedef watched as Sorka returned to the kitchen before turning back to her.

"You looked confused. Did something I said not make sense?"

"Yeah." She said, leaning one elbow on the table and propping her chin in her hand. "That whole 'Lights' and 'Shadows' bit. What's that?"

Tzedef blinked at her.

"You don't... oh, yes, ancestor worship. You likely wouldn't, would you. Apologies. 'Light' and 'Shadow' are the two philosophies that are guided by the Fourteen. The Great Gods that created the world and all things in it. All gods, whether Great, greater, or lesser, fall within the Duality, and are thus governed by the principles of Light or the principles of Shadow."

"And those are... what?" Casey asked, "Good and evil?"

"*No!*" Tzedef nearly yelped, then hastily lowered his voice. "No, absolutely not, and please do not let anyone hear you say that. Wars have been fought over that particular kind of thinking."

"O...kay?" She said slowly, and Sorecco leaned forward against the table, one finger tapping the wooden surface gently.

"So if it's not like that," he said, "then what is it? This seems a lot more complicated than keeping track of umpteen generations of ancestors."

One of Tzedef's ears flicked as he thought. "The way I am familiar with it starts with the Wheel of Fourteen."

"What's that?" Sorka asks, coming back with her own bowl of stew and mug of tea. "What about the Wheel?"

"My companions were asking about the clerical ranks," Tzedef explained, eyeing his stew dubiously. "And then it came up that Casey did not know about the Duality, so I was explaining."

Sorka stared at Tzedef for a moment, then transferred her incredulous gaze to Casey. "How do you not know about the Duality?!"

"I'm from Permani!" Casey snapped, the tips of her ears going pink.

Sorka's incredulity melted away. "Oh, well that explains it. Nevermind, then."

Sorecco arched one eyebrow. "Just like that?"

"Just like that." Sorka agreed, "honestly, if you just don't know, then that's an improvement on some of the people we've had here from Permani before. Half the time they seem to think that we're out here sacrificing babies or some such madness. We don't, by the way," she added hastily, "just in case you were wondering."

"Right..." Sorecco drawled, his finger still tapping the table quietly. "Okay, so... what's the Wheel of Fourteen, then?"

"Well," Sorka said slowly, obviously trying to organize her thoughts, "It starts with the fourteen gods, and those're divided into two philosophies, the Lights and the Shadows. They aren't opposites, exactly, but they can conflict. For example, one of the Lights is science. Rational thought, basing work in evidence and in the natural world. That's what a lot of apothecaries and doctors follow."

"To counter that," Tzedef said, "is the Shadow, magic. As a Shadow aligned cleric, my healing is based fundamentally in belief and faith. However, I have augmented it by thorough study of the science behind how my healing works. I have studied the body and how it works. This is the way that the two philosophies lean on one another."

"And… that's not unusual?" Casey asked, frowning slightly, "using things from both sides of the… philosophies?"

"Not at all." Sorka shook her head. "In fact, most people don't truly dedicate themselves to one of the Great Fourteen, because they all have so many overlaps that it's almost impossible to truly separate out what is fully one or the other."

"Which is where the smaller gods come in." Tzedef agreed. "They tend to claim smaller domains on either side of the philosophies which makes it easier to figure out what you're dedicating yourself to. Things like knowledge, or animals, or the harvest."

Sorecco tipped his head curiously, having finished his tea at some point and apparently feeling well enough to start poking cautiously at his fish. "What about yours?"

Tzedef hesitated, then forced himself to speak.

"Hecate is a crossroads goddess. A goddess of liminal spaces and transitions. She falls under Magic, which is a Shadow philosophy, so I am affiliated with Shadows."

"Neat!" Casey declared, beaming at him, and Tzedef inclined his head, smothering his guilt.

It wasn't a lie.

It just wasn't necessarily the whole truth.

He poked at his stew a few times, stomach churning uneasily, then put his spoon down and stood.

"I believe I would like to turn in. Are there rooms available for myself and my companions, or need we find an inn?"

"There's rooms." Sorka said, glancing from his still-full bowl up to his face. "Liam is supposed to be in charge of managing them this week. He's..."

She twisted, turning around in her seat to scan the dining hall, and perked up when she saw whomever she was looking for.

"Liam!" Her voice carried across the hall, and the small plantfolk turned in his seat to 'look' over at them, then slid off his seat on the bench and shuffled over.

"Yes?" The soft, rustling voice wisped out of what looked like a pile of forest detritus- leaves in varying states of life and death, and twigs, all piled together higglety-pigglety with no visible eyes, or mouth.

"Liam, are there any rooms made up right now? We've three guests at the moment..."

"Separate?" He asked, and Sorka glanced over at Tzedef, then Casey and Sorecco.

Tzedef glanced over at them as well, and shrugged. "Either is fine to me."

"It's only for a day or so, right?" Casey checked, and Tzedef nodded, then tilted his head slightly and shrugged.

"That depends entirely on how long it takes to get a weather reading. If we must wait a week, then it will be a week."

Casey grimaced. "I don't want to make more work for anyone, but a week...Separate rooms? Please?"

Liam rustled softly. "Yes. It is fine. I will show."

"Excellent." Tzedef nodded, and stooped to drag his

bag and shield out from the bottom of the pile of travel packs, slinging the bag over his shoulder as he stood, then reaching back to hook his shield into place.

Liam waited until he was done, then sat there expectantly until Casey 'Oh'ed suddenly and stood as well, grabbing her bag, then Sorecco's.

"Sorecco, we're being shown rooms. I've got your bag."

"Ah." He said, understanding dawning, and stood as well, climbing over the bench and leaning down to fumble for his staff.

Once all three of them were situated, Liam's upper half bobbed forward a little bit and, radiating satisfaction, the little pile of leaves and twigs turned and shuffled away.

Liam led them out of the dining hall and down several quiet hallways before stopping in front of a wooden door.

"Here. A suite. Separate rooms are inside, yes. A bathing room, too, and privy."

Casey lit up, and Sorecco perked up as well.

Tzedef simply sighed. He should have expected this. It wasn't like Sorka had been *subtle* in the dining hall, and, if he was being honest with himself, he hadn't exactly been the most subtle either. He'd been healing for almost six straight hours; not many people at lower ranks could manage that.

"About my clothing…" Tzedef said quietly, and Liam turned to him with a soft rustle.

"Yes?"

"I needed to give what I was wearing to the launderer. Do you know how long it will be before I get it back?"

Liam's upper… pile… tilted very slightly to one side, like a humanoid cocking their head as they thought.

"Tomorrow." He decided, and Tzedef blinked.

"Tomorrow? That's rather quick. Are you sure?"

"Tomorrow." Liam said again, firmly. "Morning. Yes."

Tzedef blinked again. "Very well. If you're sure, then you have my thanks."

Liam's upper half bobbed again, and he turned and started shuffling away.

Tzedef only watched him go for a moment, but Casey didn't even manage that and pulled the door open eagerly; desperate to get to a proper bath and bed.

The door opened up into a comfortably appointed sitting room with several thick rugs laid out across the stone floor. A couple of squishy looking couches and a couple of armchairs were all arranged so that their occupants could speak to and see each other without difficulty, while still getting the benefit of the fireplace that was set in the wall opposite the door.

There were four doors along the walls, one on each side, and then one on either side of the fireplace. All were closed, but Casey apparently had no compunctions about tossing her bag onto one of the couches and striding over to peek inside.

"Bedroom!" She announced, and then, without any

hesitation, "Dibs!"

"Casey," Sorecco sighed, stepping into the room and tapping his staff gently on the floor to make his bell ring. "You can't just call dibs. At least let us get an idea of what there is, too."

"Nope." Casey said resolutely, "I saw it first, it's fine, it's mine."

"Casey…" Sorecco groaned, and Tzedef shrugged.

"I do not mind. The rooms are likely all similar, anyway, so it makes no difference to me."

Not, he admitted privately, that he would have cared even if there *was* a difference. No, anything more opulent than an inn room made his scales crawl and set his teeth on edge. Even the fact that they'd been given a suite was making him edgy, though for Casey's obvious delight, he'd keep that to himself.

"Fine." Sorecco said, and then grinned wickedly, shifting his grip on his staff to tap it again. "Then I've got dibs on the first bath!"

"Wait what?!" Casey yelped from the bedroom, and poked her head through the doorway. "Hang on, that's not fair!"

"It's perfectly fair." Sorecco retorted, "I've been ill for days, and the bucket baths were okay, but I want a proper, real, *actual* bath."

"You-!" Casey started, then stopped, shut her mouth, and scowled. "Fine. But I get second!"

Tzedef grimaced, but said nothing. His scales were itching from the sea salt that even bucket baths couldn't entirely clean away, and he *longed* for the warmth of a proper bath, but he didn't feel like arguing with either of the siblings about it. Instead, he headed over to the door opposite the room Casey had claimed, and opened it, peeking inside.

Thankfully the room was relatively simply furnished. There was a bed, of course, and a nightstand with an unlit light crystal on it, and a desk and chair pushed up against the wall. The stone floor was cushioned by more of the thick, colorful rugs that decorated the sitting room, and a few small tapestries hung on the walls, presumably adding color to the windowless room.

A crystal brazier sat in one corner, the heat crystals in the brass bowl also inactive, and Tzedef sighed.

It would be a cold, grey night then, with the stone walls sapping the heat of the room away and him unable to light either light crystal or brazier. And likely no bath, either, if the temple was relying on crystals instead of bringing the water in by hand. He'd need to check.

Into the bedroom he went, taking off his backpack as he went and tucking it up against the wall near the head of the bed on the side furthest from the door. He'd sleep on that side as well, with his mace and shield in easy reach.

Colors faded away in the dark room, but the light from the sitting room let him see enough to notice that the nightstand was dust free, and the linens and quilt on the bed were fresh. That must have been what Sorka meant when she'd said that Liam was in charge of managing the rooms for the week; keeping them fresh and clean in case of visitors.

"Found the bathing room!" Casey shouted, her voice muffled, and Tzedef headed towards the sitting room again, curious. "This is so weird, it's in the same room as the privy!"

"Is it really?" Sorecco demanded, poking his head out of the door to the right of the fireplace.

"Yeah!" Casey called back, and Sorecco's face twisted with disgust.

"That's gross... Hang on, let me come bell at it. I want to see."

Tzedef stood in the doorway to his room, watching with no small amount of amusement as the siblings explored the bathing room.

"Oh hey, there's a door between them." Sorecco said, surprised.

"Well, yeah, at least they did that much right. But still, if you open the door any smell is gonna come in, and that's just disgusting!"

"But it's one of the vanishing privy pots, isn't it?" Sorecco pointed out, "So at least it'll be clean."

"That won't stop smells though." Casey argued, and Tzedef chuckled quietly as he turned back into his room, leaving them to argue over the bathing room. If he was lucky, he might be able to get a bit of sleep before it was his turn.

The army around him marched, silent but for the rattle of weapons and unmaintained armor, and shuffling feet. The sun blazed down on them, but the stench no longer bothered him.

There was nothing but his mission.

Tremaine had gone too far. Not even at their worst would Yaelin direct strikes at the enemy medics. The camps, yes. Supply trains, most certainly. The medics?

Never.

They marched.
Tzedef didn't eat.
He didn't hunger.
He didn't drink.
He didn't thirst.
Hecate's power sustained him, just as, through him, it sustained the army.

Tremaine would fall.
He would see to it.

Quiet knocking on the bedroom door jolted Tzedef awake, and for a moment he lay there, his stomach churning, until another quiet knock got his attention.

"Tzedef?" Sorecco called quietly, "Are you in there?"

"Yes." Tzedef rasped, then cleared his throat roughly and tried again. "I am. Was there something you needed, Sorecco?"

"It's your turn for the bath."

Tzedef blinked. He didn't even remember falling asleep. Huh.

"Tub's already full." Sorecco continued seamlessly,

"I figured you wouldn't want to wait."

Tzedef blinked again. That...

He sat up, swinging his legs off the side of the bed. "Thank you."

"No problem." Sorecco said, and Tzedef heard him turn and step away, the familiar little chimes of his bell growing fainter as he moved away.

Sure enough, the bath was full of clean, steaming water, and Tzedef stood there, staring at it, utterly bemused.

He could see the water stone on the inside rim of the tub. That was definitely how it would have been filled, and he just as definitely wouldn't have been able to use it. And Sorecco had just... done it for him. And then made an excuse so that Tzedef could save face about it.

That was kind of him.

And, Tzedef had to admit, completely unexpected. Most people completely forgot about his limitation. The fact that Sorecco had not only remembered, but made an accommodation for it...

He paused in the middle of lifting the borrowed robe over his head, and sighed, calling himself an idiot.

Of course Sorecco would remember. He was likely used to people doing the same thing to *him*!

The water was deliciously hot, and Tzedef luxuriated in it for as long as he dared before scrubbing down with the soaps that the temple provided, getting the grit of salt out from between his scales.

It was a much more relaxed Tzedef who emerged from the bath wrapped in a clean, fluffy, robe and wandered through the dark sitting room back over to the bedroom he'd claimed. Apparently both of the siblings had decided to turn in after their baths. He couldn't blame them, it had been evening when he'd finished with the healings, and it was even la—

He paused in the doorway, surprised.

The brazier had been activated, and the softly glowing crystals were giving off a careful, gentle heat that was slowly warming the room.

And.

There was a candle, in a holder, over on the nightstand, already lit and casting just enough light to keep the grey from his vision.

His tail curled as a mix of embarrassment and quiet pleasure swept through him, making him hunch his shoulders as he stepped into the room and closed the door behind himself, quiet as could be.

CHAPTER THIRTEEN

The Storm Queen's Temple

"Keep up, DeLansere!"
"Yessir!"

"Don't touch the potions, DeLansere!"
"Yessir."

"DeLansere! Get me the bandages! Now!"

"De... Lansere... Stop. Evacuate with the others."
"Sorry, sir. You can court martial me later."
Blood splattered his face from a ragged, gasping cough from the man under his hands, but Tzedef didn't pause, frantically trying to stop the bleeding. All he needed was a little more time. A little more skill.

A little **more**—
The potion in his hand darkened into unusable sludge, and Tzedef threw it away with a curse. He should have known better than to try.

"Stay with me, sir. We're going to need our chief

medic after this, right? Just hang on—!"

Blood bubbled at the corners of his commanding officer's mouth, and Tzedef despaired.

The cannonball that had landed in the middle of the camp had exploded into shrapnel and shredded through tents and soldiers alike, and now Tzedef was dealing with the results, bleeding from several small wounds of his own as he tried to save his commander's life.

"Little dragon..." The voice that slipped into his mind was female, and unfamiliar, and speaking a language that pressed its meaning directly into his thoughts.

"Little dragon, I can help you..."

Tzedef froze, just for a moment, then swore again and scrambled to try to staunch the bleeding.

"Little dragon, let me help you."

*"If you're going to help, then **help me!**" Tzedef nearly roared, and sparks of light **bloomed** in his mind, the closest of which was under his hands, barely an ember which, as he watched, winked out.*

What was left of his commander's chest stopped moving, and Tzedef gritted his teeth, then glanced around, searching, matching embers to the bodies littering the ground around him.

The commander was dead. Fine. Deal with it later. For now? Triage.

The feeling of metal biting into his palm slowly roused Tzedef, drawing him out of memories and back to the present.

Somehow, he'd gone from his bed to one of the couches in the sitting room, where he'd apparently been staring into the low flames in the fireplace for… quite a while, judging from the dryness of his eyeballs. And he was clutching his amulet like it was his only lifeline.

His hand ached as he forced his fingers to uncurl, and Tzedef sighed.

He hadn't had a memory storm like that in a long while, but apparently the hard birth and the packed infirmary had stirred things up a bit.

Well.

There would be no getting back to sleep after that.

Instead of trying, Tzedef went and dressed, and then slipped out of the suite and went wandering the dark, early morning halls, looking for something to do.

Something to do found him in the dining hall, where a tiny blue dragonkin who introduced herself briefly as Vali pressganged him into service in the kitchen, helping to make the breakfasts for everyone who would soon be rising.

"I'm supposed to have help." She complained disgruntledly as Tzedef reached up to the top shelf of a cupboard for a large mixing bowl, something that was over even *his* head. "But Jasper and Rietta like to sleep late, and they take the dinner shifts on their own if I don't complain about the breakfast shifts, so…"

"That still seems rather unfair." Tzedef observed, handing Vali the bowl and watching as she poured a truly exorbitant amount of flour into it, added some other powders and spices from various jars and small bags, and then started cracking eggs into the mixture.

"It is, and it isn't." She sighed. "I don't actually mind cooking. It's just that whoever designed this kitchen was an idiot. A *tall* idiot. And I can't reorganize it, because then no one will be able to find anything! Hand me the milk out of the cold cupboard?"

Tzedef blinked, but did so, and watched with interest as she poured a generous measure into the bowl and started to mix.

"What are you making?"

"Pancakes. They're a kind of fried sweet bread."

"And that will be enough for everyone?"

"Everyone who shows up on time." Vali nodded, whisking furiously.

"Then what will the rest eat?"

"Porridge." She said simply, and tipped her head towards the large, covered cauldron over the fire that Tzedef hadn't registered before. "Speaking of which, could you stir that, and then dump those bowls of chopped fruit and nuts in and stir some more?"

"Of course."

By the time he was finished with stirring the additions into the porridge, she had six cakes sizzling away on a griddle on the stove, right next to another griddle that was frying up sausages and ground meat patties.

Not long after the second batch of everything was cooking away on the stove, the first of the initiates stumbled in, sleep rumpled and barely awake.

"Porridge should be done," Vali informed him absently, "put it over here, in the counter, and then you can go eat, too."

"Thank you." Tzedef said, and did as he was told, sliding the cauldron into a cutout slot in the counter that left the lip even with the surface.

"Great." Vali beamed up at him. "Thanks so much for your help. Now get out."

He snorted, amused, and got out.

The few early risers had already gotten their food already, so Tzedef grabbed a bowl, served himself a bit of the porridge and a fair few of the sausages, then headed for a seat.

He would need to find the Storm Queen's temple today, to get a weather reading. Now that it was firmly autumn, he needed to know if the weather would hold long enough to get them to Vraka, or if it would be safer to stay in Tyona until spring. A weather reading would likely be expensive, but it would be worth it- knowing what was coming would allow them to pa—

But the Storm Queen's temple had been smote.

Tzedef grimaced, then glanced up as footsteps approached his table, and snorted softly with amusement.

Casey and Sorecco were coming over, Casey with two trays and Sorecco with his stick, and both of them looked as though they'd been dragged backwards through a hedge.

"I take it neither of you slept well, then."

"Not in the slightest." Sorecco mumbled, stumbling the last few steps to the table, catching himself with his stick, and then all but collapsing onto the bench. "I kept waking up thinking Casey was dead because I couldn't hear her breathing."

Casey grimaced, putting one tray in front of Sorecco. "Honestly? Same here. I didn't realize how used to sleeping in the same room we were. Spoon's on the flat right." She informed Sorecco, "sausages are at the bottom left. Juice is at the top left, and there's fruit at the top right. Porridge is bang in the middle."

"Thanks." He muttered, and yawned widely. "Ugh... do I even *want* to know how early you got up?"

The question was obviously directed at Tzedef, and Tzedef considered it carefully.

"Probably not." He said eventually. "I did not sleep well either. Although..."

He hesitated, his tail curling. "Thank you for the bath. And the brazier. And the candle."

Sorecco flushed a little, but shrugged, affecting nonchalance. "It wasn't a big deal. You have every right to be as comfortable as everyone else."

Tzedef blinked, and held his tongue against the myriad of responses that that brought up.

There was no need to embarrass the man further.

"So what's on the agenda for today?" Casey asked, artlessly changing the subject.

Tzedef hummed quietly, watching Sorecco for a moment longer before turning his attention to the woman.

"I need to get a weather reading. According to Sorka, the Storm Queen's temple was smote recently, and badly enough that there were injured, so I am unsure if it is even possible, but if it is, then we need one to be sure it will be safe to make the trip up to Vraka this late in the year."

"What happens if you can't get one?" Casey asks around a mouthful of sausage, and Tzedef shrugs.

"Then I check in with the harbor's weathermaster and see if *they* are willing to grant me a reading. Likely it won't be quite as helpful, because the weathermasters usually focus on what the weather at *sea* will be like, but hopefully they will be able to at least give us an idea of the conditions up to Vraka."

"And if that doesn't work?" Sorecco asks, head cocked slightly to one side.

"Then we will discuss our options further. It is autumn; if we feel as though we can get up to Vraka before winter hits in truth, then it may behoove us to try, if only to keep what funds we have available ready for looking for lodging there. If, on the other hand, we feel as though we cannot, then it may be safer to overwinter here in Tyona. Stopping to overwinter in a village on the way is an option, but would likely eat into our coinpurses quite heavily, since I doubt there would be unaffiliated temples there for me to earn our stay with healing services."

"Alright." Casey said slowly, nodding. "Alright then. We'll figure it out once we know if we'll have a weather reading, then. Do you want us to come with you?"

"No," Tzedef shook his head, "there is no need, and it will likely be quite boring, besides."

"Alright." She said again, and glanced over at Sorecco, "What do you think, 'Recco? Stay here? Or go out and see what we can see?"

"I'm fine going out." Sorecco said easily, "Hells, there's probably bards here. Maybe I can trade for a story or two off one of them!"

"That sounds reasonable." Tzedef agreed, and scraped up the last of his porridge. "Alright. I will be going, then. Hopefully I will return before dinner, but if not, then I will definitely be back before dark."

"Alright." Casey agreed comfortably, and Sorecco nodded, his mouth full.

Tzedef nodded back, paused, called himself an idiot, and stood up without bothering to speak.

It didn't take him long to stop back at the suite and gather his bag, mace, and shield, and once he was more settled he headed for the gate out of the temple compound and out into the city. The sooner he got this done, the sooner he would know if they would be leaving, or if he would need to hunt down Lady Pelmin's Second to negotiate for a longer term stay.

Luckily, the Storm Queen typically preferred her temples to be on relatively high ground, so it shouldn't be too hard to find.

Two hours later, he gave it up as a bad job and asked for directions.

Tzedef stared at the ruined temple in disbelief. When Sorka had said that the building had been blown in half, he'd expected that it would be mostly intact, with a large fissure through the roof perhaps.

This was nothing like he'd expected.

The temple was so much rubble, with people climbing over it here and there.

Arcanists were already at work, lifting stone chunks back into the proper places and using magic to shape the stone into pieces that fit easily together, but even from where he stood Tzedef could see scorch marks. Apparently whatever wood had been inside the building had caught fire at some point.

"Excuse me," The voice was light, and neutral. Polite, but disaffected. "Is there something you need?"

Tzedef turned, and found himself bemusedly looking up at the half giant that was standing next to him, clad in a shirt in the faded blue of the Storm Queen, and worn brown trousers that were covered in soot smudges and stone dust.

"Apologies," Tzedef said and glanced back toward the building. "I arrived in town yesterday and heard about your temple. I had been planning to come and ask if your seers knew what the traveling conditions would be like on the way to Vraka for the next while."

"Ah." He blinked down at Tzedef placidly. "You need a weather reading, then?"

"If possible, yes. I have a small amount of coin, or I can pay in kind. My goddess specializes in liminality, crossroads, and magic, so I might be of some use here."

"Three specialties?" The half giant looked mildly

surprised. "That's unusual. Still, I believe we have things mostly under control here. If you want to buy a weather reading, our seers are being housed at Meskli's Temple."

"I see." Tzedef considered that, then nodded slowly. "How much do your readings typically cost?"

"Depends on the time frame you want looked at." He said mildly, "But for something from here to Vraka... that's a good month, month and a half on foot. Call it about two gold? Maybe three, depending on who's doing it. The initiates aren't quite as precise as the clerics can be, so they'd be a bit cheaper."

Tzedef hid his wince and nodded. "Thank you. That's very helpful. I just have one additional question."

The half-giant made a questioning noise, and Tzedef smiled crookedly at him. "Where is Meskli's temple located?"

The half-giant laughed, a low, rolling sound like distant thunder, and gave him directions.

Meskli's temple turned out to be a series of buildings in a small compound near the harbor. The largest building was made of white and grey stone, expertly carved with reliefs of waves and ships on the outside, with a beaten copper rooftop that gleamed in the sunlight. The three smaller buildings were made of wood and stone, similarly to the unaffiliated temple, and it was to the third of these smaller buildings that Tzedef was directed to when he stopped a passing priest to ask.

"Look for Freida." He was told, "she's got green hair.

You can't miss her."

And sure enough, he found a green haired young woman with little trouble, sitting at one of the round tables in the dining hall and wolfing down her lunch with the eagerness of someone who'd been using quite a bit of magic recently.

"You need a weather reading?" The young firbolg blinked up at him, surprised. "I mean, the latest one just went out a week ago. I can get that one for you, if you like?"

"Is that for the general region? Or just for Tyona?" Tzedef asked, and she shrugged.

"It's for the general region around Tyona. It doesn't go up to the Lorinn Mountains, but it's pretty close!"

Tzedef hummed thoughtfully, then shook his head. "No, thank you. I believe I will need a reading. I plan on heading up toward Vraka in the near future, and I've no wish to be unprepared for any early storms that might sweep down out of the mountains."

"Right." She nodded firmly, "I can do that for you, unless you'd like one of the older clerics to do it? Most of them are busy with the temple right now, but I think Master Virgil might be available."

"I'm sure you will perform admirably." Tzedef said, and Freida beamed at him.

"Thanks! Then I'll do you up a reading as soon as I'm done eating, all right? Would you like to join me? There's plenty of food, I think."

"No, thank you." Tzedef shook his head. "I ate recently."

"Okay, then lemme just—" She turned back to her food and shoveled a couple more bites into her mouth, chewing furiously as she turned back to him and stood up.

"Oh," Tzedef blinked, consternated. "I didn't mean that you had to— You should finish your meal."

"Nah," Freida's voice was garbled, and she held up one finger toward him, 'wait', then swallowed hard. "Nah. It's fine. I was almost done anyway, and honestly, I've been itching for a chance to do a good reading. They're so much fun!"

Tzedef blinked at her, slightly bemused, then took a step back and gestured for her to precede him. "Then by all means, lead the way."

Freida grinned at him, and, bouncing slightly, led the way.

The room she led him to was a small hall off the main temple; the white stone was covered in well made tapestries depicting more oceanic scenes, mostly of ships sailing on deep blue threads, while sea monsters lurked deep below. There were small, padded benches scattered across the room, and odd, stiff looking round cushions scattered here and there. Two braziers in the back corners gave off enough heat to chase the chill of the stone away and over it all there was a comfortable sort of silence. Not heavy, or expectant, just comfortable.

Freida led him to one of the small benches and turned in place, sitting down in one smooth motion before gesturing for Tzedef to sit on the bench across from her.

"Now. Here's the really fun part. Do you wanna

watch?"

Tzedef blinked, settling himself down on the low seat. "I had assumed I would be watching you, yes. Unless there's need for me to be elsewhere during the process?"

"No!" She waved that thought away, then grinned at him. "I mean, do you want to watch? I can…" she wrinkled her nose, thinking, "I can sort of… pull you along, I guess, and show you what we're looking at? You probably won't understand it, really. It took ages before I could really understand even a fraction of what I was looking at, and I still miss things sometimes, but I'm much, much better than when I started! Master Desmi even thinks I'll be able to take my cleric's trials soon!"

"That's wonderful." Tzedef said quietly, considering the offer. "You have my congratulations. I think, yes. I would like to watch, if it is no additional trouble to you."

"Nope!" Her grin widened, "It's not any trouble at all, especially if you already know how to meditate."

She paused.

"Do you already know how to meditate? It's fine if you don't, it just makes it a little easier."

"I do." He nodded, and Freida sighed happily, settling down into a relaxed position.

"Great. Then what we're going to do is we're both gonna start meditating, okay? And in a few minutes you're going to feel a bit of a tug, but it's going to feel a bit odd, 'cause it'll be more mental than physical, if you get what I mean?"

Tzedef nodded again, more slowly this time. "I

believe I do."

"Awesome!" She chirped, then took a deep breath and visibly calmed herself. "Okay, so let's go then. This is gonna be great, you'll love it."

Tzedef took his own deep breath and, as he let it out, centered himself, falling quickly into a light meditation that left his outside awareness slightly muted.

He wasn't sure quite how long he waited, but a touch on his shoulder drew him out of the meditation, and he opened his eyes to see Freida looking at him concernedly.

"Hey, are you okay?"

Tzedef tilted his head. "Yes, why? Is there something wrong?"

She frowned, looking a little worried. "I couldn't find you in the aether. Are you sure you feel all right?"

"Quite sure." Tzedef said, now thoroughly puzzled. "Does this mean I won't be able to watch?"

"No, it's fine. I just can't pull you out with me. I'll have to walk you through how to do it on your own, if you still want to watch. It'll take a little longer, but if you're okay with that, then I don't mind!"

Tzedef frowned slightly, then shook his head slowly, "I do not think that I have the time to spend on learning a new spell. Still…"

He paused, thinking.

"I believe, if I ask for help from my goddess, then she may grant me the ability temporarily. Though it may help if you could walk me through the basic principles of the technique?"

"I can do that," Freida nodded, and settled herself more comfortably, dropping her hands into her lap. "All right, so the first thing you need to know is that astral projection doesn't really um... it's not... it's not movement, right? You don't actually go anywhere. All that moves is your soul. Your essence. So what you want to do is kind of push yourself out of your skin."

Tzedef stared at her.

"On balance, I do not believe that that explanation cleared anything up in the slightest."

Freida flushed. "Look," she said, slightly defensively, "usually that explanation is paired with someone being able to help pull you out of your body. Getting the feel of it really helps, okay! I don't know why it won't work with you!"

"Peace," Tzedef held up his hands disarmingly. "I meant no disrespect. Perhaps that will be enough to go on. Fall into your meditation again. I will follow and then you may attempt to pull me out again. Perhaps my goddess will intervene and allow it to work this time."

"What goddess do you follow that might be able to do that?" Freida wanted to know, and Tzedef shrugged.

"One aligned with Magic."

Freida 'ah'd softly, and resettled herself, resting her hands palm up on her knees and closing her eyes.

Tzedef, after a moment, followed suit.

Oh lady of the crossroads, permit me, your servant, to tread the boundary between life and death for this short time. Allow me to cast forth my soul from this physical form and see with ethereal eyes.

Something tugged on him. An indescribable feeling, almost like the impression of a touch. A memory of a memory.

For a moment he resisted. But this was normal. She had said to expect this, and she wouldn't be allowed to continue doing this if she was doing it incorrectly.

So instead he let go and fell out, and up, and into the world.

The aether was the world, and it went by at a thousand miles an hour, swirling and spinning and wheeling about until he was dizzy and disoriented.

And then, suddenly, it all stopped at once, leaving him staring down at a blue and green sphere, floating in a black void and glowing with a soft, comforting light.

"Whoops." Freida's voice was a bit sheepish, and he looked around to see her, ghostly and monochrome, floating a little ways to his right. *"Little too far, there. Come on, we need to get closer."*

And closer they went, swooping down towards what Tzedef realized was the planet below them until they were floating above the continent of Malfeir.

"All right. Here comes the cool bit."

Tzedef stared in breathless awe as the clouds along the mountains in the north rolled back, pulling away from the land and out to sea, shifting and growing and shrinking and swirling as they went.

"Hmmm..."

Fog rose from the ocean, then fell against the

ground, and clouds swirled across the continent, growing and fading and dying and growing again.

"Is this the future?" He asked, and Freida laughed.

"No. We can't see the future like this. The past is easy. It's already happened, after all, but the future? No. All we can do is make predictions. Watch, we're getting close to the present."

A storm raged across Tyona, extending out to sea a little ways, but not far enough. Not as far as he'd expected a storm like that to go.

Lightning flickered between the clouds, fast and thick and furious in reds and purples and blues, and Tzedef wondered which of the strikes was the one to destroy the temple. If he could even see it.

Before he could ask, the storm broke up, shattering into individual clouds that scudded sulkily across the sky like a flock of angry grey sheep.

The scene paused.

Or rather, Tzedef realized abruptly, watching as a cloud slowly blossomed above the bay, it slowed down.

"How long was that?"

"About six weeks." Freida said absently, *"Now hush. I need to concentrate."*

Tzedef hushed, and watched as the wisp of a cloud bloomed into a fluffy white thing and, as the wind pushed it away from the bay, started working on turning itself into a neat little thunderhead.

"All right." Freida said after a while, *"I think I have what we need. Come on, let's head back."*

Tzedef nodded, and followed the gentle tug on his

soul, watching as the world grew larger and larger and more and more defined, until they were passing through city walls and buildings, swooping in on the familiarity of Meskli's temple.

Tzedef slammed with intangible force back into his body, and his eyes flew open.

Freida was watching him with a wide smile.

"That was…" Tzedef floundered for words for a moment. "Incredible."

She laughed, wide and delighted, and rocked back and forth with glee.

"Isn't it though? Isn't it one of the most beautiful things you've ever seen? I love it so much, and it's always just… it's so good. It's so wonderful. It's our home! For real, that is Chaelu! We live there! Here! And we can look at it! At the whole thing! We can see Fernil, and Malfeir, and Jelwynth, and Anselterre, and all the little islands and things! Did you see the ice? Did you see the ice cap along the north pole? Did you know that it grows and shrinks with the seasons? And that in the deeper Shadow months there's one in the south!? I love it so much! Our planet is so wonderful! I want to see all of it!"

Tzedef blinked, dumbstruck by this outpouring of enthusiasm.

"Ah…" he tried, then closed his mouth and, when Freida gave him a quizzical look, tried again. "Does that mean you have the weather reading ready?"

"Oh right!" She scrambled to her feet, then reached down to offer Tzedef a hand up.

Tzedef pretended not to notice it, and rose smoothly to his own feet, dusting off his trousers.

"So now I have to go look at some things, and those are kind of secret," Freida said apologetically, "So... do you wanna go back to the dining hall and have a cup of tea or something while I do that?"

"I can return to the dining hall, yes." Tzedef said, and turned to follow her out of the meditation room when she paused.

"I forgot to ask. Do you want the report written? Or oral?"

"Written is fine." He said, and she flashed a smile at him before bouncing her way out the door.

"All right then, the dining hall is just down this corridor, then take the third right, and the second left!"

Tzedef nodded, and watched with a small smile as the ebullient young woman bounded away before turning to follow her directions.

That had been... Awe inspiring.

CHAPTER FOURTEEN

The Weather Reading

To Tzedef's surprise, the sunlight slanting through the windows in the dining hall showed that it was only just gone noonish, and the initiates gathering around the tables nearest the kitchen for lunch helped to prove it.

Blinking owlishly, he glanced around the room then found one of the empty tables and sat, staring down at his hands.

Never before had he seen Chaelu in such a manner.

Never before had he felt so very, very small.

He had known, in the way that everyone knows, that the world was quite large. That he was but one tiny part of a much larger system, and that his life, while worthwhile in and of itself, was ultimately as fleeting as a snowflake in sunlight.

But never had it been driven home quite so firmly.

Chaelu was so very large, and so very beautiful.

"I know that look."

The voice was somewhat familiar. Rough, and a bit

irritable, but exasperatedly fond.

"Freida gave you a special, didn't she?"

The demonkin priest that had directed him to speak to Freida in the first place pulled out a chair and sat down across from him.

Tzedef blinked at them.

"What?"

"A special," he said, "she took you up with her to watch, didn't she?"

"Oh. Yes."

He laughed softly, and his eyes softened. "Yeah. You had that look about you. Incredible, isn't it?"

"It is, yes." Tzedef murmured, and glanced down at his hands again, flexing his fingers.

He'd only been intangible for that short time, but even now he thought he could feel the aetheric wind whispering around his fingers.

"Is that a service that is often offered?" Tzedef asked, "I've received weather readings before, but never have any of the readers offered to let me observe."

"No." He shook his head, idly drawing patterns on the tabletop with one finger. "Freida's special. See, the being out of your body part? That's actually pretty dangerous. If you're out for too long, your body forgets how to have a soul in it. Stay out long enough and you can die.

"If you do it on your own, then there's a feeling you get when you start getting close to that point. A weakening feeling, almost. But Freida? She can feel that for other people. It's her Gift; she knows how long it's safe to have other people watching her, and she's decided that she wants to show as many people that view as she can."

"I see," Tzedef said, and he wasn't quite sure how he felt about not having been told the risks of being led out of his body in the first place, even though it was, apparently, mostly safe.

Apparently, his unease was obvious enough that the demonkin blinked, then sighed.

"She didn't tell you that, did she."

"She did not, no."

He sighed quietly, and reached up to pinch the bridge of his nose. "Lady *bless*—"

He cut himself off, and shook his head. "And people wonder why she's still only an initiate of the fifth…"

"I take it this is something she forgets to mention often, then?" Tzedef asked, his voice wry, and the demonkin nodded wearily.

"Pretty much every time." He said, resigned, and opened his mouth to speak more, only to snap it shut again when Freida barged over cheerfully, grinning at them and holding a large roll of paper.

"Tauril! Hi!"

"Hello Freida." The demonkin, Tauril, apparently, said with weary fondness. "I see you've made a new friend."

"Yeah!" She chirped, beaming as she began to spread the roll of paper across the table between them. "He came in for a weather reading!"

"And you absolutely remembered to warn him about the risks before you invited him along with you, right?"

Freida froze, then grimaced. "No. I forgot."

"Again." Tauril sighed, and she winced.

"Again." Freida agreed. "I'm sorry. And I'm sorry to you, too, sir. I completely forgot to give you the warning."

Tzedef blinked, then shook his head. "Tauril," he glanced over at the demonkin, who inclined his head slightly, "Tauril told me that your gift renders most of the warnings moot. I will admit, I would rather have known before performing the viewing for myself, but your forgetfulness is understandable, at least on some level."

"Still," She sighs, "I really need to stop forgetting."

"Nevertheless..." Tzedef said, then directed her attention down to the paper on the table with a nod. "Is this the reading?"

"Oh, right!" Freida said, apparently suddenly remembering what she'd been doing and brushing her hands across it to smooth it out more.

It was a sketched map of the route between Tyona and Vraka, overlaid with lines in different colors that swept across it at various angles.

"Okay, so," she said, and traced her finger along the roads between the two cities. "It's a bit of a long way, and there's no direct route between us, so you've got choices. The first route will have you essentially doubling back a little bit, here, but it'll take you through this village here, then this town, and finally to the capitol of Nazelm. Lindham is... well."

Freida looked uneasy for a moment, then shook the expression off and continued. "This second route, here, will take you through that same first village, but you'll branch off here and go to Leeward, then Morkrit, and then you'll hit Galemsville before heading east to Vraka.

"The last route takes you through Leeward, but then heads a bit south before going north again toward Lalbis and then straight to Vraka from there. That way is the longest route."

"I see." Tzedef studied the map carefully, then traced one of the colored lines. "And these?"

"Those are weather patterns." Freida told him. "Predictions based on the recent past and the weather patterns of this time of year in years past. Things are never exactly the same, but the patterns are there, if you know how to look. So look, here, the longest route will take you over two months to get to Vraka from here. The shortest route will take just about a month and a half. Based on that, you can expect heavy rain in the latter half of your journey from here, through here."

She gestured on the map, and Tzedef leaned closer, watching intently.

Carefully, Freida laid out the potential weather patterns for the next two months for him, explaining what to look for that might shift things one way or another and cautioning him against taking the reading as set in stone fact.

"It's really, really not." She warned. "There's all kinds of things that can throw a reading off, especially one that goes so far out in the future. But this is a good overview of what to expect, and I don't think things should be much worse than some heavy rain, so as long as you're smart about it, you should be fine."

"Thank you." Tzedef said, surveying the reading for a long moment before going fishing through his pocket for his coinpurse. "How much do I owe you?"

"Two and a half gold." Freida said promptly, and he nodded and paid the woman, who grinned at him as he gathered up the reading, rolling it up carefully and stashing it in his bag.

"Thank you for your business!"

It was nearly dark by the time he got back to the unaffiliated temple, and the dining hall was bustling with the initiates he'd seen the night before. Somehow, the noise and bustle didn't bother him as much as it might have, though he'd spent the last couple of hours wading through throngs of people, trying to find the appropriate rain gear.

"There you are!" Casey called, waving Tzedef over to the table where she and Sorecco were sitting. "What took you?"

"I was delayed." Tzedef said as he slipped onto the bench across from Casey, next to Sorecco, who snorted.

"Obviously. Did something we need to worry about happen?"

"No." Tzedef shook his head. "Getting the weather reading took longer than expected, and I stopped off to find some things that will assist us, should the weather turn as the reader predicted. What about you? Did you have a good day?"

"It was glorious," Sorecco said dreamily, "There was so much music, Tzedef, and so much joy in the songs. I can't wait to get to the bardic college if that's the kind of thing they teach there."

Tzedef hummed softly, then glanced over toward the kitchen, checking to see what was being served. "I'm sure that, although the songs might be taught there, the passion is that of the singer."

Casey nodded, casting a fondly exasperated look at her brother. "Honestly, I was really surprised at how enthusiastic some of those bards were. They were singing in bars, for ancestor's sake. Not in concert halls."

"Perhaps to a passionate singer, any venue is a concert hall?" Tzedef suggested, then slid off the bench. "A moment. I wish to get a meal."

"Oh, I'll come with you. Me and Sorecco haven't eaten in ages." Casey stood as well, and the two of them made their way over to the window through which the food was being portioned.

Supper turned out to be some kind of individual meat pie, stuffed with gravy and potatoes and herbs, with a dark red wine to wash it all down with.

"So what was it like, getting the weather reading?" Casey asked as they moved through the line, picking up cutlery and napkins before moving off back toward where Sorecco was waiting for them.

"It was… interesting." Tzedef said. "The initiate who did it for me allowed me to watch. The experience was… singular."

Casey blinked at him. "What do you mean, 'singular'?"

"What was singular?" Sorecco asked as they arrived back at the table and Casey deposited his plate in front of him.

"The weather reading, apparently." Casey told him, and he cocked his head, curious.

"How was that singular? Usually it's just a bunch of sitting around while an elder communes with the ancestors, isn't it?"

"Not here." Tzedef informed him, "Remember, ancestor worship is not as widespread on the mainland as it is in Permani."

"Right, yeah." Sorecco agreed, waving that detail off, "Okay, so how does it work, then?"

"Before today," Tzedef said, "I couldn't have told you. I wouldn't have known. After... well. It is difficult to describe with just words. The initiate I was directed to helped me understand what needed to be done to leave my body, and she showed me the world. All of Chaelu, floating in a void. Glowing. It was indescribably beautiful, but incredibly humbling. Never before have I seen anything like it, and, unless I come back for another reading, I doubt I will ever see anything like it again."

"Huh." Casey said, watching him thoughtfully, "It was really that good?"

"Yes."

"Well, maybe next time I'll come too. We can't be letting you have all the fun to yourself, after all."

Tzedef snorted softly, but without heat, and dug into his pie. "Shadows forbid that I have some small enjoyment without including you, Casey."

"Exactly!" She pointed her fork at him, grinning. "And don't you forget it!"

"Hey!" Sorecco complained, his lips twitching in a smile, "What about me?"

"You are a bard." Tzedef deadpanned. "Your participation was a forgone conclusion."

Sorecco froze for a second, processing that, then broke out in a broad, pleased grin. "Well alright then. As long as you don't forget it."

Tzedef snorted again, and did his best to make sure his crooked smile was in his voice. "As if I could."

Casey chortled into her pie, and Sorecco preened, then turned back to his own food. For a time the three of them ate in companionable silence, then something occurred to Tzedef and he glanced up at Sorecco.

"You were going to look for any new spells you might learn, correct? Did you find anything?"

"Someone offered me a light spell," Sorecco said around a mouthful of food, "I think it's a cantrip? I mean, I took it, but light's basically useless to me, so I don't know when or if I'll ever use it. No, what I'm really excited about is the Sleepsong. Apparently the woman who taught me the basics of it works part time in a nursery, and she says it comes in seriously useful for getting crying kids to calm down and pass out."

"Interesting," Tzedef mused. "Does it force one to

stay asleep? Or merely encourage one to fall asleep?"

"A little of both," he said, "she said that if you just sing it and then be done, all it does is encourage sleep, but that if you sing it and *keep* singing it, then it'll hold the listeners asleep."

"Huh." Tzedef blinked. "That is interesting indeed. I wonder—"

"Alright, folks!!!" The loud voice from behind Tzedef made him clamp his mouth shut, twitching slightly.

When he turned to look, it was to see a gnomish man standing on a table, grinning broadly and holding a flat box in one hand. "You all know the drill, but for our guests," He bowed elaborately towards Tzedef, Casey, and Sorecco, "I'll explain! The ever patient Jasper and Rietta have made dinner, and we need the kitchen cleaned up for Vali in the morning! So! Everyone who helped out in the last three days? Out! Begone! Everyone else?"

His grin turned evil as he hopped down from the table. "Let's *play*."

The game, it turned out, was dominos, and there were spare sets for Tzedef and Casey. Sorecco, it was decided, was exempt, since he didn't know the kitchen layout, and Casey decided that if she was going to have to clean if she lost, then *all* of her was going to play, so the other two Caseys got sets as well.

Vali interrupted before the games really got started and proclaimed that Tzedef was exempt from having to help clean because he'd helped her with breakfast, much to the disgruntled mutterings of some of the initiates. They had, from what Tzedef had heard from them as the games were being set up, been looking forward to beating such a high ranked cleric and watching him do dishes.

Still, the games were set up, and soon enough the click of ivory on wood was interspersed with good natured teasing and groans of dismay.

It was, Tzedef decided, a good time for him to make himself scarce, but as he turned for the door, his eyes landed on Sorecco. The other man was leaning against the wall with his stick tucked into the crook of his elbow, his face blank, but his posture irritated, and Tzedef found himself heading over there instead.

"Copper for them?" He said quietly, leaning on the wall as well, and Sorecco snorted.

"It's nothing, I'm just being pissy."

"Oh?"

"I just…" He sighed, and Tzedef remained quiet, watching as Sorecco gathered his thoughts. "I hate being excluded from things, just because people think I can't do them. Sure, I don't know the kitchen layout, but I can wash or dry just as well as anyone else!"

"You can." Tzedef agreed, and cocked his head. "Do you *want* to assist with the clean up?"

Sorecco sagged. "Not really. I just… it's the principle of the thing, you know? I hate it when *other people* decide I can't do something just because I can't see."

"Understandable." Tzedef said quietly. "Having others enforce limitations is irritating."

"It really is."

Tzedef hummed softly, but said nothing more, listening to the click of dominos as the games were played.

"I was planning on going back to the suite." He said eventually, and glanced over at Sorecco. "Would you care to join me? Or would you prefer to stay here and fume?"

Sorecco went still for a moment, then sighed, and most of the tension leeched out of his body as he leaned a little harder on his stick, rather than the wall. "I might as well come with you."

Tzedef hummed again, pleased this time, and the two of them headed for the door, Sorecco's bell chiming softly with every step.

The suite was dimly lit, and cool with the fire banked, and Tzedef went over to stoke it again, stirring the embers until they caught on the wood and it started to burn properly.

"So." Sorecco said, sitting down on the couch with his stick propped against the arm, then sprawling out.

"So." Tzedef echoed, mildly amused as he retreated from the fire to one of the armchairs.

"Was there a reason you wanted to come back here? Or was it just to get away from everyone?"

"Mostly just to get away," he admitted. "Today has been rather full of people."

"Yeah." Sorecco sighed happily. "It's been great."

Tzedef chuckled softly, and Sorecco grinned over at him.

"I am glad that you've had a good time."

"Honestly?" Sorecco said, his grin fading, "I'm really glad we left Natari, and Yunxing in general. I wasn't sure if it was the right choice, but now… Things really seem to be looking up. I haven't heard Casey so happy in years."

Tzedef cocked his head, curious. "What about you?"

"What about me?"

"Are you happy?" Tzedef asked, then shook his head. "Ah, forgive me, that is—"

"Yeah." Sorecco said, his smile warm. "Yeah, I am. This is nice. It's good to not have to worry about Missus Halven, or the guild, or Casey's work following her home. So yeah. I'm happy."

"Good." Tzedef said after a long moment. "That's good."

CHAPTER FIFTEEN

The Road to Maplemore

With the weather reading in his pack, and all the supplies that they needed obtained, Tzedef was of the opinion that they were ready to depart the next morning. Casey and Sorecco, on the other hand, informed him in no uncertain terms if he thought they were going to pack up and leave after only two days of rest, then he was out of his mind.

So instead, two days later, early in the morning, the three travelers set out from the eastern gate of Tyona.

The road was a wide, cobbled thing, and by the time the sun was high, the air was thick with humidity.

Tzedef loved it, and he kept to the middle of the road, as much in the sunlight as he could get so that he could soak up every scrap of warmth.

"I thought dragonkin were warm-blooded." Casey said, fanning herself with a limp hand as she trekked through the shade on the side of the road. "How are you not roasting?"

"Dragonkin are warm-blooded." Tzedef rumbled, his eyes half closed in contentment. "But, as you surmised when we first met, I am not just dragonkin. The demon in me relishes the heat and despises the cold. This weather is perfect."

"Perfectly awful." Sorecco said tartly, the bell on his stick, now unbound from the cloth that had kept it silent in the city, chiming softly with every step he took, "I'm sweltering over here!"

"Don't we have a water stone somewhere?" Casey asked, pulling her pack around to her front to start digging through it. "A good dousing might be just what we need."

"Oh yeah," Sorecco agreed instantly, "That sounds amazing. Do me, too, Case? Please?"

"Sure." She said absently, still rummaging. "Though… did we put the stone in your bag? I'm not finding it here."

"Ummm…" Sorecco pulled his bag around and stuck his hand under the flap, frowning slightly.

"Ah!" His face brightened. "Apparently yes. Here."

He pulled out a small, smooth, apricot sized stone that shone dull blue in the sunlight, and held it out toward his sister.

"You might as well douse yourself, first." She pointed out, not reaching out to take it, and Sorecco paused, then grinned sheepishly.

"Right."

He stopped walking and bent over, flipping his braid over his shoulder so that it hung down in front of himself before holding the stone approximately over his own head and activating it with a flicker of light that was barely visible in the bright sun.

Immediately, a stream of water poured out from between his fingers, splattering down onto his head and soaking his hair.

"Oh that's nice," he sighed, and moved the stone slightly so it would soak more of his head before the stream of water stopped and he stood upright again. Immediately, the shoulders of his pale brown shirt turned dark with damp, and he held out the stone to his sister again, who took it.

"Having hair must be terribly inconvenient." Tzedef mused, watching as Sorecco tucked his stick into the crook of his arm and started squeezing water out of his braid.

"It's not so bad," Casey said, dousing her own shoulder length hair quickly before shaking the excess water out of it and sending droplets scattering everywhere. "I always thought that not having hair was a little odd. Doesn't your head get cold?"

"No more so than my face." Tzedef answered, "and there are hats and scarves should I get too cold to bear."

"Fair enough!" Casey laughed, and tucked the water stone into her own bag before starting to walk again.

Tzedef waited for Sorecco, then fell in step with the siblings.

"So." Casey said, drawing the word out long and slow, "What are we supposed to do while we walk? Because I'm going to be honest, walking in dead silence is going to be *really boring* after the first hour or so."

"You could practice that thing Inral was showing you," Sorecco said, "or we could talk. I bet Tzedef hasn't heard a load of the stories from Permani, and I know I don't know too many stories from off Yunxing."

Tzedef shifted his pack. "I do not know many tales. Stories were not considered particularly important as I was growing up, and most of the tales I *do* know are soldier's tales. Rumors that have been blown out of all proportion and taken on mythical status."

Casey blinked, turning to stare at him as she walked backwards.

"Soldier's tales?"

Tzedef blinked back at her. "Yes?"

"You were in the military?"

He blinked again. "Yes? Did I never...?"

"No!" Casey exclaimed, "you never mentioned that at all!"

"But then, where did you think I obtained my shield?" Tzedef asked, bemused, and Casey threw her hands up in the air, exasperated.

"I don't know! I thought it was a family heirloom or something!"

Tzedef snorted, his lips twisting in a wry smile. "Not hardly. No, the shield and mace I bear were issued to me by the Yaelin military."

"Where's Yaelin?"

"Near the center of Fernil," Tzedef said, "It's quite a small country, comparatively."

"What's it like?" Sorecco asked, interested, and Tzedef blinked.

"Fernil? Or Yaelin?"

"Yes." Casey said before Sorecco could say anything, and Tzedef raised one brow ridge at her, but answered anyway.

"From what I know, Fernil and Malfeir are roughly the same size, although Fernil is more divided up by different countries, and where Malfeir has the desert they call the Sand Sea in the center, Fernil has the Lekato Sea near the center."

"Wait, you have an *actual* sea in the center of your continent?"

Tzedef chuckled, the sound low and rolling and amused. "Yes. Why? Is that truly so strange?"

"Yes!" Casey exclaimed, waving her hands around again, and again, Tzedef laughed.

"What about Yaelin?" Sorecco asked, "What's that like?"

"Yaelin is… interesting. It is a small country, as I said, and, much like I have heard of Wethfren, where Vraka lies, it relies mostly on trade. The spices and precious stones that come through Yaelin are of some of the highest quality in the world, and the people who live there know it. It has caused a lot of problems in the past."

"Problems like what?"

"Like several of the larger countries that surrounded us thinking that we were an easy target." Tzedef said grimly. "We were too small to host a standing military, to their mind, and so we would be easy pickings. Once we were conquered, they would have access to our trade routes, and they would be all the richer."

Sorecco winced. "That sounds bad."

"It was unpleasant." Tzedef said, his voice flat. "But Yaelin remains free, and I am no longer beholden to the military. The war is over, and we won. Last I heard, the reparations the crown was demanding from Tremaine were quite steep, and should prevent another attempted annexation from that front for some time."

"Oh." Casey said quietly, and Tzedef shook himself.

"But that is in the past. As I said, I am not beholden to the military any longer, and so I travel in search of my goddess' request."

Sorecco nods slowly, then shakes himself as well. "Well, if all you know are stories from the military, then obviously we have to fix that, so pick! Learning Stories, or Ancestor's tales?"

Tzedef blinked. "What?"

"Learning Stories, or Ancestor's Tales?" Sorecco repeated, and Casey jumped in.

"Don't pick the Ancestor's Tales, I swear they're *so boring*. We need to keep walking, not fall asleep!"

"Very well?" Tzedef said, mildly bemused. "Do I get to know what those options *mean* before I choose?"

"Oh, right, you wouldn't... Okay, so the Learning Stories are things like, why the sea has foam, or how the stars came to shine. Things about the world, right?" Sorecco explained, "while the Ancestor's Tales are history.

Actual history, I mean, things that happened in the past that are important enough that they should be remembered in the now, you know?"

"I see." He said, and glanced over at Casey who was making big, exaggerated 'no' gestures at him. "Perhaps one of the Learning Stories, then?"

Sorecco grinned. "Alright! Here we go, then! 'A long, long time ago, before the endless wheel started to turn from the weight of souls, when the world was brand new...'"

Tzedef let the words wash over him, keeping his eyes on the trees and bushes to either side of the road, and looking for a decent place to camp as the sun slowly started to set.

Sorecco's voice was a soothing background sound, and the simple, childlike tale eased something in Tzedef. When Sorecco finished, Tzedef clapped softly.

"Are all of your tales like that?"

"The Learning Stories are." Sorecco said, and tilted his head slightly, listening to the returning echoes of his bell. "I know other tales, but the Learning Stories are my favorite. They have this cadence to them, you know? It's almost songlike, but I've never been able to put one to music properly."

"Maybe you will learn how at the college." Tzedef suggested, and Sorecco perked up.

"Maybe! That would be amazing, actually. I'd really like that!"

"Do you wish to tell another?"

"Sure!" Sorecco grinned, and started weaving another tale.

Tzedef listened as Sorecco spun words into a tapestry that told of a golden haired girl that wished for the moons, and her father who would have done anything for his daughter, but couldn't do this.

Sharp red eyes caught a gap in the foliage ahead and to the side of the road, large enough for a small cart to pull through, and he quietly sped up and went to it to investigate, not interrupting the flow of words from Sorecco until he'd peered beyond the encircling brush and found a nice, neat little camp site that seemed well used, though currently empty.

"A moment." He said, and Sorecco paused his tale as he and Casey caught up to him. "There's a place to camp just here. Would you like to stop? Or shall we press on and hope to find another place before it's fully dark?"

"Stop here," Casey said instantly, glancing over at where the sun was touching the tops of the trees, before peering past him at the little camp. "This seems like a nice enough spot, and it'll be dark soon."

"I vote for stopping too," Sorecco agreed.

"Then we'll stop here." Tzedef nodded, and stepped off the road and into the cooler shade of the trees.

The three of them worked around each other, trying to set up the camp in their own ways and stumbling over how the others were trying to help until finally Casey had enough and directed Sorecco to build the fire and Tzedef to put up the tarp he'd bought.

"And I'll go hunt down some firewood before it's properly dark." She said firmly, and turned to march off into the forest.

Tzedef watched her go, mildly bemused, then shrugged, glanced over at Sorecco, who was muttering to himself irritably, and went to put up the tarp.

She came back later with an armload of sticks that she dropped by the fire with a small clatter, and Tzedef glanced them over.

For someone who claimed she'd never been outside of a city in her life, Casey had managed to get a selection of decent wood, though a couple of pieces looked too green to burn well until the fire was much more established.

Still, she'd done what she'd said she was going to do, and done a decent enough job at it, so he had no room to criticize her efforts. She'd done well.

Each of them munched on their rations as they sat around the fire in the ever deepening twilight, and Tzedef watched as Casey and Sorecco chatted companionably with each other, sometimes bickering gently over this or that, but mostly staying friendly; laughing about past experiences, or people they'd met.

In the end though, the rations were gone and the fire was casting its light out in a circle around the camp, and the three of them were sitting in a kind of comfortable, sleepy silence that was broken only by the sounds of the forest around them waking up for the night.

With a soft sigh, Tzedef hauled himself to his feet and walked to the edge of the firelight.

"Are we ready to settle for the night?" He asked quietly, his voice a low rumble, and Casey blinked sleepily over at him.

"I think so, why?"

"I'm going to set up a small ward." Tzedef said, starting to pace around the circle, his steps slow and even. "It won't do much to keep anyone out, but if anyone wishing us harm crosses it, then I will wake."

"A ward?" Sorecco perked up, twisting around to face where Tzedef had last spoken. "Can you teach me?"

Tzedef paused, glancing over at him.

"I don't know? It is an ability gifted to me by my goddess. It may not be teachable."

"Oh." Sorecco drooped, and Tzedef took another few steps, considering the matter carefully.

"That is not a no," He said. "I did truly mean it that I do not know. It will take some thought to see if this is something that could be… translated, so to speak, out of prayer and into the arcane."

"Oh!" Sorecco said again, and perked up again. "Will you, then? I'd love to learn something new."

"I will do my best." Tzedef agreed after another moment's thought. "Though I cannot guarantee that it will work."

"Of course, of course." Sorecco said hastily, "I wouldn't expect you to just pull a working arcane version of a god's gift out of your butt. That would be ridiculous."

Tzedef snorted softly, amused, and kept pacing his way around the circle.

Goddess of liminality, guard this space so that those who pass through might be judged. Allow me to awaken should threat present itself, that I might defend myself and my companions.

The circle closed with a soft snap of power; an electric tingle that fizzed on his tongue for a moment until he sighed it away.

"That should do to protect us, but, should you wish it, we could also stand watches during the night."

"Nah." Casey said easily, rolling to her feet and staggering slightly as she headed for the bedrolls under where the tarp was strung up. "I'm sure nothing'll come at us in the middle of the night. And besides, even if something did, I'm sure we could handle it."

Tzedef wasn't so sure, but Sorecco and Casey both seemed perfectly content to trust in his spell, so he settled himself back down next to the fire.

"I will sleep in a while, then. For now, rest well."

"Thank you, Tzedef." Casey yawned, and pulled off her boots so that she could slide into her bedroll.

Sorecco's bell chimed softly as he made his way over to his own bedroll next to Casey's and Tzedef turned his attention toward the fire as the siblings settled.

He didn't know whether to find their faith in him heartening or frighteningly naive. Still, either way, he had promised to see them safely to Vraka, so that is what he would do.

Tzedef sat there until the siblings were both softly

snoring and the campsite was illuminated by the light of the twin moons filtering through the tree branches. Then he sighed, banked the fire, stood up, and went to bed.

The next morning dawned cool and foggy, with mist clinging to everything in swirling waves of damp air. It made getting the fire going again something of a chore, and by the time they were back on the road all three of them were short tempered and snappish.

By the time noon rolled around, the sun had burned off most of the clinging fog, and the cloaks that each had bundled in to help escape the damp had been discarded in favor of complaining about the heat.

This set the tone for the next few weeks of travel. Each morning dawned cooler than the last, and each afternoon, though warm, was also cooler, until the three of them were forgoing the tarp altogether in favor of huddling close to the fire to sleep at night.

Still, Tzedef didn't worry about it. The weather reading he'd gotten had forecasted rain only during the latter half of their journey, and they weren't even quite to the end of the Lorinn Mountain range yet. It would be fine. They would be fine.

He didn't worry, and he resolutely *kept* not worrying until the morning when they woke up and there was frost on the ground.

As if that were some sort of sign, the leaves on the trees around them started to turn over the next few days and soon the three travelers were wearing their cloaks all day, trying to ward off a biting chill in the air that hadn't been there when they'd set out.

"There's a village along this route soon, right?" Casey asked one morning, her breath steaming in the cold air. "I'm getting pretty tired of sleeping on the ground every night. It's absolutely frigid!"

"There is, yes." Tzedef paused in putting his bedroll away and pulled out the map instead, unrolling it and holding it so that Casey, who moved over to stand next to him, could see. "We should be reaching it within the next day or two, see?"

Casey frowned at the map, then pointed. "So we're… here?"

"Here," Tzedef took hold of her finger and moved it slightly north along the road. "approximately."

"I see." She frowned, then squinted back down the road the way they'd come. "How far do we usually go in a day?"

"About this far," Tzedef showed her, using two fingers to measure a space on the map. "We started about here, yesterday."

"So… if we walk really fast today…?"

"Then we will exhaust ourselves and still possibly not make it to the village by nightfall." Tzedef said firmly, and rolled the map back up, tucking it away in his pack before putting his bedroll in on top of it. "If we keep to our usual pace, then we will be sure to make the village by tomorrow at the latest. Be patient."

"I am perfectly patient," Casey protested, and drew her cloak more firmly about herself. "I'm just also cold."

"Then walking will warm you." Tzedef pointed out, slinging his pack on his back and glancing over at Sorecco, who had kept uncharacteristically silent through the whole exchange. "Are you all right, Sorecco?"

"Just fine." He rasped, straightening up and turning to smile crookedly at Tzedef, who frowned.

"You don't sound fine." Casey said, frowning over at her brother as well, "you sound like you're getting sick."

"I do not!" Sorecco barked, scowling at Casey before turning with a chime of his bell toward the road. "Let's go. We're almost there, right? No time to waste."

Tzedef sighed. Hecate save him from people who insisted on toughing things out when there were solutions right to hand. Still, far be it from him to force a healing on someone who didn't want one.

If Sorecco wanted a healing, then he'd ask. And if he got too sick to ask, then Tzedef would heal him anyway, and Sorecco could shout at him afterwards.

Casey huffed at Sorecco, but let the subject drop, and the three of them set out along the road, huddled in coats and each with a warm canteen.

That was a trick that Tzedef had picked up in the military- if you filled a canteen with boiling soup in the evening and closed it well, then you had a bedwarmer for the night, and still-warm soup in the morning to eat for breakfast. The principle here was the same; he'd made soup that morning when he'd woken up, well before Casey and

Sorecco woke, and filled canteens with it. It would keep each of them warm while the air was still cold, and they'd have warm soup when they stopped for lunch.

By the time lunch rolled around, however, the light had gone dim and grey, and the air was heavy with damp. The sky above was covered in thick, dark clouds, and, as Tzedef cast them a wary look, they began to sprinkle a light mist of rain.

"Oh come on!" Casey cried, and glared up at the sky, her frustrated shout drifting away in a white plume of steam. "Seriously? We're almost there, and now we're getting rain? It couldn't hold off for *one day*?!"

"Relax." Tzedef said quietly, "Our cloaks are well waxed, and our boots are sturdy. We may get a bit damp, but we will not get soaked."

"We won't." Casey grumbled. "But what about tonight's campsite? Any wood we find'll be wet, too, which means no fire for us."

Tzedef winced. She was right about that. He hadn't thought to start collecting wood yet, since the reading had said that the rain would come during the latter half of their journey, and wood was heavy.

He should have anyway. The siblings had the magic bags, which would have made the weight a negligible concern, but he wasn't used to having bottomless bags available, and now all three of them would be paying for his oversight.

"It'll be fine," Sorecco croaked, pulling his hood further forward to try to block the misty rain from his face.

"We just have to move faster, and we'll reach the village in time to sleep."

Tzedef grimaced. Just what he wanted. A forced march through frigid temperatures. Precisely what he wanted to do when his every instinct was screaming at him to den down somewhere and surround himself with furs and braziers to keep the chill away.

But the siblings had a point. If they moved faster, there was a chance that they'd reach the village that night, and his previous point about possibly not reaching the village wasn't going to hold up to the lure of a soft bed in a warm inn. Especially not when weighed against a cold campsite with no fire.

"Very well." He said, shifting his pack higher on his back and peering further up the road, as though that would give him a better idea of how much further they had to go. "We'll speed up. Not so fast that you wear yourself out, mind, but if we can reach the village tonight, then that's all the better."

Two hours later, the rain turned to snow.

CHAPTER SIXTEEN

Maplemore and the First Snow

By the time they reached the village, it was fully dark and all three of them were too tired to talk, more focused on putting one foot in front of the other and not falling over than in trading barbs or witticisms.

Sorecco, in particular, seemed to be struggling; swaying on his feet as his breath rasped harshly, and Tzedef resolved privately to heal the man of whatever illness was taking hold of him before breakfast the next day.

All three of them were covered in snow, and though the ground had been too warm for it to stick properly when the first wispy flakes had fallen, now there were puddles of mostly-melted slush everywhere that were accumulating small drifts of white on top.

The village gate was shut.

Tzedef stared at it then groaned softly, reaching up to massage his forehead with his thumb. He should have thought of that. With it being so late, of *course* any gates would be shut.

This gate was a small thing, just large enough to let an average sized cart in or out, and based on the pulleys that Tzedef could see, the whole thing lifted out of the way when it was open. The wall it was set in stopped a good five feet over his head, but there didn't seem to be anyone guarding it, which meant that, more than likely, it was meant to keep out wild animals more than people.

"Of course." he muttered, "Of course it couldn't be that easy."

"Maybe if we knock?" Casey said, a touch desperately, and Sorecco reached out, overextended slightly, and fell over to bang up awkwardly against the gate.

"Ho the gate," Tzedef called, as Casey reached out to help Sorecco get his feet back under himself properly, hoping that perhaps, if there was a night guard, they would hear him.

Casey took the opportunity to knock as well, and, after a moment, Tzedef heard the creaking of wood. Not long after that, a small head popped over the top of the wall, peering down at them curiously as lantern light spilled down the wall to shine on them.

"Hey there, strangers!" The voice was young, and a bit squeaky, and the owner ducked out of sight for a moment, which was immediately followed by furious throat clearing sounds before the head came back into sight.

"Who goes there?"

This time the voice was almost comically deep, and Casey stifled a tired giggle, smothering it with her hand as she turned away so the young person up on the wall couldn't see.

"Three travelers." Sorecco croaked upwards, "We've been walking all day. Can we come in?"

Tzedef eyed the young man at the top of the wall as he considered that, then ducked out of sight again, and a moment later the gate slowly creaked upwards.

Casey and Sorecco both stumbled through the open gateway gratefully, and Tzedef followed on their heels. They were greeted on the other side by a young gnomish man in ill-fitting leather armor, swathed in a thick woolen cloak and clutching a spear that was large enough on him to more properly be called a pike.

"This all of you?" He asked, his voice cracking slightly, and there was a sigh from above and behind them as the gate lowered into place again.

"Min, I've told you. You don't gotta be so uptight. Just give the poor folks directions to Amarie's place and let 'em be on their way."

"But they could be spies! Or scouts for a bandit tribe! Look! This one's even got a weapon! And a shield!"

The second voice sighed even more heavily, and boots clomped down the steep, ladder-like staircase that led up to a walkway that was attached to the wall itself.

"Min. They been traveling. O'course they got weapons."

A couple of steps brought the owner of that voice

into the light, revealing him to be a large half orc, with thick dark hair and well fitted leather armor. He too, was swathed in a thick woolen cloak, and he glanced over at the teenager with resigned patience.

"Don't give the village a bad name. We're likely the first stop they've had in a good while."

"You are, yes." Tzedef agreed, wishing he had a staff to lean on in the same way that Sorecco was leaning on his stick. "Please, which way is it to your inn? We've been on the go since dawn."

"It's been a really long walk from Tyona." Casey added through softly chattering teeth. "I just wanna get warm again."

The half orc glanced over at the teenager, and made a sort of 'go on' gesture with his hands.

"Amarie's place isn't far." The teenager said grudgingly, and half turned away so that he could point down the main street. "It's just there, on the corner of the third street down, but the door's on the other road, not this one, so you gotta go 'round the corner, okay?"

"Right." Tzedef agreed, and Min frowned up at him.

"No, it's on the left. Over there, see? 'S still got its light on."

"No, I meant—" Tzedef started, then sighed wearily. "Very well. Thank you. Are there any local laws that we should be particularly aware of?"

After the last time he'd entered a village only to nearly be strung up because of something absolutely *inane*, he was never not asking again.

The teenager blinked at him for a moment, then puffed himself up proudly. "Yeah! There are! You gotta call me Lo—"

"Min!" The half orc barked sharply, and the boy deflated, scowling. "I'm sorry about him. It's his first week. I'm Bren, this is Minalo. We're the night guards here, so if you see anything off, please don't hesitate to let us know. There are not any unusual laws in place here, though we do ask that if you have any ill party members, that you stop by our shrine for a small blessing. There was some trouble with a nasty bout of pox a couple of years back and people are still a bit wary."

Tzedef cast a sidelong glance at Sorecco, then nodded at Bren. "I'm a cleric, myself. Would there be any trouble if I took care of the matter myself before we moved on?"

"That'd be fine, too." Bren nodded, and Tzedef turned toward Sorecco.

"Sorecco."

"I'm—" Sorecco started, then turned away, coughing harshly into his elbow.

Tzedef waited patiently for the coughing fit to pass, then cleared his throat meaningfully.

"Oh fine." The younger man grumbled, and held out the hand not holding onto his stick.

Tzedef took it and murmured a quick prayer to Hecate that resulted in a soft saffron glow around their joined hands, and a sudden, incredibly harsh coughing fit that left Sorecco gasping for breath but breathing easier and looking visibly better.

"Alright?" Tzedef asked Bren, pointedly ignoring Minalo's attempts to puff himself up.

"Alright." Bren nodded, looking satisfied. "Thanks for that."

"It was no trouble." Tzedef nodded back.

"Give Amarie my best." Bren said, waving them off, and Tzedef hummed a small agreement before setting off down the road, Sorecco's bell chiming gently off the small buildings in the near distance as he and Casey followed.

Amarie's place turned out to be a small building with small, lumpy glass windows that prevented any view of the inside, but that nonetheless glowed from within with the comforting yellow light of a warm fire and many light crystals.

Inside was just as warm as the windows promised, and Casey groaned softly at the sight of the crackling fire, starting toward it before Tzedef caught her shoulder and tugged her back.

"Just a moment." He murmured softly. "We must introduce ourselves, first. It's only polite."

Casey moaned quietly in disappointment but followed him over to the bar instead, casting longing glances toward the fire as the snow on her cloak started to melt.

The three of them left a small trail of melting slush and water on the floor as they made their way over to the bar, and the greying, dark-faced, catling woman behind the bar looked quietly dismayed at the mess.

"Apologies." Tzedef said quietly, coming to a halt before her, "We three are travelers seeking lodging. Do you perhaps have rooms available?"

She hesitated, and Casey spoke up. "Bren sends his best, too, by the way."

"He does?" The woman brightened slightly, then nodded firmly. "Alright then. I'm Amarie. I've got two rooms available right now. Will you be wanting both?"

"Yes." "No."

Tzedef glanced at Sorecco, surprised.

"It's cheaper to share a room," he said, "and that way we'll have more funds when we get to Vraka."

"Ah." Tzedef considered that, then nodded slowly. "Very well. If that's how you wish to do things, I have no objection."

"The rooms only have two beds." Amarie warned, glancing between the three of them, and Casey groaned quietly even as Sorecco nodded.

"That's fine. Casey and I can share."

"Sorecco no... You kick! I just want some actual sleep in a warm bed... Please..."

Sorecco scowled, looking mulish, and Tzedef cut in before he could argue about the kicking comment.

"One night with two rooms should be fine. The snow should stop overnight and we'll be able to carry on. If money is a concern, I'm sure there will be plenty of opportunity for the three of us to earn some coin along the way."

Sorecco's frown deepened, but Casey tugged softly

on his sleeve.

"Please?"

He deflated with a sigh and nodded reluctantly. "How much are the rooms?"

"One sil per night, per person." Amarie said promptly, "Though if you want a meal in the morning, that's an additional three cop."

Sorecco hid his small grimace well enough, but Tzedef caught the edges of it even as he nodded again. "Two rooms, then. Please."

"Alright!" Amarie clapped her hands once, then reached under the bar and pulled out a large ledger, a small pot of ink, and a wooden, ink-stained pen.

"Make your marks here, please!" She turned the book toward them and pointed at three separate, consecutive lines.

Tzedef took the pen, dipped it, and scrawled his signature across the first line, then held out the pen to Sorecco, who didn't take it.

After a long moment, Casey coughed slightly. "Tzedef. Um…"

Tzedef blinked, then heartily resisted the urge to call himself nine kinds of stupid as Sorecco sighed heavily.

He held the pen out to Casey instead, who took it and signed on the line beneath his, her handwriting a soft, flowing script.

Sorecco managed to wait until after Casey had put the pen into his hand and guided him to the right place to make his mark before rounding on Tzedef, amusement writ large on his face.

"Did you seriously forget!?"

Tzedef stayed silent. He wasn't positive, but he didn't think there was a correct answer to this question.

"He did." Casey snickered, fishing in her pocket for her coinpurse. "Sat there for a good ten seconds, waiting for you to take the pen."

"In my defense," Tzedef said, slightly stiffly, and then paused, thinking it through.

Nope. There was no good way to end that sentence.

"Nevermind." He sighed as Sorecco held out his hand and Amarie dropped a key into his palm.

Casey took the other key, and Amarie pointed them across the room at a small hallway that led out of the common room.

"The rooms are just over there," she said, pointing "Just down that hall. One on the left, the other on the right, just past the privy. "

"Thank you." Sorecco said gratefully, and tapped his stick on the ground, letting the bell jingle before turning toward the hallway and leading the way across the room.

Casey followed him eagerly, but Tzedef didn't move, watching his companions head toward the rooms for a moment before turning back to Amarie, who looked puzzled.

"Was there something else you needed?"

"Yes," Tzedef said, "and no. Bren mentioned that there had been a pox somewhat recently. I am a healer, accredited through the Halls of Healing in Yaelin. Are there any ill or injured people in the village currently? I'm willing to assist as much as I can before we must move on."

Amarie blinked. "Well, the pox was a year, year and a half ago, so we're well shot of that, and our own herbalist usually keeps decently well on top of any normal injuries. I think we're good, sir, but I thank you."

That was something of a relief. Moral obligation to offer assistance aside, trying to take care of the ills of an entire village would have taken more time than he was willing to set aside from their travel. This way, his obligation was fulfilled and they wouldn't be delayed.

Sighing quietly with relief, he bade the woman goodnight then wandered after the siblings and down the hall Amarie had indicated.

Casey's voice called out to him from the first door he knocked on, so he entered the other room with a soft announcement of his presence and slung his pack and shield to the floor at the end of one of the beds.

Sorecco was already in the process of changing into dry things, and Tzedef rapidly followed his example, falling into bed a few minutes later with weary relief.

His sleep that night was dreamless, for the first time in a long time.

Tzedef woke the next day to the scent of bacon drifting through the air, with just enough dim grey light shining through the window to give him the impression that he'd woken decently early. Sorecco, however, was already gone, which was an oddity in itself; the other man usually preferred to sleep as long as possible before getting up.

When he left the bedroom and entered the inn's common room, he spotted Casey and Sorecco both sitting at a table near the fire, each with a plate and a softly steaming mug in front of them. From the look of the plates they'd been lingering for a while, and while neither of them looked particularly pleased, neither did they look irritated that he'd slept past them for once. In fact, Casey perked up as he approached.

"Good morning, Tzedef!"

"Morning, Tzedef." Sorecco's greeting was slightly more subdued, but still not anywhere near as irritated as Tzedef might have expected if he'd egregiously overslept.

He glanced toward the windows and the weak, grey light that was filtering through them as he took a seat. Maybe the siblings had just woken early, for once? Perhaps they were eager to get on the road?

"Good morning."

"So." Casey said, pushing her plate over toward him; a silent offer of bacon. "We have a problem."

Tzedef paused, frozen in the act of reaching for a strip of salty deliciousness. "We do?"

"We do." Sorecco confirmed. "How easy is it to travel in snow?"

Tzedef blinked. "Well, that rather depends on how deep the snow is, and how long you're going to be traveling for. Why?"

He had a sinking feeling he knew, but he had to ask anyway, just in case. It couldn't possibly have snowed that much over night, could it have?

"There's six inches of snow on the ground outside." Casey reported grimly, "And it's still coming down."

Tzedef frowned. That… was unlikely. More than unlikely, it was explicitly not what the weather reading he'd gotten from Freida had said, and the Storm Queen's weather readers tended to be spectacularly reliable.

"How long have you been awake?" He asked, picking up a piece of the offered bacon and taking a bite.

"Hours." Sorecco said. "Since just after dawn for me, at least according to Casey."

"I've been up a little longer than him." Casey put in, propping one elbow on the table and putting her chin in her hand. "I haven't checked outside in the last while. Amarie asked me to stop letting out all the warm air, but when those guys came in I saw outside and it was definitely still snowing."

'Those guys' were a small, mixed kin group that were clustered around one of the other tables a bit away. Tzedef recognized Minalo and Bren, and, going off of that, guessed that the others were guards for any other gates the village might have.

"I see."

His frown deepened as he munched thoughtfully on the bacon. If it was truly snowing as badly as Casey was saying, then continuing on would be a bad idea. Sorecco and Casey had little experience in traveling, and Tzedef himself didn't have the kind of magic that would help with keeping warm or keeping the snow off of them. They would be cold, and wet, and while Tzedef *could* prevent the loss of fingers or toes due to frostbite, it would still be utterly miserable.

"Do we keep going?" Sorecco asked, a little nervously.

"Do *you* want to keep going?" Tzedef asked, probing for their opinions.

"Not really," Casey admitted immediately, "It should blow over soon enough, right? It's still only mid-autumn. There's no way the weather is usually this bad this early."

"Yeah, they would have warned us at the temple if it was, right? Or the weather reading would have said." Sorecco agreed, "And I'd rather not travel in the snow if we can help it. It should blow over in a day or three."

Tzedef hummed, then glanced over at the group of weary looking kin. "A moment."

He stood up and headed over to them, tail swaying behind him as he went.

Each of the people glanced up as he drew closer, and Bren smiled in greeting.

"Good morning, Bren," Tzedef said quietly, "I apologize for disturbing your meal, but I had a question about the current weather."

One of the others groaned, and Minalo snorted.

"We all do." Bren admitted, shifting in his seat to turn so that he could better look over at Tzedef. "But what can I help you with, sir?"

"Call me Tzedef," he introduced himself, "I was wondering if this kind of weather is typical for the region at this time of year."

"It's not." Bren said bluntly, "We don't usually get much snow at all, and that's only in the depths of the shadow months."

"It's great!" Min said enthusiastically, "I've never seen so much snow here before!"

"Shaddup, kid." One of the men groaned, scrubbing at his face wearily, "Weather like this… the fields're gonna be frozen. None o' the winter crops're gonna make it unless we're real damn lucky and a druid or something comes along."

Min looks abashed, sinking back in his chair. "Oh."

"Yeah, 'oh'." One of the women at the table said snarkily, then sighed. "Yeah, we don't get snow like this hardly ever."

Tzedef nodded, and thanked the group, then returned to his own table and re-settled himself in his chair, thinking hard.

"Well?" Casey asked, "Did you find out anything interesting?"

"Not interesting, as such." Tzedef admitted. "They say that they don't get snow like this often. This is an oddity to them, as well."

"Dust…" Sorecco muttered, idly tapping his stick on the floor and listening to the soft chiming of his bell. "I don't suppose they have a weather reader here?"

"It's not likely." Tzedef said, "On the map this village seemed to be quite small, and Bren only mentioned a shrine. Unless one of the Storm Queen's clergy has decided to post up here, which I doubt considering how close Tyona is, then we're out of luck…"

He trailed off thoughtfully, then looked sharply over at Casey. "Actually, we may have an alternative. I'm no weather reader, but the reader back in Tyona did show me something potentially useful. I may be able to check and see approximately how long this snow is going to hold out, so we will know when it might be safe to carry on."

"You can do that?" Sorecco asked, cocking his head curiously, "Really?"

"I don't know." Tzedef admitted, "I succeeded once, with assistance. I may be able to replicate the feat, but there's no guarantee that anything I interpret from it will be worth anything."

Casey shrugged. "I don't see why you shouldn't, unless failing is going to end up with you hurt somehow?"

Tzedef frowned. "It shouldn't. As long as I'm careful, I believe I should be safe enough."

"All right then." Casey said, shrugging again. "Why not, then. Having any information is better than none."

"Very well." Tzedef said, and reached out to swipe the last piece of bacon off Casey's plate. "I may as well do that now, then."

"Do you need anything?" Sorecco asked, and Tzedef shook his head.

"No. I do not believe so, at least. Simply some time to myself and a chance to breathe. I will retire back to our room for this, I think. Please do not disturb me unless I have not emerged by dinner."

Casey's eyes widened slightly incredulously, but she said nothing as he stood and stretched, then headed back toward the bedroom.

This would take concentration, he knew, but he had a sinking feeling that they would need all the information he could glean from his amateur reading.

The bed was too comfortable for him to meditate on, he found. The softness and the chill in the air were too good at luring him into laying down and wrapping up in the blankets again. Instead he sat on the floor and leaned back against the bed, his tail slipping underneath it.

Gradually, his breathing slowed; falling into a smooth, careful rhythm that set his mind adrift, and Tzedef started trying to cast himself out of his body.

In the end it took another invocation to his Goddess to force the shift between physical and aetheric, and Tzedef gasped for non-existent air as he floated in the air next to his own body.

Without someone to guide him or chivvy him on, he took a moment to absorb his surroundings; to take in the faintly faded coloration of the room around him. To see how the bright colors of the rag-quilt were ever-so-slightly washed out. To feel the abrupt lack of chill in the air.

Then he turned and, purposefully, walked through the wall and back out into the main room of the inn.

The group of night guards was dispersing, people drifting away from the table and leaving coins beside their plates for Amarie to collect with the dishes.

Casey was eying the coin speculatively, and Tzedef wondered what she was thinking. If she was thinking about how easy it might be to take some of the coin, and whether or not she'd be caught in the theft.

He could tell the moment she dismissed whatever she'd been thinking; she turned back to the fresh plate of bacon on the table and picked up a piece.

"Hey Sorecco?"

"Hmm?" Sorecco slid his hand across the table, seeking, and found the plate, taking his own piece.

"You ever think we mighta bit off more than we can chew?"

"Mmf," Sorecco swallowed hard, then propped his head up on the heel of his other hand. "You mean with Tzedef?"

Tzedef hesitated, then resolutely turned and marched through the outer wall of the inn.

Still, as he was going he heard Casey's affirmative hum and Sorecco's derisive scoff.

"Nah. Tzedef's a go—"

Outside he waded through snow that offered no resistance to him. He felt no chill as fat, wet flakes fell through him, and, when he looked up, it was to be greeted with a low ceiling of clouds, thick and fat and grey.

The question was, he thought, how to get up there.

And as simply as that, he was. Drifting amongst the grey with no frame of reference for up or down.

It took some experimentation before he worked out that it was willpower that moved him, and soon he was drifting to and fro, popping up through the top of the clouds into a sunlit paradise of towering fluffy white clouds, or down through the bottom to inspect the snow-covered landscape below.

In the end, though, he was on a mission. He needed to know how long the snow would last, and if this seemed to be a fluke. A one-off freak weather occurrence that wouldn't further impact their travel plans.

Surely it was. Frieda had seemed to be quite skilled. He didn't think she would be *that* wrong.

So up he went. Further and further and further, until the sky around him dimmed from blue to black, and the stars burned like pinpricks of fire against the inky darkness of the void.

He looked down.

CHAPTER SEVENTEEN

A Sea of Clouds

"What do you mean there isn't an end in sight!?"
Lucas Miller, the headman of Maplemore, squawked, and
Tzedef sighed internally as he set about explaining it
again.

"I was looking at the weather in much the same way
a weather reader does." He said patiently, "the clouds
stretch from the middle of the ocean out over the Sea of
Sand, from the northern pole to the lowest reaches of
Silsharn. There are no gaps. There is no end. Winter is
here, and I do not believe it will be leaving anytime soon."

Lynn, Lucas's wife and the village herbalist, gaped
at Tzedef, horrified. "But you're not a weather reader, right?
You could be wrong!"

"I very well could be." Tzedef agreed, "In fact, I
fervently hope I am. I highly doubt anyone is prepared for a
winter such as the one I greatly fear we are facing."

"We don't have a local reader," Lucas fretted, "and
our priest is basically useless, she's only good for small

blessings and—"

He broke off with a yelp as his wife smacked his arm.

"You be nice! Poor Maria is doing her best! It's not her fault her god is so small!"

Tzedef winced. In times like this, having a small god was almost worse than having no god at all.

The Lesser Gods required followers and worship to exist, and the more followers and worship a god got the more powerful it, and by extension its priests and clerics, were.

Small gods with few followers often puffed themselves up to make themselves seem greater or more powerful than they were, which often resulted in their followers ending up in sticky situations.

More than once he'd heard that it had ended in death for whatever cleric had been trying to overreach their god's abilities.

"And don't you start, either!" Lynn rounded on Tzedef. "Maria's had more than enough on her plate without some high and mighty cleric coming 'round and judging her none!"

"Ma'am, that was honestly the last thing on my mind." Tzedef said honestly, "My god is quite small as well, and her domains are not conducive to assisting on a religious or magical level with this situation."

"Domains?" Lucas demanded, "Your 'small god' has multiple domains? What are they?"

Tzedef grimaced internally. He hadn't meant to say

that.

"Magic, crossroads, and the grave." He admitted. Hopefully that would keep—

"Graves?!" Lucas exclaimed, his voice going shrill, and Tzedef sighed, his expression going flat and resigned.

"Good," Lynn interrupted her husband before he could gear up any further for the rant Tzedef could see brewing.

"Good?" Lucas turned to Lynn, his voice plaintive, and Lynn nodded firmly.

"Good. Maria and I're both Light aligned. You say your goddess is magic, crossroads, and graves? That means you're Shadow aligned, right?" She glanced over at Tzedef, but kept most of her attention on her husband.

"Correct." Tzedef said, wondering where she was going with this.

"Good." She said again. "You aren't going anywhere if the weather's as bad as you say it's going to be, and we're going to end up with a lot of ill and injured people this winter if it turns out badly. You'll be useful as a healer, and, if the worst comes to pass, then your goddess's grave domain allows you to lay spirits to rest, yes?"

"Correct." He said again, rather taken aback by how quickly Lynn had taken charge. "I have the ability to ease restless spirits and perform burials that will appease most dead. But how did you know I was a healer?"

"Bren told me." She said simply, and tossed him a quick smile. "He keeps me up to date on any healers that announce themselves as they pass through, just in case I need to tap them to work with me in an emergency.

"Now." She looked dead into her husband's eyes. "This young man and his friends'll be staying here until the weather clears. Whether that's in a couple days or a few weeks, we'll see, but if it does turn out as bad as he's fearing, then I don't want to be caught all on my lonesome with just poor Maria doing her best to help out, all right?"

Lucas nodded, a trifle glumly. "Yes, dear."

"And you won't cause any trouble for this nice young man based on his goddess?"

"No, dear."

The look he shot Tzedef didn't promise good things in his future, but Lucas seemed genuine enough when he looked down at his wife, so as long as he didn't try to attack Tzedef in the middle of the night, he was content to leave it lie.

"Good." Lynn said again, and nodded, seemingly perfectly satisfied as she turned to more fully face Tzedef.

"I work out of our home, and we've no room for another person to stay." she said plainly, "I can have a word with Amarie about letting you stay if you don't have the coin for a long term stay, but your traveling companions will have to make their own arrangements."

"It would be appreciated." Tzedef nodded. "I'll inform the others."

He turned to go, then paused when Lucas cleared his throat, turning back to look at the man.

"How do we know this isn't some sort of scam?" Lucas asked bluntly.

Tzedef blinked at him, surprised. "Isn't the purpose of a scam to get money, goods, or services for free or reduced prices?"

"Typically, yeah."

"Then why would this be a scam?" Tzedef asked, honestly puzzled, "I came to warn you, and did not request any special treatment or compensation. The only special treatment that was mentioned was offered by Missus Miller, here, not me. Not to mention, if I am lying then it will quickly become apparent."

Lucas frowned, but nodded reluctantly. "That's all true, I guess."

"Further," Tzedef pressed, "I do not expect to not earn my keep in the same way that my companions might. You can rest assured that I will be working to earn my stay here, should we need to stay past when our coin runs out."

"All right," Lucas's frown deepened, "but something about this doesn't seem right. I'll be watching you."

"Of course." Tzedef bowed shallowly, hiding the sardonic look on his face, and turned and strode away.

"So what did they say?" Sorecco asked as soon as Tzedef stepped back into their shared room.

"Not very much." Tzedef admitted. "There was an assumption made that we would be staying in the village until the weather clears, which, given the distances involved in traveling either to the next village or back to Tyona, seems reasonable."

"Yeah," Casey sighed, glancing out the window at

the barely discernible snow still coming down. "Way too long to get back to Tyona, and at least what, a week to get to Leeward? It's not happening while the snow is coming down like this."

"But we don't have the money to pay for an extended stay. Not without dipping into the funds that were supposed to help us get started in Vraka." Sorecco pointed out, and Casey grimaced.

"We each should be able to find work that will allow us to remain housed and fed. The herbalist here wishes for my assistance should it become necessary. She seems to be under the impression that the weather will clear in a week or two."

"Do you think she's right?" Casey asked, leaning forward from where she was sitting on Sorecco's bed, and Tzedef shrugged helplessly.

"I don't know. I'm not a weather reader. I do not know how to turn back time in the way I was shown, and I don't know how to extrapolate the patterns they see. For all I know, I am seeing problems where there are none and the clouds will clear tomorrow."

"Part of me really hopes you're wrong about this." Casey admitted, "But a lot of me is afraid you aren't."

"Me too." Tzedef murmured, reaching up to rub absently at his amulet.

Snow fell for the next two weeks, sometimes coming down thick and fast, other times so lightly that one would almost have thought it had stopped. But it hadn't, and it didn't, and by the time the third week had passed with no sign of it slowing down, the villagers had given up on hoping that the winter crops were going to make it, and had started settling in grimly for a long, hard winter.

Luckily, both Casey and Sorecco had skills that were valuable enough that they were able to earn enough money from the villagers to pay Amarie for their stay; Sorecco was often followed around by a gaggle of children, eager to hear one of his seemingly endless supply of tales or songs, and Casey found herself under Amarie's direction, helping in the kitchen or around the bar during the day, and entertaining 'guests' in her room in the evenings.

Tzedef himself ended up helping most often with the small village guard, usually keeping watch over one or the other of the village gates, and, as he was found to have the most unflappable disposition of anyone but Bren, he was often partnered with Minalo.

Every morning, Tzedef checked again to see when the interminable snow was going to end, and every morning he saw more clouds on the horizon, pouring down out of the north with no end in sight. Even the gaps between storms were only brief interludes that allowed the villagers a chance to get some of the most necessary outdoor chores done.

Without the bolstering effect of the winter crops, food began to run low near the end of the month of War, and with spring nowhere in sight, Lucas called Maria and Tzedef both to meet with him.

"We're running low on food." Lucas said bluntly, looking ever so slightly haggard. "You're both priests. Do something about it."

Tzedef stared at the man, dumbfounded, then glanced sideway at Maria, who was twisting her hands nervously.

"Do something about it." He echoed, turning back to stare at Lucas, red eyes pinning the man in place. "Something like what?"

"I don't know!" Lucas blustered, "Make food! Ask your gods for a miracle!"

Ah.

That's where this was going.

"That won't work." Tzedef said flatly. "I cannot create food or drink in any way other than the mundane."

"What!? What kind of cleric can't summon food and drink!?" Lucas puffed himself up, and Tzedef scowled.

"The kind who doesn't worship a harvest goddess!" he snapped, "the kind who worships a goddess of the crossroads and the grave! Now, I can certainly *try* to summon food and drink, but I can almost guarantee you that it will be inedible at best and actively rotting at worst!"

Lucas paled, but soldiered on, blustering with all the pomp of an offended melli bird. "You're a cleric! You have a duty to the people! We've taken you in, fed you, housed you! You owe—"

"I'm going to stop you right there." Tzedef said, his voice like ice. "I owe you nothing. I have worked to earn my keep, and I have kept you appraised of any changes the weather might make as soon as I am aware of them. I have checked for you, daily. Sometimes more than once.

Anything I might have owed you is more than paid off."

Lucas scowled, and opened his mouth to retort, only for Maria to interrupt.

"He's right."

Tzedef half turned, looking at the normally shy woman in surprise.

"Tzedef is right." She said, her voice shaking, twisting her fingers in the hem of the heavy coat she was wearing. "He doesn't owe you anything. I'm the village priest. It's my job to help see the people through the hard times. My god is a small one, but he isn't a grave god. I can at least try to intercede with him for food. It might even work. I think."

Lucas narrowed his eyes at her. "You *think*. You can *try*. It *might* work. Are you ever certain of anything, girl? What use are you as a priest if you've got all the backbone of a over-saturated earthworm!?"

Maria shrank into herself, flushing miserably.

"There is no call for that." Tzedef rumbled warningly, then stopped as Maria shook her head.

"I'll see what I can do with Nelthys." She said quietly, "We might be able to work something out."

"See that you do." Lucas said, still scowling. "Or we're all going to be in big trouble."

Tzedef didn't even bother with a farewell to the pompous fool, just turned on his heel and strode with military precision toward the door.

Soft, hurried footsteps told him that Maria was following, and when he got to the door he held it open for her, silently pleased by the way Lucas shivered in the gust of cold air that blew in.

Maria glanced up at him as she passed, ducking her head gratefully as she stepped out into the bitter cold and turned to hurry toward her little shrine.

"He had no call to say that to you." Tzedef said, and Maria stopped in her tracks, then turned to look at him with a wan smile.

"He's right, though. I do have all the spine of an over-saturated earthworm."

"Nevertheless," Tzedef started, and stopped when Maria shook her head.

"It's fine. I'm working on it. It's something that drives Nelthys up the wall too. He's always telling me that I should stand up to people more, or that I need to learn to say 'no'. We're working on it."

Tzedef blinked at her slowly, taking that in.

Apparently the young woman had a closer connection to her god than he'd thought. That was good. It would most likely stand her in good stead should she come to difficulty beyond the headman grousing at her.

"If you insist." He said eventually, and the smile Maria flashed at him was more genuine and less tired.

"I do." She said. "But thank you for your concern. It's nice, having someone physical stand up for me."

Tzedef shrugged, then glanced up at the sky which was swiftly clouding back over.

"We'd best get back inside. I mislike the look of those clouds, and I think the temperature is dropping again."

"Right." Maria said, glancing up as well before huddling deeper into her coat. "I'll just... go, then."

"Yes." Tzedef inclined his head toward her, and watched as she turned and hurried down the street that was only marginally kept clear due to the combined efforts of several of the villagers.

Only once she was out of sight did Tzedef allow himself a long sigh and a dirty look at the closed door of the headman's house.

Lucas had, over the last few months, proven himself to be a petty, small minded, prejudiced idiot whose two redeeming features were the fact that he happened to actually be excellent at his job, and his wife.

Truly, Tzedef wasn't sure why the woman wasn't running the village herself; she seemed to have her husband well in hand whenever she was actually around.

Which, thinking about it, was probably why she was nowhere to be seen during Lucas' little meeting.

He shot the door another dirty look, then shivered and reached back to adjust the sleeve that one of the other guards had knitted for him to wear over his tail. It wasn't the most comfortable thing, but it was warm, and that was what mattered right now.

Silently, he turned and headed back toward the inn, cursing his own heritage the whole way.

Skaal wouldn't need a tail sleeve, nor would Tekla. They'd gotten the working parts of both sides of their heritage- cold resistance from their father, and heat resistance from their mother.

But Tzedef? Oh no. He'd gotten nothing. Nothing but frostbite and heatstroke until they'd realized that here, too, was something he'd failed at.

Nevermind the fact that it wasn't something he could possibly have succeeded at in the first place.

Now thoroughly irritated, he opened the door to the inn and slipped inside, glancing around. It was relatively busy, with Sorecco entertaining a gaggle of children over to one side, and a group of adults over at the bar, chatting with the air of people partaking in a particularly good gossip session.

Exactly what they had to gossip about, Tzedef hadn't the faintest clue, but with everyone holed up out of the storms for so long a bit of gossip was probably the least of any evils that might come about. Still, it wasn't anything he was interested in, so he ignored it in favor of heading toward his and Sorecco's room.

Despite what he'd told Lucas, he didn't actually know for sure what results he would get from asking Hecate for food. On the one hand, it was entirely likely that he would get rotting food. She'd probably think it was funny.

On the other hand, people made offerings of food to graves all the time. If that qualified as food, to her, then it stood to reason that he might be able to summon at least small portions of things typically left at gravesides.

Which, in his experience, was usually alcohol.

But small portions of alcohol might not be a bad thing to be able to summon, actually. It could be useful to sterilize wounds, if nothing else...

Now thoughtful, Tzedef stripped out of his outdoor wear, tossing it onto the various hooks that Amarie had installed when it became apparent that their stay was going to be a long term one. Then, clad only in his soft under-trousers and the loose, grey-green shirt that he favored, he settled on the floor between the beds and closed his eyes to meditate.

CHAPTER EIGHTEEN

Spring

Winter passed with an interminable slowness, broken only by flurries of near-frantic activity whenever the weather allowed- usually with hunters going out and returning with game birds or, if they were lucky, a deer or elk.

It wasn't much, but it was enough to keep food in people's mouths, and that, coupled with the way that Nelthys and Maria had pulled through on miracling up enough food for the children to stay fed, was enough that people were staying cautiously hopeful.

Several people fell ill around the turn of the Month of Self, badly enough that Lynn called Tzedef in to help with curing them, but aside from that and a couple of broken bones from slipping on ice, things were relatively calm through the end of winter.

Spring came slowly, in drips and drabs, in warmer days and snowless nights, and with it came the thaw.

Tzedef rapidly grew used to the sound of trickling water on the roof of the inn, and the streets all nearly flooded as the snow that'd been piled to the eaves melted. It was a mucky, muddy, disgusting mess, and there was a sort of hesitance among the farmers about whether or not the weather had cleared enough to start working on getting the early spring crops in the ground.

Eventually, however, the decision was taken out of their hands.

The amount of divinity that Maria needed to channel to produce the food for the children was taxing, and she couldn't summon enough to feed the whole village, which meant that even though everyone else had tightened their belts, normal food was growing dangerously scarce.

They would have to get the spring crops in the ground sooner, rather than later, and hope that enough of the seed made it through the damp that they'd be able to eat.

Tzedef watched from his post at the south gate as the farmers went to work in the fields, oxen hitched to plows, turning over the sodden, muddy earth.

He didn't know much about farming, but from what he'd overheard in the common room of the inn over the last few days, the seed rotting in the earth was a distinct, worrying possibility that was outside of his ability to do anything about.

He was no druid. No land-healer. His goddess had no

links to the natural world that would enable him to help with this.

He would have to simply hope and pray that the land dried out quickly enough for the seed to sprout well. Just like everyone else.

And indeed, it seemed as though the hopes and prayers were having a positive effect; there was no more snow, no rain, and very few clouds for the next few days, leaving the sky clear for the sun to beam down with all its might on the wet ground.

Slowly the ground began to dry out, and the seeds that the farmers had so carefully planted began to send up shoots, spreading like a soft green mist across the fields that surrounded the village.

Which, it turned out, was a problem.

The first indication Tzedef had that something was wrong was Bren stiffening next to him.

The second indication came when he followed the other man's gaze and saw the rag-tag group of people approaching the village, some dressed in mismatched armor, but most in normal farmer's wear, or hunting gear.

"Trouble?" He murmured, and Bren nodded.

"Those aren't guards from the mountain, and they ain't from Leeward or Tyona either. I know what that armor looks like, an' they keep it a lot better than that."

"Mercenaries, maybe?" Tzedef suggested, though, looking at the poorly kept and, in some cases, rusty, armor, he doubted it.

"Nah…" Bren murmured, dismissing the possibility as well, which left just one possibility.

"Bandits, then."

Bren nodded again, his eyes fixed on the approaching group. "Min, go get the headman, and let Rose know that we might need backup."

Minalo nodded, pale-faced and silent for once, and hurried down the ladder, darting away once he was on solid ground.

"I count thirty-two." Tzedef said quietly as the group came to a halt about a hundred feet from the gate.

"Thirty-five." Bren corrected him, "There's a few gnomes hiding 'round the back of the group."

"Lovely." Tzedef sighed, and glanced down at the loaded crossbow that sat next to him on the walkway, leaning against the wall.

"Open the gate!" The woman at the front of the group shouted. She was elven and haggard, her hair hanging in limp hanks around her face, and her voice was hoarse and cracked. Still, the sword at her hip was one of the few in an actual sheathe, and that meant something, though he wasn't sure what just yet.

Tzedef kept his face impassive.

"On what grounds?" Bren called back, and his hand tightened around the tiller of his own crossbow.

"On the grounds of you lot have food, an' we needs it!" someone closer to the back of the group shouted, and the woman turned, making a sharp gesture that made the group shift uneasily, and fall quiet again.

"We're hungry." She called, "We got starving kids what needs food. You lot, you've got your spring crops in." She gestured toward the fields misted with green sprouts. "You must have spare. Seed stock, animals. Anything."

"An' you need weapons t'come 'round as neighbors? And armor?" Bren asked skeptically, and the woman shoved back a hank of hair, revealing a too-thin face and sallow skin.

"The roads're dangerous." Her voice was flat, but it carried up to them still, and Tzedef sighed.

Desperation hung about the group in a haze of emotion that Tzedef could almost taste, even clear up on the wall as he was. It made them more dangerous than an army, in some ways. Dangerous like a rat, cornered and without any escape.

They were tired. Hungry. Desperate.

And they were convinced that the village had food.

"We don't have any extra." Bren called down, and Tzedef winced as a low, discontented susurrus rippled through the crowd.

"Bullshit!" One man snarled, stomping forward out of the group and coming to a halt just shy of the elven woman. "Ye've seeds in the earth, which means ye've animals. We've all et ours! Ye can spare a few!"

"What's all this? What's going on!?" Lucas's voice was shrill with panic, and he scrambled up the ladder to look over the edge of the wall.

Rose, Bren's second, followed him up the ladder and whistled through her teeth at the gathering in front of the gate.

"They want food." Bren informed them quietly, and Lucas puffed himself up, leaning over the wall to shout down.

"We don't have any food for thieves and vagabonds! Go away!"

"Thieves!" The elven woman shouted back indignantly, "Lucas Miller you'd best be talking about someone else right now, or you can come down here and say that to my face, you spineless wimp!"

Lucas squeaked, and pulled back out of sight.

"Why didn't you say Isabeta was here?" he hissed angrily at Bren, and Bren blinked.

"Wait that's *Isabeta!?*" He leaned back out over the edge of the wall. "Izzy? Is that *you?!*"

"Of course it's me, you brainless nit!" She shouted, now verging on incensed. "Who the hells did you *think* I was?!"

"Shit." Bren said softly, staring down at the woman with a complicated look on his face.

Tzedef grimaced.

Just what they needed. Not only were there bandits, now they were *known*. They were, potentially, *friends*.

Fuck.

"They need food." Bren said, and Rose hissed slightly as she sucked air between her teeth.

"We don't have enough for them, and their families. We barely have enough to last us through until the spring crops start coming in. And that's a maybe at best." Lucas snapped, and Rose turned to scowl at him.

"So we'll tighten our belts," she said. "Skip more meals. These people are our friends! We can't just leave them to fend for themselves!"

"We can." Lucas said grimly, "And we have to. If people start skipping more meals, who'll have the strength to get out and harvest the spring crops? Who'll help keep the fields vermin free? Who'll put the next rotation in the ground, when it's time?"

Rose scowled at him, but said nothing, turning her attention back down onto the crowd that was, slowly, starting to mutter discontentedly.

"What's wrong?" Maria's voice was soft and worried, but it carried up to the top of the wall easily enough. Lucas looked over his shoulder down at her, his face dismissive.

"Noth-"

He paused midword, a calculating look on his face as he gazed down at her, then peeked over the edge of the wall again.

Tzedef arched one brow ridge as Lucas turned his back on the outside of the wall entirely, looking down at Maria.

"Have you already summoned the food for the children?"

"Of course!" She looked almost offended. "I do that first thing in the morning, you know that."

"Right, yes, of course." He waved her offense away. "Can you do it again?"

"Um." She blinked. "No? I haven't... We aren't..."

Tzedef cast a glance over at Lucas, who was looking increasingly impatient, then sighed and slid down the ladder.

"There are people outside," He informed her quietly, "led by a woman named Isabeta. They are hungry, and they say that they have hungry children back at their homes. The village cannot afford to feed them all, but if you can entreat Nelthys for another miracle, then we can ensure that they are fed for the next day."

"But why *me?!*" She cried, "You're a cleric! You're much more powerful than I am! I've seen you! You do miracles as easily as *breathing!*"

Tzedef's shoulders slumped. "I am a cleric, yes. But I cannot do this."

"You haven't even tried!" She exclaimed, and Tzedef looked down at her to meet her eyes steadily, facing the accusation there with tired resignation.

Carefully, he lifted one hand, holding it palm up in front of her so that she could see that it was empty.

"Great goddess, keeper of the crossroads, cast forth your blessing that I might feed the hungry. Grant me the grace to ensure that those with most need of your succor receive it."

The words weren't rote. They weren't rattled off with the ease of a priest giving a catch-all blessing.

But they were delivered in a flat, lifeless tone, and Maria recoiled as a dinner roll appeared on his hand in front of her face. Crawling with maggots and covered in blue-green mold.

"What in Nelthys' name?!"

"My goddess is the protector of the *grave*." He said flatly. "I have tried, ever since the idea was first brought up, to summon food that might help. To ease your burden, if nothing else. But this is the best I can do. Rotten, decaying food. Food fit for the dead, and none other."

He flung the maggot covered roll away, hiding a grimace as he wiped his hand on his cloak.

"Do you see? You are the only option, here. If you are afraid, I will go out with you. I will not let harm come to you, I swear it, but offering your assistance may be the only thing that prevents us from having a battle on our hands."

Maria hesitated, then glanced up at where Lucas was watching her, his face faintly derisive.

"I…" She hesitated. "I haven't tried to cast it a second time in a day after the first week. I don't know what'll happen."

"All we can ask is that you try." Tzedef said quietly. "Nelthys… I am sure that he has faith in you, just as much as you have faith in him."

Maria glanced up at Lucas again, then took a deep breath and firmed her spine.

"Okay."

"Okay?" Tzedef asked, and Maria nodded.

"Okay. I'll try. I mean, they're hungry, right? I can't just stand back and do *nothing.*" She hesitated, then looked up at him. "But you'll still come out with me, won't you?"

"As I said." Tzedef nodded. "I will."

"Right." Maria took a deep breath, then let it out slowly, and Tzedef glanced up at Lucas.

"We will try to feed them. Hopefully there will be enough food for them to take home, as well."

Bren glanced down outside the wall, then down at Tzedef, a conflicted look on his face.

"We can't... we can't just let them in. Not with them armed to the teeth and ready to do Lights knows what if we can't feed them."

"So get some tables and bring them out here. They need not go any further than this. If you believe it will help, call out the rest of the guards and have them stand ready at the streets into the rest of the village." Tzedef said simply, and turned to face Maria again as Bren, Rose, and Lucas all conferred on top of the wall.

"What do you need to entreat your god for a miracle?"

"Nothing," She said, shaking her head. "Just... prayer, and belief. He's not quite so small that he requires sacrifice."

"Right." Tzedef said, and glanced up at the trio on the wall. He could hear the group outside the gate getting louder, their discontent making them clear even through the thick logs that formed the wall.

A few moments later, Min scrambled down the ladder again and raced off into the village, and Bren leaned over the outer edge of the wall.

"All right, you lot. We're going to try something. You know Maria? Well her and Nelthys have been working on a way to feed people. She's been keeping the little 'uns fed as food's been gettin' low. She ent been able to cast it more'n once a day, yet, but she's willing to give it a shot to try and get you enough food for all of you and your people back home." He paused, and Tzedef could picture the hard look he was giving them. "This ent a guarantee. We don't know if it'll work. But you're all friends. We don't want you going hungry, and we don't want deaths, here. So."

There was a low mutter of agreement from the other side of the wall, and Bren nodded, his face grim as he pulled back and reached for the crank that would raise the gate.

The gate creaked up slowly, and Tzedef watched as the shifting crowd of people behind it was revealed.

Up close, he could see that the majority of the weapons on offer were either repurposed farming tools or rusty, blunted old pieces that hadn't seen proper care in decades at the kindest. Only Isabeta's sword seemed to be in good repair- the sheathe well oiled leather, and the hilt free of any rust or damage.

"Come." He gestured, and the elven woman, Isabeta, stepped forward, eyeing him warily.

"You're new."

"A traveler," He replied. "stuck here for the winter. I am a temporary member of the guard."

"I see." She eyed him even more warily, taking in his shield and the way he stood with his mace casually hanging at his hip. "What brings a soldier all the way out here?"

"Is this not the main thoroughfare between Tyona

and Vraka?" Tzedef inquired mildly, glancing past her as the others milled past her.

Every person in the group had the look of someone who had lost far too much weight far too quickly. The winter had not been kind.

"It is." She admitted, and glanced over his shoulder to where Maria was standing, looking increasingly nervous as more people came through the gate. "Can she really do what he said? Create food from nothing?"

Tzedef shrugged, turning away. "We shall see, won't we?"

A few steps took him to Maria's side, and the woman shrank back to stand in his shadow. It was almost a relief when Min reappeared, hauling a large table with the help of one of the other guards. They set it down not far from where Tzedef was standing, and Maria almost gratefully stepped over to it, her hands fluttering over the wooden surface nervously.

Tzedef glanced around, checking the streets that led out of the wider 'entrance' area of the village, and nodding slightly when he spotted Mattias, Niko, Ramble, and the others standing in them, their eyes on the group that was starting to mill around the table and Maria.

"It would um…" Maria started, her voice thin and hesitant, "It would help if you could all… um… excuse me?"

Only those closest to her even heard her, and of those, only Isabeta turned to listen to her.

"You're going to need to speak up, girl." The woman

said bluntly, and Maria flushed miserably, ducking her head.

"Sorry."

"Don't be sorry." Isabeta chided her. "You're the priest. You deserve respect, so don't just stand around waiting to be handed it. *Command it.*"

Maria's flush deepened, but she took a deep breath and looked up.

"Ex- *Excuse me!*" The shout got everyone's attention, and Maria faltered at being under so many eyes at once, shrinking back.

Only Tzedef's hand on her back, careful and supportive, kept her from turning to flee, and she took another deep breath, then let it out slowly.

"It w-would help if everyone could join hands around the table." She said, and managed to modulate her voice enough so that she could be heard without shouting.

"Why?" One of the gnomes asked bluntly, and Maria's hands twisted in front of her.

"Because she's the priest and she said so." Isabeta snapped. "Get your head out of your arse, Rhimbac."

The gnome grumbled, but moved closer to the table, and soon it was obvious that there were too many people to fit comfortably around the table.

"Two rings." Maria said finally, "And the- the two people closest to me in the outer ring will have to hold my shoulders."

Tzedef nodded and stepped out of the way. He was already spoken for, and he doubted his goddess having a hand in this would end well for anyone present.

Slowly, with much shuffling and no small amount of shoving and swearing, all thirty-six people were arrayed around the table. Isabeta was holding Maria's hand on one side, and a dusky orange demonkin had her other. Sheer mechanics meant that a pair of human men had her shoulders, and Tzedef could see her trembling, forcing herself not to flee the attention of so many desperate people.

"Nelthys, god of small works, please grant us your blessing. Give us the nourishment we require to continue our own works in every way, big and small."

The prayer was short, and simple, but Tzedef could hear the faith that Maria poured into it, the absolute confidence that her god wouldn't let her down. That while she might fail, Nelthys wouldn't.

And as the last syllable left her mouth, green fire flashed at her fingertips, racing around the circles like caged lightning until it reached her again and poured up her arms to wrap around her throat.

Almost as one, the circles broke, people letting go of each other's hands with muted curses, stepping back warily until someone let out a triumphant shout.

"Food!"

Sure enough, the table was laden with food. Simple, hearty fare. A cauldron of stew. Loaves of thick, crusty bread. Jars of milk, thick with cream.

Maria stepped back as the would-be bandits fell on it with barely concealed desperation.

Only Isabeta held back, turning to look at Maria with calculating eyes.

"Congratulations."

"Th-thank you." Maria said, looking stunned, and Tzedef stepped forward.

"You should help yourself, before it's all gone." He said simply, and Isabeta nodded, then turned to join her fellows at the table.

Only once the elven woman was preoccupied did he turn his attention to the shellshocked young woman at his side.

"Congratulations." He echoed and Maria turned huge brown eyes up to meet his, looking a bare breath away from full on panic.

"Did that really just happen?" She croaked, one hand going up to her throat and the dark green vine that twined around it now, the color sunk into her skin in a way that no magic or knife could remove. "Did he really- am I *really-?*"

"You really are." Tzedef confirmed, and smiled slightly. "Did you not know he was so close to requiring a High Priestess?"

"No!" Maria wailed quietly, "How could I have known? I thought if he chose anyone, it would be one of the women from my home village! They were always so much better than I was at- at *everything!* Why would he choose *me!?*"

"Because you love him." Tzedef said simply. "And your love shines through in your worship."

Maria stumbled over her next words and fell silent, staring up at Tzedef and completely unable to refute his words.

"Maria, Tzedef." Bren's voice was tense as he called down to them. "Come here."

Tzedef glanced up at the half-orc on the wall, his eyes narrowing slightly, and he nodded, turning to follow Maria as she hurried around the crowd.

Maria had some small difficulty getting up the ladder, mostly due to her skirts, thick and heavy to keep out the cold, and in the end Bren reached down to grasp one of her wrists and pulled her the rest of the way up. She squeaked as he put her down gently on top of the wall, then again when he grasped her shoulders to turn her to look out toward the fields.

Tzedef took the rungs two at a time, hurrying to the top of the wall, then froze when he spotted what had made Bren call them up.

Frost Wheat, pale cream and beautiful, swayed in waves as the wind rippled across the more distant fields.

Leafy greens rustled in the breeze in the closer fields, and, in the closest fields, wildflowers bloomed, ready to feed the bees that had been starting to stir from their hives in the last few weeks.

Maria stared, mouth slightly agape as she took in the sudden bounty. Stunned nearly senseless.

"Well now," Tzedef murmured approvingly, "*that* is a miracle worthy of a high priestess."

CHAPTER NINETEEN

A Miracle Harvest

Lucas turned a calculating gaze on the priest, his face blank before he started rapping out orders.

"Bren, get Agatha and Cecil out here. We're going to need to see if that's all ripe and if it is bring it all in as quickly as possible. Rose, go down, talk to them see if any of them are willing to help bring it in in exchange for portions to take home. Maria, *can you do that again?*"

"I don't—" Maria stammered, her eyes still fixed on the over-full fields, "I don't *know*! Nelthys… that isn't his domain, but I— I don't see how we *could* have, without a do —"

Her voice cut off and her eyes went distant, and Lucas scowled, opening his mouth to say something before Tzedef cut him off with a sharp motion of his hand.

"It's… He has a new domain." She breathed, blinking out of the light trance she'd fallen into.

"That happens." Tzedef nodded, "If enough worship comes from those with particular inclinations, new domains may be gained that lean more towards assisting those worshipers."

"Wonderful," Lucas said, slightly sarcastically, "What is it? Is it useful?"

Maria, much to Tzedef's surprise, glared at the man.

"I don't know," she said, her voice thick with sarcasm as she gestured out towards the fields. "Do you think *agriculture* is useful?"

Lucas's eyes sharpened. "Agriculture. So you could encourage the cows to calve easier? Or the sheep to bear more lambs? The fowl to lay more?"

Maria's eyes went wide, and she shrank back, all bravado vanishing in the face of Lucas's sudden questioning.

"I- yes? Probably? It would take some checking, I think. We don't know the limits of the domain, yet."

"Good." Lucas said, "Fine. That's fine. Test away. Do whatever you need to to figure out your limits. If you can cast blessings like *that* on *their* fields," he jerked his head down at the still eating farmers, "Then we won't have a repeat of this situation."

"Right." Maria glanced down at the farmers, then shook out her skirts and headed for the ladder. "I'll just- I'll go check on the barns, I think."

"Do that." Lucas nodded, then glanced over at Tzedef, almost dismissively. "Take *him* with you. I wouldn't put it past some of that lot to try to 'convince' you to leave with them. Especially once they see the fields."

Maria quailed at that thought and nodded faintly,

glancing up at Tzedef to see if he had any objections.

He had none, and so followed the woman down the ladder.

"Ey!" the dusky-orange demonkin called, glancing up from his meal and catching sight of Maria and Tzedef as they made their way across the square. "Maria, right? Thanks! And thanks to your god, too!"

Maria nodded, her eyes wide, and stammered something, then all but fled down the streets toward the barns where the majority of the animals that called the village home were kept.

She only slowed down once she was safely out of sight of the grateful farmers, and Tzedef paused with her as she let out a long, shuddering breath.

"That's..." She started, then floundered. "How do you-? Why are they so-?"

"They are grateful to you." Tzedef said, and Maria huffed softly.

"I know that, and I'm not trying to dismiss it. I just..." She made a helpless, flailing sort of gesture and Tzedef sighed.

"You are unused to the adulation that comes from performing the kind of miracles you just performed, yes?"

"*Yes!*" She cried. "I didn't do it! It was Nelthys! So why are they thanking me!?"

"Because you are here, visible and tangible, and Nelthys isn't." Tzedef said, and turned to keep walking toward the barns.

Maria blinked after him, then hurried to catch up.

"What do you mean? Nelthys is here! He just gave them food! He grew the crops!"

"Through you." Tzedef said implacably. "People-ordinary people with little contact with the gods- they understand that the gods exist, but to them it is an abstract concept. They worship who their parents worshiped, because that is how they were raised. Sometimes they might get some small blessing or another from a village priest, or they might have a good harvest while around them their neighbors' crops fail. Things to reinforce their belief in the gods of the fathers.

"Still, those things? Those blessings? Happen through the priests. The clerics. We are the visible representations of our gods on this plane of existence. People see us, and they understand that our gods may act through us. Belief in our deeds becomes belief in our gods, which strengthens our gods in turn. The more faith people have in our gods, the greater the miracles they can accomplish through us. We are the conduits through which the gods act, and people see and judge us for those acts. Good, helpful, and kind acts breed thanks, respect, and faith, which in turn brings renewed strength to the cycle."

"But what about you, then?" She asked, peering up at his face, and Tzedef glanced down at her, puzzled.

"What about me?"

"You've been here for nine months, and you haven't done *anything*."

Tzedef snorted, a wry smile tugging at the corners of his mouth, and Maria hastily amended her statement.

"Nothing cleric-y, I mean. You haven't given any blessings. No prayers. You haven't even tried to spread word of your goddess. It's *strange*."

"Is it?" He asked, slightly bemused. "I have been informed in no uncertain terms that my welcome here is conditional on my keeping my goddess and my practices to myself. We have been fortunate that there have been no deaths over the winter, or I would have asked if you would prefer I step in for the burial blessings."

"Are the blessings from a grave goddess so much different from that of other gods?" Maria asked, sounding fascinated, and Tzedef shrugged.

"Yes, and no. Our blessings are the same in that we offer prayers to guide the soul to the Dark Lady's domain, but we also offer prayers that are meant to keep the bodies where they are. To keep them from rising as undead and allow them their final rest. As well, should there be no family, or no one versed in the preparation of the body for burial, it is our job to do so. To see that things are done properly, so that the soul might rest easy."

"Oh." Maria fell silent for a few moments as they crossed the street that led into the green. "But all of that sounds fine. It sounds really helpful, actually! Why would you have to keep it to yourself?"

Tzedef scoffed. "Because there are those that believe that those who follow the path of the grave also follow the path of *defiling* the grave. Necromancy." He clarified, catching her uncomprehending look. "They believe that those who choose to give succor to the dying and dead do so only for nefarious purposes."

"Well that's stupid!" Maria declared, frowning. "You're a good person! You wouldn't do something like that!"

Tzedef's tail twitched, and he glanced down at her.

"You wouldn't!" She insisted, catching his look and hurrying up slightly to get in front of him and stop, forcing him to halt as well. "You're a good person! I've *seen* it. You don't even shout at Min, and *everyone* shouts at Min!"

Tzedef snorted again, amused. "Minalo simply has a surplus of energy, coupled with a desire to be seen as older than he actually is. It is a phase he will grow out of, in time, and for now it is easily mitigated by giving him jobs that allow him to feel as though he is providing a valuable service that only he can provide."

Maria blinked, processing that. "Huh. Really?" she shook her head, "That's not the point! The point is, you defend me against Lucas, you don't shout at Min, you're careful around the littles and I don't think I've ever seen you even raise your *voice!* You're *kind,* Tzedef. Much too kind to do something like *necromancy.*"

For a long moment, Tzedef was silent, his red eyes studying the earnest face of the woman in front of him, then he inclined his head slightly, bowing before her determination.

"Thank you." He said simply. "You are… very kind, yourself."

Maria flushed, and turned away, starting back across the green toward the farmyard and barns.

"I'm afraid." She said, her words barely carrying

over her shoulder to reach his ears. "It's easy to be nice when you're afraid of what will happen if you aren't."

"Perhaps." Tzedef allowed. "But I did not say you are nice, I said you are *kind,* and that is an entirely different animal."

Maria huffed softly, but didn't say anything as she reached for the small side door to the closest barn and hauled it open.

Tzedef watched as Maria stepped carefully through the mud, heading back towards the gate square where Lucas was, presumably, waiting.

She had checked the animals thoroughly, from geese to hogs, to goats, to cows, and when Tzedef had expressed surprise that she seemed so knowledgeable about them, she'd laughed a bit self consciously.

"I was a farm girl, back home." Maria had explained, "I grew up learning how to care for my family's animals, and Ma made sure that all of us knew how to make sure the animals were healthy. I can't give them all a good, in depth check right now, but I can at least make sure there's nothing *obviously* wrong."

Tzedef had nodded and left her to it, loitering near the side door that was the entrance most people used.

It had taken a few hours for her to check all the animals in each of the barns, and several of the hens had flown up into the eaves of the barn rather than let her check them over, which had made her laugh and tell them that if they were well enough to fly, then they were likely well enough to last until their people could check them properly.

Which led to now, walking back down the streets with a much happier seeming Maria as the sun began to make its descent.

"You seem more at ease." Tzedef remarked, and Maria's stride faltered as she glanced up at him in surprise.

"Oh, do I?"

"Yes."

"Oh." She said again, and shrugged a bit awkwardly. "I guess just... being around the animals like that, it reminded me of home. It was nice. I could say something like, 'animals are easier than people', but they aren't. They're just different, and sometimes that means it's harder to understand them and what they need, and sometimes that means it's easier."

"You seemed to do well enough." Tzedef observed, and Maria smiled, slightly sheepishly.

"Ma taught me enough to get by on my own, I think; for if I'd decided to start up my own farm, but Nelthys called me, and I answered, and here we are."

"I see." He did, sort of. "I would likely still be in the military in Yaelin, if Hecate had not called for me."

"You were in the military?" Maria blinked up at him, surprised, and Tzedef nodded, reaching to his back and pulling his shield around to show her the etching: a flaming mace breaking an anvil in two.

"This is the symbol of my company." He said, tracing the flames coming off the mace. "Eks Company."

"Oh." She said, and waited until he'd swung his shield back onto his back before starting to walk again. "So did you leave because Hecate called you?"

"No." Tzedef said, his mouth twisting wryly. "Not at all. I was a field medic by training before I ever came to Hecate, and the abilities granted to me after I found her let me heal more and better than I had before. I… retired from duty after the war Yaelin was fighting reached a ceasefire."

"Oh." Maria said again, and didn't say anything else as they rounded the corner into the entrance square, too busy staring at the hustle and bustle that had taken over.

The table had been moved to one side and had been joined by several others, and they were piled high with onions and garlic, all being busily braided into strings to cure by the older children and younger teens.

Through the gate, people were bringing in cartloads of frost wheat, and cabbages, and bundles of lettuces.

Even the over-winter crops that had been put into the ground just after the first snow, the ones that the farmers had written off as a loss, seemed to have grown, and grown well, though Tzedef couldn't have told you what they actually *were*.

Overall, the atmosphere had changed from tense and wary to something very much like a kicked over ant hill.

"There's so much…" Maria breathed, the fingers of her hands pressed to her lips.

Tzedef nodded. "You did well. You and Nelthys both."

Slowly, Maria nodded, following a loaded cart with

her eyes as it rolled down the street and out of sight.

"Maria!" Lucas's voice cracked like a whip over the noise, and Maria startled.

"Coming!" She called, and hurried across the square, winding her way between people as she made her way to the ladder that led up onto the wall.

Tzedef watched as people paused, giving way before the new high priestess, then followed, his pace more leisurely, and he reached the bottom of the ladder as Bren helped Maria up again.

Brown eyes met red as Bren glanced down at Tzedef, and Tzedef nodded to him before leaning back against the wall, watching the industriousness of the farmers of the village, and their visitors.

He listened with half an ear as Maria told Lucas the results of her checks on the animals, the rest of his attention on calculating how likely it would be that there would be enough spare food for himself, Casey, and Sorecco to make rations that would carry them through the last month of their journey to Vraka.

It didn't seem likely, and Tzedef sighed. They would need to stay partway through the summer, then, which meant more guard duty for him. Joy.

Then again, if things were going to be kicking off with regards to the farming season, then injuries would most likely be more common, and need to be taken care of more quickly than Lynn would be able to heal them. It would, at least, be a break in the monotony.

Raised voices from the top of the wall caught his

attention again, and his ears twitched, swiveling slightly to better hear the argument.

"I'm telling you, there's no way to induce twins at this stage! They're too far along already! You're just going to have to content yourself with good, healthy animals, and easy births!"

"That's not good enough!" Lucas snarled, and Tzedef turned, one hand on the rungs of the ladder before Bren's voice made him still.

"That's enough, Lucas." The half-orc's voice was a low, warning rumble, "The girl's doing her best. Healthy animals and easy births is nothing to sneeze at, especially considering the winter we've just had."

Lucas spluttered something, then huffed. "Fine! But I expect you to keep earning your keep around here, girl. Don't think that just because you've got that fancy band that you can get away with doing nothing!"

"Doing *noth—!*" Maria's voice rose in an aborted shriek, and a moment later Tzedef had to hastily step to the side as she all but fell down the ladder, her skirts whirling around her as she turned and fled.

Again, people paused in their steps, making way for the young woman, and again, she didn't seem to notice. This time too distraught to pay attention to anything but her next footstep.

"You're a moron." Bren said bluntly, but that was all Tzedef heard as he heaved a silent sigh and followed after Maria.

His long legs ate up the distance easily enough, and

apparently she'd slowed down a bit once she'd gotten out of the square, because he caught up to her several houses later; falling in step with her.

A quick glance down showed him the tears streaming down her cheeks, and Tzedef winced internally.

"That was ill-done of Lucas." He said after walking in silence with her for a while.

Maria sniffed hard, then scrubbed at her eyes.

"I'm not upset." She said, and Tzedef's eye ridges arched incredulously.

"I mean, I am, but I'm not *sad*. I'm just... I'm so *angry!* How could he say that? *Why* would he say that?!"

She sniffled. "I work hard. I really do. Maybe it doesn't seem like it, but I do! There's always someone needing *something* from me, and I barely get a moment's peace to myself, and I'm always working with Nelthys on *something*, even if it's just trying to figure out the best way to distribute blessings so that we don't upset anyone and everyone gets what they need! I work-" her voice hitched.

"I work really, really hard to earn my tithe, and then he just... he has the nerve to act like I don't do *anything?*"

Tzedef sighed.

"Lucas is what we in the military would have called 'an asshole'." He said bluntly, startling a watery giggle out of Maria. "He has no idea about how certain things work, nor does he wish to know. I would not say that he delights in his ignorance, but he certainly does not hesitate to air it at every turn."

"Normally I'd say he's not that bad." Maria said

quietly, "But this… now… I'm just so angry! I don't know what to do!"

"Well," Tzedef considered her for a moment. "You could always leave. If he isn't going to respect your position as the village priest, then he can find out what it's like to deal with a village with *no* priest."

But Maria was already shaking her head. "I can't leave just because of Lucas. That's not fair to everybody else, and they've all been wonderful to me. Even though I'm new, they've been so welcoming, and kind… I couldn't leave them just because of him."

"Well," Tzedef said, "You could always move to have him removed as the head of the village. If he isn't in charge, then his words won't have weight with the people and he won't have a chance to try to turn them against you."

"Turn them against me?" Maria glanced up at Tzedef, astonishment writ large on her face. "Why would he do that?"

"To attempt to force more miracles out of you." Tzedef said, "To force you to do as he wishes. To bend you to his will. There are many reasons why he might do so. None of them are good for you."

"He wouldn't do that." She said, but she sounded uncertain, and Tzedef paused, turning to look her full in the face.

"Lucas is a small-minded, petty, self-centered man. If he thought it would somehow increase his standing, or increase his sway, then he absolutely would."

Maria made a soft, distressed noise, but didn't say

anything else, and after a moment, Tzedef turned and starting walking again.

This time, she fell in step beside him, and the two of them walked for a while in silence before she paused in front of a small, two story building, turning to go up the walk.

The front garden was a riot of colorful flowers and she carefully skirted some that hung over the path before pulling out a key and opening the door.

"Oh. Is this the shrine?"

"Yep." Maria paused, "You've never been here, have you?"

"No." Tzedef confirmed. "I thought it best to keep away from the shrine, just in case Lucas decided that my presence here meant that I was attempting to 'corrupt' people."

Maria scowled. "That's ridiculous. As if you could. 'Corrupting people'. *Really*. How stupid."

Tzedef smiled crookedly, and Maria huffed quietly.

"Well, you're here now, so would you like to come in?"

Tzedef tipped his head to one side, thinking, then nodded. "Yes. I am interested in seeing what kind of shrine a god of small works has."

"And agriculture!" Maria chirped, grinning, and Tzedef inclined his head.

"Small works and agriculture."

CHAPTER TWENTY

The Shrine of Nelthys

The inside of the shrine was clean, lit well with crystals that shed a clear, white-gold light, and cluttered with *things*.

Maria crossed the room to a small stove at one side of the room, and opened the front, poking around the still-glowing embers with a small bit of wood out of the small box to one side.

"Feel free to look around." She said, slightly absently, and Tzedef nodded, turning his attention to the rest of the room.

It wasn't, as he'd first thought, overwhelmingly cluttered, but the small space made it seem so. On second look, the space was actually used quite well.

Comfortable chairs, cleaned and polished, with lovingly patched cushions, were scattered through the room with no apparent rhyme or reason. Pillows and cushions littered the floor between and around the chairs, all well worn and equally carefully patched and cleaned.

Tzedef carefully made his way around the room, inspecting the small sculptures that covered nearly every flat surface. Many of them were poorly made, or badly fired, but as he moved around the room they increased in detail and quality until he was looking at incredibly detailed sculptures of a male figure with six arms. In most of the sculptures, each hand held a different object.

A pen.

A feather duster.

A needle.

This one cradled a small bundle that Tzedef guessed was supposed to be an infant to his chest.

That one over there wore spectacles and peered down at something held in one hand, the other five holding various tools.

"It's Nelthys." Maria spoke up from behind him, and Tzedef carefully didn't jump, though his teeth gritted sharply. "I've been sculpting him since I was a child. Small works is such a broad domain, there's always something new that I realize falls under his remit, and I have to sculpt it."

She glanced over at the more poorly made sculptures and laughed a little. "Or, you know, try to."

"This is impressive." Tzedef said honestly, turning to look at her. "Your shrine is one of comfort and peace. It is admirable that you have managed to foster such an environment, even through the hardships of the last nine months."

Maria flushed, her cheeks going dark as she glanced

away.

"Thanks."

Tzedef nodded, then glanced around again, breathing in the environment before sighing.

"I must return to my post before Lucas takes it upon himself to start harassing my traveling companions for my whereabouts."

The admission was reluctant, and Maria winced, but nodded. "Thank you, Tzedef, for playing escort for me today. It's been nice, talking to someone who can understand what it's like."

Tzedef inclined his head gravely. "The pleasure was mine. You are welcome."

He let her escort him to the door, then stepped out and into the crisp air of the early evening, exchanging polite goodbyes with the woman. It took until he was two houses down before he heard the door click shut and could allow himself to let out a long, tired exhale.

Guarding Personages of Importance was exhausting, and Maria, as the newly recognized high priestess of a village's deity *definitely* qualified.

He'd been lucky that, for the most part, his position as medic had precluded his participation in some of the more onerous guard rotations, but that didn't mean he'd been able to escape *all* of them. Granted- Maria was not as difficult as some of the visiting nobles had been, or even some of the higher ups from the military, but emotions were... difficult for him to handle, particularly when they were someone else's, and Maria was nothing if not *emotional.*

For a moment he considered heading back to the inn, then he sighed and resignedly headed back toward the gate.

They must be seen as contributing to the community, or the community could easily turn on them.

As it grew darker, large light crystals were unearthed from the village hall and brought out by the middle teenagers, held on poles long enough that, when one end was resting on the ground, the other was several feet above even the tallest of those working to bring in the harvest.

They lit up the fields that were already beginning to look barren, and with the artificial light people worked long into the night.

By the time the first rays of the sun peeked over the horizon, everyone was exhausted, but the fields were picked clean, the produce was in one of the storage barns, and the crystals were being taken back into storage.

"Go get some rest." Bren clapped his hand on Tzedef's back as he passed him, yawning widely. "Everyone's back in the walls, and you've been running since early yesterday. Have you even eaten?"

"Minalo brought me something." Tzedef said, shifting to the side until Bren's hand fell away. "Around midnight."

"Get some food in you, then, and get some rest." Bren repeated and moved off.

Tzedef sighed, rolling his shoulders to loosen them

a bit, then turned and headed for the inn.

Casey and Sorecco were sitting together at one of the tables when Tzedef got back to the inn, Casey smudged with mud and looking exhausted, and Sorecco nursing a mug of tea that smelled of healing herbs.

"There you are." Casey sighed, "Did they finally let you off the wall?"

"Yes." Tzedef said, pulling out a chair and sitting with a grateful sigh. "Are you well? I saw you bringing in full wheelbarrows."

Casey winces. "Well, once Cecil caught sight of my hands he made me switch over to water duty, but…"

She held her hands out to him, revealing a mass of blisters; some already broken open and starting to scab over, others fresh and puffy.

Tzedef winced, reaching out to take one of her hands in his, turning it gently this way and that to examine the damage. "You've never done any farm work, have you?"

She shook her head. "Nope. I'm a proper city girl, I am. Cecil gave me the easiest jobs he could, but apparently even that was—"

She broke off with a pained hiss as Tzedef covered her palm with his own, doing his best to keep the touch as light as he could.

A murmured prayer and a muted flare of saffron light later, and Tzedef was holding out his hands expectantly for her other, still damaged, hand.

Casey stared at him for a long moment, then sighed and, smiling softly, slipped her hand into his.

"There will likely be other injuries." Tzedef said casually once her other hand was healed, turning it over in his hands to check and make sure he hadn't missed anything.

"There are." Casey nodded. "One of the guys out there cut the crap out of his leg with his scythe."

Tzedef frowned. He'd missed that. "Do you know where he is?"

Casey shrugged. "I think they took him to Lynn's. Get him all bandaged up and cleaned up, you know."

He nodded slightly. "Then I suppose I will have to stop by Mistress Miller's domain at some point to offer my assistance."

"Do that." Sorecco croaked, and Tzedef turned to him, surprise writ large on his face.

"What happened to your voice? Are you falling ill again?"

The bard shook his head and took another sip of his drink. "The kids had me writing a song for Nelthys ever since they heard about the fields."

Which would have been at roughly the same time the adults had heard of it, meaning that Sorecco would have been singing, hopefully off and on, since early in the day *yesterday*.

Casey stared at him, horrified. "Sorecco, it's almost been a full day!"

"I know." He rasped, and slumped against the table. "I got lucky. Someone came around and collected them a few hours ago, and Amarie gave me this tea to help. I could barely speak at all until just before you two got back."

"Man." Casey said, shaking her head, "Those kids are relentless. Still, you've been doing a really good job with them all winter. They really like you."

"I hope so." Sorecco sighed, "After I spent all that time coming up with stories and games to keep them out of the way while their parents tried to keep the snow manageable?"

"Would you like me to heal you?" Tzedef asked, concerned, and Sorecco hesitated, then shook his head.

"Not tonight. If it's not better by tomorrow night, then yes please, but I'd rather give the brats an idea of the consequences their actions have. They wouldn't stop going on about the song today, so they don't get any songs tomorrow, you know?"

Despite his words, his tone was fond as he spoke about the children, and Tzedef slowly nodded.

He didn't quite understand the chain of logic, but Sorecco was the one who'd been interacting with the children of the village the most. He would know better than Tzedef would.

"All right." He murmured, "If you're sure. I just don't wish for you to incur permanent damage before achieving your dream."

"Nah," Sorecco smiled crookedly, "I'll be fine, but thanks. Like I said, if it's not better by tomorrow night, then I'll gladly accept a healing."

Amarie swept past the table and dropped off a plate in front of each of them, each topped with a few small green bundles that smelled heavily of herbs.

Casey startled, looking around after Amarie, then looked down at the little bundles. "What in the world?"

"Dinner, I would assume." Tzedef said mildly, poking at one of the bundles with a careful finger.

Clear liquid oozed out of the bundle and Tzedef tilted his head, curious, before picking one up and turning it over to examine it.

"Cabbage, I believe." He announced after some thought. "So… some sort of cabbage roll?"

"Oh." Casey glanced down at her own plate, then shifted Sorecco's so that it was more in front of him. "Straight ahead." She told him, "They're in the center of the plate. Why cabbage rolls?"

Tzedef shrugged. "I believe that cabbage was one of the crops that was grown with the miracle. I saw several wheelbarrows full of cabbage wheeled into the village."

"That part makes sense," Casey agreed, prodding at one of her own rolls. "But aren't they usually filled with meat? I thought we ran out of meat a month and a half ago."

"Yes." Tzedef said, "Which is why I'm quite curious as to what they have been stuffed with."

And so saying, he took a bite out of the one he'd been examining.

It was surprisingly good, even with the lack of meat. Amarie had taken fresh carrots and chopped them fine, then mixed them with mashed potatoes and a variety of herbs that Tzedef couldn't have hoped to have named.

All in all, it was a surprisingly tasty meal, and he

was rather disappointed to only get three, but it made sense. They were still on short rations, after all, and Amarie had to make what food she was allocated stretch.

The three of them ate in relative silence, and once the last of his cabbage rolls was gone, Tzedef sighed wearily.

"I need sleep." He said bluntly. "I'll be going to bed, now, I think."

"Ah," Amarie called as he started to get up, and she hurried out from behind the bar over to their table. "Sorry Tzedef, Casey, Sorecco. I need to talk with you for a moment, if you don't mind."

Sorecco tilted his head, "Is something the matter?"

"No," Amarie shook her head, "But also yes. Lucas came around and asked if I'd be willing to put the travelers up for the day, since they worked so hard getting the harvest in. I don't technically have the rooms for their full group, but I was hoping the three of you wouldn't mind tripling up?"

Casey glanced at Tzedef, then Sorecco, then shrugged. "I don't mind, but I don't know how we're going to get a third bed into one of those rooms. They're tiny."

"I know," Amarie sighed, "But I can't really just leave people out to freeze all night. Or day," she added wryly, glancing at the gradually lightening windows. "I expect I'll be spreading pallets out here, as well, unless Lucas manages to talk some of the others into opening their homes."

Sorecco sighed, but nodded. "All right. Casey can

share my bed. We'll make do."

"Thank you," Amarie smiled gratefully at them, "Casey, if you could…?"

She trailed off hopefully, and Casey nodded. "I'll get my stuff out of the room and give it a clean. It should be ready by noon, does that work?"

"Perfectly." Amarie nodded, and glanced up as some more people poured into the inn through the front door. "Thanks so much, you three. I really appreciate it."

She hurried away before any of them could speak, and slipped behind the bar just as the first few people reached it.

"I'd better get that started." Casey said, standing with a weary sigh. "Thanks, Sorecco."

"Don't mention it." He waved her off, "It's nothing we haven't done before, after all."

"Right." Casey said, and reached out to squeeze his shoulder before striding toward the hallway that led to the rooms and vanishing down it.

Sleeping in the same room would be cramped, Tzedef knew, but he would rather have the siblings close, where he could ensure that none of the would-be bandits might get any ideas.

Not that he thought they would, per se— Three travelers wouldn't exactly make the best hostages, what with having little connection to the village or villagers, but still, it was a comfort to have both of his friends closer, where he could ensure their safety.

Tzedef paused.

Something about that thought… He frowned, then shook his head. It wasn't important.

What was, was that Sorecco had just asked him a question, and he'd missed it.

"Pardon?"

"I said, do you think we'll be able to get on the road to Vraka any time soon?" Sorecco repeated patiently, his voice as harsh as a raven's caw. "With the snow thawing and everything, I thought we might head out soon?"

Tzedef winced, "I… don't know how possible that is. We ate all of our stored rations, and with the whole village short on food, there's nowhere for us to get more. I'm not like Maria; I can't just intercede with my goddess for food."

Sorecco slumped. "So we're stuck here."

"Possibly until mid-summer, yes." Tzedef confirmed, and winced again at the crestfallen look on Sorecco's face.

"That's…" He started, then stopped and sighed despondently. "All right."

"I am sorry." Tzedef said quietly, "If there was a way for us to be on our way sooner, I would take it. But for now the safest option for us is to wait until mid-summer. At that point there should be enough of a food surplus that we can get what we need and go."

"Right." Sorecco sighed again, fingers tapping out a rhythm on the table. "All right, I suppose. There's nothing we can really do about it. I'll just… hopefully the bardic colleges take students year round."

"I don't see why not." Tzedef said in what he hoped was a sympathetic voice, and Sorecco nodded, then smiled wanly in his direction.

"Thanks, Tzedef."

For what, he wondered, but only said, "you're welcome," as Sorecco pushed away from the table and stood, taking up his stick as he did.

Tzedef watched him head towards the room, shuffling carefully around the larger groups, then bumping into someone as the noise in the room muffled the tone of his bell too much for him to utilize his Gift properly.

For a moment it looked like it was going to lead to a fight, then Sorecco said something that put a surprised look on the other man's face and he burst into laughter, clapping Sorecco on the shoulder before moving out of his way.

Tension leeched out of Sorecco's posture as Tzedef watched, and a moment later he, too, disappeared down the hallway that led into the bedrooms.

CHAPTER TWENTY-ONE

Judgement

The next few days were hectic, with Lucas pushing
Maria hard to bless the other fields as the farmers tilled the
empty fields back under and started planting the next crops
in their rotation.

Maria did her best, but after the second time she
ended up unconscious from trying to channel too much
divinity in one day, Tzedef stepped in to put his foot down.

"You cannot keep pushing her this hard." Tzedef
said, glaring at the man over the limp body in his arms.

A crowd was forming around them, the farmers that
had been ready to start harvesting the fields Maria was to
bless gathering around to find out what'd gone wrong.

Lucas scoffed. "She and her god have been
freeloading off this village for a year and a half now. It's
about damn time she was able to finally contribute
something."

"She has been working as hard as any priest of a
small god could feasibly be expected to work." Tzedef said

flatly. "You are expecting too much from her. Not even the larger gods would be able to keep up with your demands."

Lucas sneered at him. "What would you know about the larger gods? Your goddess is so small that she can't even grant her follower the grace of *food*."

Tzedef gritted his teeth. "Do not." He hissed, "Presume to know what my goddess can and cannot do. She has granted me powers that far surpass anything your feeble mind could possibly comprehend."

Lucas scoffed. "Regardless. You're a healer. Heal her so she can get back to work."

Tzedef stared at him, completely flabbergasted by the man's complete and utter *gall,* and a low angry mutter rippled through the group surrounding them.

"No." His voice was completely flat. "I will not. Maria is going back to her home. She is going to rest, possibly for the rest of the week, and *you will not bother her.*" He shifted the woman in his arms carefully, absently noting that her eyes were clenched shut and her lips were moving silently.

"*If* she decides to bless the rest of the fields, it will be on her terms, not yours."

"Says who?" Lucas snarled, "You? You're nobody! Nothing! If it weren't for Lynn and I, you'd have starved or frozen to death once your coin ran out!"

There was another low, dissatisfied murmur from the farmers around them, and Maria's expression went stricken as her eyes opened and her head turned weakly to watch Lucas. It took Tzedef a moment to see what she was looking at, and when he spotted it, grim satisfaction rushed through him.

Yes. That was an appropriate punishment.

Something blacker than pitch, darker than jet, was etching itself onto the back of Lucas' right hand.

"You may be correct." Tzedef allowed. "Though I like to think that my companions and I would have found ways to work with Amarie to earn our keep just as well. However, you are incorrect in your assertion that I am 'nobody.'"

Tzedef smiled, baring his teeth at the man across from him.

"I am not a high priest, and to be frank, I do not wish to be. To be bound to one temple is akin to a slow death, to me. However, I *am* a cleric of Hecate. Moreover, I am a *favored* cleric of Hecate, and that allows me certain abilities and freedoms. You have insulted myself, my goddess, and the high priestess of another god. You have abused and besieged a high priestess of another god. You have threatened the life and livelihood of both myself and the high priestess of another god. As the ranking cleric present, *I call Judgment on you.*"

Gasps rippled through the crowd, and people shuffled, getting further back away from Lucas as he paled drastically.

Weight pressed down on Tzedef's shoulders as a vast, unknowable *attention* fell on him, Maria, and Lucas.

Lucas's knees buckled, but somehow he kept his feet, and, as was his nature, he opened his mouth and started talking.

"Now let's be reasonable here! There's no call to go as far as a Judgment! We can work this out! So maybe I was a little hard on the girl, but honestly, she's much stronger for it, now, isn't she? I bet she wouldn't even have been chosen as High Priestess if I hadn't pushed her a bit! I-"

He cut himself off with a scream of pain, falling to his knees and clutching his left wrist as the flesh on the back of his left hand sizzled, another sigil scorching itself into his skin.

Tzedef looked at the sigil with mild interest, reading the lines easily as his goddess whispered their meanings into his mind.

He couldn't read the sigil on Lucas's right hand, but judging by the paleness of Maria's face, she could and it likely said much the same thing that the sigil on his left did.

The crowd around the three of them muttered, shifting anxiously on their feet and Tzedef saw several people glancing worriedly at each other.

"Judgment has been passed." He said calmly as Lucas fell forward onto his hands, staring at the burnt-black sigils on the backs of his hands and panting, shaking with residual pain. "Lucas Miller, you are twice cursed. Twice will you pass on everything you own to the gods you have insulted. Twice will you make pilgrimages, once each to the Seats of the House of the gods you have offended. Until such time that you fulfill these acts, your endeavors will fail. Any farms you manage will lie fallow. Any animals you own will not bear young. Should you die before completing your tasks, your soul will wander Chaelu for twice the number of years you have walked the land. No other god may grant you succor. No other being may lift this curse. This is the Judgment of the Goddess Hecate."

Maria shifted in his arms, her face pale, but resolute, and she shifted again until Tzedef got the hint and lowered her to her feet.

"Lucas Miller," her voice shook, and she leaned on Tzedef heavily, but her words were clearly heard even in the back of the crowd. "You are twice-cursed. Twice will you pass on everything you own to the gods you have insulted. Twice will you make pilgrimages, once each to the Seats of the House of the gods you have offended. Until such time that you fulfill these acts, your endeavors will fail. Any farms you manage will lie fallow. Any animals you own will not bear young. Should you die before completing your tasks, your soul will wander Chaelu for twice the number of years you have walked the land. No other god may grant you succor. No other being may lift this curse. This is the Judgment of the God Nelthys."

Lucas stared at the two of them, then, slowly, turned his head down to look at the backs of his hands, the left one reddened and burned, the right smooth and dark.

The crowd muttered softly, and Maria turned sharply, trying to march away from Lucas, and the farmers, and Tzedef, only to waver and nearly fall again as her knees gave out under her.

Tzedef caught her, and helped her back upright, and the two of them made their way out of the crowd and back into the village.

Maria kept it together until they were in the shrine, then she burst into tears.

Tzedef stared at her.

"What is wrong?"

"I didn't want that to happen!" She wailed, "I was arguing with Nelthys, begging him not to, and he did it anyway! Now everyone is going to hate me! They're going to be so scared of me!"

Tzedef sighed, and helped her down into one of the more comfortable seats next to the fire, then sat down himself.

"Maria." His voice was calm, and quiet, and it still managed to get her attention. "How long has Lucas been tormenting you?"

"He wasn't-!"

"Maria." Tzedef met her eyes steadily, and she sagged, then sniffled.

"Since I got here... He was always after me to do more, to draw on Nelthys more, to work harder, and take on more responsibilities."

"Was that fair to you?" Tzedef asked, then held up one hand, pausing her response. "Was that fair to *Nelthys?* Making him watch that happen to you day in and day out?"

Maria wavered. "No..."

"Then can you blame Nelthys for doing his best to protect you? You were unconscious. Again. In the mud. *Again.* For the second time in two days. Because Lucas kept pushing you. Because he wouldn't take no for an answer.

Because he wouldn't accept your physical limits."

Maria winced at the reminder of the mud, glancing down and plucking at her dirty skirts, then reached up to touch her muddy hair and winced again when dried mud sprinkled down out of it.

"But now people will be scared of me. They'll hate me."

"They may be afraid." Tzedef allowed. "But I doubt they will hate you. Lucas was hardly well-loved himself, and anyone with eyes could see how he was abusing your good will."

"But—" Maria started, then jumped when someone knocked on the door.

Tzedef sighed, but stood, giving the woman a stern look when she moved to stand, and she subsided meekly.

When Tzedef opened the door, he found Isabeta on the other side, now looking slightly less gaunt and significantly less haggard than she had the first time he'd seen her.

"Is Lady Maria well?" She asked, looking up at Tzedef, who nodded.

"She will be. She requires rest, now. The Judgment, along with the field blessings, took a lot out of her."

"May I speak with her?"

Tzedef arched on brow ridge, then glanced back at Maria, who gave him a small nod, and made a beckoning motion at him.

"For a short time only." He cautioned, and stepped back out of the way.

Isabeta ducked her head at him and stomped field mud off her boots, then stepped into the shrine and strode over to Maria.

Maria watched her apprehensively, chewing worriedly on her bottom lip as her hands twisted in her lap.

"Lady Maria, you don't know me, aside from these last few days." Isabeta said, standing in front of her, "My name is Isabeta. Me and my group, we come from the area around the village of Farley."

Maria blinked. "Farley? I don't think I've heard of that village."

Isabeta smiled wryly. "You wouldn't. We're a couple of days off the beaten path. About a week's journey from here."

"Okay." She said cautiously, "That's nice, I suppose... was there something you needed?"

"Our village doesn't have a priest." Isabeta said bluntly, "and we're so small, and so far off the main roads, we don't often have wandering clerics come through. We, that is to say, I, but the others agree as well, wanted to extend the offer to you to come to Farley. And live."

Maria gaped at her.

Tzedef stifled a smile.

In the end, it turned out that the village of Farley had fallen on hard times recently. Aside from the awful winter, hunting had been increasingly hard as the game animals either died off or were hunted to oblivion. Their crops had suffered a mild blight toward the end of the growing season, and they'd had to slaughter just about every animal they owned just to make it through the winter. Only the fowl had been spared, as many families had brought them into their homes, letting the birds keep laying through much of the cold months.

It was a heartbreaking story, and Tzedef could see Maria growing more and more torn as Isabeta spoke.

In the end, Maria begged for a couple of days to consider it, to see how the Maplemore villagers would respond to the Judgment, before she made a decision.

Isabeta bowed, wished her well, and left.

The moment the door closed behind the elven woman, Maria rounded on him.

"What do I do!?"

Tzedef let his amusement ring clear in his voice.

"Whatever you want. You now have options, Maria, and that is a precious, precious thing to have. Best of all, you also have *time*. You need not make up your mind now. Only think on it, and have your decision ready in a few days. Just ensure that your heart is set on whatever you decide because it is unlikely that you'll be able to take it back once it is made."

"R-right..." Maria stammered, and slumped back in her chair, still in shock.

Tzedef lingered for another few minutes. Long enough for Maria to shake out of her reverie, remember the mud in her hair and on her dress, and shoo him out of the shrine with a promise that she felt much better and that she would call for help should that change.

Tzedef simply nodded and took his leave with good grace. He too, was muddy after all, and a change of clothes was something he was quite looking forward to.

But a quiet change of clothes wasn't to be.

Casey was in their room, one of her laid out on the bed she and Sorecco shared, another of her sitting on Tzedef's bed on the other side of the small room, and both of her jumped when he opened the door, startling guiltily.

"Oh, it's you, Tzedef." The Casey on the bed sighed, relieved, and the Casey lounging on her and Sorecco's bed lifted her head to look at him and frowned. "What happened to you?"

"Lucas was being himself, and Maria ended up unconscious. Again." Tzedef said crisply, shucking out of his shirt and going to his bag to dig out another one.

Luckily, his trousers were mostly untouched, and what little mud there was on them was dried and easily brushed away.

Casey sat up, frowning worriedly. "Is she okay? Will she be alright?"

"She is fine." Tzedef said, hand elbow deep in his pack as he searched. "Lucas, however, is not. He crossed a line, today, and I called Judgment on him. Nelthys was apparently angry enough about his treatment of Maria that the curse was already starting to take before I did anything. Ah."

Out his hand came, clutching a dark grey shirt, which he pulled over his head, working carefully to avoid snagging it on his horns. The last thing he needed right now was to spend time mending a carelessly torn shirt.

When he emerged, it was to see Casey watching him, a puzzled look on her face.

"What's Judgment?"

Tzedef blinked. "You… don't have Judgment?"

Casey shook her head. "Not that I know of? Going off the way it *sounds*, it's some kind of trial?"

Tzedef winced, then waggled a hand in the air, side to side. "Of a sort? It's… when someone acts against a god, or a chosen of a god, then the gods can act against them. Usually they don't, unless a mortal calls for their Judgment. Then, the acts of the person will be weighed, and the harm that they've done is weighed, and the gods pass a judgment on them, making the punishment fit the crime."

Casey scowled. "But that's ridiculous! What's to stop someone from calling for a judgment for every little thing! Like, what if someone accidentally stepped on a priest's toes? Or doesn't give a cleric the respect she thinks she's due?"

Tzedef shook his head. "It doesn't work like that. Judgment judges not only the one it was called against, but also the caller. If the gods decide that the reason was petty, or selfish, or not worthy of a member of their order, then the judgment passes to *them*, instead. Because of that, Judgment is rarely used. No one wishes to be cursed because their god decides that they have been called for reasons unworthy of their attention."

"Oh." Casey considered that, then shook her head ruefully. "That's so weird. Back on Permani we didn't have anything like that. If you insulted people's ancestors, then you'd probably get in a fight or something, but the ancestors themselves didn't really care. They were more worried about the stuff that happened back when *they* were alive. It's why some marriages were so hard to arrange- because the ancestors on both sides had some kind of feud that the living folks had long since forgotten about. The ancestors would *insist* on some sort of reparations, and it'd be up to their descendants to negotiate until the ancestors were satisfied."

Tzedef blinked again. "That... sounds painful."

"Oh it was," Casey nodded emphatically, "You wouldn't *believe* some of the stuff the ancestors demand. Stuff like 'Find a rare flower that only grows on this one island.' But it turns out that the island was scoured by a tsunami two generations ago and the flower's gone extinct, but will they accept a substitute or offer a different task? Nope! They want that flower, and they wanted it *six generations ago*, so by the ancestors, they're going to get it!'"

He winced, a full body cringe that even had his tail curling in sympathy. "That sounds awful. How do situations like that end up getting resolved?"

"Oh, who knows." Casey shrugged. "It's always different. Sometimes it doesn't, and the families end up parting ways. Sometimes the kids would get married anyway and just deal with the complaining until the ancestors on both sides got too distracted by 'Ooo! Grandbabies!' to remember what they were feuding over. Sometimes the kids would actually manage to complete the reparations. It just depends."

"I see." He said, a bit dubiously. "That sounds…"

"Completely bonkers, right?" Casey laughed, "Don't worry, it's a pain to us, too, but that's life, right?"

"I suppose it is." Tzedef agreed after a long moment, then he shrugged. "I apologize for startling you, when I came in. I hope I'm not interrupting…?"

Casey's cheeks colored a little, but she waved him off. "Nah, no. You're not. I was just… practicing."

"With your Gift?"

"No, not that. It's that trick that Inral was showing me, back on the ship. I've been working on it all winter, here and there, and I think I've finally got the hang of it."

The trick Inral…?

Tzedef's heart sank.

Apportation.

Curse it all.

He'd thought that Casey had forgotten about that when she hadn't brought it up again once they were off the ship.

"You've been working on it so long?"

Casey colored further. "I'm not a genius like Sorecco is. It takes me longer to learn things."

Tzedef grimaced. "That is not what I meant. I was more surprised by your persistence. I would have expected most to have given up by now."

"Oh." She blinked, then shrugged, and the Casey on his bed tossed a small stone up into the air, caught it, then tossed it again, and the Casey on her own bed made a small tugging gesture, and the stone vanished midair, only to appear in the air above her free hand and fall into it with a soft smack. "It's still not very good; I still need to do the movement, which'll be a problem if I'm trying to be subtle."

Tzedef stared at her, then sighed and covered his face with his hand.

"Hecate save me from geniuses…"

"I'm not a genius!"

"Casey. You cast the spell without any words, and with barely a sign. Even if you *have* been practicing for nine months, that's more than some can manage in nine *years*."

"… it is?" Casey asked, her voice tiny, and Tzedef lowered his hand to look at both of her in turn.

"It truly is."

"…Oh."

CHAPTER TWENTY-TWO

Leaving Maplemore

Casey fell into a contemplative silence after that, rejoining herself so that Tzedef's bed was empty and he could lay down to relax.

The likelihood of the people of Maplemore turning against Maria was slim, he thought. She was too kind. Too genuinely likable.

She worked hard, and that hard work was apparent to everyone except, perhaps, Lucas. The fact that now she was a high priest should have brought anyone that *was* on the fence around, at least because of the fact that being able to boast a high priest was, for many villages, a mark of pride that no one wanted to see driven away.

Maria would be fine, regardless of her fears.

Sure enough, contrary to Maria's worries, the people of Maplemore didn't turn against her. In fact, they rallied around her, and Tzedef saw no fewer than five people over the course of a single day heading in the direction of the shrine with small gifts and tokens for Nelthys, or Maria, or both.

Apparently some people had had their reservations about their new priest and the god she'd brought with her, and seeing that he was perfectly willing to defend her and that she had the spine to deliver the edict herself had brought them around to land firmly in her camp.

All that aside, however, Tzedef wasn't expecting it when, after a day of guarding the fields as the farmers worked to re-plant, Lynn cornered him at Amarie's, plopping into the chair across from him with all the weariness of a seasoned traveler finally coming to rest.

"You certainly kicked a hornet's nest." She sighed, and Tzedef frowned uncertainly.

"I will not apologize."

Lynn waved him off. "I don't expect you to. No. Lucas made his bed. He can lie in it. If I'd known how badly he was tormenting that poor girl I'd've kicked him out on his ass myself. I did not marry a bully."

Tzedef arched an eye ridge at her. "Madam, people do not just *become* bullies. If he was not bullying you, it was only because he had others on which to vent his spleen."

Lynn stiffened, looking ready to object, then she sighed and sagged back against the back of the chair. "You're probably right, there."

Tzedef watched the halfling woman for a long moment, idly drumming his fingers on the tabletop as the tip of his tail twitched back and forth.

Lynn broke the silence first, sighing again before sitting up straight and looking him dead in the eye. "So you know, I'm not here as the herbalist. I'm here as the acting Head of Maplemore. Lucas voluntarily resigned the position after several people pointed out to him that, as the village head, he technically managed all the farms connected directly to the village. Or at least, they were worried that the curse might see it that way. No one wants to risk a famine on top of the winter we've just had."

Tzedef nodded slowly, taking that in. "All right. And what does the Acting Head of Maplemore want with a traveling cleric?"

"It's not so much what I want with you," Lynn said, "as what you want with *me*."

Tzedef blinked. "That... I was not aware I wanted anything from you?"

She smiled wryly, and fished a small pouch out of the purse at her belt. It jingled when she put it down on the table between the two of them.

"This is what Lucas was supposed to be paying you, for your work as a guard."

Tzedef blinked again.

"Your weather reading, as amateur as it was, helped prevent quite a few deaths and circumvented many other dangers. It was more than enough to 'pay' for your room and board over the course of the winter. That you then went out of your way to also stand guard in a rotation with our own small guard, well... It garnered you a lot of goodwill with the people. Especially the other guards.

"Lucas was supposed to be paying you a guard's wage, and when he resigned I ended up going over the books, just to make sure there were no discrepancies. The guard's expenditure never went up, and when I confronted him, he admitted that he'd been attempting to keep costs down by not paying you as he should have."

Lynn pointed at the small pouch. "That is your back-pay for the work you've done over the winter, plus a small amount as an apology."

"I... see." Tzedef said slowly, reaching out to pick up the pouch and weighing it in his hand. "Well then, I thank you for your swift action in redressing that wrong. With that in mind, however, what will become of Lucas?"

"That's a bit of a tricky question." Lynn said, leaning back. "Some would say that the curses are enough punishment. Others might say that he was only punished for what he did to you and Maria in your roles as cleric and priestess and that he deserves to face punishment for what he's done to you in your role as a member of the community."

"But I am not part of your community." Tzedef protested mildly, and Lynn arched an eyebrow at him.

"Are you not?" She asked, "Did you not stand watch in the worst of the winter storms? Did you not provide healing when your fellow guards ended up with frostbite? When Gerard had that stroke? Do you not now have friends here?"

"I did." Tzedef acknowledged, "I do. But I would think that one would have to be a permanent resident to be considered a member of the community."

Her nose wrinkled, and she waved him off. "That's just splitting hairs. You've lived here. You've helped out wherever you could. You're a member of this community for as long as you're here. But that's beside the point. We were talking about what would become of Lucas."

Lynn sighed wearily, and leaned forward, propping her elbow on the table and her chin on the heel of her palm. "I believe he will voluntarily leave the village, once road conditions are better and there's more supplies to go around. He has no home with me, anymore, and word has been spreading about Isabeta's offer to Maria. People are angry with him, and for good reason. To lose a priest so soon after gaining one? Well…" She shook her head grimly. "People are angry."

"If he has no home with you, where will he stay?" Tzedef asked, "I wish him punished, but not to the point of freezing or falling deathly ill, and the nights are still fairly cold."

"Most likely? Here at the inn." Lynn shrugged. "He can take a pallet just as well as any other."

"Ah, yes." Tzedef nodded, then glanced around. The pallets were all stacked neatly against the back wall, blankets folded neatly and packs piled haphazardly nearby. Various pieces of armor and 'ancestral blades' were piled even more haphazardly nearby, making Tzedef's inner soldier wince.

"A question," he said abruptly as something occurred to him. "Isabeta said that they had starving children back in Farley, yet they still linger. Has something been done about that?"

Lynn nodded. "After the first harvest we sent a wagon back with Mattias and a couple of them from Farley, loaded up with what Lucas thought we could spare. It wasn't much, but I'm working on getting things set up to send another few wagonloads of food and seed down south. At this point, I'm hoping that whatever Maria decides, she's willing to head down there for a couple of weeks and get them well started on their growing season."

Tzedef hummed thoughtfully, thinking that over. "It's likely that Maria will agree. She is a kind hearted person and, from what I've seen of her, hates to see anyone suffer. Nelthys, on the other hand…"

"I know." Lynn sighed, "I'm working on it, but trying to figure out how to appease a god when his high priestess just insists that everything is fine is… difficult."

Tzedef winced. "That is spectacularly unhelpful, yes. Would you like me to have a talk with her?"

"Not yet, I don't think." Lynn said, "I think I've almost gotten through to her about it, but we'll see."

He nodded and settled back in his chair, his tail curling slightly around the leg of the chair as he thought.

With Tzedef having received his back-pay, Lucas being effectively neutered, the farmers from Farley well on the way to being taken care of, and Maria being gradually taught what people would expect from her in her role as high priestess, there wasn't really anything else he could think of that Lynn might need to speak to him about. There was, however, something that *he* needed to speak to *her* about.

"I estimate that it will take until mid-summer before there will be enough supplies for my companions and I to stock up without putting a strain on the resources of the village." He said slowly, and Lynne looked up at him attentively. "But I know little of farming, and I am not in charge of the resource distribution, so it is merely an estimate. How close to reality am I?"

Lynn blinked, then leaned back herself, thinking. "Well, we're getting one field's worth of harvest every four, five days with Nelthys's blessing. It's plain that, even with the boost in power he's gotten, he's still a small god, and doing the fields takes a lot out of Maria, too. Then there's the fact that unless we follow the rotation right, we're gonna end up with tired soil. If Nelthys continues to bless the fields until we've gotten one full spring's worth of harvest, fixing, and rest, which I'm not banking on, to be clear, there should be enough supplies for you three to be on your way in, say, a month? Maybe two?"

Tzedef blinked. Even though the snow had persisted well into spring, a month or two only took them through the very beginning of summer.

"That soon?" He asked cautiously, and Lynn grinned at him.

"That soon. We've plenty of fields around here, and with how fast we're getting things grown and harvested we're not losing any to insects or beasties or drought or anything. We'll have a gracious plenty soon enough, and then we can go back to our regular planting and growing schedule."

"I see." Tzedef said, cautiously starting to rearrange plans in his mind. "Shall we just continue on as we have been, then?"

Lynn shrugged. "The way I see it, your living arrangements now are between you and Amarie. There's little risk of you three dying in our streets now, so I can't in good conscience tell her that she needs to keep you on without some sort of exchange. If what you've been doing is good enough for her, then that's all to the good."

"I see. We'll have to speak to Amarie and see if she's willing to continue the current arrangement, then. Either way, it should be fine. Will I continue to be paid for guard work?"

"Sure." Lynn shrugged again. "As long as you're doing the work, you'll get paid."

"Right." Tzedef agreed, nodding to himself before turning his attention back to Lynn. "Was there anything else?"

"Nope." She said easily. "Anything else you needed from me?"

"Not that I can think of." Tzedef admitted, and Lynn nodded, sliding off the chair and brushing her skirts off with businesslike determination.

"Good. That's all settled then. If you need anything else, you know where to find me."

"Of course."

Red eyes watched her on her way out of the inn, then turned contemplatively towards the fire.

He hadn't expected her to remove herself so thoroughly from Lucas, but he supposed that finding out the abuses he'd put Maria through would have put anyone off.

After all, if he was willing to do that to someone that was supposed to be well respected, then how long would it be before that same attitude was turned against Lynn herself?

Two months.

He could handle two months, though he would have to let Casey and Sorecco know as soon as possible.

Two months seemed to fly by.

Amarie had been amicable to having Casey continue to work at the inn for her and Sorecco's stay and food, and Sorecco had continued to entertain those children who were too young to assist in the fields. That brought in supplies from an unexpected quarter- the parents who no longer had to worry about keeping an eye on young children paid him in things. Food like fresh cheeses, or soft bread, or a couple of coins here or there, or, to his utter joy, fresh batts of clean, creamy white wool.

Sorecco had run his fingers over the carded layers of soft wool, delighting in the texture before somewhat reluctantly folding it carefully and tucking it into his magic bag.

Tzedef, meanwhile, continued to work on the guard

rotation, earning what coin he could before they would inevitably need to buy their supplies to get back on the road.

Maria kept blessing the fields, and the harvests kept rolling in, keeping those who were processing the grain busy as more and more wheat piled up in the storage barns.

Gradually the air of quiet desperation that had begun to pervade the village faded away, replaced by an air of cheerful industry.

The pastures around the village were full of cows with new calves, and sheep with new lambs, and the pens in the barnyards had several sows with piglets on the teat.

All in all, Maplemore was the picture of a thriving village by the time Tzedef was confident that they had all the supplies they needed to leave.

But leaving, it turned out, was the hard part.

People, it seemed, had gotten attached to them, and for the three days leading up to their departure, people would hunt them down and press gifts on them. Gifts of food, or drink, or coin, or other small sundries. It left Tzedef utterly baffled.

Granted, he admitted to himself, he hadn't stayed in one place for very long after leaving the military, and even when he'd been in one place for a few weeks, he'd mostly kept to himself. Still, even his military leavetaking hadn't been this drawn out. In fact, it had been much more akin to a handshake, a coinpurse, and an admonishment to not let the door close on his tail on his way out.

Eventually, however, Casey, Sorecco, and Tzedef found themselves setting out of the north gate just as the sun was rising one morning.

CHAPTER TWENTY-THREE

The Road to Vraka

Maria caught up with them a couple of miles outside town, cantering up on a stocky pony that was built like a four-legged brick, with a frown on her face.

The little group paused as Maria pulled the pony to a halt next to them and slid out of the saddle, adjusting the small pouch at her hip as she automatically went to arrange her skirts and ended up brushing at the trousers she was wearing instead.

Tzedef blinked at her, and Casey grinned.

"Hi Maria! Nice horse!"

"Thank you," She said distractedly, and crossed her arms across her chest, still scowling at Tzedef.

"Is… something the matter?" He asked, somewhat bewildered. "Did we forget something? Is someone severely injured?"

"No, you didn't forget anything, at least, not that I know of. And nobody's hurt, either." She said, and Tzedef's confusion only grew as her toe began to tap impatiently.

"Then... what are you doing here? Did you wish to join us on the journey to Vraka?"

"No! Dear Nelthys, no!" Maria exclaimed exasperatedly, "You left without saying goodbye!"

Tzedef blinked again, dumbfounded. "You... rode out after us. Because I did not say goodbye?"

"Of course I did! I have things for you!"

"Oh?" Casey cocked her head to one side, eying the other woman speculatively, "How come you didn't just give 'em to us before we left, then? Or is it something *special* for Tzedef?"

Her grin was a bit sly, and Maria reddened slightly, but drew herself up with dignified aplomb.

"I was *busy*." She said, "Ever since the Judgment, people have been keeping me run off my feet. I tried to catch you at the inn this morning, but Amarie said you'd left before I got there. Anyway, here."

She opened the pouch at her hip, and pulled out a small, fat, palm sized, bronze pigeon, simply made, but well polished to a warm, golden color.

"Sorecco, this is for you. It was an offering to Nelthys, but he thought you'd put it to better use than just sitting around gathering dust in the shrine. He's practical like that, you know?"

Sorecco made a soft, surprised sound and held out his empty hand, closing it around the body of the pigeon when she put it into his hand, before tucking his stick into the crook of his arm so that he could run the fingers of his other hand over the smooth metal and fine details.

"Thank you."

"Mmhm. It's a guide, so it should help keep you from getting lost in Vraka."

She turned to Casey, then, and held out a pair of earrings. Simple silver hoops that gleamed in the sunlight. "Nelthys blessed these for you. He said they should let you understand more people, even if they don't speak Common for some reason."

Casey smiled. "That's great! thank you so much Maria, Nelthys!"

Maria beamed at her, then turned to Tzedef and started chewing nervously at her lower lip. "For you, Tzedef... well... I made you this. I hope you and Hecate like it."

The statuette she pulled out of the pouch was small, only about a hand's length tall, and carefully made, then fired. It was unpainted, but shone with a clear glaze.

It was a woman.

A woman dressed in flowing cloth, holding a torch in one hand, with her other hand resting on the head of a large dog.

Carefully, he reached out and lifted the statuette out of Maria's hands.

He turned the statue.

Another woman stared at him, her back to a column between herself and the other, a dagger in one hand.

He turned it again, and a third woman looked back at him, her back to the column as well, a snake winding around her neck while one hand supported the long body of the serpent.

Tzedef stared at it, and Maria shifted anxiously. "Do… do you like it?"

"You… sculpted Hecate." His voice was slightly hoarse.

"Is that allowed?" She asked, "Nelthys said it should be fine, and he told me what she looks like, and I really tried to do a good job, but I'm not sure I got the details right, and I—"

"It's perfect." Tzedef interrupted her, still staring down at the little figure.

It was radiating a bit of divinity. Nothing particularly strong, but definitely there, and Tzedef finally pulled his eyes away from it to look at Maria.

"There is… a blessing?"

She nodded. "I don't know what for, exactly. Nelthys just said it was for a little bit of extra luck. It shouldn't interfere with your prayers, if you end up wanting to use it while you're traveling."

"I usually pray to my amulet." Tzedef admitted. "This is…"

He shook his head, "This is wonderful. Thank you, Maria. Truly."

Maria flushed slightly, and nodded, ducking her head a bit as if to avoid his gratitude. "You're welcome."

For a moment she stood there, shifting slightly, then she clapped her hands together, making Sorecco jump.

"Well then! That's all your gifts! I hope you enjoy them, but I should be heading back now."

"Right." Tzedef agreed, and stepped back slightly. "Farewell, Maria. I hope you succeed in your endeavors. May you and Nelthys flourish."

She smiled at him, brief, but bright, and turned to mount the pony again as Casey nodded.

"Seriously, thank you Maria. Both for the gifts, and for riding out to give them to us. These'll probably come in handy!"

"Agreed," Sorecco said, still clutching the bird in one hand. "This is great."

Maria's flush darkened, but her smile was pleased.

"You're all very welcome. Please, if you're ever coming back this way, stop and say hi, okay? You've got a place in Maplemore, if you want it."

And saying that, she turned the pony's nose back toward the village, and urged it forward, breaking into a walk, then trot, then an easy, loping canter that rapidly took her out of hearing distance.

For a long few minutes, the three travelers, just stood there, then Casey sighed and tucked the earrings into her pack, and Sorecco seemed to shake himself out of his reverie, tucking his bird into the pouch he wore at his hip.

"Tzedef? Should we get going?"

Tzedef looked up, his face blank for a moment before he caught up mentally with the question Sorecco had asked.

"Oh. Yes. We should."

He swung his pack down off of his shoulders and opened it, carefully nestling the statuette in amongst his clothing before closing it back up and putting it back on.

"Let's go."

The weather on the road through Leeward to Vraka stayed reasonably in season the whole way, something that Tzedef had privately doubted would be the case. There were a few drizzly days, but for the most part it was sunny and breezy— weather that was perfect for both walking and camping. Sure, the relatively constant breeze made it colder than it otherwise would have been, but cloaks and coats helped to keep things reasonable, and the days quickly warmed up as summer truly took hold.

It was without any sort of fanfare that they crossed the border into Wethfren, and though they happened across several trading caravans on the same route toward Vraka, it seemed easier and faster to continue on as they were. So they did, walking steadily north until, around noon one day, they arrived at the gates of the Trading City of Vraka.

The guards barely glanced twice at them as they passed through the gates, and although Tzedef got a moderately long look from one of them, nothing came of it.

"We're here," Casey grinned, following Tzedef over to the side of the gate, out of the general flow of traffic, "finally. What did we want to do first? Find an inn? Hit up a bar for some food? Find the bardic college?"

"Find the bardic college!" Sorecco pounced on that suggestion as he wound a strip of cloth around the clapper of his little bell. "Please, I need to know if they'll take me, I need—"

"To bathe." Tzedef said, calmly cutting him off. "So that you can look your best when you go to the college. Appearances matter, especially to the bards. I doubt you will get as good a reception were you to show up covered in road dust and smelling of travel."

Sorecco drooped. "Oh. Right. That's a good point."

"Then, an inn?" Casey suggested, "And, if we're going to stay, maybe we should try scoping out any empty houses, or seeing if there's any empty flats around? Though I don't know who we'd start to ask about that sort of thing…"

"An inn, first." Tzedef nodded. "And once we're settled we can see about looking into places to bathe. Tomorrow we can begin to look into more permanent housing for the two of you. I can delay going to the college for information for a few days, at least."

"Great!" Casey chirped, clapping her hands once, and turning back towards the guards, "Then give me a second, and I'll get us some directions!"

Tzedef nodded, and Sorecco made a discontented noise as she marched away, then turned his face toward Tzedef.

"Do you mind if I hold your elbow? Now that we're back in a city it's a bit loud for my bell."

"I do not mind," Tzedef said cautiously. "but I have no experience as a guide."

"That's fine," Sorecco waved that away, "just don't let me trip or something, okay?"

"Very well."

It took a moment of fumbling, and a bit of adjusting on Sorecco's part, but eventually Sorecco's hand was tucked properly in the crook of Tzedef's arm and the two of them followed Casey over to the guards.

"—place to stay for a few nights? There's a few around. You need anything specific?"

"Some place close to a bath house." Casey said firmly, "We've been on the road for *forever*, and I'm *sick* of road dust."

The guard she was speaking to, a dwarven man with a thick, black beard, and a nose shaped like a tomato laughed, nodding. "Completely understandable. There's a couple of places like that around, but the one that's closest to a bathhouse would be Twists and Turns. They've got a bathhouse attached to the inn itself."

"Twists and Turns." Casey nodded, "That's certainly... a name."

"It's because of the route to get there." He explained, "The place is a nightmare to find because half the route is down alleyways that're practically invisible. I'm pretty sure the majority of their income comes from locals going to use the bathhouse."

Sorecco frowns. "That's rather unhelpful, then. Are there any others that are *close* to bathhouses? Ones that are easier to get to?"

"Sure." The guard shrugged. "There's The Courier's Rest. That one's not to far from the Karlyl bathhouse."

"And where is that?" Tzedef asked intently.

"On the west side," The guard said easily, and gave a

series of directions that referenced something called 'The Pit' several times as a landmark. Mostly in the form of 'if you reach The Pit, you've gone too far.'

"Thank you very much!" Casey said once he was done, and the guard waved her off.

"Just doing my job. Wouldn't be right to leave a bunch of travelers wandering around with nowhere to go. Did you need anything else?"

Sorecco hesitated, then opened his mouth, and Casey cut him off.

"No, thanks. I think we can pick up any other information we need by asking around at the inn, right?"

"Pretty much, yeah." The guard nodded. "The innkeepers around here know more than us guards, a lot of the time. Just make sure you stay out of trouble, all right?"

"All right!" Casey grinned at him, and turned to head away.

The guard's eyes flicked back over the next group of people coming through the gate, and Tzedef watched as he thoroughly dismissed them from his mind.

Tzedef turned, and he and Sorecco hurried after Casey, who slowed down after about half a block and waited for them to catch up with her.

"All right," She said once they caught up. "So where do we want to go?"

"The Courier's Rest sounded fine to me," Sorecco said, shrugging.

Tzedef shrugged as well. "We may as well? It would be pointless to ask for directions without then taking them, wouldn't it?"

"Yeah," Casey said, "I was just wondering if you wanted to try looking for that Twists and Turns place. It might be cheaper, if only locals go there for the baths."

"Nah," Sorecco waved that idea off. "I'd rather not get lost half a dozen times in the first week of being here. The other place might be a little more pricey, but at least it'll be easier to *find*."

"Fair enough!" Casey agreed, and turned to lead the way down the street again, peering at the signs on the buildings, and searching for the side streets the guard had mentioned.

Luckily, the route he had given them was relatively easy to follow, and they wound their way through the city towards the west side. They never came across anything that could possibly be construed as a pit, much less one that would garner so much emphasis when it was being spoken about, which was, Tzedef supposed, a good thing, since it meant they were likely following the directions properly. Sure enough, they found the inn just about where the guard had told them they'd find it.

It was a relatively large building, taking up a good quarter of the block, with a round, tower-like addition to one side of it. Pane-less windows circled that part of the building at irregular intervals and the occasional bird fluttered either in through one of the higher windows or out of one of the lower windows.

"Well, the name makes *some* sense, now." Casey said, watching as a pigeon fluttered down into a window, a small scroll case attached to its leg. "If they get messages here, then I guess couriers stop in a lot."

"Probably." Sorecco agreed, his nose wrinkled against the stink of bird droppings, "Though, if the inside smells like this, we're finding somewhere else to stay."

Tzedef made a noise of agreement as the three of them took the short flight of steps down to the door that seemed to lead into the inn proper.

The inside, fortunately, did not smell like droppings. In fact, it smelled rather heavily of food and beer and people. Which was, Tzedef admitted to himself, completely fair, considering how many people were crammed into the underground room.

Judging from the size of the room, it had originally been the basement of the building above it. Stone pillars reinforced the ceiling above them and light crystals grew out of and around the pillars in elegant, geometric shapes that lit up the room with a cozy glow.

"Oop," An Ursine woman that towered over even Tzedef paused in front of them, the look on her bear-like face apologetic. "Lemme just get past ya there."

Casey scrambled to get out of the woman's way as Tzedef steered Sorecco to the other side and she slipped past them with a grateful nod, her cinnamon-brown fur compressing as she squeezed her way through the doorway.

Casey stared after her, then accidentally caught Tzedef's eye and flushed slightly before turning back to the bustling room. Tzedef arched one brow ridge, but did the same, letting Sorecco set the pace down the last couple of stairs into the room proper as he took it in.

For the most part it seemed to be a normal inn common room, albeit one that was significantly busier than most others he'd seen outside of festivals or parties. It was only when he looked again that he spotted several discrepancies.

First, the majority of the people in the room were wearing leather bandoleers with a varying amount of pouches and pockets on them.

Second, along the wall that corresponded with the tower outside there were a series of polished brass tubes, their ends all capped with little flaps above small brass trays. There was a small counter in front of the tubes, and, as Tzedef watched, one of the flaps wiggled and something fell into the little tray beneath it.

A small lapinkin, previously unnoticed due to the fact that he'd been sitting on a stool with his nose buried in a book, stood up and retrieved the thing, checked the tube it'd come from, then glanced at the ends of what turned out to be a little cylinder.

"Parcel from the Merchant's Guild for delivery to the Woodworker's Guild!" He shouted above the general babble of noise in the room, "Thirty pounds or more!"

Three quarters of the people who'd stood up from their chairs at the first half of the call sat back down looking disgruntled, and there was a brief stare off between those that remained until finally a large lizardfolk who seemed like they might be related in some way to an alligator made their way over to the counter and retrieved the chit.

They spoke quietly with the lapinkin for a moment, then nodded and made their way toward the door, reaching it just as Tzedef, Casey, and Sorecco reached the bar.

"Just a mo." The dwarf behind the bar said distractedly, carefully pouring something red down the back of a spoon to pool on top of another liquid in an already mostly full glass. A moment later, she glanced up removing the spoon entirely and handed the glass over the bar to a young elebensis who was holding a tray.

"Table eleven, Jash."

The elebensis nodded, and the bartender watched him go for a moment before turning to look properly at them.

"Right, thanks for that. What can I do for you folks?"

CHAPTER TWENTY-FOUR

The Bardic College- Trials and Tribulations

Getting a couple of rooms and directions to the nearest bathhouse was as easy as asking for them and paying, and Tzedef settled into his upstairs room with a weary sigh. Casey and Sorecco had decided to share this time, leaving Tzedef on his own and he couldn't decide if that was more of a relief or a disappointment. On the one hand, he'd gotten used to sleeping with the breathing of another person nearby. Eleven-ish months in close quarters will do that, after all. But on the other, this way he wouldn't disturb anyone if he wished to do a bit of meditation. Or if he had more nightmares.

Luckily, Sorecco had been a heavy enough sleeper that Tzedef hadn't disturbed him often during their stint in Maplemore. Still, the few times that he *had* woken the other man had been unpleasant to explain, especially since he hadn't wanted to simply brush him off. With that in mind, he decided to be glad for the room of his own, and set about making himself comfortable.

First his shield came off his pack, and he put it down at the end of the bed, resting it against the foot so that it stayed upright. Then his cloak came off, and his pack was dropped to the floor with a soft sigh of relief.

Second, the little statuette of Hecate came out of his bag, where he'd wrapped it in several layers of spare clothing to help protect it from the bumps and jostling of travel. It ended up set on the small nightstand next to the bed, just in front of the dormant light crystal that, he presumed, was meant to light the room once the sun set.

He would have to remember to ask for a candle if he didn't want to rely solely on his night vision.

Tzedef could, faintly, hear Casey and Sorecco in the next room over, bickering cheerfully with each other as they settled in. They would be wanting to bathe soon, and while Tzedef would have loved nothing more than to stay in his room and get in some much needed meditation, he too, wanted a bath quite badly.

Sure enough, less than ten minutes later Casey knocked on his door.

"Tzedeeeeef!" She called through the wood, "Come on! We're going to go find the bathhouse!"

"Coming," he called back, and glanced speculatively at his cloak before dismissing it. It was warm enough, and the walk should be short enough that he wouldn't need it.

The bathhouse, the bartender had assured them, wasn't very far. Only about five minutes away, and the three travelers found that to be true as they followed the directions they'd been given to a long, squat building made of brick. Long windows just under the eaves let out billows of lightly scented steam that made the whole street smell vaguely damp and soapy, and Sorecco sighed happily as the group approached.

"Oh yes. This is going to be excellent."

The inside smelled just as clean as the street outside, and they were greeted by a cheerfully bouncy cervid who took their money, passed them towels, and asked if they needed any soaps or other toiletries.

Each of them opted to try different soaps, and they were directed through a pair of small doors toward changing rooms.

"Make sure you take your clothes in with you!" The cervid chirped as they headed for the doors, her deer-like ears flicking slightly, "There's cubbies to hold them along the walls once you get in so you can keep an eye on your things."

Tzedef nodded, and passed through the door.

The bathing room itself was a communal room that took up the majority of the building, with unglazed clay tiles as flooring, and glazed tiles lining the walls in intricate mosaics that depicted oceanic vistas and underwater scenery.

Showerheads lined one wall, and there was an array of individual pools full of steaming water, all separated from the large main pool in which several people were already soaking.

Someone giggled behind him, and Tzedef turned to

see Casey, wrapped in her towel, looking at the mosaics with a gleeful grin.

Tzedef blinked, and turned to look at the tiled walls again. They seemed normal? There wasn't anything particularly funny about them that he could see, and when he turned a quizzical look back at Casey and caught her eye, her grin widened.

"It's sea-nery." She explained, and burst into laughter at the look on his face.

Sorecco made a questioning noise as he steps out of the changing room, his robes bundled in one hand, his stick in the other. "What's funny?"

"There's these mosaics," Casey explained, padding over toward the cubbies on the wall, "On the wall. All ocean scenes and stuff. So it's *sea*-nery."

She burst into giggles again as Sorecco groaned softly. "Where are those cubbies the clerk mentioned?"

"Just here." Casey said, "Off to your left. There's showers on your right, and there's a main pool that's absolutely *massive* and a bunch of smaller ones further forward."

"Think we're supposed to shower before we get in the pools?" He asked, following her voice toward the wall with his stick questing cautiously in front of him.

"Most likely." Tzedef said, following him over to the cubbies and tucking his clothing into one that he was reasonably sure he'd have a good view of the whole time.

"Great." He sighed, "Are there at least shelves for the soaps?"

"Um..." Casey turned, squinting over toward the showers. "Yeah, I think so. You should be fine."

"Great." Sorecco said again, and roughly bundled his clothes into one of the cubbies.

His stick, he held on to uncertainly. As though he wasn't sure if he should take it with him or leave it propped up against the wall.

In the end, he propped it up against the cubbies and took Casey's elbow, letting her guide him around the room, chattering all the while.

Bathing was nice. Tzedef hadn't shared a communal bath since he'd left the army in Yaelin, but this was much more relaxed than that had been and he relished the way the hot water of the shower beat against his scales.

The baths themselves were luxurious, though some of the smaller pools had warnings around them stating that one should only enter if one was particularly resistant to heat or cold.

Tzedef was neither, and so, by unspoken consensus, the three travelers ended up in the large pool together, leaning back against the rim of the pool and enjoying the way the heat sank into their bones.

They stayed for just over an hour before rumbling stomachs drove them from the water and into the dressing rooms again, and a few minutes after that they were back on the street heading back toward the Courier's Rest.

Dinner was interesting; the room never really emptied out, but couriers cycled through almost constantly.

People came and went, and only rarely did Tzedef see a person leave and then return again.

The food was hearty, and filling, though not particularly good. Still, it wasn't bad, either. Tzedef had certainly had worse, so he wasn't going to be complaining, and neither, apparently, were Casey or Sorecco.

They ate without lingering, and then, by mutual accord, headed up to their rooms when they finished, splitting up with quiet good-nights and well wishes.

Tzedef, however, didn't immediately go to sleep. Instead, he settled on the bed cross legged, facing the statuette of Hecate. He had, over the course of the winter, spent quite a bit of time meditating, but never had he had anything more representative of his goddess than his amulet. Her holy symbol.

Now, though...

He reached up and pulled the amulet over his head, then reached over to prop it up against the statuette.

There. That would work nicely.

Hopefully she wouldn't be offended by him praying to an effigy blessed by another god. She hadn't seemed to have a problem casting a Judgment with Nelthys though, so it would probably be fine.

He lost track of how long he sat there, the candle he'd requisitioned from the bartender burning lower and lower as he dwelt on Hecate and the quest she'd granted him— the progress he'd made. The setbacks. The difficulties.

He was so close to finding out where he needed to go

that he could almost taste it.

Tomorrow would bring the information he sought. He knew it.

Eventually, once the candle had burned to about the midpoint, Tzedef sighed softly, content, and blew it out.

Sleep came in a soft, inexorable wave.

'Tomorrow' started before dawn, with Sorecco knocking on his door and practically vibrating with nerves.

"What is wrong?" Tzedef leaned against the doorjamb, doing his best to suppress a yawn before giving up and letting loose with one that cracked his jaw.

Sorecco paused, his face blank. "Are- are you okay? That sounded painful."

"I'm fine." Tzedef assured him, "But I doubt you came here to ask that. What is wrong?"

"Nothing's wrong, exactly." He temporized, and Tzedef arched a brow ridge at him before remembering and sighing.

"What *isn't* wrong, then?"

Sorecco hesitated, and Tzedef sighed quietly. "I will not judge you. Nor will I think you are somehow lesser for having trouble with something. So. What is wrong?"

For a moment, Sorecco was silent. Then he sighed, leaning on his stick slightly.

"I can't sleep." The admission seemed to cost him something. "I keep wondering what's going to happen at the College tomorrow."

"Today." Tzedef corrected him absently, and

Sorecco winced.

"It's that late?"

Tzedef frowned, then peered closer at Sorecco, taking in the dark circles under his eyes and the pale cast to his skin.

"You have not slept at all, have you." It wasn't a question, but Sorecco shook his head anyway.

"I told you. I can't sleep."

Tzedef sighed again. "You will be doing yourself no favors with your application to the college if you do not sleep."

"I know!" Sorecco snapped, then deflated, looking abashed. "I'm sorry, I'm just... Just..."

"Nervous?" Tzedef supplied, and Sorecco nodded reluctantly.

"Yeah. What if they don't like me? What if they decide that I'm too hard to teach? What if they say no?"

"Then you would be welcome to continue traveling with me, should you so desire." Tzedef offered automatically, then paused, blinking.

That wasn't something he'd actually considered offering to Casey and Sorecco before, but now that it was out of his mouth he couldn't bring himself to take it back.

"I am sure that you will be able to find more people to learn from and learn more stories and songs on the way to wherever it turns out that I need to go." Tzedef added, slowly feeling out the idea and finding it more and more to his liking. "It is possible that you would find more fulfillment in an ad hoc education than something more structured."

"Maybe." Sorecco admitted, sounding slightly defeated, and Tzedef scrambled to reassure him.

"Not that I think you will not make it in. Your voice is good, your memory impressive, and your willingness to learn is one of your best qualities. I cannot think of any way that a reasonable person might bar you from entry."

Sorecco cocked his head at Tzedef, a faint hint of color rising in his cheeks as a slow smile spread across his mouth.

"You think so?"

"I do." Tzedef confirmed. "There is no reason why they should reject you."

"He said *what?!*" Casey's voice was a low, venomous hiss, and she looked about ready to march past Sorecco and into the office he'd just left.

" 'A cripple like you could never be a proper bard.' " Sorecco said hollowly, his face almost white with shock. " 'You'd be better off sticking to your street corner and collecting coin from passing suckers.' Casey... Casey he didn't even let me *try*."

He looked near tears, and Tzedef found himself bristling, glaring at the door as though he could in any way help this situation. Only the fact that him intervening would do absolutely nothing good kept him from walking into the office and demanding that the hawk-like birdfolk give Sorecco a fair chance.

Casey, apparently, had no such compunctions holding her back and she brushed past Sorecco and stomped toward the door, her footsteps loud on the tile.

"Casey, wait! Where are you going?"

"To give that complete *bastard* a piece of my mind!" Casey spat, and Sorecco made a halfhearted gesture in her direction; as though he wanted to stop her but couldn't quite bring himself to really try.

"You shouldn't—"

The office door slamming open cut him off, and Sorecco flinched, clutching his stick tighter.

Tzedef got a momentary glimpse of a darkly feathered man looking up indignantly, his plumage poofing out in irritation, and then the door slammed shut.

Sorecco flinched again.

For a long few minutes there was silence. Then, slowly growing louder and louder, Tzedef heard shouting from the office and Sorecco started to cringe, shrinking in on himself and looking miserable.

"Can we— can we just go." He croaked, his knuckles white around his stick, and Tzedef winced as Casey's voice, recognizable even through the thick wooden door, hit a pitch he'd previously thought only dogs were capable of hearing.

Tzedef hesitated, then shifted and stood up from the tiny, uncomfortable chair he'd crammed himself into.

"Let's go." He agreed, his voice a deep, displeased rumble.

Sorecco sagged, relieved, then stiffened when

another door slammed open and a woman stuck her head out.

"What is going *on* out here?!"

CHAPTER TWENTY-FIVE

Cestra and Beech

"Well?" The woman demanded when neither Tzedef nor Sorecco responded right away. "What's going on out here?"

"I—" Sorecco started, then faltered. "My sister—"

"Is that the harpy that's currently screaming at Roderick?"

"Yes?"

"Why?" The woman asked, and exited the office fully.

Tzedef's eyes widened.

From the waist up, the woman was a typical example of a human woman, albeit a particularly well muscled one.

From the waist *down* however, she was a snake. Golden brown patches broken up with black and orange outlines, the snake body that propelled her forward was long and sinuous and rippling with muscle. Coupled with her dark skin, darker hair, and orange eyes, she was strikingly beautiful.

"Well?" She said again, looking impatient, and Sorecco opened his mouth, then closed it again, unwilling to speak his rejection from the college into reality again.

"The registrar," Tzedef began, "you said his name is Roderick?"

She nodded, slightly impatiently, gesturing for him to get on with it.

"Roderick refused to grant Sorecco entrance to the college, citing his lack of sight as the reason."

Orange eyes flitted to Sorecco, glancing him up and down before narrowing.

"You're blind?"

"Yeah." Sorecco said, slightly defensively, "What of it? I can still sing. I can tell tales. If someone would give me a *chance* I know I could learn an instrument."

She waved that off. "Anyone can sing, and most anyone can tell tales. It's called lying, boy, and most people do that as easily as breathing. The *real* question is can you keep time. Do you have an ear? Can you *learn,* and what do you do with that learning?"

"I…" Sorecco hesitated, then lifted his chin and shifted his grip on his stick. "I can learn. I have a good ear. My memorization skills are sharper than most people I know."

The woman eyed him for a moment longer, then nodded firmly. "My name is Cestra Vislani. I'm the dean of the bardic college in Vraka. Give me a moment, and then we'll go speak in my office."

Sorecco paled sharply, and Tzedef's eyebrow ridges

rose as she turned toward Roderick's office and didn't bother knocking on the door before flinging it open, cutting Casey off mid-word.

"Roderick, you can't keep rejecting prospective students out of hand just because you don't like them!"

Cestra swept into the office like an avenging goddess, absently chivvying Casey out before shutting the door in her face with a flick of her tail.

Casey stared at the closed door for a moment, then turned around and gestured questioningly at the door, half angry, half confused.

"What the hells?!?"

"That would be the dean." Tzedef told her, "She wishes to speak with Sorecco when she finishes with the registrar."

Casey's eyes widened. "What do you mean that's the dean?! I thought that guy was the dean!"

"No." Sorecco croaked, then cleared his throat roughly. "No. He's the registrar. I... I don't understand what's going on. Isn't he the one who decides who can enroll?"

"Apparently there are standards he must adhere to." Tzedef guessed, "Standards that he was circumventing in dismissing you out of hand."

"And that means the dean wants to talk to you?" Casey asked, looking at Sorecco with something very much like hope in her eyes.

"Apparently." Sorecco said, still slightly stunned. "I —"

The door to the registrar's office swung open again, much less violently this time, and Cestra glided out with an irritated look on her face.

"Right." She said, rather sharply. "*That's* taken care of. You. Sorecco. My office."

She moved past the small group, her scales rasping softly on the stone floor, and Sorecco hesitated then followed her, his stick sweeping ahead of him as he walked.

"To your right." She directed him absently, sweeping ahead of him and through the still open door, and Sorecco turned into the office as well.

The door shutting sounded almost unnaturally loud.

For a long moment Casey stared at the door, then she turned toward Tzedef and flailed silently at the door.

"I suppose we wait." He said, answering her unasked question and gesturing at the uncomfortable wooden chairs along the wall.

And so, they waited.

And waited.

And *waited.*

When the door swung open almost an hour and a half later and Sorecco emerged looking somewhat shellshocked, Casey sprang to her feet.

She barely waited until the door behind him swung closed.

"Well? Did you do it? Are you in? How'd it go?"

"I—" Sorecco started in a shaking voice, his knuckles white around his stick. "It went... well? I think?

Gods above, I need a drink."

"Then a drink you shall have." Tzedef said calmly, climbing to his feet and dusting down his trousers. "I believe I saw a pub on the way here. It will likely be full of students, but if you are to attend this college, then that is something you will quickly grow accustomed to."

"Right." Sorecco took a shaky breath, then let it out slowly, and Tzedef watched him force his shoulders to relax down and away from his ears.

"Let's go, then!" Casey grinned, tugging on Sorecco's sleeve, "C'mon! And on the way you can tell us if we're drinking to celebrate or forget!"

"Okay, Casey, okay! You don't have to pull at me! Fine, let's go get a drink and a meal, and I'll tell you how it went."

The Bardic College, was not, as the name implied, one building or one course of learning. In fact, it would have been more apt to call it a university, with multiple colleges all under the auspices of some of the best, most learned wizards, bards, musicians, storytellers, historians, and researchers of both magical and mundane subjects in the world.

And it was all located in what the locals called The Pit. A massive circular bite that had been taken out of the near-center of the city and destroyed the old University District in the process. The circumference was so clean cut that it looked very much like someone or something had taken an enormous cookie cutter and simply punched out a piece of the city.

That circumference, though, was broken up by the absolutely massive trees that grew along the edges of The Pit, their roots winding in and out of the walls and providing support to the dirt and stone there. Ferns, vines, creepers, moss, and other greenery crept along the walls as well; every little bit helping to keep the sides of The Pit from washing down into it and taking even more of the city down with it.

Several long ramps were carved into the walls of The Pit, sloping gently down and around so that people, wagons, carts, and carriages could get down into the New University District with ease. Roughly equidistantly around the circumference there were also the lifts; magical platforms between the ramps that ferried things and people relatively quickly from the top of The Pit to the bottom, with no stops along the way.

Some enterprising souls had carved homes and shops into the stone that made up the walls under where the dirt cut off, placing windows and doors around where roots clung with grim determination to every cranny in the stone. It was toward those walls that Tzedef led them, heading for a tavern that he'd spotted on the way to the Registrar's office.

Along the way, however, the scent of roasting meat, thick with spices, caught their attention, and they paused, Sorecco's stomach rumbling unhappily. They paused, turning and Tzedef turned his face into the wind to get a better idea of where the scent was coming from.

"Okay," Sorecco started, "I know I said I wanted a

drink, but that smells *really good.*"

"And you skipped breakfast." Casey said knowingly, and Sorecco turned to scowl in her direction.

"I did not! ...I had a piece of toast." The last bit was mumbled, and Casey sighed.

"You can't just *not eat* because you're nervous, 'Recco..."

"I know..." he said mournfully, "I just- I thought it'd be fine, and I'd get something on the way, but then I felt like I was gonna puke just *thinking* about eating, so I just... didn't."

"Well, we'll get something now, then." Casey said, "And hopefully something to drink, too, to wash all that out of our mouths."

"That sounds nice." Sorecco admitted, then scowled. "Stupid registrar..."

His stick stabbed at the cobbles more viciously than absolutely necessary as he turned toward where the scent of grilling meat was coming from.

"You know you are better than that." Tzedef said calmly, stepping forward to take his place on Sorecco's left and Casey nodded earnestly as she started guiding him toward where she thought the smell was coming from.

"You really are." She said. "You're *smart,* 'Recco. *Really* smart! I bet you knocked the soc—" she paused, "Um. Tail? Whatever. Point is, I bet you really impressed the dean!"

"Maybe." Sorecco fretted, his grip on Casey's elbow tightening. "I couldn't tell. She has *incredible* vocal control. I couldn't tell what she was thinking at all."

"Then did you not get in?" Tzedef asked, frowning, and Sorecco sighed.

"I don't know."

Casey paused midstep, making Sorecco stumble slightly. "What do you *mean* you don't know?!"

"I mean I don't know!" He snapped, clutching his stick tightly, "Dammit Casey, don't just stop like that!"

"Right, sorry!" She waited until Sorecco was re-situated, then started walking again. "How can you not know? Did she just talk to you for a while and then kick you out? Are we supposed to be waiting on a messenger? A letter or something?"

"No." He shook his head. "No, I'm... apparently there's a two part application for the bardic colleges? Part one is an interview, but part two is- it's an *audition*. I have to come up with a performance, and put it on, and if I do well enough on both parts, *then* I'm in. She told me to come back in a week."

"A week!" Casey squawked, "That's practically nothing!"

"It's a lot longer than I'd usually get, out in the world." Sorecco pointed out. "Unless I find a wealthy patron my usual gigs'd be bars, pubs, or inns, and I'd have to assess the crowd with only a short lead time, then tailor my performance to them on the spot."

Tzedef nodded. "It's true. Many of the bards I have encountered have been fascinatingly changeable. I have watched several bring audiences back from anger and impatience to laughter and camaraderie. Bards are masters of emotion, as well as word and song."

Casey frowned, then nodded slowly. "You're right. I hadn't really noticed before, but now that I think about it, there's been a couple of times where I've seen some musicians just… turn on a plat, and their audiences turned with them."

Sorecco sighed. "That's going to be harder, for me. Judging the crowd will rely almost entirely on what I can hear from them, and if I'm playing an instrument, well. That would make it rather hard."

"True." Tzedef nodded, "However, if you are playing an instrument that would be a series of pure tones, correct? Your Gift could just as easily tell you if people are leaving or getting restless, yes?"

Sorecco hesitated. "I don't know. I've held a guitar before; there was bard that was playing at Over Easy once, and she didn't mind letting me hold it, but she didn't have time to teach me how to do much more than that."

"It is surprising that she allowed you to hold the instrument." Tzedef observed, turning a corner, and Sorecco nodded.

"I was surprised too, but she was really nice. Lilia, her name was. She moved on not long after that, so I've no idea what happened to her."

"Perhaps you could find out at the college?"

Sorecco shrugged. "Maybe, though honestly it really isn't that important. I doubt she'd remember some random person she was kind to a few years ago."

"Oh hey, there it is!" Casey grinned, bouncing a little bit as a large pavilion tent came into sight, an absolutely tiny roofed wagon at the side.

Sure enough, the delicious smells were emanating from the wagon, and when they got closer, Tzedef saw that there was a wide window on the side of the wagon and odd tables with benches joined to them spread out under the tent.

"Mothers above, that smells so good." Sorecco sighed, following his nose toward the wagon as Casey guided him around obstacles until they came to a stop just in front of the window.

"Hey there!" The gnomish woman inside the wagon grinned widely at them, her teeth bright against her dark skin. "Ain't seen you folks around before! Welcome to The Pop Up!"

"Thanks," Casey smiled back, "We smelled you from three blocks away. What're you cooking?"

The woman beamed at Casey. "Oh honey, what *ain't* I cooking! I got pottage, I got sausage rolls, I got lamb, I got goat, I got beef, an' pork, an' chicken; I got *everything!*"

She eyed Casey and Sorecco for a moment, then switched her gaze to Tzedef.

"You two look like students, if I don't miss my guess, an' you sir, are you with the guard?"

Tzedef blinked, a bit startled. "I am not, ma'am."

She eyed him for a moment longer, then smiled again, all good cheer again. "Excellent!"

"We're not students, either." Sorecco said, and Casey

jabbed him in the ribs with her elbow.

"Yet."

Sorecco sighed, "That I know of."

The gnome's eyes bounced between the two of them, looking mildly amused as the siblings went back and forth.

"Not students, then. All right, so how kin I help you?"

"Food?" Casey said, making piteous eyes at the woman, who burst out laughing.

"Oh my dear, ain't that a face! All right, food it is. Pick your poison!"

"What do you have?" Sorecco asked cautiously, and the woman arched an eyebrow at him.

"Dincha hear me say I got everything? I said it, an' I *meant* it! Name somethin', anything, an' I'll betcha I kin whip it up for ya."

Sorecco hummed thoughtfully, "All right. See if you know this one, then. When she and I were kids, our parents used to make these dumplings. They'd get steamed in a pot, then fried crispy, and they were stuffed with ground pork and spices. I'm pretty sure it's a recipe from Hakui Island, but I don't know what they're called."

The woman stared out into the distance, her eyes flicking back and forth as though she was reading something, and once Sorecco stopped talking, she jerked into motion.

"I think I kin getcha something like that, but it'll be a bit, that okay with you?"

Sorecco tipped his head. "Sorry?"

"I kin do it," the woman repeated, speaking clearly, "But it'll take me a while. You okay with waitin'?"

"Oh." Sorecco sounded dumbfounded, then shook himself. "How much will it cost?"

"One sil." The woman said promptly, and Sorecco hesitated. "Would be more, but I think I actually got all the ingredients on hand!"

Curiosity won out over frugality, and Sorecco nodded. "All right, I'm fine with waiting."

"Good!" She said, and turned her attention to Casey, who looked wistful.

"I never could get that recipe right… All of mine stuck to the pot too much, or fell apart. Can I have that, too?"

"Of course! It'll still be a bit of a wait, but I gotcha covered."

Sorecco withdrew two silver coins from his belt pouch and handed them to Casey, who laid them on the windowsill.

The gnome made them disappear, then turned to look expectantly at Tzedef, who hesitated.

"I have not had a boiled pudding in many years." He admitted slowly. "Perhaps that, with whatever fruit you have on hand?"

The woman nodded cheerfully. "I gotcha. That'll be five cop."

Tzedef nodded, and fished his coin string out of his pocket, unlooping it for long enough to slide five of the largest coins off before tying it up again.

The copper jingled as he dumped them into the woman's waiting palm, and her grin was all but splitting her face as she tucked the money away.

"Right! You three go have a sit, and I'll bring it out to ya when it's ready."

With that, she turned and walked out of view, something that Tzedef was almost certain wasn't possible considering the fact that the window they were standing at stretched nearly wall to wall.

Tzedef craned his head, then stared as the view inside the wagon warped and shifted, then expanded until he was looking into a space many times the size of the wagon itself; a fully kitted out kitchen, with everything in it all appropriately sized for gnomes.

His eyes went wide and, very carefully, Tzedef took a step back away from the wagon.

He didn't want to see what happened if that much space suddenly lost the magic that was keeping it folded down into that tiny of a footprint.

"Well," Sorecco said, oblivious to Tzedef's consternation, "she said go sit, so… Where's the seats?"

"Over here." Casey said, and the two of them headed for the odd table-benches under the pavilion tent.

Tzedef took one last look into the wagon, then followed.

"So." Casey said once they were all situated at the table, "You've got a week."

"Yeah." Sorecco sighed. "A week to put together a performance that'll wow the dean of the *entire* university and whoever else she decides to bring around. I don't even know where to *start*. Hells, I don't even— wait. Do people this far inland know the sea tales?"

Casey clapped, grinning. "Probably not! You could tell a couple of those, and then sing that one song, you know, the one about the woman's sailor lover?"

"Yeah." Sorecco said thoughtfully, "That could work out well, I think. Do a general sea theme. Most of the songs don't need instruments, so they won't sound too odd being sung alone. Yeah." He said again, more confidently. "Yeah, that'll work nicely, I think. Thanks Case."

"No problem!" She replied promptly, and leaned sideways against him. "This is your dream. I'll do anything I can to help you achieve it."

She paused, then wrinkled her nose as something occurred to her. "I need a job."

Sorecco winced. "I should probably figure out something, too."

"You'll be going to school!" Casey protested, "That's practically a full time job as it is!"

"And?" Sorecco retorted, "I can still do something in the evenings. Maybe spinning, again, if I can get permission from the local weaver's guild."

Slowly, Casey nodded. "As long as you actually can *get* permission, then yeah. I don't see why that wouldn't work. You're certainly good at it."

Sorecco nodded, then tipped his head in Tzedef's direction. "What about you? You were all excited to come to Vraka before, but you've barely said two words about what you want to do now that we're here."

"I have been thinking." Tzedef said mildly, watching with no small amount of amusement as an absolutely massive centaur bent over awkwardly to talk to the woman in the wagon.

"Thinking about what?"

"Thinking about how I am to find the information I need. I was told that if anywhere would likely have it, it would be the Bardic College of Vraka, but now that I am here, I find myself unsure of where to begin looking."

"Wouldn't the library be a good place?" Casey asked, and Tzedef shrugged.

"It would, though I am unsure if going up to a random librarian and asking if they know anything about an 'Ambered Castle' would do any—"

Rapid hoofbeats beat a tattoo against the cobbles, and suddenly there was a centaur at the end of their table, her eyes fixed on Tzedef and lit up with almost feverish glee.

"Did you say the Ambered Castle?" she demanded, leaning eagerly into Tzedef's space and unintentionally looming over him.

Tzedef leaned back, then scooted sideways on the bench until the woman abruptly seemed to realize what she'd been doing and straightened up with an apologetic look on her face.

"Did you say the Ambered Castle?" she asked again, and Tzedef nodded slowly.

"I did, why do you wish to know?"

"Hi my name is Beech nice to meet you." The centaur said very rapidly, and did an odd half bow that involved cocking one foreleg up and across the other before continuing at a slightly slower pace. "I've been researching the Ambered Castle for the last couple of years! Well, trying to anyway, but the stupid bureaucrats in Reyfil Mountain won't grant me access, and I keep running out of money and having to come back and apply for more grants and then there's the travel time back and forth and honestly I swear I've traveled the road up there so many times now I could do it in my *sleep* and—"

Casey stared at the chattering woman then turned her head slowly to look at Tzedef, who looked back at her helplessly.

"You know about the Ambered Castle, then?" He interjected, half hoping to halt the deluge of words.

"No." The woman sagged comically, "I don't know *anything* about it."

Tzedef stared at her.

"No really," she said, catching his look. "I honestly don't. I haven't managed to get so much as a *finger* on the amber, and I've been trying for years."

"But you know where it is, and who to speak to to gain access to it." Tzedef pressed, and Beech shrugged.

"Oh, sure, I know that stuff. But that's all the easy part. It's the *getting access* part that's the hard part. The Ambered Castle is a… wossname… thing… National treasure! That's it! Anyway, yeah, it's a national treasure of the Dwarven Kingdom of Reyfil Mountain, so they're just a *biiiit* touchy about outsiders wanting to come in and study it. But I'm getting there! I'm wearing 'em down! I've got new grant money and I'm not afraid to use it!"

Casey burst into laughter, and, after a moment Beech grinned sheepishly, reaching up to fiddle with a lock of her black hair.

"Ah, sorry. I get a little overenthusiastic sometimes. Do you mind if I join you?"

"Not at all!" Casey grinned back at her, "We're just waiting on our food."

"Me too," Beech said comfortably, settling easily. "Jenna is an *amazing* cook, and I don't think I've ever seen anyone stump her. What'd you guys get?"

"Dumplings," Sorecco said easily, "Can't remember the name for the life of me, but our mom used to make them when we were young."

"Ooo," Beech said appreciatively, her ears twitching this way and that. "That sounds good! I've got a sweet curry coming. I love how she makes it."

Tzedef blinked at her. "A… sweet? Curry?"

She nodded happily. "Oh yeah, it's got apples in it instead of potatoes."

"Interesting." Tzedef said, and Beech beamed at him.

"So, anyway. The Ambered Castle. Why're you interested in it?"

"I am searching for a particular magic that I have been reliably informed may be found in the Ambered Castle."

Beech ooo-ed appropriately, sounding interested. "Magic? Really? I mean, I guess that makes sense, seeing as there's an *entire castle* trapped in amber it's probably *got* to have some kind of really cool magic stuff inside it! Hey! Maybe that's what happened to trap it in amber! Someone was researching a new spell and it went *really* wrong!"

Tzedef blinked at her. "I— Does that often happen, here?"

Beech shrugged. "Not really, but man the screw ups can be *doozies* when they happen! Either way, that's really neat that you know about anything that's inside the castle. What's your source? Can I interview them?"

"It— I—" Tzedef scrambled for an answer, and Casey stepped in.

"His goddess told him!"

Beech's face screwed up like she'd tasted something sour. "Ugh. Gods. Really?"

Tzedef blinked again. "Yes. Gods. Why? Do you take issue with the gods?"

"Nah," Beech shook her head, then grimaced and waggled a hand from side to side. "Kinda? I mean, I'm grateful to the harvest gods and the Storm Queen and all; gods know the world wouldn't work as well without them, but... I can't cite 'divine revelation' in a paper, y'know? It's gotta be verifiable *evidence*. Stuff that other people without super closer relationships with the gods can replicate."

Tzedef ah-ed softly. It made sense. Not everyone was close to the gods. Not everyone could simply call on divine knowledge. It made sense.

"But anyway," Beech said cheerfully, her ears swiveling towards the food cart as the door swung open, "That's an aside. You're heading north, right? Do you have a guide yet?"

"I hadn't planned on hiring one." Tzedef admitted, and thanked Jenna quietly as she slid a bowl full of boiled pudding in front of him, along with a small pitcher of cream.

Beech guffawed and then, when Tzedef didn't laugh, slowly trailed off into awkward silence.

"Oh you're serious. Um. Well that's... not great."

"Is it really that dangerous?" Sorecco asked worriedly, and Beech nodded emphatically.

"It really is. If you aren't running into bandits on the road, then there's the frost trolls once you get further north, and that's not even *mentioning* the damvar in the villages that you *have* to keep an eye out for because those things are *seriously* nasty. I'm not even joking; I once saw someone who'd been in contact with a damvar for like, a month and the guy was absolutely nuts. Just *raving*. Not even a falshi could help fix him."

Tzedef frowned. "I do not recognize those names. Damvar, and falshi. What are they?"

Beech shrugged. "Cat spirit things, I guess. Damvar drive people mad in the dark of winter up north, and falshi are basically the opposite. They can help people that've been hunted by a damvar, and they keep things clean and stuff. I dunno. I've never actually seen a falshi in person.

Anyway, the point is, you *probably* need a guide. At least to keep you from getting your spleen eaten."

"What would eat his spleen?" Casey asked, leaning forward with eager interest.

Beech shrugged again. "Maybe nothing, maybe a troupe of Bujoun finds him while he's asleep. Then he never wakes up again."

Tzedef opened his mouth to ask what a Bujoun was, but Beech cut him off.

"Either way, you really should get a guide. It won't hurt you any, and it'll probably help quite a bit."

He sighed. "As useful as a guide might be, the fact of the matter is that hiring a guide would likely decimate what small amount of money I have for provisioning and travel expenses. I thank you for your concern, Miss Beech, but I believe I will be fine on my own."

Beech scowled at him, then perked up as Jenna returned, sliding a large bowl of rice and curry in front of her, then placed a plate of dumplings in front of both Sorecco and Casey.

"There you are, my dears!" She grinned, "Now go on, you two. See if I got it right."

Cautiously, Casey reached out for one of the dumplings with her fork, murmuring directions to Sorecco as he felt around for his.

As one, the siblings popped their dumplings into their mouths, and chewed.

And swallowed.

Sorecco turned to Jenna.

"Milady, I am but a humble student, but I would be the luckiest man alive if you would do me the honor of marrying me."

Jenna stared at him for a moment, then burst into cackling laughter, slapping her thighs and laughing until tears streamed down her cheeks.

"I take it I got it right, then?" She gasped, and Sorecco nodded as Casey stuffed another dumpling into her mouth.

"You certainly did. I was skeptical, I admit, but you hit the nail exactly on the head. Thank you, Missus Jenna."

"You're quite welcome." She grinned at him, "I suspect that, if you're a student, I'm gonna be seeing quite a bit more of you, yes?"

"*Yes*." Sorecco agreed fervently, and Jenna's grin widened.

"Good."

And she turned and headed back into her little cart, leaving the four of them to eat in peace.

Carefully, Tzedef drizzled cream over his pudding, then cut into it, letting out a rush of steam and the scent of warm berries.

For a time, the four of them ate quietly, each enjoying their meal in their own way.

But from the way Beech's ears were twitching and flicking, she was thinking, and thinking hard.

An assumption that was borne out when she put her fork down and turned more towards Tzedef.

"All right. So you're going north. And I'm going

north. And you look like a generally tough guy, right? So how about this; why don't we travel up to Reyfil Mountain together. Like I said earlier, I could probably make the trip with my eyes closed at this point, but I don't like to travel alone, so this'd be killing two birds with one stone!"

Tzedef considered that, slowly chewing his bite of pudding.

It wasn't a bad idea. If Beech truly was as experienced as she claimed, then it *would* be useful to have her around on the journey up.

And, he had to be honest with himself, he had rather gotten used to traveling with companions over the last while. To go back to traveling alone would be doable, but it wasn't something that he necessarily looked forward to.

"Very well." He nodded to Beech, putting down his fork and extending his hand to shake hers. "I accept your offer. We will travel to Reyfil Mountain together."

CHAPTER TWENTY-SIX

The Storm Queen's Approval

Tzedef spent the next week alternating between speaking with Beech about what route they might take and what equipment they might need, and wandering the city.

It wasn't quite aimless wandering; he'd managed to pick up a couple of odd jobs that had made him a bit of money while not taking up too much time or energy, and he'd learned a great deal about the city. Not all of it was particularly relevant to himself, but he'd passed on the local scuttlebutt to Casey and Sorecco, giving them a heads up about the local politics, areas to avoid, or places that might be hiring or renting.

Casey soaked it up like a sponge, but for the most part Sorecco was distracted, too busy putting together his performance for his audition to pay attention to anything else.

He'd decided to abandon the idea of the sea-tales, and was instead working on a performance based on the last winter. Occasionally he would try out this turn of phrase or that particular twist on an old idiom on whoever was closest at the time, and though Tzedef did *try* to give him helpful feedback, there wasn't much that he could say. Sorecco was a good storyteller, and Tzedef... well. Tzedef was just content to listen.

Today, however, Tzedef's wandering feet took him to the temple district.

It was unusual for him to not have made his way there sooner, but between Sorecco's anxiety over the audition, and the little statuette that he kept stored safely in the pack he carried with him, Tzedef hadn't felt as though it was particularly urgent that he find a temple proper.

Now it was the last regular district of the city he had yet to set foot in, and he was starting to feel antsy. Some time meditating in a proper temple, with incense smoke in his lungs and the cool press of thick stone walls around him would help settle him, he thought.

The temple district was a large area, full of parks and green spaces, and buildings great and small.

Some of the temples were tiny, single room buildings made of wood or brick. Others were large, sprawling stone things that obviously housed not only their own dedicates, but others as well.

There was an air of calm industry to the whole district. As though everyone he passed on the streets knew where they were going, and what they were doing, but knew there was no real hurry to it. As though there was a widespread feeling that things would get done in their own time, and it was pointless to worry about it because in the end they would get done.

"*There* you are!"

The sharp, exasperated, hurried voice that caught his attention made Tzedef pause briefly, glancing around to see who might be speaking, and to whom.

The fact that the elderly cervid woman who was hurrying down the marble steps was coming toward *him* was a surprise, and she must have read it on his face because she hurried faster.

"Yes, you. Don't you go anywhere, now, I've a message for you, and you are *appallingly* late!"

Tzedef blinked, then glanced at the temple behind her— a relatively modest building made of storm grey marble and carved with various weather phenomena— before looking back down at the woman as she drew closer.

"Madam, I do not believe—"

"That sounds like a you problem." She said, briskly cutting him off, "Now. My Lady said something about a statuette? Let's see it, then."

Tzedef blinked at her again.

"I hardly think—"

"Well that's not a particularly appealing quality." She interrupted again, "But then, I can't particularly judge, now, can I. My Lady obviously sees something in you, since she's told me to give you her blessing."

Tzedef stared at the woman, baffled beyond words, and her fuzzy ears flicked irritably as she held her hand out.

"The statuette?"

"What possible reason would the Storm Queen have for offering *me* a blessing?" Tzedef asked, and was relieved when he managed to get the whole sentence out without being interrupted.

Big, dark eyes looked up at him, skepticism writ large on the woman's softly pointed face. "Do you *really* need to ask that?"

"I wouldn't have if I didn't mean to." Tzedef said flatly, a thread of irritation in his voice, and the woman scoffed.

"So you *didn't* perform ad hoc weather readings for a village without a reader over this last winter?"

Tzedef blinked a third time. "I did…" he said cautiously. That wasn't something he'd thought was particularly worthy of a blessing, though.

"You probably saved their lives." The woman said bluntly. "Many villages were decimated by the sudden turn of the weather and the severity of the storms. The fact that you used knowledge gained from one of our own to help save even *one* village… well. She can't bless you as her cleric since you're already spoken for, but she *can* give you a little something that might help you out in the future."

Tzedef nodded slowly. "I suppose I can see that, but… it seems counterintuitive. Why would she change the weather so sharply, then reward someone for preventing the loss of life that her decision would have caused?"

"She didn't change the weather!" The snap in the cervid's voice made his eyes widen, but the woman didn't seem to notice, too embroiled in her own fury. "Just because she's the goddess of the weather systems doesn't mean it's her fault when something goes screwy! It's not her fault! She didn't do it, and if you say she did then orders or not, you'll not be getting a blessing from me!"

"Very well," Tzedef said, taken aback, "but you realize that that leads to the question that if she did not change the weather, then what, or who, did? As far as I know, there is nothing natural about how quickly the weather turned, or how intense those storms were. Or how many there were."

The cervid's nose twitched, and she frowned up at him severely. "Do you want your blessing or not? I have things I need to take care of that are more important than standing out here in the sun nattering on like some old woman."

Tzedef carefully did not point out the silver streaking the fur around her nose and mouth. Instead, he swung his pack around off his shoulders and dug through the layers of clothing to find the carefully tucked away statuette of Hecate.

"Right." The deer-like woman said once it was in her hands, and she frowned down at the statuette for a moment before closing her eyes.

Her lips moved silently— in prayer, Tzedef supposed— and divine power swelled around her before flowing smoothly into the little clay statue.

For a moment the power twisted, seeming almost alive as it worked its way around the edges of Nelthys' blessing, before settling in place with a feeling very much like a soft sigh.

"There." The woman said firmly, and unceremoniously handed the statuette back to Tzedef. "Blessing delivered. Have a nice day."

Tzedef nodded and opened his mouth to thank her, only to be cut off as she turned around and marched back into her temple, hooves clicking quietly on the marble steps.

He watched her go, bemused, then glanced down at the small statue of his goddess.

It was odd, he thought, that now two gods had blessed the same statue, and not even one that was of one of them, but a statue that was of an entirely different *third* god.

Still, Hecate hadn't objected, and the two blessings hadn't seemed to conflict or do anything at all, really, so he supposed they were just there more as a symbolic thank you for his deeds rather than anything that would actually affect anything.

Much like the medals that Yaelin's king had sometimes handed out to certain soldiers, he thought with a snort of bitter amusement as he tucked the statuette back into his pack deep among his clothing.

He swung the pack back up and on, and started walking again until he reached the small building that bore the mark of the unaffiliated temples.

"At last." He murmured, and headed inside.

A few hours later he emerged into the dying sunlight

of a summer evening, the set of his shoulders relaxed, with the scent of a particularly musky incense clinging to his clothes. He had been right. Some meditation in a semi-familiar setting had been just what he'd needed.

Making his way back to the Courier's Rest didn't take long— the inn was on the same side of the city as the temple district, after all— but it did mean cutting through the noble's district to get there. It was lucky that the nobles of Wethfren, or at least those nobles who dwelt in Vraka, were more relaxed about things like that. In fact, Tzedef hadn't so much as seen a noble order a person beaten for delaying them, though he had spotted one of their carriages drawn up short by an old man who had fallen into the carriage's path, scattering his shopping everywhere.

The driver had seemed resigned, and the old man had been highly apologetic, but the whip at the driver's side had remained untouched, and the old man unscathed.

Perhaps the laws here were different. Perhaps they applied to the nobility just as much as the common folk.

Or perhaps he was reading too much in to a simple exchange that ought not be read into.

The streets grew busier as Tzedef left the area of the Noble's district; people emerging from their homes to enjoy the last light of day as the air cooled, bustling about to do shopping or meet up with friends.

And through it all, flickers of movement at the rooftops kept catching the corner of his eye.

Nothing was ever there when he turned to look properly, though, and so he tried to put it out of his mind, reaching up to rub at his amulet absently even as the relaxation he'd managed to cultivate from his meditation vanished.

By the time he reached the Courier's Rest and slipped inside he was as tense as a bowstring, his every nerve vibrating with the ruthlessly crushed desire to fight or flee.

Luckily Casey was at the bar chatting with the dwarven bartender, Kendra, and Tzedef made his way over to her.

"Oh! Tzedef! Welcome back!" Casey half turned to greet him, grinning widely, and Tzedef tensed further at the sight of the long scrape across the side of her face and the blossoming bruise around her right eye.

"What. Happened." He asked tersely, and Casey's grin turned smug.

"I punched a half-giant in the face!"

Tzedef paused.

That was. Not in the realm of responses he had expected.

"How did you *reach?*" the words slipped out of his mouth without so much as a by-your-leave, and Casey burst out laughing.

"He was all bent over to get in my face," She explained. "And he was being an asshole to one of the girls at the bar I was at, so I punched him in the face!"

Tzedef blinked, processing that.

"All... right." He said cautiously. "And that led to your face...?"

"Well he didn't like getting punched in the face, right?" Casey said matter-of-factly, "So he hit me back, and one thing led to another and I managed to get him into that wrist lock that Inral showed me back on the ship and got him out of the bar and now I've got a job!"

"As a waitress?" Tzedef asked hopefully.

"As a *bouncer!*" Casey said with no small amount of glee, and Tzedef internally despaired.

Casey turned back to Kendra, who had been watching the whole exchange with a highly amused expression on her face. "So yeah, like I was saying, I wanna celebrate! What do you recommend?"

"Well, we've got a quite nice pale ale that's just come in from the north brewery." She said, "Or there's an Asparian spirit they call Frostwine, that's pretty good. Strong, but pretty good."

Casey hummed thoughtfully, then shrugged. "I always like a nice ale, so let's go with that. Tzedef? What do you want?"

Tzedef paused for a moment, then glanced down at the dwarven woman behind the bar. "I don't suppose you have any Ruby Dragon's Breath?"

Kendra's eyebrows hit her hairline. "Now *that's* a wine! You've got expensive tastes, though. I've only got the one bottle, and you'll have to buy the whole thing if you want any."

"I assumed as much." Tzedef said, "But the price?"

She named a number that made him wince and Casey gape, and, reluctantly, he shook his head.

"I think not, then." He said regretfully, "The pale ale will do me fine, I believe."

"And a wine for Sorecco." Casey put in. "He liked that red that you served with dinner the other day, you know, the one with the elk stew?"

"I know the one you're talking about." Kendra nodded easily, "And sure. I'll have Jash bring it out to you in a few. Were you wanting an evening meal, too?"

"Please." Tzedef nodded, feeling his empty stomach twist on itself. "What do you have this evening?"

"Stew's on, as usual." She said, "And I've got some nice fowl on the spits, and potatoes slow roasting in the oven."

"Sounds great!" Casey said with a satisfied nod. "I'll take some of the bird and a bowl of the stew, please."

Kendra nodded, then looked up at Tzedef expectantly.

"I will have the same." He told her.

The bartender nodded again, and Casey leaned forward before she could turn away.

"The same as me for Sorecco, mmkay? If he wants more, he'll come get it himself."

"Alright." Kendra agreed, and turned away from the two of them to head back into the kitchen.

"Right," Casey said, looking thoroughly satisfied with herself as she turned around to survey the crowded common room. "Sorecco's over there. Let's go!"

Tzedef nodded, and followed Casey through the room until they reached the table next to the wall where

Sorecco was waiting for them.

"It's us." Casey said, pulling out the chair that would put her back to the room and sitting, leaving the one facing the front door for Tzedef.

Quietly thankful, Tzedef sent her a grateful look as he sat; finagling his tail through the gap that was left for it in the back of the chair.

"Good evening, Sorecco." He said, and Sorecco smiled crookedly.

"Hey Tzedef, welcome back. Did Casey tell you about her new job?"

"She did," Tzedef said, leaning back with a quiet sigh, "although she did not tell me where."

"It's a little place closer to The Pit." Casey said, "A student bar called the Thrush and Nightingale. I'm going to see if there's any places near-ish there that we can rent, too, so we'd be closer to the university and my work."

"That'd be good." Sorecco said, and paused when Jash came over with a tray full of food and drinks, which he distributed swiftly. "Thanks, Jash."

"Yeah." The young elebensis ducked his heavy head, and hurried away.

"But yeah, finding somewhere close to school and your work is a good idea." Sorecco continued, then hesitated, "hopefully I actually get in."

"You'll get in." Casey said confidently, "you're *good* at this, Sorecco. You really are. Little kids are *ruthless*, and you kept a whole group of 'em entertained all winter. Well enough that their parents were giving you gifts to thank you!"

"Yeah." Sorecco said, his voice tight, "yeah, it's fine. It'll be fine. I'm fine. I've got everything set up, I've got the performance memorized, it'll be *fine*."

"It will be." Tzedef agreed, and for a fair while, they each focused on their own meals.

"Okay," Sorecco said, putting down his spoon abruptly, "But what if this is a mistake? What if Cestra wasn't the dean? What if—?"

Tzedef interrupted him with a snort, "I do not think you need to worry about *that*. Not just anyone would feel as though they have the authority to reprimand the registrar, and she did. On your behalf, even."

Sorecco gulped, then nodded. "But what if—"

"You will be fine." Tzedef interrupted again, "you have practiced your performance as much as you could for the last week. If they do not grant you entry, then they are fools and you're better off without them. Do not forget, Sorecco, you have options. And if those options do not appeal, then you will travel with me and once I have found the candle magic, I will take you back to Yaelin and you may enroll in the Bardic College *there*."

Sorecco took a deep breath and steadied himself.

"Options. Right. I have options. This is fine. Everything is fine. Right."

"Everything is fine." Tzedef repeated softly. "You will be fine, regardless of the outcome."

"Right." Sorecco said again, and sighed, picked up his spoon, and worked on finishing his meal.

CHAPTER TWENTY-SEVEN

Kaz

The next morning found Sorecco fretting himself into such a state that Casey ended up sitting him down, handing him a glass of spiced wine, and standing over him until he drank the whole thing down and relaxed a little.

"Okay." He said, faux calmly, "I'm fine. I'm calm. Everything's fine. It's going to be fine."

"It will be." Tzedef agreed, "And, as I said last night, you have options. Do not forget that, Sorecco."

"Right," he agreed, and stood up, clutching his stick with both hands. "Okay, let's go."

"Ah," Tzedef said slightly awkwardly, "I will not be joining you. I must meet with Beech to finalize some of our plans. If everything is prepared, then we will be leaving in the morning."

"You're leaving so soon?" Casey asked, dismayed, and Tzedef nodded.

"My goddess has been more than patient with me, but I am still searching for the candle magic. If the

Ambered Castle lies in Reyfil Mountain as Beech says, then I must go there."

"Oh." Sorecco said softly, "I know you just met Beech, and I was there and everything, but somehow I'd forgotten that that meant you'd be leaving."

He shook himself. "Well then! Good luck with your meeting! Hopefully we'll see you tonight?"

"If possible, yes." Tzedef nodded and Casey leaned forward, catching his attention.

"You should write to us." She told him firmly. "And we'll write back to you. We're friends, and friends keep in contact, yeah? So write to us. Let us know when you find your candle magic. I'll let you know when we have a proper flat, so come back and visit any time, okay?"

Tzedef blinked at her.

That was somewhat unexpected. He'd expected that the siblings would be... not necessarily glad to be rid of him, but certainly at least somewhat relieved.

But now Casey was staring at him expectantly, and Sorecco had his head tilted slightly, birdlike. Both of them waiting on his reply.

"I suppose?" He said, somewhat baffled. "I will write. Though I do not believe that mail travels with any true regularity between Fernil and Malfeir, so if I return to Fernil, there will likely be long delays."

"That's okay." Casey said, leaning back and nodding firmly, "Who knows! Maybe one day we'll come visit you!"

"No!" The snap in Tzedef's voice made her recoil and Sorecco jump, Tzedef winced, modulating his tone.

"I... do not have a permanent residence. I tend to wander, so there would be nowhere for you to stay."

"Oh." Casey looked concerned, but on glancing at his face again, visibly decided not to ask the question at the tip of her tongue. "Okay. If you say so."

"I do." Tzedef said firmly. "I do not mind the idea of escorting either of you to specific places, but traveling around the world just for a social call is... inadvisable."

Casey nodded slowly, then glanced sideways at Sorecco. "All right. Then I guess we're on our own for your audition."

"Yes." Tzedef confirmed. "Please accept my apologies for not being able to be there."

"It's fine." Sorecco said with a slightly sickly smile. "I'll just... I'll do my best, and we'll meet up for dinner?"

"If possible, as I said. Otherwise, I will leave a message here for you. But I do not believe that Beech will wish to travel overnight, so leaving on the morrow is the most likely option."

"Great." Casey nodded, then planted her hand in the center of Sorecco's back, propelling him gently toward the door. "We have to go, or you're going to be late. Tzedef, we'll see you later!"

Tzedef nodded, his eyes lingering on Sorecco's still pale face. "Fare well."

The siblings vanished through the door, and Tzedef sighed as it swung shut behind them. He truly had intended to be there for Sorecco's audition, but his quest had to take precedence, and Beech had asked to meet up to finalize their plans.

Speaking of which; he also needed to leave, or he risked being late.

A quick check ensured that he had everything he might need on him; he hadn't really unpacked into the inn room, after all, and then he too was out the door and into the street.

The open air market that Beech had given him directions to was near the south gate, and as Tzedef made his way through Vraka's busy streets, he couldn't quite shake a vague feeling of unease.

Sorecco would be fine, and now Tzedef had to focus on his own mission. His own quest.

Beech stood out easily, towering over the surrounding crowds as she did, and Tzedef made his way across the open square to where she was waiting for him next to a neatly packed row of vegetable stalls.

"Hey there!" She grinned down at him as he drew closer, and Tzedef smiled faintly back.

"Hello. I hope I have not kept you waiting long?"

"Nope! I've only been here five minutes or so."

"Good." Tzedef nodded, then glanced around. "You wished to meet. Why?"

"Oh, right." Beech shifted on her hooves, and her upper body twisted around to where a pair of satchels were slung across her back.

A moment's rummaging gave her a slightly crumpled sheet of paper, and she turned back around to hand it to him, shifting on her hooves again.

"I wanted to make sure we had everything. I thought we could compare notes!"

Tzedef took the sheet of paper, blinking down at the carelessly scrawled list before looking back up at Beech.

"Did we not just do this yesterday? I was under the impression that that was the final check."

"We did," Beech admitted, her ears flicking nervously, "I ah… added some things?"

"You did?" Tzedef glanced down at the list again, frowning slightly as he puzzled through Beech's 'handwriting'. "What could we possibly ne—"

He stopped, staring at the list, then turned a flat look on Beech herself.

"A cart."

She shifted again, nearly prancing with nerves. "Yes, I- well, I thought that it would be easier, you know? Toss anything that won't fit into the magic bags, and your things, in the back, and then you could ride in the cart and I'd pull it. Toss a tarp over everything and it'd keep it all from getting wet if it rains or snows, and we'd be able to travel faster. No offense, but you two-leggers are slow. This way would just be easier."

Tzedef blinked. "And you're all right with that idea?"

"Sure?" She tilted her head, her ears swiveling to point towards him. "Why not? If we're going to be traveling together then it only makes sense, right?"

"I suppose…" Tzedef said slowly, and glanced down

at the list again to buy himself some time to think.

Every centaur he'd worked with before had been adamantly against pulling carts or carrying more than their own gear. Sure, they had if they'd been ordered, but for the most part, the centaur contingent had stubbornly refused to carry or haul more than 'their fair share'.

The fact that what they considered their 'fair share' to be the same amount as a smaller humanoid was a subject of much contention among the rest of the rank and file, many of whom actually did haul sledges or drive carts filled with extra supplies for the camps.

"What about food?" He asked, "You will need more than what we had spoken about if you are going to be working harder.

"Got that covered!" Beech said cheerfully, and she turned to rummage through her bags again, coming back a moment later with a jar of thumb-sized lozenges in different colors and shapes.

"Candy?" He asked, puzzled, "I fail to see how sweets will help...?"

"They aren't sweets." Beech said, grinning widely, "They're a new way of transporting and consuming rations that a friend of mine at the university has been working on developing. I talked to them yesterday after I thought about getting a cart, and they agreed to hook me up with a supply! I've got four jars like this, and Kaz swears that they'll last me a month per jar if I have two per day."

Tzedef frowned. "Will that be enough? How do they work?"

"I'm… not really sure," Beech grimaced apologetically, "but hey, if you want, I can introduce you to them? Kaz is great, and I'm sure they'd sell you some if you'd like, too. They're always looking for new testers, and new streams of income!"

Tzedef nodded. "Yes, I think I would like that. I wish to know how they work, so if there is a potential point of failure it is known about before hand and we can plan around it."

"That's completely fair!" Beech nodded, and turned to tuck the jar back into her bag before turning around entirely and starting to stride off, her gait long and smooth. "Come on, then! I'm sure they're still in their lab. They almost never leave."

Tzedef hurried after her, tucking the list into his pocket for further perusal later, just in case he'd missed anything.

Beech led him on a winding path through the city that avoided most of the main streets and they ended up in front of a slightly more worn building in the Pit, with a carved stone sign out front that proclaimed this to be the 'Varlius Memorial Research Laboratories'.

Beech snorted when he paused to look at it.

"Ignore that." She advised. "Lord Varlius is still alive and kicking. He's just weird. Still, he pours a lot of money into the research and development of new magical techniques and spells, so the University lets him get away with pretty much whatever he wants. Come on, Kaz is on the fourth floor."

Tzedef followed her into the building, past open doors with odd sounds coming out of them, and closed doors with strange smoke leaking out from under them, up three flights of wide, shallow stairs and down the hallway to a large set of double doors.

She paused for a moment, and knocked on the door.

"Kaz?" She called, "You in?"

"Depends!" A voice called back, a slight hissing overtone making the 's' just the tiniest bit sibilant. "Who's asking?"

"It's Beech! I brought a friend, you know, that guy I was telling you about?"

"Hang on!" the voice said at once, "Let me get the cauldrons covered before you come in. I don't want hair in anything!"

"Sure." Beech nodded to nothing, and settled back on her hooves, content to wait for however long it took.

After a few moments of clattering from behind the doors, the left one swung open inward to reveal a bright blue lizardfolk with lime green stripes zig-zagging wildly across their scales and bright orange eyes. The scent of roasting meat and fresh baked bread and poached fish flooding past them and out into the corridor.

"Heya Beech, Beech's friend." They nodded at Tzedef, and stepped back out of the way, "Come on in. Whatcha need?"

Beech pouted as she ducked under the lintel, pushing the right side of the door open as well to let her step carefully into the lab. "I don't only come around when

I need something!"

"No," The lizardfolk, who Tzedef assumed was Kaz, said easily, "You don't. But you do come around more often right before you head out on another pointless trip up north, so. Whatcha need?"

Beech's pout increased, and her ears drooped low. "Stop knowing me so well!" she complained, and Kaz laughed.

"No."

Beech sighed dramatically, then took a couple of steps to the side and gestured Tzedef inside. "C'mon. Nothing in here bites, I promise. Seriously, Kaz is a genius, you're going to love it."

Cautiously, Tzedef stepped into the lab, glancing around.

He half expected to see beakers and glassware and piping and tubes everywhere, full of bubbling liquids and half finished potions.

Instead, to his surprise, the scene inside made the scents that had originally escaped the room make much more sense.

It was a massive kitchen.

There were four large fireplaces along the outside wall, each with carefully lidded cauldrons sitting in, near, or above the fire.

There were two ovens, one next to the other, along the far right wall, both closed, with the scent of baking bread nearly overpowering the scent of whatever was in the cauldrons.

Two large tables were pushed together in the middle of the room, and one side had what looked like a veritable feast laid out on it, while the other had what looked like the makings of a second in the midst of being prepared.

It smelled delicious.

It looked incredible.

And it was absolutely sweltering.

"Kaz," Beech complained mildly, flapping her tunic to try to get air against her skin. "Can't you crack a window?"

"Nope." Kaz said unrepentantly, "I use less fuel this way. Sorry."

"It's fine…" Beech sighed, and gave up flapping her tunic as a bad job, glancing around instead. "Oh, did we catch you just as you were about to make another batch?"

"Mmhm." Kaz nodded, moving over toward the table with the feast on it.

"What're you testing this time?"

"Whether or not having the food actually prepared does anything to the nutritional value of the Consumable." They said promptly, "If it doesn't then you could theoretically just dump all the constituent ingredients into a pot and candy them and still get a meal."

"Oh?" Beech took several long strides after her friend, Tzedef in tow. Both of them watching with interest as Kaz lifted their hands and started to chant.

Magic welled up between their fingers, and spilled out across the table, and bit by bit, the food on the plates and platters and in the bowls and tureens shimmered, and shrank, and hardened, until all that was left was about a dozen thumb-sized lozenges, all a rich amber color.

"There." Kaz said, satisfied as they picked one up and examined it. "Perfect."

They glanced at Beech, then at Tzedef. "Are either of you hungry?"

Tzedef blinked.

"I could eat." He said cautiously, and Kaz grinned, tossing him the lozenge.

He caught it, nearly fumbling the candy in surprise, and glanced from the lozenge to the grinning lizardfolk.

"Go on," They urged, "Put it in your mouth. Don't crunch it until the last little bit. It's safe, I know that much for sure. I'm just fine-tuning the details right now."

Tzedef glanced over at Beech, who nodded encouragingly to him, and he sighed, and slipped the candy into his mouth.

The taste of venison flowed across his tongue, making his eyes widen as he sucked on the 'sweet'.

"It's not sweet." He mumbled around the lozenge, and Kaz's grin widened.

"It wouldn't be," The say, "There's no sweetener in the process of making them aside from what's in the food itself. What's it taste like?"

"Venison." Tzedef reported, then, "Potatoes, now, as well. And gravy. Roasted carrots. Honey glazed figs."

He glanced over at Kaz. "It's delicious."

His frank assessment made them beam at him, and Tzedef turned his attention back to the lozenge he was sucking, noting with no small surprise that his stomach was filling as if he were actually working his way through a regular sized meal that had each of those flavors as constituent parts.

The lozenge dissolved faster than a hard candy of the same size, and by the time it was a small, brittle disc in his mouth, he was pleasantly full.

"That is truly incredible." He said, looking over at Kaz, then at the lozenges that were scattered across the table. "You are going to revolutionize the way people travel, especially on shipboard."

"You think?" Kaz looked delighted, reaching over to start gathering up the lozenges. "Mostly I just wanted a way to store food that wouldn't let it go bad over long periods of time. These'll keep basically forever, I think, as long as you don't get them wet."

Tzedef nodded slowly. "So how does it work?"

Beech winced as Kaz lit up, launching into an excited explanation of the exact magical principles behind the spell.

From what little Tzedef could understand of the explanation, it boiled down to this: one part of the spell checked to see what the caster could safely consume. A second part checked to ensure that what was safely consumable was in range, and, if it was, activated the third part of the spell, which started the candying process. The shape and color of the resultant lozenge was determined at that point, and the caster could also influence size and flavor at that point if they so chose. Once the candying was complete, any non-consumable items in the spells range were left behind.

"I don't usually mess with the flavor." Kaz said easily, pouring the gathered lozenges into a jar and capping it tightly. "I'm a decent cook, so I don't feel like I need to, but if you're somewhere where the cooking is absolutely awful, then it works like a charm. The only problem is, if you determine the flavor yourself, then it only tastes like one thing, and I can't figure out why."

"It's a great spell anyway," Beech said cheerfully, "I'm sure you'll figure it out sooner or later!"

Tzedef, however, was stuck on something. "You used the word consumable several times in your explanation, not just 'food'. Is there a reason for that?"

Kaz grinned widely. "Yup! Because it doesn't just work on food! It works on anything the caster can safely consume! Food, water, wine, air, potions… anything!"

Tzedef stared at them, and Kaz beamed, well pleased with themself.

One spell.

This one spell would utterly revolutionize warfare. Supply lines would dwindle to a few carts at a time. Medicine would no longer have shelf lives, meaning that potions that usually required consumption immediately upon completion would be available on demand.

This was incredible.

And terrifying.

"How much would it cost to have you make me the same amount of meal lozenges that you made Beech?" He asked, red eyes intent, and Kaz cackled gleefully.

"Now we're talking!"

Tzedef and Beech left the building half an hour later with four new jars tucked carefully into his pack, wrapped in rags to keep them from banging into each other and shattering.

"That." Tzedef said, "Was well worth it. Thank you for introducing me to your friend, Beech."

Beech grinned as she tucked a small handful of translucent candies into the pouch she wore around her neck, "Kaz is great, aren't they? And it was smart to ask them to just candy the rations you already had. They'd've charged so much more if they'd've had to've cooked all that food themself."

Tzedef grimaced. As it was, the cost of the spells themselves had just about wiped out the rest of his gold. Still, with the way the spells worked, it was well worth it. It brought down the weight of his food supply by a significant amount, which meant, in turn, that he could carry more, or bring along other supplies that he hadn't bought because he didn't have the room for them. Now he did, and so, he could.

Beech glanced up at the sky as she stepped carefully down the cobbled streets of the university district.

"Looks like it's just after noon." She observed, and glanced at him. "Want to catch lunch?"

Tzedef smiled crookedly. "I just 'ate' remember? Thank you, but no. However, do you know where auditions for new bardic students might be held?"

"Auditions?" Beech paused, looking around at the buildings around them, one finger tapping her chin thoughtfully.

"Yes." Tzedef nodded. "I have a... friend auditioning today. I would like to be there, if I can, though it is likely that the audition is already over. Still, I would like to at least try."

"You'll probably want to try Tetral Hall, then." She says, and turns, pointing down a nearby side street. "It's that way, over near the administration building. Want me to show you where?"

"That would be appreciated, yes." Tzedef nodded, and Beech beckoned him to follow her.

"Come on, then!"

Tetral Hall was not, as the name suggested, a hall. Nor was it a building in the traditional sense.

No.

Tetral Hall was an amphitheater, a half circle set into the ground, with terraces serving as benches all the way down to just shy of a stage.

A young catling was standing in the center of the stage, sawing industriously away at a fiddle and somehow managing to produce sounds not unlike the wails of the damned from the poor, abused instrument.

A few people sat scattered through the terraces, many with sheaves of paper on their laps or nearby. A few of them were making notes, though, from the grimaces that

Tzedef could see from where he stood, he doubted they were complimentary.

"I don't see Sorecco anywhere," Beech murmured, and Tzedef glanced around again, then nodded.

"Nor do I. I must have missed his audition entirely."

"That's rough." She said sympathetically, and Tzedef shrugged.

"I already apologized for needing to miss it. Getting to catch even a small part would have been a pleasant surprise."

Beech blinked down at him, then shrugged her broad shoulders and turned away from the amphitheater. "Fair enough. So what did you think of the cart idea? You never actually said."

"Ah," Tzedef blinked, and, on thinking back, realized that no, he hadn't actually. "My apologies. I forgot. If you do not mind pulling a cart, then I can hardly complain about the additional space for supplies."

"Great!" Beech cheered, her ears perking up happily. "I know someone who'll lend me a cart, so all I've gotta do is head over and pick it up!"

Tzedef nodded. "Are we still planning on leaving tomorrow morning? Or would you prefer an extra day to stock up on additional supplies?"

She waved him off, her tail swishing playfully, "Don't worry, we can still leave in the morning. I'll get the cart, pack it all up, and meet you in front of your inn in the morning. You're still at the Courier's Rest, right?"

"Yes."

"Great, then I'll meet you there, say… an hour after dawn?"

Inwardly, Tzedef despaired over his lost sleep, but externally he nodded. "An hour after dawn, then. I will ensure that I am ready."

"Perfect!" She smiled, "I'll see you then, then!"

With that she turned and trotted off, her hoofbeats rapidly fading into the distance.

CHAPTER TWENTY-EIGHT

Acceptance

With nothing else to do with his afternoon, Tzedef slowly made his way out of the Pit and back to the Courier's Rest. He stopped occasionally to examine the wares of the shops he passed, but, with the majority of the shops in the Pit geared toward the students that lived, worked, and learned there, none of it was particularly interesting to him.

So it was that he arrived back at the inn just as the sun was touching the top edge of the wall to the west and the shadows were lengthening into evening.

He had to step to one side rather briskly as a pair of whip-thin lizardfolk in the courier's uniform darted out the door and up the stairs, but after that, the way seemed clear, and he ducked into the inn's main floor with a small amount of relief.

Busy though it usually was, he could generally count on not being jostled in the inn. The same couldn't be said for the streets outside, and keeping an eye on his belongings to ensure that nothing vanished into hungry pockets was exhausting after a while.

Today, however, the interior of the inn was sedate. Calm, with a low murmur of voices as the waiting couriers chatted and ate and drank with one another, and Tzedef's shoulders gradually unclenched as he looked around for Casey and Sorecco.

He didn't see either of them, and, with a slight frown, he headed for the stairs up to where the rooms were. He would check their room to see if they were there, and, if they weren't, he would make a thorough check of his own room to ensure that everything was packed away in preparation for tomorrow.

Sorecco yanked open the door at the first knock, his eyes wild, his usually neatly braided hair in disarray.

"What?" He demanded, and Tzedef blinked.

"It is I," Tzedef said cautiously, and Sorecco sagged.

"Oh good, you're back. Welcome back, by the way." And he fumbled around for a moment, then dragged Tzedef into the room by his shirt sleeve.

Tzedef blinked, but went willingly enough, and spotted Casey, perched on one of the two beds in the room.

"Just let him get it out of his system." She advised him dryly. "He's been like this since the audition."

Tzedef blinked again. "Why? Did something happen?"

"They said my performance was passé!" Sorecco proclaimed, throwing the hand holding Tzedef's sleeve up dramatically. "They said it was prosaic and banal, and that they see a hundred performances just like it every year!"

Tzedef frowned. "But… you were recounting this last winter, yes? And the drama with Lucas and Mary? How could they have heard stories like that a hundred times before?"

"I don't know!" Sorecco cried, turning and stalking a few steps away from Tzedef and then running into the other bed.

Swearing, Sorecco moved slightly until he had positioned himself in the aisle between the two beds, then pointed imperiously at the bed he'd just run into.

"Sit down. I need to pace."

Tzedef glanced at Casey, who shrugged, an amused half smile on her face, and gestured for him to do as he pleased.

Tzedef sat, and Sorecco started to pace.

"I did everything right! I kept cadence through the whole thing, I stayed in tune, I *know* they were interested, I could *feel* it! It was a good tale! *I wrote a good tale, dammit!*"

Tzedef frowned, "Does this mean you were not accepted?"

"Oh no," Sorecco waved that fear away. "I got in alright, they told me that straight off. Apparently I 'have potential'. And then they ripped my performance to shreds! I was pitchy when I sang about Nelthys, and in the fourth stanza my rhyme scheme was a syllable off, and I should have had accompaniment- even just a drum would have worked, *apparently.*"

Sorecco paused, his chest heaving, a flush of anger

high on his cheekbones.

"Overall, they said, it 'needs work' but they 'have faith that in time I will be a credit to their institution.' BAH!" Sorecco shouted, making Tzedef's eyes widen. "Screw their institution! And screw them!"

"Does… that mean you do not wish to attend school here?" Tzedef asked cautiously, and Sorecco swung around to point at him.

"Absolutely *not!*" he declared, "I am going to take their precious 'institution' and shove it so far up their overly polished behinds that they'll be able to *taste* my skill!"

"Not likely," Casey interjected dryly, and Sorecco turned on her, his mouth open indignantly. But Casey kept going. "Their heads are so far up there that the institution wouldn't fit."

Sorecco paused, then let out a rough bark of laughter and sat down abruptly, landing with a thwump next to Tzedef.

"You're not wrong." He said wryly, and abruptly, it seemed as though all the energy had gone out of him. "Ancestors, that— *Those—!*"

"Extremely well educated people that are going to be in charge of your future for the next few years?" Casey suggested, and Sorecco sagged, slumping sideways to lean on Tzedef's shoulder.

"Yeah." He admitted. "Them. Ugh."

"Perhaps it is another part of the audition?" Tzedef theorized, trying not to jostle Sorecco as he spoke, "To see if one can handle criticism, whether deserved or not? After all, one's audiences are not always going to be agreeable, correct?"

Sorecco's nose wrinkled. "You might be right. That'd be just like them, wouldn't it? Tests inside of tests inside of tests… This school is going to be a nightmare, isn't it."

Oddly enough, he sounded happy about that.

"Possibly." Tzedef agreed. "But I am sure you are up to the task."

"Of course I am!" Sorecco sat up straight again, leaving Tzedef's arm cold as he stretched. "I'm Sorecco, after all!"

"Sure." Casey agreed, smiling fondly at her brother. "Now that you've got all that out of your system, do you want to eat? We still need to celebrate your acceptance."

"Right!" Sorecco realized, and grinned, "Yeah, that'd be great!"

Dinner was a raucous affair, with Sorecco performing snatches of his much lambasted tale and getting progressively more drunk as the other patrons of the tavern plied the nascent bard with glass after glass of wine.

Not all of the laughter was good natured when Sorecco stumbled over this table leg or that outstretched foot, and Tzedef turned cold red eyes on those that laughed loudest and longest.

Eventually, however, Sorecco found his way back over to Tzedef's table and fumbled his way into the chair across the table from him, beaming and bright-faced.

"You are in good spirits." Tzedef observed, and Sorecco's grin widened.

"I *am!*"

"It is a relief, then? Knowing that you are accepted at the College?"

Sorecco nodded vigorously. "Very much so! I didn't realize how much I was worrying about it until I just… *stopped*. This… all of this has been unbelievable. First you show up, and then we're moving, and then that *winter*, and now I'm *here*, and I'm finally- I can go to the college. *I'm going to the Bardic College!*"

Tzedef winced at the joyous whoop, and the cheer that rose up to follow it, but smiled nonetheless.

"But you." Sorecco said heavily, suddenly serious as hc leaned on the table and stared somewhere to the right of Tzedef's head. "You, my *friend*. This is all because of you. Everything- everything that's happened, it's all because of *you*! And you still haven't found your castle of amber. You haven't found your- your candle magic, yet. Have you?" He asked, looking suddenly worried that Tzedef might have found the candle magic and simply not told them.

"I have not." Tzedef assured him. "I leave in the morning to seek it, remember?"

"I remember!" Sorecco sounded almost offended, then dropped his voice and leaned closer. "I'm not actually *quite* as drunk as I seem. But drinking seemingly endless amounts of wine without any ill effects the next day is, supposedly, a skill one must have if one is to be any sort of *proper* bard, so."

He grinned and sat back in his chair, and Tzedef observed him, somewhat impressed.

"I see." Tzedef allowed his voice to warm slightly, hoping it would betray his admiration to the man across from him before he continued to speak. "But returning to the subject at hand, yes. I will be leaving in the morning."

Sorecco frowned, tapping at the tabletop with one finger.

"Did you know," he said slowly, "that the university doesn't officially begin offering classes until the month of Honor?"

Tzedef hadn't, and he frowned slightly, wondering where Sorecco was going with this.

"That's five months from now." Sorecco continued thoughtfully. "And while the university offers project space and things for established students, for the most part the dean said that they expect the bardic students to go out into the world and apply what they've learned. I'm a new student, so I can't really do that, either."

Comprehension slowly dawned on Tzedef, and his eyes widened slightly.

Five months. That would be two hundred ten days.

Beech said that it would take two months on the absolute outside to get up to Reyfil Mountain, and that was *if* everything went wrong.

Two months there, two months back, and a full month to just… do whatever struck their fancy in the mean time.

"You cannot seriously be thinking of accompanying me to Reyfil Mountain." Tzedef said incredulously, and Sorecco cocked his head, curious.

"Why not?" He paused for a moment, then continued before Tzedef could answer. "No, really, why not? I don't have anything to do. I don't *need* to be here until Honor, and it's not like there's job opportunities thick on the ground for a man like me. This, at least, would be *interesting*. And it would give me fresh material for tales and songs. First hand material, too, which is always best."

Tzedef stared at him. "But…" his voice failed him, and he fumbled for words, searching for anything that could make the man in front of him see sense.

"You don't have supplies. Beech and I are going north, and although it is summer it will be significantly colder than either you or I are accustomed to. You would need new clothing, more rations, a thicker bedroll, better boots…"

Tzedef trailed off, his mind whirling with all the ways that taking Sorecco along would be difficult even as a goodly portion of him was countering his objections as soon as he raised them.

"I have warm clothes from this last winter." Sorecco countered calmly, with an odd half smile on his face. "Amarie, Lynn, and Tabitha were more than eager to see everyone clad in the warmest clothing they could manage. I believe even some of your own kit came from them."

That much was true, and Tzedef's tail twitched with the reminder.

"Rations and a bedroll can be bought easily enough," Sorecco continued, "either tonight or tomorrow morning. Plus, I heard about a cobbler-enchanter that sells magic boots that size themselves automatically and keep your feet the perfect temperature. Those would be a good purchase for me regardless of if I go with you or not."

"I—" Tzedef started, and snapped his mouth shut as Casey careened over, bouncing off someone else before coming to a halt and flinging herself into one of the remaining empty seats at the table. Somehow, through all of that, she avoided spilling from either of the two wooden mugs she carried.

"Hey! It's Casey, here to save you two gloomy guts from yourselves!" She chirped, depositing the mugs in front of each of them. "Sorecco, you're missing your party! Center right, by the way. I gotcha a light ale."

"I'm just taking a break," Sorecco informed her, one hand questing for the mug. "And talking to Tzedef about what I'm going to do with my break before classes."

"Oh?" She cocked her head, curious. "Did you finally decide on something? I still think you could at least apply to the Weaver's Guild. Your yarn is definitely good enough for journeyman."

Sorecco sighed. "No, Case, I told you. I don't want to bother with Guild garbage when I'm trying to go to classes and everything."

Casey frowned, and Tzedef took a drink of his ale, halfway hoping that the mug would protect him from Casey's wrath.

"Alright, so… what do you want to do, then?"

"I'm going to go with Tzedef up to Aspari."

"The hell you are!"

Casey's shriek cut through the cheerful chatter and for a moment, a ringing silence filled the common room.

Casey was too busy staring at Sorecco with wide, terrified eyes to notice that everyone in the place was either staring at her, or craning their necks, trying to see what everyone else was looking at.

Tzedef put his mug back down with a small thunk, and swept his eyes around the room, meeting curious eyes with his own flat, disinterested gaze.

Only a few met his eyes for longer than a moment.

Bit by bit, sound returned to the common room, and the people around their table returned to their own conversations and occupations.

Only once the room was *almost* back to its previous volume did Sorecco respond.

"That's not up to you."

Casey's eyes flicked over to Tzedef, and when she spoke it was in an almost reptilian hiss.

"Tell him he's not going. Tell him you won't take him."

Tzedef shifted uncomfortably.

"I…" He started, and then stopped again, doing his best to choose his words carefully. "I cannot, in any meaningful way, stop him from going. Whether it is with myself and Beech, or with a caravan, or even on his own. Sorecco is his own man, and he will do as he pleases."

The half surprised smile that curled Sorecco's lips made Casey growl in frustration, then huff bitterly.

"Fine. *Fine.* I'll just... I'll let Victor know that I quit, and I'll go get packed, and—"

"Casey, no!" Sorecco said, alarmed for the first time, and Casey glared at him, a hint of furious tears in her eyes.

"What? You think I'm going to let you go off to fucking *Aspari* on your own!? We've already waltzed across a third of the continent. Why *not* go to the Frozen fucking North while we're at it!?"

"Casey," Sorecco tried again, "you were so happy about that job! You can't just quit! And weren't you talking about looking for apartments soon?"

"Yeah!" Casey snapped, *"With you!* Because we were going to live in one *together!"*

"We still *are.*" Sorecco protested, "I just want to go on a bit of a trip. I want to experience more! I want to get more first hand knowledge. More first hand adventures! Things I can turn into tales and songs!"

"And what if those adventures you want mean you don't come home?" Casey said quietly, her voice vicious. "What then? You'll be dead somewhere up in the Frozen North and I'll be none the wiser, just waiting for you to come home day, after day, after *day.*"

Sorecco flinched, and let go of his mug, his hands curling into fists on the table.

"You say that as though I would permit that to happen." Tzedef said mildly, "Or that Beech would."

"I don't think you'd *let* it happen." Casey admitted

heavily, wiping at her eyes before turning to look at Tzedef. "But you're not a god. You can't prevent everything."

Tzedef nodded slowly, then spread his hands. "But I can promise you that Beech is experienced with this route, and you *know* I am a competent guard, and Sorecco himself is not helpless. Indeed, his Gift alone renders us most unlikely to be ambushed along the way."

Casey hesitated. Wavered.

"Casey." Sorecco said quietly, "I'll be okay. You don't need to worry about me. Stay here. Find an apartment. Keep your job. Please. I want... I *need* this. I'll be back before the end of fall, so just... please."

She broke.

"Fine. Go. You're right. I can't stop you. And you're going to need someplace to come *back* to when you're done gallivanting across half of Malfeir. But you'd better come back with stories!" Casey said, her voice harsh, "And presents! And- and a *girlfriend*! I can't always be the one corralling you, y'know?"

Sorecco choked, and Tzedef eyed Casey with something akin to alarm.

"Casey, that's a bit much!" Sorecco protested, and Casey shook her head, folding her arms stubbornly.

"Nope, I mean it. If you're going to be traveling, then you need someone around to watch your back. If you won't let me do it, then I want you to find someone who you will, got it?"

Sorecco groaned softly, and slumped. "All right. I'll look. But no guarantees that I'll come home with someone, all right? I still want to focus on school once I get back!"

"Deal." Casey said, nodding firmly.

Dawn came rather more quickly than Tzedef would have preferred, but, aside from a few things that could be gotten on the way out of the city, Sorecco was ready to accompany Beech and him on their way to Reyfil Mountain.

Beech looked somewhat surprised to see three of them waiting for her when she clopped up to the inn as the sun crested the horizon, but took it relatively well when Sorecco informed her that he wanted to travel with them as well.

"I don't mind," She agreed easily, "But are you sure you've got everything you need? There aren't a lot of places to restock on the way up there. Aspari's pretty barren."

"I still need to pick up a couple things on the way out of the city." Sorecco admitted, "But it shouldn't take long, as long as I'm willing to take what people have in stock."

"Alright," Beech shrugged, "if you're sure, then toss your stuff into the cart and let's get going."

Sorecco tapped his staff and listened to the chime of his bell before slinging his bag into the cart that Beech was harnessed to. It thumped loudly on the floor, and he smiled, satisfied, before yipping softly in surprise as Casey pulled him around to face her.

"Be careful." Casey said, tugging her brother into a fierce hug. "Don't do anything stupid, okay?"

"I won't." Sorecco promised, hugging her back as

Tzedef stood awkwardly off to one side. "I'll see you in the fall, alright, Case?"

"Alright." She muttered, and squeezed once more before letting him go and stepping back. "I love you."

"Love you, too." Sorecco said, smiling fondly. "Be safe, Casey."

"I will." She promised, and watched as Sorecco tapped his stick on the ground, making his bell chime before heading over to Tzedef and slipping his hand into the crook of his elbow.

"Fare well, Casey." Tzedef inclined his head at her, and got a nod back in return.

"You too, Tzedef. Take care of my baby brother, okay?"

"I will do my best."

"Good. Travel safe."

Tzedef inclined his head again, then turned toward Beech and made a sort of 'after you' gesture that made her laugh and shift in place with much creaking of the leather harness that attached the cart to her.

"Off we go, then!" She grinned, and, with a small grunt of effort, started down the street at a walking pace, the cart clattering on the cobbles behind her.

Sorecco winced at the noise, but firmed his expression and his grip on Tzedef's elbow, and the two of them followed.

They made three stops on the way through Vraka to the north gate, each time pausing for a short while to allow

Sorecco to enter a shop and make whatever purchases he needed to.

The last stop was the cobbler-enchanter, and Sorecco came out wearing his new boots with a happy spring in his step.

"That's the last stop." He said, reaching into the cart and searching for his bag.

Tzedef glanced over and pushed the bag into his hand.

"Ah, thanks." He said absently, opening it and stuffing his old boots in before flipping the top closed.

"So we're good to go, then?" Beech asked, twisting around to look at Tzedef and Sorecco, who nodded.

"Yup. I'm pretty sure I've got everything that I need to survive a trip up through Aspari."

"Good!" Beech said, and turned back around to start forward again. "Because after this next block or two, we're in the walled fields, and there's no more shops."

"The walled fields?" Sorecco asked, keeping one hand on the cart so that he could keep pace with it as the streets filled with people.

Tzedef fell in on the other side of the cart, listening intently as Beech explained.

"Oh, okay, so originally the city was a lot smaller, you know? Just a couple of temples, the beginnings of the university, and a bunch of houses. So the walls were a lot smaller, and there were farms and things outside the walls. As the city got bigger, though, the walls needed to be moved. So we moved 'em. Bought up a bunch of the farms, cleared more of the forest around for new farms, and built new walls. But the city kept growing, and so we needed new walls again. So we did the same thing, bought up the farms, cleared more land, and moved the walls. The last couple of times we moved the walls, though, we didn't tear down all the farmland that ended up inside the new walls. So there's still farmland and orchards and stuff inside the walls. We call 'em the walled fields."

Tzedef arched one eyebrow ridge. "Interesting."

"Mmhm." She nodded. "They actually take up most of the north-western third of the city. We'll be cutting through a narrow bit to get to the gate."

Sure enough, a couple of blocks later the buildings fell away abruptly to reveal large, flat fields full of greenery that rustled in the early summer breeze. In the distance, maybe a quarter of a mile away, Tzedef could see the gate. Dotting the road between it and them were various carts and people, some heading for the gate, others heading toward the city proper, and still others angling away from the road to take what Tzedef assumed were other, smaller roads through the fields.

His guess was borne out when they passed a small turnout that led to a narrow dirt road that stretched into the distance through the field.

Beech and Sorecco kept up a lively stream of chatter as they headed toward the gate- one which Tzedef listened to with idle enjoyment as they spoke about, apparently, anything that popped into their heads.

Passing through the gate was as easy as waving at

the guard in the guardhouse, and without any fanfare whatsoever the three of them were on their way to Aspari.

CHAPTER TWENTY-NINE

The Dwarves of Reyfil Mountain

Traveling with Beech and Sorecco went surprisingly well. Both of them were pleasant company, and they kept each other entertained more often than not, allowing Tzedef to simply listen to the conversation and throw his two copper in as he pleased.

But he was not allowed to remain in the background forever.

"So Tzedef." Beech said comfortably one evening, laying by the fire and running her hands through her hair. Her magic twitched across her skin in a ripple of blue-green fire that left her coat gleaming, clean of the day's road dust.

"Hmm?" Tzedef glanced up at her from where he was securing the cart.

"What's your story?" She asked, then winced and frowned, working her fingers through the knot she'd hit in her hair. "I mean, sure, you're looking for candle magic at the Ambered Castle, I get that, you've said, after all, but what's your story? Where're you from?"

Distantly, Tzedef was aware of Sorecco perking up and turning in his direction.

He had been lucky in that Sorecco and Casey had been perfectly content not to pry into his background as they had traveled together. Apparently, Beech was not anywhere near as satisfied with allowing him his privacy.

Tzedef sighed, finished shoving the block into place, and stood up straight.

"Why do you wish to know?" He asked evenly, doing his best to ignore the way his tail twitched with badly hidden agitation.

Beech shrugged. "I figure, if we're gonna be stuck together for the next while on the way up there, it'd be nice to get to know you a little bit, you know?"

She... had a point. Tzedef admitted to himself reluctantly, and glanced over at Sorecco, who was industriously making sure that his own bedroll was perfectly placed.

Tzedef sighed again and settled next to the fire.

"I am from a city called Yaelin, which is the capital of a small country that is also called Yaelin. And yes, it does, occasionally, get confusing." He cracked a small smile as Beech snorted.

"That sounds familiar... it's over on Fernil, right?" She asked, and Tzedef nodded.

"On the western side of the continent, yes."

"Wait," Sorecco said, frowning, "if it's on the western side, then why didn't you just take a boat from there over to Lowast and come to Malfeir that way?"

"Because I didn't know I was coming to Malfeir in the first place." Tzedef said mildly, "and then because I was already in the area of Hagenia and it seemed easier to take a ship from there."

"Ah," Sorecco grinned sheepishly, "Yeah, that'd do it."

Beech, however, was frowning thoughtfully. "Yaelin, Yaelin... I know the name from somewhere, but what...? Oh!"

She clapped her hands loudly, making Sorecco jump. "Jade! Yaelin trades in some of the best jade in the world! Wow, you're really lucky."

Tzedef snorted. "It isn't as though I in particular had any dealings with jade. No. I was a mere military medic."

Beech snorted disbelievingly. "Pull the other one, it's got bells. There's no way some random military medic talks like you. No way, no how."

Tzedef grimaced. Caught.

"I was merely a military medic." He said again, and continued slowly. "But before that, I was Tzedef Evelotae DeLansere, the second child of Lady Yenlari DeLansere and Lord Teromestalrex DeLansere."

Beech blinked at him, then grimaced sympathetically. "Dragon father?"

Tzedef startled. "Yes, how did you know?"

"Only a dragon could manage to sound that officious with just their name."

Sorecco burst out laughing.

For a moment Tzedef stared at her, then a snicker escaped him, and before he knew it, he was laughing too.

When they finally wound down, Beech was grinning at him unrepentantly.

"So, you were the spare, then." She said. "How come you ended up in the military, then? Don't nobs usually keep their heirs and the spares close to hand?"

Tzedef shrugged. "Possibly, but the Lord and Lady's marriage was a marriage of convenience. Both were particularly powerful mages in their own right, and desired offspring that were equally, if not more, powerful. My older brother was a success, and became the Lady's heir, but the Lord still desired his own heir."

"Oh no..." Sorecco breathed, looking horrified, and Tzedef smiled grimly.

"Just so. My sister is a particularly gifted Luminologist, and became the Lord's heir. Meanwhile, I was sent to the military to bring what little honor I could to the family name."

"But you're a cleric!" Sorecco protested, and Beech made an interested noise. "A *good* cleric!"

"Yes." Tzedef said gently, "And therein lies the problem. I am a cleric. My power comes not from myself, but from someone else. To the Lord and Lady, that makes me no better than a leech. A bottom feeder, subsisting on the scraps others deign to give me. They could not bear the 'dishonor', and so I was cast out. Now I am merely Tzedef, the ex-battlefield medic."

For a long moment, there was no sound but the crackling of the fire and slowly fading birdsong in the summer twilight. Then Beech stirred.

"Well that sucks. Anyone ever tell you that your parents are assholes?"

Sorecco burst out laughing again, and Tzedef's muzzle twitched as he suppressed a smile.

"The fact has been brought to my attention, yes, though never quite so bluntly."

"Well they are." She said firmly, and reached out to poke the fire with a stick.

"What about you, then?" Sorecco asked, tilting his head curiously. "You're basically obsessed with getting in to see the Ambered Castle, right? Why? What's the big deal about it?"

"Well," Beech said, resettling herself comfortably, "you know I'm a geologist, right?"

"No." Tzedef and Sorecco chorused in unison, and she startled.

"No?"

"You had not actually mentioned what your particular field of study was until just now." Tzedef told her, privately enjoying the look of chagrin on her face.

"Oh. But I was talking about grants and research papers and all that and…" she trailed off, looking bewildered. "Why didn't you ask?"

"I assumed that, had you wanted me to know, you would have told me." Tzedef said calmly. "It hadn't occurred to me that you thought you already had."

"Oh." She said again, looking nonplussed. "Well… I mean… I'm a geologist."

"Alright." Sorecco said with a shrug. "So what's a geologist so interested in amber for? Isn't that from trees?"

"Technically yes, but also no." Beech informed him. "Originally, yes. It's tree sap. Except then it sits in one place for a ridiculously long time, and gets buried, and it goes from sap or resin, to amber. And I'm interested in this particular deposit of amber because it's impossible."

Tzedef blinked at Beech. "Impossible how?"

"Well, there's a couple of reasons." She said, and started ticking them off on her fingers. "First, there's no trees that grow up that far north. Granted, the weather witches that like to study the distant past say that there were, in fact, trees up there way back when, when it was warmer. That might make that point null, but then there's the fact that the Ambered Castle is in a freaking volcano. Not on. In. Anything organic would have been incinerated while it was building itself, not fossilized."

"Alright…" Tzedef said slowly, considering all of that as Beech took a deep breath.

"Thirdly, there's the fact that the Ambered Castle is not hyperbole. It is a large chunk of a literal castle, trapped in a substance that, to the naked eye, looks like amber. There's no tree on Chaelu that could give off that much sap, and the chance of it all fossilizing properly is slim to basically none."

Beech holds up a fourth finger. "And then there's the fact that the amber is magic."

"Magic how?" Sorecco asked, leaning forward interestedly. He tched impatiently as his braid fell forward over his shoulder, and tossed it back. "What does it do?"

"I don't know." Beech said, her voice thick with frustration. "The dwarves won't say, and they don't let anyone without a pass close enough to examine it, and they wouldn't even give me a sample last time I was up there. I mean," She added, gesturing widely with her hands, "the stuff glows! Brightly enough that it's a visible light source down in the City proper! It's obviously magical, but Shadows forbid that anyone get an idea of what it's actually capable of! No! That's asking too much!"

She huffed, crossing her arms in front of herself and scowling.

"Does it perhaps have some kind of religious or cultural significance?" Tzedef asked. "Something that would prevent the dwarves from allowing outsiders near?"

"Not any more than the rest of the mountain does, I think." Beech said sulkily, and Sorecco cocked his head to the side.

"How do you mean?"

"Well all of Reyfil is sacred to the dwarves, isn't it?" Beech said matter-of-factly. "So it stands to reason that the ambered castle wouldn't be any more or less sacred than any other part of the mountain, right?"

Tzedef blinked. "Go back to the part about the mountain being sacred?" he requested, and Sorecco chimed in eagerly.

"Yeah, that sounds like a story worth hearing!"

Beech arched an eyebrow, glancing between the two of them. "You actually want to hear…? Okay. Alright then. Sure, why not."

A long long time ago, before humans started writing everything down and the gnomes rose out of the earth, the dwarves were a prosperous, plentiful people. Every mountain in the land held a dwarven kingdom, and dwarven crafts ruled supreme.

But there was a problem.

The dwarven people were too prosperous. Too numerous. They were running out of space in their strongholds, and metals to work with, and gems to mine and craft with.

And so it was that it was decided that the dwarves would split up and explore the rest of the world. Three clans would go south, three would go north, three east, and three west. Thus would the clans that remained have more space, and the ones that went would (hopefully) have new veins to uncover.

The clans that went to the far, frozen, north discovered a land bridge, a strip of land that crossed the sea, and they ended up in what seemed to be an endless wasteland of ice and snow. Their supplies were dwindling. They didn't have enough to turn and go back, so all they could do was keep Ibris at their backs and try to make their way south in the hopes of finding warmer, more plentiful land.

But it wasn't to be. They walked for weeks, and their supplies dwindled further and further until finally, distraught, they called upon the gods for help. One god heard their plea and was so moved by their tenacity that he reached down and formed a mountain of fire in the land of ice. This place, he told the dwarves was for them and them alone. A new home full of the riches of the earth and warmed by molten rock, it would supply them with all they would need to live.

And so it came to pass that the three wandering dwarven clans became the dwarves of Reyfil Mountain.

"Granted," Beech added, "they've really relaxed the 'no non-dwarves in the mountain' bit in the last few centuries, I've heard. Apparently it used to be that anyone who wasn't a dwarf had to conduct their business outside the mountain. Honestly, I believe it. There's a town set up basically on Reyfil's front doorstep, and it's been there a good long while. Still, the King's authority stops where the mountain does, so Reyfilton is full of a lot of outcasts, or people that've been denied access to the mountain for one reason or another."

Huh… Tzedef sat back, gazing into the fire and thinking. That may or may not make things harder. If the mountain really was sacred, and they refused access to the ambered castle for any reason, then he would have a nearly impossible time finding the candle magic that Hecate had told him lay within.

Maybe he could ask for an exception on religious grounds? But that wasn't too likely to work. It wasn't as though he would look too favorably on someone coming up to him and asking for access to a spiritually significant place or artifact because a different god told them that something important was therein.

Sorecco's voice jolted him out of his racing thoughts, and Tzedef turned his attention back to the conversation just in time to hear Beech make a bawdy joke that had Sorecco curled up in stitches on his bedroll. Apparently they had moved on from the ambered castle while he'd been thinking.

The conversation wandered for a while more, until the sun was fully down and the only light was provided by the fire and the moons in the sky. Only then did Tzedef lay down his alarm ward and Sorecco climb into his bedroll as Beech tossed a blanket over her lower half and wrapped a thick cloak around her upper half.

"We'll find a way to get you both to the ambered castle." Sorecco promised sleepily. "There's a way. We just have to find it."

CHAPTER THIRTY

The Thorn Vine

The next week or so went surprisingly smoothly. Tzedef found himself chiming into the conversations more, and found, to his quiet pleasure, that his additions were welcome, even if they did occasionally mean that he received some small amount of teasing from Beech or Sorecco. Usually about his overly formal mode of speech.

Still, it seemed to be meant in good humor, and so Tzedef paid no mind to it.

"—I still think that if she were going to marry anyone she should have married the crane." Sorecco said, his bell chiming with each step as they walked, "Crane wives are notoriously loyal. But noooo, had to go with the tailor who got her cursed in the first place. Did she just forget about that? Did he enchant her? Seriously, what's the deal with that?"

Beech laughed, then paused for a split second, her ears perking up and swiveling to face forward, where the road curved sharply behind some trees.

Tzedef's ears perked as well, and his eyes narrowed at the sound of grumbling and the creak of leather.

The bell chimed again, and Sorecco frowned, his grip on his stick tightening.

All three of them were rather tense when a pair of men dressed in leather armor came around the corner, scowling and grumbling to each other.

As soon as they saw Tzedef and his group, the one on the right snorted and called out to them. "You might as well go back to the last turn off. This road's blocked."

"Blocked?" Beech blinked, slowing gradually to let the cart come to a halt. "Blocked how?"

"There's a fuckoff big hedge in the way." The man on the left said looking mightily irritated. "Got thorns the size of knives, it do, and the damn thing grows back bigger and meaner if ya try to cut it down."

"Reckon the folks on the other side've been at it for a solid week." The first man grumbled. "It's gotta be at least twenty yards thick by now."

His traveling companion nodded emphatically, "So yeah, there's no getting to Girtwood through here. We're heading back to the crossroads at Eifale, ourselves. It'll take a fuck load longer to get up to Oprenway, but what can you do? The thing's like to be there until some druid or something can convince it to move, or someone finds something that'll kill it."

Beech frowned, glancing around. "There's nowhere to turn around, here, the road's too narrow. Is there a spot up ahead? I don't want to walk the four miles back to where we last camped backwards if I can help it."

"Eh…" The man on the left grimaced, trying to recall. "Maybe? Dunno. I wasn't paying attention. Anyway, good luck to you folks, you're like to need it."

With that ever-so-helpful admonishment, the two men fell into line with one another and headed past Beech and the cart, then down the road back toward Eifale.

Tzedef glanced up at Beech, then over at Sorecco, both of whom were frowning.

"We may as well continue onwards and see if there is a place to turn." He said after a moment. "Perhaps the hedge is not quite so bad as they thought?"

"If it wasn't that bad, they'd've gone around. The forest in these parts isn't that thick." Beech pointed out, and sighed, dragging the cart forward again until the wheels started rolling slowly. "Still, we might as well check. Sorecco? Everything okay?"

"Hmm?" Sorecco shook himself slightly, then nodded. "Oh, yes. I'm fine. I was just wondering what sort of vine would have thorns the size of knives and grow as quickly as they were saying."

"A magical one, I would assume." Tzedef said dryly, and sighed. "Sometimes I wonder if casters have more power than sense. Blocking off a main road like this is a serious problem."

"Probably." Beech agreed, "And yeah, if they figure out whoever blocked off this road, they're probably gonna be in a decent bit of trouble, but that's a pretty big if. Those guys said the road's been blocked for a week? The caster's probably long gone."

Tzedef sighed again, and fell in beside the cart, the fingertips of one hand resting on his amulet while his other hand rested on his mace.

There wasn't anything there when they rounded the corner, but Tzedef could see a splotch of green on the road in the distance.

"It looks as though the hedge is quite a bit further ahead than we thought." He observed, and glanced around. "No turnarounds here, though. Shall we continue onwards? I would like to get a look at it, if neither of you mind."

Beech shrugged. "I don't mind if you and Sorecco don't mind."

"I don't mind." Sorecco said after a moment's silence, and that seemed to be that.

Tzedef stared blankly at the hedge.

The hedge, not having eyes, refused to meet his gaze.

"I don't think you can actually call this a hedge…" Beech said slowly, and Sorecco frowned, tapping his stick on the ground to get a better idea of what she and Tzedef were looking at.

The 'hedge' was a fifteen foot tall, impenetrable monstrosity that stretched not only across the road, but into the forest on either side of the road and out of sight.

"No." Tzedef agreed, watching the thorns on the slowly shifting vines warily. "I believe this qualifies more as a natural disaster."

He frowned, his ears flicking as something caught his attention from the other side of the hedge.

Faint, muffled, swearing.

"You hear that?" Beech asked, her ears swiveling, and Tzedef nodded.

"Hear what?" Sorecco asked, cocking his head to one side.

"There are people on the other side of the hedge." Tzedef informed him. "One person, at least."

"Oh." Sorecco said, "The people that those guys mentioned, maybe?"

"Most likely." Tzedef nodded, and Beech frowned.

"They said that the people on the other side had been at this for a solid week. You'd think they'd have figured out some way to keep the hedge from growing back... or at least they'd've stopped cutting at it..."

Tzedef shrugged, reaching out to prod at one thick vine between the thorns.

Nothing happened when he touched it, and so, more boldly, he ran his fingers along the woody stem.

"OI!" Beech bellowed, and Tzedef and Sorecco both jumped, Sorecco dropping his stick with a clatter of his bell against the ground.

Tzedef turned to glare at the woman, only to find her paying absolutely zero attention to either of her traveling companions.

"OI!" She shouted again, "You! On the other side! What the hells is going on!?"

The muffled swearing got louder for a moment, then stopped, and a moment later a man's voice shouted back.

"Bitch of an 'edge-witch cursed the road!"

"What?"

"Bitch of an 'edge-witch cursed the road!" The man bellowed, and Beech frowned.

"Why!?"

"Bitch slept with my daughter!" the man shouted back, "I took 'er in and fed and 'oused 'er, and she defiled my girl!"

Beech snorted, a wry grin on her face. "So he went to chase the hedge-witch off, and the witch panicked and, well... grew a hedge. Poor thing."

"Indeed." Tzedef said, and reached out to touch one of the vines again. "Well, they don't seem to be inherently magical."

"They've gotta be at least a little." Beech contradicted him. "Or else they wouldn't grow back so quickly or so thick."

"True." Tzedef admitted, and glanced at the vine he was touching, which, unlike the vines around it, was perfectly still. "Some sort of conditional magic, then?"

Beech shrugged. "I wouldn't know. I'm not a spell researcher or anything, remember? I'm a geologist."

"Right." Tzedef sighed. "Sorecco? Can your Gift give us any idea of how thick the hedge is, now?"

Sorecco straightened up, his grip on his stick shifting slightly. "Maybe? It depends on how thick it is, I think. If the sound can't travel very far..."

"Understood." Tzedef nodded. "Please try?"

"Sure."

Sorecco tapped his stick on the ground, and his bell chimed once.

He frowned, and tapped again.

And again.

"Well…" he said slowly, "there's good news and bad news."

"What is the bad news?" Tzedef asked wearily.

"Well," Sorecco said. "First of all, the guy on the other side? Still trying to cut down the hedge. He's got a scythe and everything, and I think he's making it mad."

"The scythe?" Beech asked, a faint note of morbid curiosity in her voice, and Sorecco shook his head.

"The hedge."

Tzedef frowned.

"One would think," He drawled, "that spending a week repeating the same actions and getting the same results would discourage one from continuing to repeat the same actions."

Beech snickered. "Yeah… some people are too stupidly stubborn for their own good."

"Yuuuup." Sorecco agreed, then tapped his stick again. "Do you want the good news now?"

"Sure." Beech said, turning her upper body towards him.

"The good news is that my Gift can reach to the other side of the hedge!"

"Great!" Beech grinned, "How far is it?"

Sorecco hummed thoughtfully, turning in a slow circle with his bell chiming, then pausing. "From about here to that tree."

He pointed at a tree about thirty yards away, and Beech grimaced.

"Great. So we can't just set it on fire and hope it burns a path through quickly enough for us to get through."

"No…" Tzedef murmured thoughtfully. "No, that wouldn't work anyway. We would have to douse the flames to get through. Beech? May I borrow your knife? I wish to see how quickly these grow back."

"Sure." Beech shrugged, and handed over a knife that was, even to Tzedef, more like a short sword.

For a moment, Tzedef eyed the hedge, looking for some place he would be able to cut without running the risk of being impaled on the thorns should the vines grow back more quickly than he thought they would.

Two quick cuts with the blade severed one of the vines, and, for a moment, nothing happened. Then, with an almost angry rustling sound, the vines around the cut location seemed to close ranks, and two new, slightly thicker, vines grew into place in front of them.

"Huh." Beech said. "So it's like a hydra, then?"

"So it seems." Tzedef said, wiping the blade of the knife clean and offering it back to her.

"What happened?" Sorecco asked, and Tzedef tuned Beech out as she started to explain, staring at the hedge with narrowed eyes and thinking furiously.

Turning around was a valid option, but it would add

significant time to their journey, which meant Sorecco might not make it back in time for the start of classes. Turning around was also made more difficult by the fact that, the entire way towards the hedge past the curve in the road, there'd been no turnouts. Nowhere to turn the cart around. Between himself, Sorecco, and Beech, they likely could get the cart turned around, but it would take a significant amount of time and effort that, frankly, he wasn't interested in putting forth. No. The simplest solution would be...

"Beech? Would you kindly ask the gentleman on the other side of the hedge to stand back, at least six yards from the hedge?"

Beech blinked at him. "What? Why? I mean, I will, sure, but why?"

"I wish to try something, and there may be ill effects should he be in contact with any portion of the hedge while I do so."

She blinked again. "O...kay? Sure. HEY GUY!"

The shout made his ears flatten to his skull, but this time neither he nor Sorecco jumped as Beech had her bellowed exchange with the man on the other side of the hedge.

It took a bit of arguing, but eventually the man agreed to step back.

When Sorecco verified that he was, indeed, well back from the hedge, Tzedef stepped forward and placed one hand on the thickest of the vines he could see.

His other hand wrapped around his amulet.

"Great Lady Hecate," he murmured, "I offer you this life, that you might gain from it what power it holds. Allow me to siphon away that which grants perpetual vitality to this hedge, that I might proceed on my quest as is my duty."

Saffron light bloomed under his palm, and the vine withered, going brittle and grey and thin.

The light spread, and as it did, so too did the withering, until the hedge across the road and off into the forest a few feet on either side of it looked as though it had been through a massive forest fire.

Tzedef stayed in position until the light faded entirely away, then nodded and pressed gently against the cracked, withered, dessicated vine.

It snapped softly, and then, with a soft whisper of sound, crumbled into ash.

And the rest of the dead part of the hedge followed suit, leaving the road clear except for a thick layer of grey-brown ash.

"There." He said, quietly satisfied when none of the vines on either side of the road made any move to re-close the gap. "Now we can proceed."

Beech lasted until they'd made it past the dumbfounded farmer and were safely out of sight and earshot before she pulled the cart to a halt and turned on him.

"What the hells was that!?"

"And will someone please explain what the hell happened?" Sorecco demanded, stabbing his stick at the ground impatiently. "One second the hedge was there, the next it's gone!"

"I am a cleric." Tzedef said calmly, and raised his voice to talk over both Beech and Sorecco when they went to interrupt. "My Goddess has several domains. Among them are magic, and the grave. I made her an offering, and she accepted."

"You killed the hedge." Beech said flatly, "As an offering to a grave goddess?"

"Just so." Tzedef nodded. "Technically, the offering was also of the magic that sustained it, so it would not simply regrow larger and more dangerous."

"Tzedef what the hell!?" Beech demanded, and Tzedef sighed.

Damn. He'd been hoping to avoid something along these lines...

"Why didn't you tell me!?" Beech demanded, "We're supposed to be traveling partners! That's vital information!"

Wait, what?

Tzedef blinked at her. "You do not fear that my goddess has dominion over the grave?"

Beech's nose wrinkled. "I mean, it's weird, and kind of creepy, but you don't have to sacrifice people for your spells, do you?"

"No!" Tzedef recoiled, and Beech nodded.

"Then it's fine. I can live with creepy and weird. I

just want to know about it before hand so that I'm not taken by surprise!"

"Wait," Sorecco broke in, looking confused. "Priests with domain over the grave are looked down on, here?"

Beech shifted slightly, looking a little uncomfortable. "Not... I mean... sort of? There's a pretty big stigma around anything to do with the grave, honestly, even though people need priests of the Dark Lady around to ensure that the dead are put to rest properly. A lot of the time, people think that people who work with the dead are only a couple of steps removed from raising the dead, or becoming undead themselves."

Sorecco shifted. "But... raising the dead is useful! I mean, sure, getting permission from the spirit is sometimes a pain, but if you get permission before they pass, then it's fine, right? How else are you supposed to work the fields all summer?"

Beech stared at him.

Sorecco shifted again, a bit awkwardly in the long silence. "You... do let your dead work the fields, right? To pick the pests away and make sure that the wild animals don't get into them?"

"No." Tzedef said after another long moment, his voice slightly strangled. "Is that... common, in Permani?"

"Sure." Sorecco shrugged. "Like I said, you need permission from the body's original inhabitant, and sometimes they don't want to be used like that after death, but most of the time people are fine with it. It's just an empty shell, after all."

Beech looked vaguely ill. "But... you let the dead handle your food?"

"It's all thoroughly washed before going to market," Sorecco assured her, "And things like grains are harvested by the living, so there's really nothing to worry about."

"But what about a person's right to rest after death!?" She demanded, "What about their family?! Doesn't it hurt to see their loved one used as- as farming equipment?"

"No? Why would it? Their family member is still there, with them. They've joined the ancestors, and they can get advice or talk to them whenever they need to. A body is just a body. It's the soul that's the important bit. The bit that's really a person."

Beech looked utterly horrified, and Tzedef stepped in.

"That does explain a great deal about Permani's culture, and while it is interesting, the sun waits for no one. Shall we carry on?"

"Y-yeah..." Beech said, still looking askance at Sorecco.

Sorecco tilted his head, a puzzled look on his face. "Did I say something wrong?"

"Most people that I have met that are not from the Permani Isles tend to think of themselves as something of an amalgamation of their body and soul." Tzedef said delicately. "That is, the soul is the self, yes, but the body is the person, and to raise the body is to defile the memory of the person. Doing that does not allow the soul to rest. It

442

is… something of a taboo to speak about, and more of a taboo to do."

Sorecco frowned, chewing on his lower lip as he thought. "But that's not how that works?"

"To you." Tzedef reminded him. "To the Permani Isles. Your gods are your ancestors. For others, their gods are different beings. Who is to say that things do not work differently depending on what you believe?"

"But magic doesn't work that way!" Sorecco exclaimed, and Tzedef raised and eye-ridge at him.

"And you know so much about magic to be able to claim that?"

Sorecco flushed. "Well, no… but wouldn't we know about it, if it worked like that?"

"Scholars might." Tzedef pointed out. "I am not a scholar. Nor are you, yet, and though Beech is, she is not a scholar of the arcane. None of us present can tell for certain who is right, or if any of us are wrong, and so we must simply accept that the others hold differing beliefs and allow that to carry us forward. Unless this cultural clash has revealed a rift so deep that we cannot travel together any longer?"

"No!" Beech exclaimed, prancing a bit in place, "No, that's not it at all. I was just… surprised. I wasn't expecting. That. I don't mind traveling with you and Sorecco, still. It's not like we're going to die on the way up to Aspari, and even if we did, there's no one around to even try to raise us from the dead, so it's okay."

Sorecco nodded quietly, and slowly the three

travelers got on their way again.

CHAPTER THIRTY-ONE

Reyfilton

That night, camped under the faint light of the stars, Tzedef sat awake, staring into the low flames of the fire they'd lit to ward off the night's slight chill. Beech and Sorecco had turned in a good hour before, and Beech's snoring filled the small turnout at the side of the road with a trumpeting racket.

It was enough to cover the sound of movement, and so Tzedef startled when Sorecco shuffled into place next to him, still wrapped in his bedroll.

"I thought you were asleep." Tzedef said quietly, glancing at Sorecco.

Sorecco shrugged.

"I wanted to talk to you."

Tzedef blinked. Part of him wanted to point out the fact that, considering the fact that they walked together all day, and had for several weeks now, Sorecco could have spoken to him at any time. The other part of him, however, glanced towards Beech where she was half leaning against a tree, dead to the world.

"About what?" He asked, and Sorecco shuffled a little closer to the fire.

"You never said what you thought, earlier."

Tzedef winced. He'd hoped that neither of his traveling companions had caught that, honestly. The longer he could go without examining that particular jar of worms, the better.

"Does it matter what I think?" He tried, and Sorecco turned the flattest look he'd ever seen on the man's face towards him.

"Your goddess is a grave goddess. You're a healer. Surely you have some opinion about what happens to the dead after they pass?"

"My opinions." Tzedef said carefully, "Are… controversial. And possibly illegal. Certainly many would consider them immoral."

"What do you mean, immoral?" Sorecco asked, "Like, raising the dead without asking? Or using them for things against their will?"

Tzedef winced again.

"I believe, personally, that once the Dark Lady takes a soul, the body is meant to return to Chaelu. What happens to the body between the time of death and the time of final decay doesn't truly matter."

Sorecco thought about that for a moment, frowning slightly. "So… you don't ask?"

Tzedef shrugged, a little awkwardly. "I do not see a reason to. I think it does more harm to pull a soul from the

Dark Lady's embrace to ask, than it does to simply do what must be done regardless."

Sorecco's frown lightened slightly. "I guess that makes sense. If your souls don't stick around, the way ours do, then it would be harder to ask, wouldn't it…"

"Quite."

"Well," Sorecco sighed. "I guess that's fine, then. At least you don't think the way we do things back home is evil or anything."

"No." Tzedef shook his head. "Your culture is itself. Just because it is different from mine does not make it lesser."

Sorecco yawned widely, then scooted around so that he was sideways to the fire, and stretched out again, basking in the warmth.

"Thanks, Tzedef."

Tzedef blinked at him. "For…?"

"Answering my question. I know it was pretty nosy."

Tzedef hesitated for a moment.

"You are my friend." He said finally. "That… is an arrangement I would like to see continue. I do not mind answering what questions you have, should circumstances allow."

Sorecco sighed softly, and when Tzedef glanced down at him, it was to see a small smile playing around the man's lips.

"That's good. I'm glad."

The journey north took the three of them through Girtwood, then a small village called Pickle (that was, completely reasonably, famous in the area for their pickled vegetables), and then across a long stretch of tundra and finally, to Reyfilton.

It was strange, Tzedef mused. He'd known intellectually that their ultimate goal was a mountain. and yet, somehow, even as Reyfil Mountain had grown on the horizon, he hadn't really registered the sheer size of the place until he was looking up at the looming wall of stone, moss, and lichen that stretched for miles in either direction.

The walls of Reyfilton, though they were made of massive blocks of stone quarried from the mountain itself, looked positively tiny compared to the mountain behind them, and the guard towers were neatly dwarfed by the foothills that embraced the town.

Luckily for them, they had made good time: it was only early afternoon, which gave them plenty of time to get in, and find a place to stay.

"Right!" Beech cheered, tossing back her fur-lined hood as they stepped through the gates, into the town proper, and out of the worst of the icy breeze that had plagued them for the last day and a half. "We're here! Now here's a question- Do we want to stay out here in the town? Or do we want to try to get a place to stay inside the mountain?"

"Is there a significant difference?" Tzedef asked curiously as he glanced around, taking in the thick walled stone buildings everywhere and the warmly bundled people that were strolling casually through the streets.

"For sure." Beech nodded, trotting forward carefully on the icy cobbles. "There's a big difference, actually. Out here they won't charge quite as much for just about anything, but you'll have to go through the checkpoint any time you want to get in to the mountain, and, of course, it's cold as shit. In the mountain, they'll charge you through the nose for everything because you aren't a dwarf, but you don't have to go through the checkpoint unless you leave and want back in. Plus, it's warmer, and you don't have to worry about the weather, and all the offices you have to visit for permits and everything are in there, too."

"Hmmm…" Tzedef frowned as a dwarf down and across the road caught his eye, nodded significantly at him, and then turned down a side road and vanished.

"Is it much louder in the mountain?" Sorecco asked, and when Tzedef glanced over at him, he spotted the white knuckled grip that Sorecco had on his stick.

A moment's thought and careful listening made him grimace. It wasn't too loud, for him, but the chiming of Sorecco's bell was getting lost in the clatter of the cart's wheels and Beech's hooves on the cobblestone, and the general murmur of conversation that drifted around and past them as they walked.

"Would you like my elbow?" He murmured, dropping back a couple of steps to walk beside Sorecco.

"Yes please." Sorecco said quietly, and after a moment's finagling, the two were walking in sync down the street after Beech.

"It's pretty loud in the mountain, yeah." She said

casually, picking up the thread of the conversation easily once they were settled. "Though I think the dwarves did something with the acoustics so that sound doesn't echo too far? Or else it'd be unbearable."

"Right." Sorecco grimaced. "I don't suppose I can put in my vote for staying out here then, can I?"

Beech shrugged. "I don't mind either way. I mean, I sort of do, 'cause the checkpoint is a pain in the ass, but I don't really, because honestly, even though inside the mountain is massive, it's still pretty claustrophobic to me."

"Claustrophobic?" Tzedef asked, "In what way?"

Beech shuddered, her skin twitching as if she were trying to get rid of a fly. "It's just… being inside, when it's supposed to be outside, I guess. Like, I can handle being in buildings. That's fine. They're supposed to be inside, right? But when I come out of a building and there's still a roof over my head, it twigs something in my brain and just… I can't deal with it. I mean, I can, sort of. I have before, but it grates on my nerves like a loose shoe. You can just tell that somehow, somewhen, something is going to go wrong."

"Hmm." Tzedef hummed, and glanced around, then up at the clear blue sky overhead. "Well, I have no particular preference either way. If the two of you would be more comfortable out here, then I see no reason why I should object."

"Great." Beech said, sounding greatly relieved. "Then, if you don't mind, we can stay at the place I usually stay when I'm up here."

"That sounds fine." Tzedef nodded, and Sorecco

nodded beside him.

"Sure. Lead the way!"

The inn that Beech led them to was a large stone building surrounded by a stone wall, with stables along one side of the courtyard, and a cart-path that led behind the building proper.

"This inn is great." Beech informed them as she parked the cart on the side of the stable away from the gate to the road and shook her way out of the harness. "They've got ground floor rooms big enough for me, which, lemme tell you? Not the easiest thing to find. Seriously, you'd think more people would be able to accommodate someone my size, considering how many giants are around these days, but apparently that's still a pretty big ask or something. Plus, they don't charge you more if you've got weird dietary requirements. Granted, if it's super out there, they'll just give you access to the kitchen and let you get on with it yourself, but that's still a lot better than most other places."

"I see." Tzedef eyed the building, then frowned as he noticed someone peering at the three of them from the front gate.

They had been followed from the front gate by, Tzedef guessed, no fewer than three separate dwarves, though for what purpose he couldn't fathom. It was making the scales at the back of his neck itch, and his fingers were beating a nervous tattoo on the head of his mace.

The only thing that had kept him from turning

around and confronting them had been the fact that, for all their sneaking around and generally shifty behavior, they hadn't actually done anything that could be construed as hostile.

Aside from following them around, the more paranoid part of him pointed out, and Tzedef gritted his teeth and crushed that voice out of existence. There were any number of reasons that curious people might follow them around.

Beech, for one, was quite large, even for her species, and her coloring was a striking blue roan that even he had never seen before.

Then there was Sorecco, with his stick and bell, and the way he had coiled his sleekly braided hair around itself until it formed a knot at the back of his head, then pinned that in place with a single stick that he had stripped of bark and rubbed smooth. He was attention grabbing in a way that even the other obvious foreigners weren't.

And then, Tzedef admitted with a private grimace, there was himself. A white dragonkin, with ears, of all things, wearing more layers than his human companion. The shield that hung over the pack on his back likely didn't help, though he doubted anyone would recognize the etching of his company's sigil on it.

All in all, they made for an odd looking group and it wouldn't have been the first time that they'd attracted attention for it, except that usually the watchers were children. Not fully grown and bearded dwarves in leather aprons.

"Is everything okay?" Sorecco asked quietly, "You're all tense."

One of Beech's ears swiveled over to point at them, and she glanced over, frowning slightly.

"I am fine." Tzedef said, then grimaced. "We were followed from the gate. It is making me... twitchy."

"We were followed?" Beech asks, straightening up from where she'd been unhooking the harness from the cart, ready to clean it up and put it away. "By who?"

"Three dwarves." Tzedef murmurs quietly. "Each dressed warmly, but with a blacksmith's apron on over their clothing. One of them is at the gate to the street. Do not loo—"

But it was too late; Beech's head swiveled around as she turned to glare over at the gate, and from the corner of his eye, Tzedef watched as the dwarf startled.

Great. Now they would be more clandestine, and it would be harder to pick them out of a cro—

The dwarf was walking over.

"What?" The word left his mouth involuntarily, and Sorecco tilted his head.

"What, what?"

"He is coming over." Tzedef murmured, and turned with Sorecco to face the dwarf head on.

"Wait a second." Beech said quietly, shifting uneasily on her hooves. "That's one of the priests. Why the hells would they be following us around? What's he even doing out of the mountain?"

Tzedef glanced sideways at her, but didn't get a

chance to ask before the dwarf came to a halt in front of them and bowed.

Beech gaped at him.

"Good afternoon?" Tzedef said cautiously, and the dwarf straightened up and nodded briskly.

"Afternoon. I hope your travels were easy and you came to no difficulty on your way up to our mountain?"

"It was easy enough." Beech nodded, her front left hoof tapping the ground nervously. "Warmer than it's been on my last couple of trips up here."

"Yes. The Storm Queen has been a fickle bitch this last year." The dwarf said, dropping any hint of formality as he turned his attention to Tzedef. "You the cleric of the interloping god Hecate?"

Tzedef blinked, taken aback. "I assure you, sir, I have no intention of any sort of proselytizing while within your mountain. I am sim—"

"Yeah, no, I don't care." The dwarf interrupted, and Tzedef's jaw snapped shut, anger rushing through him. "You got rooms yet?"

Tzedef didn't answer, gritting his teeth against the words that he so desperately wanted to say.

"Not yet. Why?" Beech asked cautiously once it became obvious that Tzedef wasn't going to respond.

"The priesthood will take care of it." He said brusquely, and gestured toward the building. "I need a word with your cleric."

Beech's tapping paused and she settled, her stance firming as she frowned down at the man in the scorched leather apron.

Somehow, Tzedef noted with the part of his mind that wasn't seething, the man had figured out how to inlay metal wires in the leather in such a way that they stayed in place. His apron was decorated with two small patterns made of different kinds of wire, both of them simple, geometric designs.

"What do you want with Tzedef?" She asked, and the dwarf glared up at her.

"None of your business. Go on, get. And take the cripple with you." He waved her off dismissively, and blood roared in Tzedef's ears.

His mace was in his hand. The flat end of the head reached out and shoved the dwarf back a few steps- a hard push in the center of his chest.

"You." Tzedef growled, "have thoroughly worn out your welcome. Leave. And do not think to bother me or my companions again."

The dwarf's eyes widened.

"Now hang on a second! I didn't mean nothing by it, and my g—"

"I. Said. *Leave.*"

His voice was a low, evil, hiss; something he'd heard more than once coming out of his brother's mouth, and only rarely from his own.

"I'm goin'!" the dwarf yelped, stumbling backwards. "I'm goin'!"

The dwarf scuttled for the gate out into the road, sending worried glances back over his shoulder until he was out of sight.

"Lights." Beech breathed once the dwarf was well gone and Tzedef had slipped his mace back into its loop. "That was…"

"Utterly reprehensible behavior. That someone in a priesthood would—!" Tzedef snarled, then took a deep breath and closed his eyes, clenching his hands into fists and squeezing tightly.

A moment later he opened his eyes, and turned toward the inn. "We should obtain rooms before it gets much later."

"Right." Beech agreed, and tossed her armful of harness across her back in a tangle of leather that Tzedef knew she was going to have a bitch of a time untangling later.

"Come on, then." She said, and trotted off toward the inn, but Tzedef didn't follow. Instead he glanced back at Sorecco, who had a complicated look on his face.

"You didn't have to do that." He said softly, tapping his stick on the ground and listening to the way his bell chimed. The walls of the courtyard, apparently, provided enough of a sound baffle for the noise of the rest of the town that he could utilize his Gift to figure out roughly what had happened.

"I didn't." Tzedef agreed. "But he insulted me, my goddess, and my companions. In short, I lost my temper. I will likely pay for that in the near future, should he actually be a member of the priesthood."

"You think he might not have been?" Sorecco said,

sounding surprised, and Tzedef shrugged as they started toward the inn.

"It's possible. I see no reason why the priesthood would seek us, or me in particular, out, so it is entirely likely that this was someone trying to take advantage of the fact that we are newly come to the area."

"Huh." Sorecco considered that. "What will you do if it turns out that he was part of the priesthood?"

"Request an apology." Tzedef said flatly. "Regardless of the fact that I am, in fact, intruding on another god's domain, the fact remains that neither I, nor you, nor Beech, have done anything to warrant such treatment. If their god condones this sort of treatment of random people, then their god is not worth following."

Sorecco stumbled. "Is- are you allowed to say that?" He squeaked, and Tzedef paused, genuinely puzzled.

"Why would I not be? If one cannot question the gods, then what can you question?"

"I just— you always seemed very… obedient." Sorecco said, and Tzedef shrugged, hunching his shoulders in his coat.

"For the most part I have no reason to question Lady Hecate. She has asked nothing of me that I was not already willing to do, and in return she has helped me to accomplish my goals. I feel I am a moral person, and thusly, I feel my goddess is a moral goddess. Certainly it's likely that that man feels the same way about his actions, and his god, but when held up against the mores of society, I find him to be severely lacking."

"Huh…" Sorecco said thinking. "All right. That makes sense, I guess. Thanks, Tzedef."

Tzedef paused. "Whatever for?"

"Being willing to explain things to me." Sorecco shrugged. "I appreciate it."

"Ah. You're welcome?"

Sorecco laughed quietly and stepped past him, his stick clacking against the step up into the inn. "Come on."

CHAPTER THIRTY-TWO

A Priest's Request

The rooms were, as Beech had promised, quite comfortable, and the three of them had agreed that it would be best to take the rest of the day to relax from the rigors of travel.

"So. The priests of... what is their god's name, anyway?" Tzedef asked, suddenly realizing that, for all the information he'd gathered about Reyfil Mountain, he still had no idea of the name of the god who had purportedly made the place.

He, Sorecco, and Beech were all gathered in Beech's room; a large space with two odd, two tiered beds. Not bunk beds, but two levels of cushioning that were only slightly offset from one another, with the top one only about a foot higher than the lower one. Beech was laying on the lower of the two, and Tzedef could see, as she leaned sideways against the cushioned side of the higher 'bed' that if she leaned forward onto it, it would neatly act as a bed for the upper half of her body.

She'd waved Sorecco and Tzedef over to the other bed when they had entered, and Sorecco had promptly made himself comfortable, kicking off his boots so he could sit cross-legged on the top part.

Tzedef had opted for the lower platform, and the sigh of relief he had let out when he leaned back against the wall had made Sorecco chuckle softly, and Beech grin.

"Nobody knows." Beech said comfortably, then caught his incredulous look and elaborated. "Oh their priests probably know, and maybe the king of Reyfil, and it might be an open secret to the *dwarves*, but nobody else knows. They keep that shit locked down *tight*."

"That makes no sense." Tzedef said, his voice flat. "Gods require worshipers. To artificially narrow the pool of worshipers in such a way is crippling. No god would consent to such hobbling."

Beech nodded, her ears perked up and forward. "Rumor has it that the founding of Reyfil Mountain is a true story, and a god actually *did* intervene directly to form Reyfil. Some people even say that it must've been one of the Fourteen."

Tzedef scoffed. "As if one of the Fourteen would break the edicts that they themselves laid down. No. More likely, if it *is* true, then it was one of the smaller gods and this secrecy regarding their name is a punishment of sorts."

"Would a smaller god do that?" Sorecco asked, interested. "Go against one of the Fourteen, I mean. Aren't the Fourteen supposed to be the gods that hold the world in balance?"

"Yes." Tzedef said, and shrugged. "I do not know why a smaller god would go against the Fourteen. It's likely that the story is incorrect, or exaggerated. It's even possible that the creation of the mountain was a miracle that one, or even several, priests gave their lives to allow their god to perform through them. Without speaking to the priests, I cannot know for sure."

"And even then it's not likely that they'll tell you anything." Beech said with an answering shrug. "These dwarves, they like to keep things like that pretty close to the chest."

Tzedef harrumphed. "Well then, what can *you* tell me about them? What ought I to know?"

Beech startled. "Why are you asking me?!"

"Because you are here, and you have been here. Multiple times, in fact. You are better placed to know things about the culture of the mountain than either Sorecco or I."

Beech shifted. "That's… true. But I can't exactly call myself an expert or anything. I honestly just stuck mostly to trying to get in to see the ambered castle. The only reason I know anything about the priests at all is because I got interviewed by one the… second? I think it was the second… might've been the third… time I came up here to try."

Tzedef said nothing; just watched her expectantly.

"All right, fine!" She caved, rather too easily, Tzedef

thought, and crossed her arms. "But you're not to take this as fact, okay? It's just stuff I've noticed!"

"Of course." Tzedef nodded and sat back, listening intently.

The dwarves, Beech explained, seemed to value *craft* above just about everything else. Everything was an opportunity to show off their craft, and so everything dwarves did was either over-engineered to the point of ludicrousness, decorated to the point where it seemed like the item in question *shouldn't function* (but it would. It always would. Dwarven pride wouldn't accept anything less.), or utilitarian to a fault.

Different clans, she said, valued different methods of showing off their craft. Hells, different *dwarves* valued different methods of showing off their craft.

"But what about the priests?" Sorecco asked, and Beech shrugged.

"They're all one clan, near as I can tell, and they're all crafters of some sort, too. The one I talked to, he introduced himself as a first tier craftsman. No idea what that actually *means*, but I got the impression he was kind of new to the whole priest thing. He wasn't... settled?" She paused, thinking about that phrasing, then shrugged again. "You know, how priests kind of get like, weirdly *certain* about things? He didn't have that."

"Huh." Sorecco murmured, frowning slightly. "Maybe the level of craftsman they are indicates their rank in the priesthood?"

"Who knows." Beech said, and a low, rumbling growl echoed through the room, closely followed by a lighter gurgling groan. "What I *do* know," she continued smoothly, "Is that I'm hungry. Time for dinner."

Without waiting for a reply, she heaved herself to her feet and strode for the door, letting Tzedef and Sorecco hurry to catch up.

Dinner, it turned out, was plain, hearty fare that the innkeeper informed them had been produced entirely from ingredients sourced from the mountain.

"Impressive." Tzedef said with a nod. "Does most of your food come from the mountain, then? I would have thought that you would have had to rely on trade for the most part."

The innkeeper, a woman by the name of Glim Headbanger, scoffed gently. "Nah. Leads to too much trouble if there's a trade interruption for some reason. Gives other nations too much power over us, too. Nah. We've got ways of providin' for ourselves."

"Everything except spices!" a smaller dwarf with only the faintest wisps of a beard on his cheeks piped up, peeking out from behind Glim, who sighed and pinched the bridge of her nose.

"Merrik…"

The child blinked. "What?"

"Aren't you supposed to be studyin' with Eliss?"

"Eliss got tired and said go home." Merrik reported, and Glim sighed again, more fondly this time.

"Alright. There's a honeybread in the cupboard for you. G'wan and let the customers eat."

The child perked up at the mention of the honeybread, and was gone almost before the last word passed Glim's lips.

"Right," She said, turning back to Tzedef and the others. "You just holler if you need anythin', all right?"

"Sure." Beech said easily, "Thank you, Missus Headbanger."

"Yes, thank you." Sorecco scrambled to say as well, and Tzedef quietly added his own thanks before Glim nodded at them, turned away, and headed back toward the bar.

After the meal, Beech and Sorecco headed back to their rooms, each claiming tiredness and a desire to be awake early in the hopes of getting into the mountain before the checkpoint got too clogged with people.

Tzedef, on the other hand, headed back out to check on the cart and lay down an alarm spell. He would, he hoped, be fast enough to get out in time to catch any would-be thief in the act. Part of him insisted that he ought to just sleep in the cart if he was that worried about it, but the other, more reasonable, part pointed out the ridiculousness of that idea and the wastefulness of paying for a room he wouldn't even sleep in.

In the end it was the lure of the soft, warm bed after a week of sleeping on the ground that did it, and Tzedef cast one last glance back at the cart before retreating inside and to bed.

The next morning when Tzedef woke and headed into the common room he spotted an elderly dwarf in the same kind of leather apron as the dwarf from the afternoon before. From where Tzedef stood, he could see no fewer than four of the wire decorations worked into the apron, each more complex than the last.

The dwarf was standing at the table that Beech and Sorecco were at, speaking to them quietly, but intently, and while neither Beech nor Sorecco looked upset or angry, neither did they look particularly happy. Tzedef sighed internally, then braced himself and strode over.

"— so you see, Gharkin does not speak for all of us." The dwarf said quietly, then paused and turned as Tzedef drew near, his expression lightening. "Ah. You must be the cleric of th— of Hecate. We were told to expect you."

"Were you." Tzedef said icily, and was quietly gratified when the dwarf in front of him winced.

"As I was just telling your companions, Gharkin does not speak for all of us, nor were his words indicative of our god's views. I apologize for the offense caused."

Tzedef's eyes flicked over to Beech and Sorecco, the former of which shrugged, then nodded, while the latter had a thoughtful frown on his face.

"Very well." Tzedef said, returning his gaze to the dwarf in front of him. "Who are you, that your words carry weight?"

"I am Ervet Godsworn." The dwarf said, pressing a fist to his chest and bowing ever so slightly. "Fifth tier Craftsman of the God of Reyfil Mountain."

Tzedef's eyes narrowed.

"What, precisely, does that mean?" He asked, his voice crisp, and Ervet blinked, looking somewhat discomfited as he glanced over at Beech and Sorecco.

"It…" He paused, visibly searching for words. "It means I am a priest of the god of Reyfil Mountain. Fifth tier is akin to a priest of the twelfth hour? That is, I am two steps removed from our high priests- the elders of the mountain."

"I see." Tzedef said quietly. "And the other man. Gharkin, you said his name was? What 'tier' is he?"

"Second." Ervet said, and gestured at the odd wire workings on his apron. "These wefan are indicators of our crafting rank, that is to say, our status in the priesthood. I have five, therefore I am fifth tier, as acknowledged by our god."

"I see." Tzedef said again, and Ervet sighed softly.

"Gharkin is… not the ideal representative of our order. Had we known he would have taken initiative to speak to you on his own, we would have sent someone else to observe instead."

"I would prefer to remain unobserved." Tzedef said flatly, and Ervet shrugged, spreading his hands helplessly.

"It cannot be helped. We require your assistance, and we needed to get an idea of the sort of man you are before Limnally was comfortable with sending people to meet with you. Gharkin's actions made the point moot, though. An apology was warranted, regardless of our feelings on the matter."

"How did you come to find out about the incident, anyway?" Tzedef asked idly.

"Gharkin came and informed us himself. He is foolish and biased, but not stupid."

"I see." Tzedef said a third time, and thought for a moment. "Very well. I'll hear you out, at the least. What is so dire that you would request help from an outsider cleric?"

"Ah." Ervet said awkwardly, and glanced sideways at where Beech was standing and Sorecco was sitting.

Tzedef sighed.

"We can speak in my room, if that will provide sufficient privacy?"

"Yes, that would be perfect." Ervet said, looking relieved. "Thank you."

"Mmm." Tzedef hummed noncommittally, and glanced over at Beech and Sorecco. "Please excuse us. I apologize for interrupting your conversation, but apparently this is pressing."

Beech smiled wryly. "It's fine. Go talk about your secrets."

"Do you want us to order you breakfast?" Sorecco asked, tilting his head toward the kitchen questioningly.

Tzedef paused, then nodded. "Yes, please. Something relatively light, if you don't mind."

"Sure." Sorecco nodded, and Tzedef turned to lead

Ervet back to his room.

Some invisible tension leeched out of the old dwarf once the door closed, and he headed without invitation to the chair next to the table against the wall.

Tzedef watched him settle, his face bland. Waiting for Ervet to start explaining.

Ervet, however, seemed perfectly content to sit there, adjusting his long, braided, steel grey beard and just generally making himself comfortable.

Eventually, Tzedef ran out of patience.

"What, pray tell, does the god of Reyfil Mountain need with me? I am, after all, only a simple traveling cleric. Not only that, but I am an *interloper* in your domain. I do not belong here, that much is *very* clear to me."

Ervet winced again, then sighed. "The fact of the matter is that it's *because* you're not associated with us that you're needed. You see…"

He paused, and silence fell, then drew on for *far* too long for Tzedef's taste.

"There is a problem." Ervet finally said, and he said it so reluctantly that it sounded as though the words were being dragged from him by force.

"That much has been made apparent." Tzedef said scathingly, and got a sharp, almost angry look from the priest.

"The problem is that our current king is *not* our *King*." Ervet snapped, and Tzedef blinked.

468

"Would you care to run that by me again?" He said, his tail twitching. That could mean any one of many things.

"I mean…" Ervet started, then sighed and waved that away. "I need to start at the beginning. Forgive me- this may be a slightly long explanation."

"Proceed." Tzedef said, leaning against the wall with his eyes fixed on Ervet.

"Right." Ervet said, and frowned, twiddling his fingers in front of himself.

"The first thing you need to know is the existence of the Ambered Castle." He says, and Tzedef nods swiftly.

"I am aware of it, yes."

"Good. That makes some things simpler. Do you know what the amber *does?*"

"No." Tzedef said impatiently, "No one does. As far as I am aware, it does not *do* anything. It is as stone. Inert."

"No." Ervet said, shaking his head. "Not at all. It is not stone, nor is it fossil. It is something else. It is called amber only because that is the closest we can compare it to."

"Fine." Tzedef said. "So then, what does this not-amber do?"

"It preserves things." Ervet said simply.

Tzedef frowned. "What do you mean, 'it preserves things'?"

"The amber," Ervet said, and his voice took on a faintly lecturing tone, "is a substance that is as hard as stone. It is relatively easily mined through manual means, and the pieces are lovely- indeed, the clarity and color makes it among the most valuable amber in the world. However, there is a flaw. A catch.

"You see, the amber does not like to be broken apart, and it is highly reactive to magic. That is to say, any magic cast on any individual piece of the amber, or the main body itself, causes *all* pieces of the amber to vanish from wherever they might be, and 'heal' the main body of the source. Trapping anything that may be between the source and the pieces forever."

Tzedef blinked. "I take it you know this from experience?"

Ervet nodded. "When it was first discovered, some thought that it the amber would make a beautifully intimidating receiving hall. They hollowed out a large area, hoarding the amber as a show of their own wealth. And then..."

"Someone cast a spell." Tzedef guessed, his voice dry, "and now everyone that was in that hollow is trapped, aren't they."

It wasn't a question.

Still, Ervet treated it as one, nodding slowly. "Just so. They have been trapped there for over a thousand years."

"Right..." Tzedef said, and frowned. "I assume there is more to this story than just that?"

Ervet nodded again. "Attempts have been made, over the years, to tunnel in and retrieve those trapped. No one knows, after all, if they are dead, or trapped, and if trapped, if they are *aware*. Every attempt has failed, either due to negligence on the part of the miners, or maliciousness on the part of outside parties. There are no fewer than a hundred and sixteen dwarves trapped in the amber at this time. Mining the amber has been forbidden for the last two hundred years or so."

Tzedef blinked slowly. That was quite a number of people trapped. The only question was...

"What do you want from *me*? I assure you that though I am quite incapable of casting magic that might activate whatever trap lies in the amber, I am also quite incapable of mining people out of it without considerable risk to their life and limb."

But Ervet shook his head. "No. We don't need you to get all of them out. Just one. You see, somewhat recently, King Nalimin discovered a new passage being carved in the amber. It was being done unobtrusively, in an out of the way area, and it was aiming not at the other dwarves, but at the castle fragment that lies within the amber. We don't know why, or how, but somehow, King Nalimin ended up encased and now his daughter, Cinnabar, rules as King."

Tzedef frowned.

"How does this involve me? If your king is dead, then it follows that his heir should rule next, does it not?"

"Not at all." Ervet shook his head again, his beard swinging slowly. "Our kings do not rule by right of birth, but by divine authority. Our god directly chooses each new king, either from the royal family, or, if none there are suitable, from the general population of the mountain. And our god has not chosen a new king."

Tzedef's eyes widened slightly. "Your king isn't dead."

"Just so." Ervet nodded, satisfied. "Though our god cannot tell if King Nalimin is aware or not; something about the amber interferes with his divine power."

"Hm." Privately, Tzedef rather doubted that. Nothing he'd ever heard of could interfere with a god's abilities save for the power of another god. "So why can you not simply mine your king out yourself?"

"We are exiled from the mountain." Ervet admitted. "Myself, Gharkin, Limnally, and a handful of other, higher ranking, priests. Princess Cinnabar decided that we were, perhaps, fomenting rebellion by refusing to accept her as the legal king and thus, here we are."

"That does sound like a rebellion to me." Tzedef pointed out mildly, and Ervet gave him a wry look.

"I didn't say she was *wrong*."

Tzedef snorted, a smile tugging at the corners of his mouth.

"Right. So you need me to… what? Locate the proper king, I assume, and extract him from the amber, preferably without alerting the usurper? How am I to do that without alerting anyone? There are guards, are there not?"

"Patrols do pass by all easy access points, yes, and it's entirely likely that Cinnabar has adjusted things to make our information obsolete. The woman is far from stupid."

"Then how do you expect me to do this?" Tzedef asked impatiently. "So far, you have provided me with ample evidence as to why it *won't* work. And, in fact, you have so far neglected to mention what *I* get out of this arrangement!"

He crossed his arms and glared at the older dwarf across from him. "All I have heard is assumptions that I will assist, and very little about the assistance I will receive. I am here, after all, on my own quest."

"I know." Ervet said. "You look for a particular magic, correct? One that is said to be found in the Ambered Castle?"

"Yes…" Tzedef said slowly, "What about it?"

"Well, there's several ways this could go." Ervet shrugged. "First, if you do agree to assist then you will have unlimited access to the amber, so long as you stay out of sight of the guards. With all of us being kept out of the mountain, we have no way of verifying what area of the amber you are mining toward. You could search for anything, and we would simply have to take on faith that you were mining towards King Nalimin."

Tzedef's eyes narrowed, and Ervet hurried on. "Secondly, if you do simply mine straight towards our King, then once he is released, we the clergy will be able to add weight to your petition to be granted legal access to the amber and the castle within. It is not guaranteed that the petition would be granted, but the support of the priesthood is nothing to sneeze at."

"Hmmm…" Tzedef thought for a moment, watching

Ervet through narrowed eyes as the dwarf watched him back anxiety barely hidden on his face.

"What of anything I find in the castle?" He finally asked, the tip of his tail twitching from side to side. "I will not spend my time mining for the magic I seek only to be stripped of whatever I find when I exit."

Ervet hesitated, and Tzedef snorted. "It is as I thought, then. No, the risk that someone will spot movement in the amber and I will end up trapped is too great. Find someone el—"

"Fine!" Ervet blurted hastily, "Anything *non-living* you find and bring out, you can keep."

"And I have your word on this?" Tzedef asked intently, "As a priest of the god of Reyfil Mountain?"

Ervet looked like he'd bitten into something sour. "Yes. You have my word as a priest of the god of Reyfil Mountain."

"Good." Tzedef smiled, the look on his face just as sharp as his teeth. "Then I will assist you and your priesthood."

CHAPTER THIRTY-THREE

Bureaucracy

Ervet took his leave not long after that, and Tzedef crossed the room to sink into the chair the dwarf had vacated, thinking hard.

He had, quite possibly, just made a very large mistake. He didn't know the anything about mining, aside from the fact that it very likely involved pickaxes. How he would be able to mine stealthily, through a very likely heavily guarded area, he hadn't the faintest clue.

On top of that, he abruptly realized, Ervet hadn't actually told him where to find the area King Nalimin was trapped in. Nor had he given him any equipment to use, or even something so basic as the usual guard rotations. Granted, Tzedef admitted to himself, Ervet had said that Cinnabar had likely changed the patrol patterns so anything he could give him was likely out of date, but still. It was the principle of the matter!

For a few moments, he sat and fumed over the

general lack of information he'd been given, then a noise from the common room caught his attention, and he scowled, forcing his irritation down.

There was nothing for it. He was going to have to dig up his own information, find his own tools, and make his own plan.

Curse it all, and curse his impulsiveness, and curse his mercenary attitude towards his fellow priest, to boot. His behavior reflected on Hecate, and they already weren't looking kindly on her, and here he was, exhibiting some of the worst parts of his nature. But he was so close, now, and the priests had trodden on his last nerve. Some part of him had been quite glad indeed to make them squirm.

In the end there was nothing he could do about it just sitting in his rented room, so Tzedef sighed, got back up and headed out into the common room.

It looked like Sorecco and Beech were just finishing up their breakfasts when he stepped out, and there was a plate of food set out at an empty third seat that he made a beeline for.

"That," He said roughly, all but throwing himself into his seat, "was singularly unhelpful."

"Welcome back." Sorecco said mildly, looking amused. "I take it your chat didn't go as well as you'd have liked?"

"It certainly went." Tzedef grumbled, picking up his fork and stabbing at the fried eggs on his plate viciously, watching them leak yolk across the ceramic.

"That good, huh?" Beech asked, half distracted, and

Tzedef snorted.

"Not in the slightest."

"Can you tell us what it was about?" Sorecco asked, and Tzedef hesitated, then, slowly, shook his head.

"I think, perhaps, it would be best if I did not."

Sorecco hummed softly, but didn't press, and Beech was so distracted by her own thoughts that she didn't seem to even notice Tzedef's reticence.

Instead, Tzedef turned his attention to eating his (now quite thoroughly cold) breakfast, eating neatly, but as quickly as he could, all with an eye toward getting into the mountain as quickly as possible. Beech, at least, seemed to appreciate it, and by the time Tzedef had finished, Sorecco had made up his mind that he was going to go with them.

"I'll be able to get an idea of the inside of the mountain without worrying about getting lost if I stick with Beech." He explained, and Tzedef nodded. The thought was logical enough, and indeed, he planned to take advantage of Beech's familiarity with the ins and outs of Reyfil mountain as much as he could. Hopefully they'd be able to get in, get whatever permits they would need to gain access to the amber, and be done by lunch.

Yes, Tzedef snorted sarcastically to himself, that sounded likely. Possibly he would spontaneously develop magical ability, too.

No. With what Ervet had told him, Tzedef highly doubted that the process would be anything resembling easy.

In the end, he was right. Applying for the permits was useless exercise in frustration. Every dwarf they spoke to sent them on to another dwarf in an endless circle of useless, pointless, aimless bureaucracy that gradually ground Tzedef's already fairly short temper down to nubs that he clung to with tooth and nail.

When they finally made their way back to the inn the sun was setting, twilight was falling, and the usually cheerful Beech was drooping and downtrodden.

"I think they made it even worse, somehow..." She sighed as Tzedef pushed open the inn door and she tromped past him with a nod of thanks. "I don't... this is insane... I thought I knew the right people to talk to from the last few times, but they're all gone. Everyone's different now... I don't— I don't know what happened."

She sounded so lost that Tzedef carefully reached over and patted her gingerly on the shoulder of her foreleg.

"You still know the places to go, do you not? And the forms to request?"

There had already been many forms.

Many, many forms.

"Well, yeah." Beech said, but she looked glum. "But I spent so much time and so much money on building up relationships with those people, and now they're gone and I have to start over, and I just don't have enough grant money to do that again! I'm starting to run out of grants I can even apply for! At this rate I'm going to have to start soliciting the nobles back home for money, and if I do that then they're going to want tangible results that're like, valuable!"

She huffed, and pawed nervously at the floor, her hoof scraping against the stone with a noise that made Tzedef's ears fold down in protest.

"Beech," Sorecco protested softly, and Beech winced.

"Sorry."

" 'Sfine." Sorecco said, and sighed. "Is it always that exhausting?"

"It was the first couple of times." She replied, "But once I started figuring stuff out, it got a lot easier. I was making *progress*, dammit!"

"I wonder if that, perhaps, is why those people no longer seem to work in the places you recall them." Tzedef said slowly. "If one were to be paranoid, then one might think that this is an attempt to sabotage your attempts to reach the amber."

"But why?" Beech burst out, stomping frustratedly. "Why go through all this trouble? What's so special about it that they have to keep outsiders away? I just want to look at it!"

Tzedef glanced at her askance, one eye ridge arched. "And touch it. And study it. And—"

"All right!" Beech interrupted, "I get it! And yeah, you're not wrong. But still!"

"So what do we do now?" Sorecco asked, leaning on his stick. "Just... give up?"

"Absolutely not!" Beech snapped, her ears going back. "I don't know about you two, but I'm going back tomorrow! I am not giving up! I've put too much time, and effort and- and money into this to give up now!"

"All right!" Sorecco said, holding up his hands defensively, "I wasn't suggesting you quit. I was just asking if you would. Most people would, I think."

Beech snorted. "Most people would have after the third time they ran out of money and had to slink back home to Vraka with their tail between their legs."

"True." Sorecco admitted. "If you're anything, it's determined."

Beech grinned, and straightened up. "You're damn right I am."

"Are there any ways that we can circumvent some of the so-called 'necessary steps'?" Tzedef asked, and Beech grimaced.

"There were, but now, with everyone all shuffled around and new, I don't think so. I managed to get away without having to do the priest interviews after my third time 'cause Helma remembered me. Jormidsarn would move things along quicker for me if I remembered to go to his office around lunch and brought him something, and Keppler was always more agreeable after a few drinks. It didn't matter what he agreed to while he was drunk, he'd always keep his word the next day."

Tzedef blinked slowly as Beech continued listing off the network of favors, friendships, and outright bribes that she'd apparently built up over her seven previous trips up to the mountain. It was, all in all, impressive, and it made Tzedef realize exactly what she'd meant when she had mentioned all the money she'd spent on these trips.

"I even remembered to bring a toy for Shoulta's youngest!" Beech cried, then groaned, long and pained. "I hope none of them are in trouble…"

Privately, Tzedef thought it was rather likely that they were. If they were so easily influenced to not do their jobs properly, then it was likely they'd either been arrested for corruption, or shuffled off somewhere where their lackadaisical approach to bureaucracy would do less 'harm'.

Though what kind of harm it would do to let people approach the amber, he failed to see. So long as no one tried to mine it, then magic would not be a risk.

Either way, it was becoming evident that there was very little chance of him getting access to the amber legally, which meant he needed to start exploring other options.

Suddenly, an idea that had been percolating in the back of his mind clicked, and his ears perked up as his eyes narrowed.

That…

Yes, that would work nicely.

"I believe I shall turn in early." He announced, and Sorecco frowned at him.

"Aren't you hungry? I know we didn't do much but stand around all day, but the sausage buns we had for lunch weren't that filling."

Even if Tzedef had eaten four of them went unsaid.

Still, Tzedef shook his head. "No, I am fine. If I wake hungry later, then I will eat."

"All right..." Sorecco said uncertainly, but nodded. "Have a good night, then."

"Thank you." Tzedef said, "Good night, Sorecco. Beech."

"Sleep well, I guess?" Beech said, looking just as uncertain as Sorecco sounded. "Do you want to come up with me in the morning? I can wake you, if you aren't already up."

"That would be fine." Tzedef nodded. "Thank you."

Beech nodded. "No problem."

Tzedef inclined his head once more, and then turned and headed to his room.

As soon as the door was shut behind him, he dropped his pack and shield at the end of the bed, kicked off his boots, and sat in the center of the bed. It took a few moments of finagling to get comfortable, but eventually he settled with his legs crossed, his back straight, and his amulet held in his cupped hands.

"Oh great lady, Queen of crossroads and liminality, thrust me out of this mortal shell so that I might see what must be seen."

Back in Maplemore, he had discovered that the astral projection that Frieda had taught him allowed him to walk through walls and see what was happening in the real world, in real time.

As he'd been coming up the road to Reyfil Mountain and listening to Beech talk about how large the Ambered Castle truly was, he'd become slightly worried about how he was supposed to find the candle magic without excavating the entire Castle.

But now there was this, and it was so obvious that he wanted to put his head through a wall.

Tzedef closed his eyes as his prayer ended, and, with the familiar feeling of simultaneously falling and going absolutely nowhere, he found himself looking down at his own body, seemingly meditating on his amulet.

Perfect.

CHAPTER THIRTY-FOUR

The Ambered Castle

The inside of Reyfil Mountain was a *sight*.

Before, Beech had hurried them through the checkpoint and into the permit offices so quickly that Tzedef hadn't had time to get more than a quick impression of pale golden light, high, arched ceilings, and the low, muted noises of an ordinary city.

Now, however, Tzedef was free to look at his leisure, so he did, passing the checkpoint through the simple means of walking through the mountainside and emerging onto the streets of Reyfil Mountain.

It was stunningly beautiful.

Every building was covered in carvings. Stone, worked into odd, multi-stranded knots, or geometric patterns, or murals depicting anything that the artisan had had in mind.

He saw proposals, and celebrations, and wars, and

even what he thought were murals depicting the story that Beech had told them on the way up, about the founding of the mountain society. All worked into stone in exacting detail, no matter how stylized the subject was.

And everywhere there was color.

Not the color of paints or pigments, no, this was the color of stones. Jaspers and quartzes. Marbles and granites. Stone buildings in every shade of grey and black, all decorated and worked with stones in every other color imaginable to create a stunning display of craftsmanship that left Tzedef nearly breathless.

Here and there he spotted gems or metals worked in among the art, but, contrary to the reputation that dwarves typically had, they were in the minority. Used as accents more than anything. In fact, it seemed almost as though the artisans had gone out of their way to *avoid* using those materials.

To prevent theft? Tzedef wondered with a small frown, but that didn't seem to track. If that were the case, then they wouldn't use them at all, even as accents.

With a shrug, he put that thought away for another time, and continued his exploration.

The streets were lit brightly with crystals every few yards, and although the sun had already set outside the mountain, inside was a bustle of activity. Tzedef passed hawkers, and merchant stalls, and shops, all open for business and doing, as best he could tell, brisk trade. Still, that wasn't what he was here for, and he kept his eyes flicking over the roof line, searching for any hint of amber.

He wandered the streets this way, invisible and intangible, for a good twenty minutes before swearing at himself and lifting off the ground as lightly as dandelion fluff.

Once he was in the air, he spotted it nearly immediately. Off in the north-east section of the cavern, next to a larger building that all but screamed 'dwarven castle', a truly enormous mass of red-gold, semi-translucent material jutted out of the stone wall. The thing stretched from floor to ceiling, and disappeared behind the cavern wall in such a way that Tzedef was positive that it extended far past where the stone blocked off his view. It was jagged, not smooth as he'd imagined, and after a moment's thought Tzedef concluded that it must have taken on the shape of the rock that had been chiseled away from it. Target found, Tzedef flew toward it at speed.

And arrived much more quickly than he'd anticipated, having forgotten just how quickly he could move in his astral state.

For a moment he just looked at it, taking in the sheer size of the thing before looking into the amber and seeing what lay within. The first thing was obvious. A large chunk of a building, complete with a section of ground, grass and all, was suspended in the amber, slightly closer to the north wall than the south wall, and relatively deep inside. The

amount of amber between him and the castle made seeing
details difficult, but from what he could see it looked like
something had simply taken a knife and shorn away part of
someone's castle and just… put it there. The edges were
clean, at least from what he could tell, and Tzedef leaned
closer, squinting. And stuck his snout straight into the
amber.

He jerked back, his eyes wide, and stared at the
completely quiescent mass for a long moment.

Nothing happened.

He stuck out his hand, and, gingerly, waved it
through the amber, and then, when nothing happened,
moved forward and stuck his entire face in.

Again, nothing happened, and slowly, a wide grin
curled the edges of Tzedef's mouth.

This was *perfect*! He'd be able to not only find King
Nalimin and plan the shortest route to retrieve him, but he
would be able to search for the candle magic without
spending any more time waiting for the wheels of
bureaucracy to turn! Granted, he wouldn't be able to
retrieve it, but even just *finding* it would be a massive step
in the right direction.

Bolder now, Tzedef slipped fully into the amber and
looked around.

It was, as he'd expected, very amber. The color tinted
everything, and although the interior was one solid mass,

there were odd ripples in it that distorted the view.

For a moment, he hesitated. Which to seek out first? The dwarven king? Or the candle magic?

In the end, it was the memory of Ervet's implication- that he would take the deal simply to mine for the castle and ignore his end of it- that made up his mind. He would seek out the dwarven king first, then the candle magic.

But first... Tzedef glanced around once more, then floated backwards and out of the amber. It was time to return to his body. This was the longest he'd ever stayed out, and the warning of the dangers of astral projection hadn't faded from his mind.

Only once Tzedef was safely ensconced back in his body and his amulet was back around his neck did he start seriously considering what he'd seen, and what he would need to do next.

It was obvious that no amount of jumping through legal hoops was going to grant him access to the amber. He probably should have figured that out when Beech had told him she'd made seven previous trips up to just *try* to get close to it.

Foolishly, he'd assumed that it was simply her size that had prevented the dwarves from granting her access. She was, after all, exceptionally large, even for a centaur, and Tzedef, never having been inside a dwarven settlement before, had assumed that they built to accommodate their own size, but no, apparently dwarven architecture lent itself more towards the grandiose.

Tzedef sighed and lay back, staring up at the ceiling but not truly seeing it as he thought.

Being inside the amber had given him a hint at how large the mass truly was. On the left side, where it was close to the wall, he'd been able to see the stone walls as dark shadows through the amber glow. But when he'd looked back, away from the main body of the cavern, or to the right, behind the 'shell' of stone that still encased the amber on that side, all he'd been able to see was amber. He hadn't even been able to tell if it was because the amber simply stretched that far back, or if there was another possible explanation. How thick must it be before one would stop being able to see through it?

He rolled over, frowning. He'd entered the amber about halfway up the wall, and the castle had been on level with him, unsupported by anything but amber and the half-sphere of soil and stone that was trapped with it. Given the fact that both the amber and the castle were quite firmly underground, and the grounds around the castle had grass, shrubs, and flowers on them, it stood to reason that the castle and it's surroundings hadn't always been underground.

It was unlikely in the extreme that the god of Reyfil Mountain had plucked part of a random castle up out of the world and placed it into the mountain they had created for their dwarves (if, of course, that is how things had happened.). It was just as unlikely that the god had created the world's largest deposit of amber, and then made it so that his chosen people couldn't make use of it. Both of those points, then, led to reason that *something* had happened that had both teleported the castle into the mountain, and formed the amber around it.

Or that something had formed the amber, and then the castle had appeared inside it?

A teleportation spell, overpowered and gone seriously wrong could account for the castle, but that left the amber- a variable that he couldn't account for. Something he couldn't explain, with effects that didn't make sense. Why create such a *large* deposit of solid amber, only to make it automatically heal itself when exposed to magic? What was the point? It did nothing except act as a flytrap for anyone caught nearby when the healing activated.

His frown deepened into a scowl. It almost seemed like a particularly cruel joke. Give the dwarves something beautiful, then make it unusable for any of the art that they so clearly cherished.

Absently, Tzedef sat up again, then reached up to his chest and rubbed at his amulet.

"Lady Hecate," he murmured, "please, grant your favored cleric clear eyes to see through the problem before me. Guide me to the correct conclusion, that I might see the workings of the world around me, and grace me with the wisdom to understand those workings."

Saffron lit up his fingertips, then faded away, and Tzedef smiled.

If he could rely on no one else in the world, he could

rely on his goddess.

Arranging himself comfortably once again, Tzedef closed his eyes, murmured another prayer, and stepped back out of his body.

This would be his last trip to the amber for the day, but if he could make even a little progress towards finding King Nalimin, then he would be satisfied.

This time his trip to the amber went quickly, and Tzedef slipped inside without hesitation. Ervet had said that the tunnel Nalimin had been investigating was a new one, being mined out covertly, which to Tzedef meant it wasn't likely to be anywhere near the dwarven castle itself. Instead, he turned his attention to the areas of amber closest to the stone walls, places where it might be easiest to conceal mining operations by tunneling through rock first.

To his surprise, there were many tunnels at varying heights, on both sides of the exposed section of amber. Most of them were dark and empty and led to nothing in the amber, but several ended up pointing him to areas where dwarves were frozen, caught in the act of mining, or talking, or, in one case, eating lunch. It was truly eerie, seeing the people simply... trapped. Without any idea of what had been about to happen to them.

Further down, on the ground floor, in front of the where the dwarven castle lay outside of the amber, but deep enough inside that Tzedef was almost positive that most people wouldn't be able to see from the outside, there was a large group of dwarves. All of them were dressed in finery and most of them were gathered around one dwarf, sitting on an ornate throne, who was frozen with his face twisted into a furious scowl.

That would likely be the group that Ervet had mentioned, which meant… sure enough, looking like they were angling toward them were several other small groups of dwarves, all with mining equipment. A couple of dwarves were wheeling seemingly empty wheelbarrows toward the outside edge of the amber, and Tzedef guessed that the wheelbarrows had likely been full of amber fragments before it had healed itself. Still, none of them seemed like a king or his guards, (except for the group deeper in,) so Tzedef turned his attention away from the miners and started scouring the edges of the amber again.

He was starting to push the edges of what he felt would probably be safe when something caught his attention- a flicker of movement a few dozen feet above and ahead of him in an area that was darker against the dark of the stone. He'd seen such spots before- they'd always signified a tunnel, and there were figures trapped in the amber near it, which meant it was worth investigating.

Curious, he drifted higher, approaching the dark spot cautiously and taking in the features of the dwarves that were trapped as he approached.

Four of them looked like they were either soldiers or bodyguards, dressed in furs and leathers to combat the chill of the mountain's interior while still providing protection, each with a weapon of some kind at their hip or on their back. The fifth, a dwarf with surprisingly hawkish features, was wearing furs and leathers as well, but also wore a thin circlet of beaten gold.

Ah... Tzedef sighed, pleased. If he wasn't mistaken, then *this* would be King Nalimin. Which meant the movement...

He glanced over, and frowned, squinting through the distortions to the outside of the amber before giving it up as a bad job and simply sliding out of the material.

Just outside the amber was a young dwarven woman, her red hair and beard gleaming in the glow of the amber. Her features were sharp, and her eyes were hard as she looked into the amber, and Tzedef cocked his head to one side when he spotted the circlet of beaten gold that rested on her head.

This then, would be 'King' Cinnabar?

Well, the name was certainly appropriate, if nothing else.

Tzedef watched her as she stared into the amber for a few minutes, then huffed, spun on her heel, and strode away.

He followed her, just far enough to see that the tunnel led out into another tunnel, which led into another tunnel, which branched off into several *other* tunnels that he was positive he didn't have enough time to map right then before he turned around and headed back into the amber. If he could just figure out where they were relative to literally anything else in the amber, he could find them again and map the tunnels backwards.

"Well you're new." The voice came from behind him, and Tzedef startled, jolting so hard that something *twanged* like a lute string snapping—

Tzedef fell off the bed.

CHAPTER THIRTY-FIVE

Victoria

For a long moment, Tzedef lay on the floor, stunned. Then he rolled to his feet and all but threw himself back onto the bed, the prayer to entreat Hecate to push him out of his body tumbling out of his mouth in a jumble of words that was only just barely intelligible.

The second his astral body formed, he was streaking back to the amber, arrowing in on where he'd been mere moments before.

It took him a bit of searching, but eventually he found the place where (the dwarf he assumed was) King Nalimin was trapped. And there, floating in the amber with a bemused look on her face, was the aetheric, monochrome form of an elven woman. Small and slight, she was wearing a simple, elegant looking dress, with elaborate embroideries along the hem, and a pendant necklace hung with a single bright gem. Even just from her bearing, it was obvious that this was no common woman.

"You're back." She sounded surprised. *"That was quick."*

"Forgive my sudden leave-taking," Tzedef said, and sketched a shallow bow. *"I was not expecting to see anyone other than myself."*

One delicate eyebrow arched, and the woman tilted her head to one side just slightly. *"It's no matter. I apologize for startling you. I hadn't realized you were so absorbed in your investigation that you hadn't noticed me."*

Tzedef stilled. He'd been being observed? For how long? For what purpose? Was this woman a guard set here by Cinnabar to keep watch over Nalimin?

He shook that last thought away. It didn't make any sense if one took into account the limitations of astral projection. What use was a guard that would only be able to stand their post for a short time before needing a break?

"Do not worry about it." He said eventually, *"any fault likely lies with me. My name is Tzedef, may I ask yours?"*

"I am Queen Victoria Fernlust." The woman smiled slightly. *"And I have been trapped here for a very long time."*

As it turned out, the piece of castle that was trapped in amber belonged to Queen Victoria, who claimed that not only was she trapped, but many of her staff were as well, and had been since the castle had appeared in the amber.

Whether the amber predated the castle's appearance, she couldn't say. All she *could* say was that the castle had appeared in the amber and all life had simply *stopped*. She was the only one of her people that she *knew* was still aware, and that was only because she seemed to be the only one that could astral project.

"I have kept an eye on the goings on in the mountain over the centuries." She admitted, *"these dwarves are different than the dwarves I am accustomed to, but they are interesting all the same. As well, I have explored much of the world, as best I am able, and learned many things. My confinement has not been all bad, for all that it has been fairly solitary."*

Tzedef frowned. *"In all that time, no one has seen you? Spoken to you?"*

Queen Victoria shrugged, the movement elegantly careless. *"There have been a few, here and there. Dwarves, all of them, and once they find out that I am one of those from the castle, they tend to steer clear again. Perhaps they believe that to speak to me is to undermine the will of whoever trapped us here."*

"Do you know who trapped you here? Or how the castle came to be embedded in the mountain?"

"I don't know. One moment I was in my own lands, the next there was an explosion of some sort, and I and half my castle was here."

Tzedef frowned. That certainly *sounded* like some sort of magical accident… though what might make a teleportation spell *explode* he had no idea.

Something occurred to him, and Tzedef perked up. *"This castle is yours, correct, your majesty?"*

"It is..." Queen Victoria blinked at him, obviously wondering where this was going.

"I wonder," Tzedef said carefully, *"if you perhaps have heard of something called 'candle magic'?"*

"Candle magic?" She hummed softly, thinking, one finger tapping her lips. *"It sounds vaguely familiar. Why?"*

Carefully, Tzedef laid out the specifics of the quest Hecate had given him, and Queen Victoria listened, a thoughtful look on her face.

"I see." She said, once he was done. *"Well, if it is supposed to be in my castle, then it will likely be in the library..."*

She paused for a long moment, then said, very slowly, *"How would you like to make a deal?"*

Tzedef's ears perked, but his eyes narrowed. Perhaps she was not simply an elf, after all. *"What sort of deal?"*

"Something simple enough, I think, though it will likely be dangerous for you."

Tzedef eyed her for a moment, then sighed. *"You wish for me to retrieve you from the amber."*

"Yes."

Tzedef sighed again. *"You realize that the castle is deeper into the amber than anyone has ever made it without being trapped?"*

"You would need to get to the castle physically eventually anyway." Queen Victoria pointed out, *"and if you do swear to retrieve me, then in the meantime I shall do everything in my power to remember the precise details of candle magic, or to locate the book or scroll on which it*

is stored, so that you needn't search more than necessary."

Tzedef hesitated, then sighed a third time. He would have to retrieve King Nalimin first, because there was no way that a mining operation that would reach out to the castle would go unnoticed, but... *"Where is your body?"*

"This way," she beckoned, and headed off through the amber toward the exposed interior of the castle.

Tzedef followed Victoria through hall after hall, drifting relatively quickly in her wake, but still doing his best to memorize the path she was taking so that he could get some idea of precisely how deep into the castle he would have to mine to find her.

"Everything truly is frozen, isn't it?" He asked rhetorically, catching a glimpse of a fireplace full of flames, caught mid-flicker, through a half open door.

"Yes." Queen Victoria answered anyway. *"My one solace is that everyone else seems to be unaware of time passing, or anything else around them. I would hate to finally manage to free my castle from this prison and return it to its rightful place only for the inhabitants to be stark raving mad."*

She came to a halt in the middle of the hallway, and moved to one side so that Tzedef could see a woman, caught mid-stride. A colorized version of the monochrome Queen standing next to him.

"This is me." She said, and Tzedef nodded slowly, circling around her trapped body to get a better idea of how he might have to go about freeing her.

Absently, he noted that even through the red-gold of the amber her hair was pure white; a stark difference from the darkness of her skin and eyes. She was also absolutely *tiny*. If she broke five feet, he would eat one of his boots.

Thinking hard, Tzedef mentally mapped the route he'd have to take from King Nalimin to Queen Victoria and winced.

"You realize that I will not reach you for quite some time, even assuming that I get permission for a prolonged mining operation?"

She nodded. *"I understand that. I am not expecting instant results. Just be aware that I will not be able to give you the candle magic until I am free of the amber."*

Tzedef nodded, then winced as something deep in his chest twinged a warning.

"I believe we have a deal, then. But for now, I am out of time. Rest assured, I will return."

Queen Victoria inclined her head regally. *"I look forward to it."*

"What do you *mean* you met the queen of the Ambered Castle!" Beech squawked the next morning over breakfast, staring at Tzedef over the table.

Tzedef sighed internally. He should have invited both Beech and Sorecco into his room and had this conversation privately, but he'd forgotten Beech's tendency to blurt things out at volume.

"Just what I said." He said quietly, doing his best to ignore the stares their table was getting from the other patrons of the inn. "Though now, I think I will explain more later. After breakfast. In your room, perhaps?"

Beech blinked at him, nonplussed, and Tzedef tilted his head, indicating their watchers.

She glanced over, winced, and nodded, "Yeah. Yeah, alright, that's fine."

Sorecco tilted his head, then tapped his stick very gently against the stone, making his bell chime quietly, and he frowned as he listened hard, trying to hear the returning sound over the general chatter of the others breaking their fasts.

"Ah…" He murmured, and his frown deepened as he rested his stick against the table again and returned to his own meal.

Tzedef thought for a moment as he cut a piece of sausage, then, casually, asked Beech about her plans for the day.

Beech perked up and, given a topic, launched into an explanation of her plan of attack on the bureaucracy of Reyfil Mountain.

He kept her going for the rest of the meal, prodding her here and there with questions to keep her talking, and Beech happily chattered away until Tzedef was positive that anyone who *had* been listening had likely given up on finding out any other useful information. Or rather, any other information that he would prefer to keep under wraps.

"Right," Sorecco said once they were safely

ensconced in Beech's room again, door shut and a prayer to ward off eavesdroppers said over the door and window. "So first of all, how'd you meet the queen?"

"I was exploring the amber—" Tzedef started, and Beech interrupted him immediately.

"How!? How did you even get *close* enough!? Did you knock out the guards? Are you a criminal now? Are we going to have to go on the run!?"

Tzedef pinched the bridge of his snout, closing his eyes.

"I did not knock out the guards. I am no more a criminal now than I was before, and no, we do not need to go on the run. There is a particular skill I was taught while in Tyona last autumn that I spent most of the winter honing with some degree of success. Astral projection allows me to travel from my body and move through physical objects, so I decided to see if I could attempt to achieve my goals without dealing with more paperwork that will, in the end, likely prove fruitless.

"With that said, I was exploring the amber when I came across another person in the aether. She introduced herself as the queen of the ambered castle, and we spoke for a time."

Sorecco frowned. "How did you know she really was the queen?"

Tzedef blinked. "I did not, for sure. I still do not, for sure, but isn't it wiser to accept one's word in cases like this? If she *is* royalty, then I will have offended no-one, and not changed my behavior one whit. If she *isn't*, then I will have, once again, offended no-one and changed my behavior not one whit. Either way, it costs me nothing to accept her at her word, so why shouldn't I?"

Sorecco opened his mouth, paused, and slowly closed it again, frowning.

"I feel like there's something wrong with that logic," He complained, "but I can't put my finger on what."

Tzedef stifled a snort of amusement. "Then perhaps there is no flaw?"

"Maybe." Sorecco said grudgingly, and Beech cut in impatiently.

"Okay, so you met someone who said she was a queen. Great. Neat. Awesome. *What was the amber like?!*"

"Very orange." Tzedef said after a moment's consideration, and chuckled at the outraged noise Beech made.

In the end, they spent most of the morning holed up in Beech's room, with Beech interrogating Tzedef up one side and down the other about everything he could remember about the amber. It was, Tzedef was surprised to find, surprisingly helpful in fixing certain details in his mind, and so he answered everything he could to the best of his ability.

Beech, however, didn't seem to find the interrogation nearly as helpful.

"This is useless." She grumbled, crossing her arms

and sulking slightly. "What's the point of a spell that lets you go anywhere and see anything if you can't interact with the world at all!? It sounds so useless!"

"The Weather Readers seem to get good use out of it." Tzedef said mildly, and the woman huffed.

"Good for them."

"Oh for pity's sake, Beech." Sorecco said from where he lay on the other oddly shaped bed. "Give it a rest. It's not his fault that the spell doesn't have tangible effects in the physical world. And it's not his fault he's not a geologist and doesn't know about half the stuff you're asking about."

"This is the closest I've come to the amber in *eight. Years.*" Beech snapped. "I will *not* just give it a rest! I am going to wring *every last scrap* of data out of him that I can!"

Tzedef blinked, slightly alarmed by the unusual vehemence in Beech's voice.

"Perhaps instead of interrogating me further," he started, and paused as Beech's head swiveled to look at him, then continued hurriedly. "You could write up a list of questions that I will do my best to find the answers to when I next go to explore the amber."

Beech eyed him for a moment before her shoulders relaxed a bit, and she nodded. "That could work, I guess. As long as I stick to purely visual qualities... yeah, that might work."

"Very well, then." Tzedef nodded, relaxing as well when it seemed as though the interrogation would not resume. "Make your list, and then perhaps it would be wise to go attempt the mountain's version of 'find the lady' again."

"What?" Beech looked at him blankly, and Sorecco made a confused noise.

"Isn't that a card game?"

"Yes, it is." Tzedef said, "I simply meant that, as a comparison, navigating Reyfil's bureaucracy is similar to playing a card game in which one must make successful guesses to win. That is all."

"Oh." Beech looked nonplussed, then shrugged. "Yeah, I guess I probably should. Getting physical access to the amber is still important. Are you two coming with me again?"

"Nah." Sorecco said, waving one hand lazily in the air above himself. "I think I'll explore Reyfilton a little bit. I had enough of just standing around being fed bullshit yesterday."

"I will not, either." Tzedef shook his head. "There are some things I must further research before I can start my search for the candle magic in earnest."

"Alright." She shrugged. "On my own again. That works fine. Will we still meet up for meals?"

"Of course?" Sorecco said questioningly. "Why wouldn't we? We're friends, aren't we?"

"Right." Something in the set of Beech's shoulders eased slightly, "Yeah, good point. Sorry."

"As well, I will still need to forward to you whatever answers I manage to glean from the amber." Tzedef reminded her. "Meeting in your room like this will likely become a regular occurrence."

"Fair enough!" Beech said happily, and leaned over toward the desk, stretching to reach the paper that lay on top, then grunting as she stretched even further to open one of the drawers and rummage inside for a moment.

"Do… you need help with something?" Sorecco asked cautiously, and Beech grunted a negative, then made a triumphant sound and relaxed out of her stretch with an explosive sound of relief.

"Got it!"

'It' was apparently a piece of charcoal mostly wrapped in a small scrap of thin leather.

Charcoal was duly applied to paper, and in no time flat Beech was scribbling away, writing question after question down as fast as she could think of them.

"Right." Sorecco said, and sat up, then stood up, bringing his stick with him. "If that's everything for now, I think I'm going to go out exploring. I'll be back for dinner."

Beech paused, distracted from her list for a moment. "What do we do if you aren't?"

"I will be." Sorecco assured her, and reached into his pocket, withdrawing a small, highly polished, bronze pigeon. "This'll guide me back."

"Oh?" Beech examined it with interest, then shrugged. "Fair enough, then. Have a good time!"

"Thanks."

Tzedef watched as Sorecco slipped out the door and closed it behind himself with a soft click, then turned back to Beech, his own plans slowly gelling.

"Did you need me for anything further?" Tzedef asked, and Beech shook her head absently.

"Nope. I'll probably have these ready for you at dinner, though, so be ready."

"Right." Tzedef nodded, stood, and took his leave as well, heading back across the common room and into his own rented bedroom.

CHAPTER THIRTY-SIX

Preparation

It took Tzedef three nights of work to properly map the network of tunnels that led from where King Nalimin was to what Tzedef thought was the most easily accessible entrance. That entrance was, unfortunately, several stories above ground at the end of a narrow, craggy path that was nearly invisible. In fact, if you didn't know it was there you could walk past it entirely; the rocks were arranged in such a way that the start of the path was almost completely concealed.

Unfortunately, the path itself being concealed from the ground below didn't mean that anyone *on* the path was similarly concealed, and Tzedef spent no small amount of time trying to figure out how to keep from being noticed on the path before reluctantly concluding that he would need to utilize a prayer for invisibility.

It wasn't something he was particularly thrilled about. In his opinion invisibility was one of the most finicky, least reliable magics in existence, and having it granted by a goddess didn't necessarily make it any better. All too often he'd seen invisibility fail at the most critical of moments, all because the user lost their concentration and started to remember themself as a person again. Even Skaal, genius as he was, had trouble holding the proper mindset for any longer than a minute or so.

Although, Tzedef admitted to himself, it was entirely likely that Skaal's difficulty came from the fact that he was a genius, and he knew it.

His older brother always *had* craved the spotlight.

With that particular hurdle at least somewhat taken care of, Tzedef turned to the next step. Not quite a hurdle, really, but certainly a *step*.

Getting the tools he'd need to chip someone out of the amber.

The problem, he realized with no small amount of dismay as he poked around a supply shop in Reyfilton, was that he had no idea what tools would be necessary.

Oh sure, a pickaxe, definitely, but anything else? What else might he need? A chisel? A hammer, maybe, for the fine details? But how would he use that to chip away at the amber around more delicate areas, like faces, without ending up gouging the ever loving shit out of the flesh that lay below?

Tzedef stared at the mining tools hanging from the wall with a frown, not really seeing them as he thought furiously.

Technically, the place was a tourist shop. Enough rich people with too much time on their hands made the trip up to Reyfil mountain regularly enough that a decent tourism industry had sprung up; with there being specific caves that tourists could wander through, and even specific areas cordoned off from the rest of the mountain where those same tourists could mine for gems of their own. None of them would end up being particularly high quality due to the inexpert nature of the miners, but it was enough to make the customers happy, and that was enough to keep the gold flowing into the mountain, which made the dwarves happy.

That said, even though the tools in the shop were for tourists, they were still of dwarven make, which meant that they were higher quality than just about anything else one could find on the market, and they were priced accordingly.

Tzedef's frown deepened into an outright scowl, then a grimace as the scales on the back of his neck itched.

"Problems, sir?"

"Shhh—!" Tzedef nearly brained the white foxling that popped up next to his elbow as he startled, and she danced deftly back and out of the way of his automatic elbow jerk.

"Ah, my apologies sir." She said, her tail swishing with such obvious amusement that Tzedef glared at her. "I was just wondering if there was anything I could help you find!"

Tzedef took a deep breath, then let it out slowly, trying to calm his racing heart.

"I am looking for mining equipment." He said, entirely unnecessarily, but the arctic foxling simply nodded, looking attentive. "I require a pick, a chisel, a hammer, and..." He hesitated, hating how uncertain he felt.

This is why he rarely stepped outside of his areas of expertise. Please, give him a body to examine, or a wound to heal. Give him a war to fight, and it would still be easier than this.

The foxling shopkeeper took pity on him.

"Are you heading in on one of the mining trips, then?"

Tzedef nodded, the lie coming easily. "Yes."

"Well then you've definitely come to the right place." She nodded firmly, and started toward the front of the shop where the counter was, beckoning him with her. "Come on, you don't want any of that. Those're souvenirs. Things for people to take home and hang on their walls and display, not to actually work with. Oh sure," she added hastily, "they'll *work*. They're good, solid, dwarven tools, after all, but they're marked up pretty steep. No. What you want's the rental equipment we've got up here. Stuff that's seen some use. A little bit of wear and tear. D'you know which cave you're heading into?"

Tzedef floundered. "Um.."

"Not yet, hmm?" She nodded again, easily accepting that. "It's always a tough choice. You want my opinion? Stick to the cave with the fewest people. People always flock to the cave where there's been a big find recently, so it's a crowded nightmare, and trying to find space to swing your pick without impaling someone else is practically impossible. No, you want one of the other caves, with fewer people."

"Ah…" Tzedef said, blinking. "Do you have any suggestions, then?"

The foxling puffed herself up, pleased as anything to be asked. "Stay out of the sapphire cave." She directed him. "Someone found a gem the size of a hen's egg in there last week, so that's where everyone's heading. The ruby cave is pretty active too, and I've heard that the emerald cave is picked pretty much clean, so they're talking about shutting that one down and opening up a new one."

She slipped behind the counter, then continued talking as she rummaged around in a series of bins there, coming up with an armful of equipment that she dumped on the counter.

"No, I'd go for the opal or the topaz cavern. You're not likely to find anything *super* valuable there, but what you do pull out'll be gorgeous."

"I see." Tzedef blinked, then glanced down at the equipment on the counter. "Is this what I would need to mine in those caves?"

"Yup!" She nodded happily, and started pointing to things, naming them and giving him a brief rundown on what he might use them for.

In the end, he left the shop several gold lighter, with an armload of equipment and a reasonable excuse for why he might be wandering around the mountain with mining equipment.

'Lost tourist' would be a pretty easy act to put on, he thought.

Once he got back to his room, he dumped everything on the bed and eyed it contemplatively.

Some of it he doubted he would need. Some of it he doubted he could *use*. The unfolding shovel, for one, stubbornly remained a stick when he tugged on it the way the foxling had shown him, and the light crystal set in the hard leather helmet had died the second he'd touched it.

In the end, he whittled the equipment down to four things: the first, a pickaxe. Plain, simple, unadorned and faintly worn, it would be what he used for the majority of the mining. The second, a chisel. The edge was wickedly sharp, and Tzedef was hesitant to use it at all, but aside from the pickaxe, he had no other way to get the amber away from the dwarves's faces. And common sense told him that trying to use the pickaxe would end in tragedy.

The third item was a hammer, and the foxling had told him that those were often used to break open promising looking stones in the geode cave, so Tzedef assumed that it could likely be used either with the chisel for detail work, or on it's own to induce fractures in the amber.

The fourth, and last, was a coil of rope. She had assured him that it was hardly ever necessary, but said that, in the event of a cave in or a floor collapse, it was better to have it than to not. Tzedef had, with some thought, agreed, so into the pack of supplies it went.

There were several other things- tools that she'd called part of the 'standard loadout'- and Tzedef, not wishing to raise suspicion by only renting what he'd thought he might need, had taken them as well, paying for the extra equipment despite the sinking feeling that the foxling had been taking ruthless advantage of his apparent lack of knowledge.

With a sigh, Tzedef packed it all away in a bag he'd retrieved from the cart (which was still unmolested, for a miracle,) and sat down on the bed, staring at the opposite wall as he rubbed absently at his amulet.

This was so far out of his area of expertise. He was a *battlefield medic*, for Hecate's sake! Not a scout! Not a spy! He wasn't *built* for reconnaissance or stealthy rescue missions! He was too big. Too noticeable. Too… *eye-catching*.

That had been part of why they'd targeted the medical tents, after all. He'd made such a lovely big target…

Tzedef growled to himself, shaking that thought away. He'd agreed to free King Nalimin, so he would do it and that's all there was to it. It was the only way he'd be able to fulfill the quest Hecate had given him, after all, and she'd done so much for him…

No. Failure was not an option, here.

"Tzedef?" Sorecco called from outside the door as he knocked. "You in there?"

"Yes." Tzedef called back. "Come in."

The door creaked open and Sorecco slipped inside, stick in hand, with a small frown on his face.

Tzedef cocked his head slightly to one side. "Is there a problem?"

"No. Not really." Sorecco paused, then wrinkled his nose and tried again. "Sort of? I don't know."

Tzedef blinked. "Alright…"

Sorecco stood there for a moment, leaning on his staff and obviously thinking, so Tzedef sat there, waiting for him to figure out whatever it was he wanted to say.

"Do… Are you…" Sorecco huffed, shaking his head. "Is everything alright? You've been… not necessarily hiding from us, but definitely avoiding me and Beech for the last few days. Is everything okay?"

Tzedef winced. "I." He started, and then stopped before trying again, choosing his words carefully. "I agreed to do a favor for the priests of Reyfil Mountain in return for their support when I petition for access to the Ambered Castle. I cannot tell you what it is, the subject matter is relatively delicate, but I have been preparing to fulfill my end of the agreement for the last few days."

"Oh." Sorecco looked vaguely puzzled, but didn't ask for clarifying details; something that Tzedef was more than a little grateful for.

"Is there anything I can do to help?" he asked

instead, and Tzedef paused, giving that some careful thought.

"I do not think so?" He said cautiously, "But I do not quite have all the details hammered out yet. It may well be that I could use your assistance. If that turns out to be the case…?"

"Then you can count on me." Sorecco smiled, and Tzedef couldn't help his answering smile, small and crooked as it was.

"Thank you."

"Any time," Sorecco said casually, and straightened up from where he'd been leaning heavily on his stick. "Anyway, that's not actually what I came in here for. I mean, it *was*, but it wasn't the only reason. Beech is back, and I think she wants to rant."

Tzedef sighed, but the sound was fond. "Of course she does. Shall I also assume that she wishes to do so over the evening meal?"

"Pretty sure, yep." Sorecco said, and Tzedef stood.

"Then let us not keep her waiting."

Sure enough, Beech was sitting at their regular table, a thunderous look on her face as she drank deeply from a mug that was approximately the size of Sorecco's head.

"Difficult time today?" Tzedef asked mildly as he slipped into a chair, his tail sliding easily along the gap left in the back for it.

"You could say that." Beech grumbled, and took

another drink as Sorecco sat as well. "You know, you'd *think* that the entire process would be streamlined. You'd *think* that the tourism that allowing even *tangential* access to the amber would bring would be worth it! You would *think*," she snarled, putting her mug down hard, "that allowing *outside experts* to verify their claims would be *important!*

"But no! The entire system is built to keep people as far away from the damn stuff as possible! It's like they don't even *want* to know anything about it!"

She huffed, her ears folded back, a furious scowl on her face.

Beech didn't speak again until after Yoru, the usual server at the inn, had come by to take their orders, and then come by again to drop off their food.

Instead, she drank in furious silence, fuming over her lack of progress.

Tzedef and Sorecco let her stew in peace, having learned over the last while that she would work herself out of the mood relatively quickly, and that any attempt to placate or problem solve would simply make things worse.

"I give up." Beech finally declared as Yoru walked away. "That's it. I give up."

Tzedef stared at her, and she hastened to clarify. "Not forever. Just for a couple of days. I need a break, or I'm gonna go nuts."

"Okay," Sorecco agreed easily. "What are you going to do instead? Explore? I found a few neat little places around Reyfilton that might interest you."

But Beech shook her head. "Nah, I was thinking of something a little more involved. Did you know that they've got caves up in the mountain where they let just anyone mine for gems and things? I mean, you gotta pay to get in, obviously, and bring your own gear, but it's still pretty neat. I hear you can find all *sorts* of impossible gems in those caves."

She took a bite and chewed for a moment, then shrugged. "Plus it's probably the closest to the amber I'm ever going to get."

Tzedef blinked.

That was true. The tourist caves were, relatively, close to the amber. Not anywhere near close enough to touch, or even to see much inside, but close enough to give the tourists a chance to bask in it's red-gold glow and see the truly massive size of it.

"That sounds like a lot of fun!" Sorecco said, sounding mightily interested. "Do you think I could come with you?"

Beech shrugged carelessly. "Sure, I don't see why not. Though um… how would you…?"

"Tell if I found anything?" Sorecco asked dryly, and sighed. "I assume that hitting a gem might feel different from hitting rock?"

Beech grimaced. "Not really? Unless it was opal or something. Those kinda… shatter."

"I would like to come too." Tzedef said, a plan

abruptly crystallizing in his mind. "It does sound enjoyable, and I would not mind acting as a spotter for you, Sorecco, if that would help."

Sorecco turned towards him, frowning slightly. "But what about you? Wouldn't you want to look for gems, too?"

"Of course," Tzedef said, "but there is no harm in taking turns, is there?"

"Well, no…" Sorecco said reluctantly, then shook his head and smiled. "I would appreciate that, actually. Thank you, Tzedef."

"Of course."

Beech blinked down at the two of them, then smiled, pleased. "Great, so we'll all three go?"

"Sounds like it!" Sorecco said cheerfully. "This'll be great! Maybe I'll be able to find something for Casey that'll get her off my back about finding a *girlfriend*."

Tzedef snorted. "Are you truly worried about that?"

"*Yes.*" Sorecco said emphatically, and pointed his fork in Tzedef's direction. "Casey is relentless. You know this. You've met her! If I come home without a girlfriend or something to distract her with, she will *absolutely* not stop until I have one at home in Vraka."

Something in Tzedef's stomach churned uneasily at that thought, and he quickly took another bite of his shepherd's pie to cover his sudden silence.

"That's true." He admitted a moment later. "She can be a bit… single minded. I suppose I should count myself lucky that she doesn't consider me a target for her matchmaking ways."

"Yet." Sorecco said darkly. "Just you wait. You'll get there."

Beech snorted with laughter, and Sorecco turned his attention to her, a small, wicked smile growing on his face.

"Actually… Hey *Beech*, are you seeing anybody?"

Tzedef choked.

After dinner, the three of them retreated to Beech's room to plan for their trip into the touristy side of the mountain. None of them were quite sure when the tours for the caverns for the tourists to mine in would happen, and so they ended up dividing things up between them.

Tzedef would head out to get the supplies (which, how he was going to explain to the foxling why he was back again, he didn't know), Beech would go scout out the way to wherever people who wanted in on the tours were supposed to meet, and Sorecco would find out how much they cost and when the next ones were.

It was all easily settled, and it was with very little trepidation that Tzedef went to bed that night. With a soft prayer, he slipped out of his body.

He had some new reconnaissance to perform.

CHAPTER THIRTY-SEVEN

Tourism

"Back again?" Queen Victoria sounded surprised as she interrupted Tzedef tracing the route between the tourist's mining caverns and the amber.

"Yes." Tzedef said, pausing politely and turning his attention towards the elven queen. *"I finally have a plan that should result in freeing King Nalimin. After that, it is just a matter of time before I am able to come free you."*

"Wonderful news." She acknowledged, and drifted closer. *"I eagerly await my release."*

Tzedef nodded, then paused, watching her carefully. *"Have you had any luck recalling anything about the candle magic? Or finding anything about it?"*

Victoria tilted her head slightly, watching him back before nodding slowly. *"I did, in fact, manage to remember how it works, though I still can't recall the exact mechanics by which one would go about preparing a candle. In short, one takes a candle and, through means that I can't remember at the moment, imbues it with spells in layers. Then, once the candle is done being imbued, when it is burned it will cast the spells in reverse order, from last imbued to first. It is quite a useful way of storing magic for later use, though most candles would likely be quite situational."*

Tzedef blinked. *"That sounds incredibly useful, yes. It would keep one from burning oneself out in emergencies."*

"True." Victoria nodded, then shrugged. *"Still, I can't recall how to imbue the candles, which is possibly the most important part. We may end up having to search the library after all."*

"After I have retrieved the king," Tzedef promised. *"Which… I should get back to charting the course I will need to take. It will not be easy, and the better I know the way, the easier it will be."*

"Very well." Victoria inclined her head. *"I will see you soon."*

Tzedef watched her turn drift away, then shook himself and turned his attention back to the route. He hadn't been lying. The better he knew it, the easier it would make the operation.

He stayed out of his body for as long as he safely could, then retreated to his physical form for a while, then sent his astral self back to walking the route. Again, and again, and again he went. Grinding the route into his mind as best he could until, when he retreated into his body for the last time, he collapsed back against the pillows on his bed and fell asleep immediately.

It would have to be enough.

The next day went as smoothly as it could. They split up in the morning, and met up again at lunch, each with something to report or hand over to the others.

"Tours are done every other day." Sorecco informed them between bites of his sandwich. "The next one's tomorrow, and it's supposed to start around noon. It's two sil each, and I already paid for us. The chits are in my bag."

Beech blinked at him. "You didn't have to do that, I could have—"

"I wanted to." Sorecco interrupted her. "Don't worry about it."

"Thank you." Tzedef said swiftly when it looked like Beech was going to try to speak again. "It is appreciated."

"No problem." Sorecco nodded, and Tzedef picked up the thread of the conversation.

"I have the equipment in my room, and your change with me, Beech."

"Great, thanks." She said, "Did you get a receipt, just in case I have to justify myself to the grant committee?"

Tzedef blinked. "No. I was unaware you might need one. Should I go back…?"

Beech waved him off. "Nah, it's fine. It's not *that* big of a deal. Just a kind of 'cover your ass' kind of thing, y'know?"

He nodded. "Yes, I understand. I needed to do something similar, occasionally, during my time in Yaelin's military."

Beech winced. "Oh man, I bet that's even worse than dealing with the grant committee. What'd you have to do? Talk to some general or something?"

Tzedef snorted, darkly amused. "Absolutely not. No, the only time I met with a general was when I was being discharged. The reports were made to the commander, who took them to the relevant people if necessary, or who simply dealt with them if no other action was needed.

She blinked. "Huh. Alright then. Anyway, *I* found out where we're supposed to meet up, and it's weirdly… something. It's just- it's weird, alright? It almost looked fake, but as far as I could tell everything was real. Real stone, real gems, real everything, you know? But it felt off. The stone didn't feel like it was carved out of the cavern walls, it felt like it was sculpted. Too smooth, you know? And the gems that were sticking out around the edges of the entrance? For sure they were real, not glass, but they didn't belong there. They'd obviously been planted there for effect. It's so strange. Like they're catering to some child's idea of what a mine is or something."

"Huh…" Sorecco said thoughtfully. "Was it like that in the mining caverns, too?"

"No idea." Beech shrugged. "I couldn't get in to see. They've got them all blocked off with a gate, and I wasn't about to try anything with a guard standing right there."

Sorecco grimaced. "Oh, yeah, no. Let's not do that. We don't want to get kicked out of the mountain before you've gotten a chance to get at the amber."

"Exactly." Beech pointed at him firmly. "*Thank* you."

Tzedef snorted very quietly, then quickly hid his amusement behind his own sandwich as one of Beech's ears swiveled around to point at him.

In the end, without anything else to do for the day, the three ended up lounging around the common room of the inn, and then, when it got too crowded for comfort with the evening customers trickling in, retreating to Beech's room to play Liar's Dice.

"Casey had these made special for me, for my sixteenth nameday." Sorecco explained, showing Beech a handful of dice with raised bumps on the faces, each corresponding to the correct number. "I think she got tired of me dragging her out to play dice games in the evenings."

"Neat," Beech said, picking one up delicately between her thumb and forefinger, and incidentally making the die look like a child's toy. "And they're balanced?"

"Yup." Sorecco nodded. "One of the guys back in Natari made me get 'em tested before he'd pay me after I won too many rounds in a row."

"Neat!" Beech said again, and handed the die back. "Well then, let's see if your luck holds true!"

Sorecco, it turned out, was an *awful* liar. Whether it was because his lack of sight meant that he couldn't see when other people were looking at him, or because he had a general lack of facial control, it was almost impossible for him to conceal his bad hands.

"I'm almost glad we aren't playing for money…"
Beech said, her eyes wide as Sorecco lost spectacularly for
the fourth time in a row.

"Do you want to?" He asked, tilting his head
slightly.

"No!" Beech said, horrified. "No offense, Sorecco,
but you're *awful* at this! Should we just switch to a different
game?"

Sorecco huffed, offended anyway, and Tzedef's eyes
narrowed.

The set of his shoulders was too amused for that
offense to be genuine.

"No no," Sorecco insisted stubbornly, "it's fine.
Come on. Let's play for coin."

"Sorecco—" Beech tried to protest, and Sorecco
overrode her, demanding a chance to play for money until
she caved.

"I believe I will sit this one out." Tzedef said, still
watching Sorecco. "But please, do not stop on my account."

"Right…" Beech said, looking resigned, and tossed
her first coin into the pot.

Sorecco followed suit, and what followed was a
merciless slaughter as Sorecco fleeced Beech for every
spare coin she had.

Tzedef smiled, leaning back against the wall and
feeling quite satisfied with himself for noticing that

something was off as he watched Sorecco's face blank out entirely, much to Beech's bewildered dismay.

"All right!" She cried, laughing, several rounds later, "Enough! You got me! You win!"

Sorecco's blank mask cracked into a wide grin, and he radiated pleased smugness as he dipped his fingers into the pot and stirred around the coins inside.

"Gotcha, didn't I."

"Oh yeah you did. How'd you learn to do that?"

"Beech." Sorecco said, fondly exasperated. "I'm a *bard*. Of *course* I know how to control my face!"

Beech laughed again, rueful and slightly embarrassed, then raised an eyebrow when Sorecco went to offer her the pot.

"You won that."

Sorecco snorted. "Don't be ridiculous. I wanted to play a joke on you, not scam you. Go on, take your money back."

"You sure?"

"Yup. Go for it."

Beech glanced at Tzedef, then shrugged and took the cup they'd been using as the pot and poured the coins into her massive palm, counting out the amount she'd bet over the rounds quickly, before pouring the rest back into the cup and handing it back to Sorecco.

"Thanks."

Sorecco grinned. "Thank *you*. That was a lot of fun. It's nice to be able to do that with someone who won't threaten to slit my throat for me."

"Someone *what?!*" Beech squawked, and Tzedef frowned. He hadn't heard anything of the sort.

"It was ages ago," Sorecco waved Beech off. "Back in Natari. Don't worry about it."

"I'm worrying about it!" Beech retorted. "Does that kind of thing happen to you *often*?!"

"Nah." He waved her off again, pouring his own coin back into his coinpurse. "Hardly ever, anymore. Seriously, don't worry about it."

Beech shifted uneasily, and glanced across the room at Tzedef, who shrugged very slightly. If Sorecco said not to worry about it, then he wouldn't worry about it until it became a problem. If it became a problem.

"Right," Sorecco said, yawning. "I'm for bed. Thanks for the games, you two."

"You are welcome." Tzedef said quietly, and slid off the other bed as Sorecco stood.

"Yeah," Beech agreed, "more than. That was fun!"

"Good." Sorecco said contentedly. "Good night, then."

"G'night!" Beech chirped, and Tzedef nodded.

"Sleep well. I believe I shall turn in as well."

"Alright," Beech said, shifting slightly to get more comfortable. "Can you hand me that pillow over there? I don't want to get up."

The pillow was duly handed over, and Beech smiled her thanks up at him, then waved as Tzedef took his leave.

Just before noon the next day, Tzedef followed Beech and Sorecco through the checkpoint. Each of them showed their tour chit to the guard there, and subsequently was directed on where to go. The directions were very clear, and Tzedef got the distinct impression that the guard had had to give out those same direction more times than she cared to count.

It wasn't very hard to wind their way through the streets- all they had to do was follow the directions, but Tzedef quietly suspected that even without the directions they would have been able to find the meetup location. All they would have had to do was follow the trickle of generally quite well dressed people, all carrying mining equipment in varying states of wear, all of whom were looking around in varying states of awe or anticipatory glee.

The look on Beech's face was a picture of disgruntled annoyance when she noticed, and Tzedef stifled a smile when she started muttering under her breath about people who wouldn't know a gneiss basalt if it bit them.

Or was that gneiss *from* basalt?

Still, she kept her muttering quiet enough that Tzedef was quite sure that he was the only one who could hear her over the clip-clopping of her hooves and the delicate chiming of Sorecco's bell, and soon enough they reached the meeting point.

Half a dozen dwarves were there, waiting, each wearing a brightly colored shirts in one of a rainbow of colors. Their hair and beards done in elaborate braids that Tzedef, in all of his intangible wanderings, had never seen before, and part of him wondered if the braids were purely for effect. The other part of him noted the carefully folded and tucked nets at their sides, and the long coils of rope over their shoulders, and wondered what they were for.

One of the dwarves, a man in a rich, dark green shirt, looked like he was counting, and, as Tzedef and a couple of people who'd been walking behind him entered the little square where the tours were supposed to start, he whistled sharply and nodded at the woman in orange-yellow who stood near the only other exit.

"All right, folks!" She called, clapping her hands sharply and producing a crack of sound that had several people wincing and made both Beech and Tzedef twitch hard. "We've got a few things to go over before we start the tours, so let's get to it! First of all, no weapons! Some of these caverns we're going to go through are very old and very delicate, so there'll be no fighting. Period. If you've brought a weapon, Yerrod will be around to collect it, and Malio will take care of it until you get back."

A younger dwarf with blue-black hair and a cheerful smile waved from one side of the square, her purple shirt making her quite eye-catching. Another dwarf, slightly older and looking surly about his task, started moving through the crowd, accepting knives and swords and daggers.

Here and there, folks tried to argue over giving up their weapon, be it sword or knife, or, in one case, wand, and in each case, Yerrod was implacable. Hand it over, or don't go on the tour. It wasn't until he got to Sorecco and started arguing with him that Tzedef realized the problem.

"I'm blind!" Sorecco snapped, clutching his stick tightly, and Yerrod's mouth flapped for a moment before he turned back toward the woman in yellow-orange, looking helpless. The woman considered that for a moment, then nodded.

"You'll want to muffle that bell, then." She called, "The acoustics in some of the caves are... well. You'll see."

Sorecco groaned slightly, but reached into his pocket for the strip of gauze he used to muffle his bell when necessary, and started to cover it.

"Sir." Yerrod looked resigned standing in front of Tzedef, and, for a moment, Tzedef hesitated. Then he sighed, removed his mace from its loop, and handed it over.

The things he was doing for these dwarves...

After that, the weapons collection went smoothly, and the woman in the yellow-orange shirt started talking again.

They would, she explained, be going through a series of caverns that the dwarves had uncovered early in their excavation of the mountain. They were each different, and all quite lovely, and she was sure that they'd enjoy them. After that, they would be given the opportunity to follow one of each of the colorfully shirted dwarves located around the square, who would lead them to the appropriate cavern where they would be given three hours to try to mine for gems of their very own. Each color corresponded to a different gem, so they were to be sure to choose carefully, and if they had any questions, they could be sure to ask!

It was all, Tzedef thought with a kind of horrified awe, so *very* practiced. So very… commercialized.

And all of the wealthier folks around the square *ate it up*.

It wasn't long before they were being chivvied into a line and the woman in yellow-orange, whose name was apparently Risma, started leading them out of the city proper and into a hole in the cavern wall that was, after the first dozen feet of darkness, dimly lit with glowing crystals that protruded from various points of the walls and ceiling.

The tunnel was long, and narrow, and barely wide and tall enough for Beech to fit through. In fact, a good portion of the time she had to stay hunched over just to avoid bashing her head on some low hanging piece of rock that hadn't been cleared away.

"We left this tunnel and the caves that came after it in as natural a state as possible." Risma said, her voice carrying easily to the back of the group where Tzedef, Sorecco, and Beech walked in single file.

The other tour guides followed much further back, not wanting to be within kicking distance should something startle the centaur, which meant only Sorecco and Tzedef, walking with Sorecco's hand in Tzedef's elbow, were close enough to hear Beech snort derisively.

"Liar." The word is a quiet mutter, and Tzedef glanced back to see Beech looking around disgustedly. "This tunnel is *sculpted.* It's not natural in the slightest. Are the caves even going to be that—"

She stopped abruptly as the tunnel widened out into a large cave, full of light that bounced around and reflected off of and shone through the hundreds of absolutely *massive* crystals that grew from floor and ceiling and walls.

"Oh *wow...*" She breathed, and stepped forward almost reverently, her head on a swivel to take in all of the crystals.

"Careful there," Risma called from the front of the group. "You don't want to get too close to the edge. The water is shallow, and those crystals are *sharp*!"

Beech blinked, and looked down, and Tzedef followed her gaze to see that the path dropped off quite abruptly into a little pond, the bottom of which was lined with gleaming white crystals spires.

"Right," Beech muttered, and backed up, sending the tour guides behind her scrambling backwards.

After that she kept her mouth shut and her eyes open, and the wonder and awe that poured off of her increased as they passed through cave after crystal-filled cave.

A couple of the caverns had no crystals at all, but instead had fabulous sculptures of stalactites and stalagmites, pillars where they joined and pure white fish and shellfish living in the shallow waters between them.

In one cavern, one of the tour guides stepped forward and sang for them, his voice a low, pure, rolling bass that echoed back from the walls, though none of them could hear the sound of his voice coming from where he stood.

Sorecco stood there, stock still, his hand like iron around Tzedef's elbow, his eyes wide as the tones echoed off the stone and built him a picture that showed him the room in a way that Tzedef could only imagine.

It was a beautiful, awe-inspiring tour, and Tzedef was feeling quite pleased that he'd come along when they were led out of the tunnel and into a brightly lit cavern made of plain, ordinary stone.

"Alright folks!" Risma called, and grinned when everyone turned to look at her. "Now's the part you've all been waiting for. You see those entrances all around in the walls? Those're the mining caves. Give all of us guides a second to get into position and then you can feel free to enter whichever cave strikes your fancy and start mining! If you don't wish to mine, the exit is to your right- it's a short passage that'll take you right back to the square in which we started."

Tzedef watched as the tour guides scattered across the cavern, with green and blue and red all close to one another, then white and grey a bit further away, and Risma, in her yellow-orange, taking up a position at a cave entrance not far from what she'd claimed was the exit.

"Sorecco? Where would you like to mine?" Tzedef asked, his eyes flicking from one guide to the next. All of them looked relatively bored, although their faces were schooled into polite smiles. "It seems as though there are sapphires, rubies, and emeralds. The shopkeeper I rented the equipment from mentioned opals and topaz, as well"

Sorecco waffled for a moment, tapping his stick nervously on the ground before turning towards Beech.

"Beech? What do you want to do?"

"I'm not sure." She admitted, looking around and shifting on her hooves. "Honestly, I'm starting to get a little claustrophobic. I wasn't expecting that tunnel to be so *small.*"

Tzedef winced. He wasn't anywhere near as large as Beech was, and it had felt a bit close for *him.* How it must have felt for *her...*

"Oh..." Sorecco sounded disappointed. "Does that mean you're going to leave?"

"No, I don't think so." She said hesitantly, then shook her head. "No. I think I'll stay. I'd like to at least get *something* out of this trip, and a nice gem would be a fun souvenir."

"Good." Tzedef said firmly, and glanced around at where people were trickling towards the caves. A disproportionate amount were heading toward the cave next to the blue-shirted dwarf.

Beech followed his gaze, and winced. "Maybe not that one. I'm so big I'll probably step on someone, and *that* would be a mess."

"Agreed." Tzedef nodded, then glanced at Sorecco. "Does Casey have a favorite color or a favorite stone? You mentioned wanting to find something for her, did you not?"

"Oh right!" Sorecco perked up. "Yeah, I did! All right, something for Casey… hmmm… She likes… yellow, I think? So that'd be topaz, you said, right?"

"Yes." Tzedef said, "Topaz sounds like a fine choice. You may wish to unmuffle your bell, though."

Sorecco grumbled softly as he adjusted his stick, then started tugging the gauze off of his bell. "Dunno why I had to muffle it in the first place… I would've liked to have seen some of those crystals, too, but they wouldn't even let me *touch*…"

"Human sweat is acidic," Beech said absently, shifting on her hooves as she unlimbered her pickaxe from her back and hefted it experimentally. "Actually all sweat is, to some degree or another. But it can eat away at some rocks. Damage them, you know?"

Sorecco paused. "Wait, are you serious?"

"Mmhm." She nodded. "Yep. It's pretty weird, huh?"

"*Yeah.*" Sorecco said emphatically, and shoved his gauze into the pocket of his robe before straightening back up. "So where are we going?"

"This way." Tzedef said, reaching over to tug his sleeve gently in the proper direction.

The sound of picks hitting stone was starting to echo through the cavern as the three of them headed toward the topaz cave, and Risma smiled cheerfully at them.

"You all ready to look for some topaz?"

"Yep!" Beech said cheerfully, then glanced with no small amount of trepidation at the entrance to the cave.

It was, technically, large enough for her to fit. But only technically.

"The cave… is it big enough for me?"

"Oh yeah, no problem." Risma assured her. "It's big enough to fit any kind of customer who might come through Reyfil Mountain."

"Great." Beech sighed, relieved, and trotted eagerly past her and into the cave.

Sorecco followed her, bell chiming softly, and Tzedef nodded to her as he went past.

CHAPTER THIRTY-EIGHT

Extraction

A few minutes later, Risma followed another couple of tourists into the cave.

"Alright!" She called cheerfully, "So, you guys can feel free to just choose a spot and start mining! If you need any help, feel free to give me a shout. I'm here to help in any way I can!"

Tzedef nodded slowly, and turned to survey the cave itself.

It was a large, irregular area, with piles of loose stone scattered here and there, and already the room was ringing with the sound of metal on stone.

"Did you want to go first?" Sorecco asked, and Tzedef half turned towards him as Risma leaned against the wall near the opening.

"Mmm…" Tzedef hummed, his mind racing as he adjusted the plan he'd come up with before. "You can," he decided, "I wish to try something when you are tired."

"Alright." Sorecco's head turned, and he frowned.

"I'm not sure where to start though…"

"Over here seems like a good area." Tzedef suggested, glancing over at where Beech was cheerfully going to town on a section of wall, before guiding Sorecco over to a relatively smooth patch that had a convenient pile of stone in between them and Risma.

"Do you remember when you asked if there was anything you could do to assist me?" He murmured into Sorecco's ear as he, entirely unnecessarily, helped Sorecco arrange his hands on the shaft of his pickaxe.

Sorecco, mouth open to protest, slowly closed it and nodded instead.

"What do you need?"

Carefully, quietly, Tzedef whispered his plan into Sorecco's ear, using the excuse of 'guiding' his pickaxe to keep close enough to him that they wouldn't be overheard.

"Alright." Sorecco said, then, slightly louder, "I think I've got it."

"Very well." Tzedef said, and backed away, over to the pile of loose stone, and sat down on the floor, settling his own mining gear on his back and crossing his legs.

Invisibility wasn't quite a spell. Oh, sure, it used magic, which meant that Tzedef had to call on Hecate for it to work, but for the most part invisibility was a *mindset*.

It relied on the 'caster' cultivating a mindset in which they were nothing but a part of the environment. Nothing abnormal. Nothing odd. Nothing out of the ordinary.

That was why it was so prone to failure; it was all too easy to see something, or think something, or *do* something that would interrupt that mindset, and then the spell would fail.

Footsteps approached from the side of the pile closest to the door, and a moment later Risma's voice sounded from just next to him.

"Everything okay over here?"

"Yes." Tzedef said calmly. "I am simply communing with the stone so that I might better find a good piece of topaz."

He could practically hear her blink, and he could imagine the slightly exasperated look on her face.

"All right then." She said. "Just as long as you aren't using magic, okay? That's cheating!"

"I will use no magic to cheat." He assured her, and she hummed, satisfied, and walked off, presumably to check on everyone else.

Nothingness.

Slowly, his sense of self faded. Slowly, his awareness of his body dimmed. Slowly, even the rhythmic sound of Sorecco chiseling away at the stone wall faded to nearly nothing.

Distantly, he was aware of Risma returning to her post near the door.

Slowly, Tzedef ceased to be.

"Now." It murmured, its voice distant and faint.

And the rhythm of the pick hitting stone changed.
"When waves are gold and sunlight greets/
The line where sea and sky must meet/
Where sailors drift and halt their race/
To join in twilight's soft embrace/
We look and see our siblings high/
Scattered brightly through the sky.

They call us one by one to sleep/
To join them in their darkness deep/
And one by one we children retire/
To dream the world as they desire."

It blocked out the song, barely whispered though it was, and rose.

It had directions, given before it was nothing. It needed—

Nothing.

It didn't need. It didn't desire.

It knew what to do.

Slowly, it moved past the yawning being at the doorway, through the cavern, and up the tunnel. Past the gate, left open for anyone who wished to leave, and then over to one side, following a side street that hugged the wall of the cavern.

It knew where to go.

It wanted—

No.

It was.

The hidden start to the path would have been hard to

find, but it had explored the area thoroughly the night before, ensuring that nothing would go wrong.

All he—

No.

It paused for a breath, then carried on. Every moment bringing it closer to its goal.

There would be guards, patrolling the tunnels.

It would need to avoid three of them.

It slowed even further.

Time had no meaning. There was only it, and the goal.

It was almost a disaster. It rounded a corner and a guard was there, stepping forward, about to run into it, and he startled, stepping back quickly out of the way.

It stopped. Its racing heart meant nothing. There was no fear. No emotion. There was no disaster, and so, when the guard poked her face warily around the corner, there was no one there.

It waited.

The guard frowned.

It waited.

She shook her head, and turned, and continued down the hall the way she had been going before.

It waited one beat. Two.

And continued on.

It ran into no other difficulties on its journey, and when it was face to face with the amber, staring in at where the king and his bodyguards were only feet away from the stone, it stopped.

Tzedef blinked, then blinked again, then shuddered from his head to the tip of his tail, shaking off the feeling of having no sense of self. He had only utilized the 'spell' a few times in his life and he had been unsure if he would even be able to maintain the appropriate mindset for long enough to get *to* the amber. Luckily it seemed that, small slips aside, he'd made it.

Good.

Working as quietly as he could, Tzedef slid his backpack off. It landed on the floor with the soft clank of metal on metal, and he flipped it open to reveal the rented chisel, pickaxe, and rope. The rope he set aside. All things being equal, he wouldn't need it. The pickaxe was hefted carefully, and the chisel was left in place.

For a long moment, Tzedef eyed the amber, his ears perked, listening for any hint of sound from the tunnels behind him. He heard nothing and so, bracing himself, he swung.

The pick part of the pickaxe dug easily into the amber, sending cracks down through the face underneath where he had struck, and Tzedef nodded to himself, satisfied, before wrenching the tool free.

Tiny fragments of amber scattered across the floor as he attacked the wall with a will.

It was strange. The stuff seemed oddly soft and pliable around his pick, and although he'd been pulling the pick toward himself, every time it bit into the amber it seemed to stretch a little before breaking apart into those little pieces. In a way, it reminded him of taffy that had gotten too cold. Just pliable enough to stretch, but just brittle enough to shatter. It didn't make sense. Ervet had said that the stuff was as hard as stone, and he didn't think the dwarf would have lied to him...

Still, he'd come this far, and he had no idea how long Sorecco's sleepsong would put Risma out for, so he had little time.

Tzedef worked as fast as he could, moving closer and closer as his pick bit deeper and deeper, until something occurred to him.

He wasn't actually mining all that well. The scattering of amber shards on the ground proved that. He'd only managed to pull small chunks away from the wall, and yet... his feet were nearly at the edge of the stone tunnel. He was almost close enough to reach out and touch the closest of the king's bodyguards.

Tzedef frowned down at the pickaxe. It wasn't magical, he was certain of that. The amber hadn't healed itself, after all, and besides, it was *him* holding it. So what...?

Experimentally, Tzedef reached forward with the pickaxe and pressed it against the amber.

It sank into the wall as though he were pressing it into quicksand. With some resistance, but no real difficulty.

That couldn't be right. If it were this viscous, then shouldn't every dwarf currently trapped in the amber have been able to simply wade their way out? Hells, if it was this viscous, then why hadn't it flooded the city cavern? It shouldn't be able to hold its shape!

The only possible explanation was that it *wasn't* actually that viscous.

Tzedef frowned doubtfully down at the pickaxe and let go of the handle, watching carefully.

If it *was* an effect of the pickaxe, then it should slowly make its way down through the amber until it reached the floor. If it wasn't, then it should stay stuck.

The pickaxe stayed still, seemingly locked in position by the amber surrounding it.

His frown deepened, and he reached out and very carefully pulled the pickaxe back out of the amber. If it wasn't the amber, and it wasn't the tool, then the only variable left was…

It was with almost dreamlike detachment that Tzedef reached out with his other hand, and slowly pressed it into the amber wall.

Amber gave way beneath his hand like putty, moving away from him even as he pressed deeper and deeper until he was in the amber up to his shoulder. Or, rather, until he *should* have been in amber up to his shoulder. Instead, he was standing on bare stone and the amber around him had moved away from him until he was in an open semicircle.

"What in Hecate's name?" He muttered, glancing around, then looking back at where his bag was on the ground, the rope coiled next to it. "Well, it certainly makes things easier."

Carefully, he retreated a few steps, watching the amber cautiously. When nothing happened, he turned around, dropped the pickaxe onto the bag, and headed back to the divot he'd left.

It wasn't until he'd stepped off the stone and onto the amber that he realized a problem; the amber moved away from him. Slowly, granted, but it did, which meant that, with no support underneath his feet, Tzedef had started to sink. It wasn't very quick, but it was a bit anxiety inducing until Tzedef had managed to get one foot up and press it into the wall like he was climbing a stair, which took him up to his previous height. After that, it was simple; all he had to do was keep climbing 'up' to stay even with the tunnel.

Luckily, the closest bodyguard was only a couple of steps away from the entrance to the tunnel, and when Tzedef reached out and grabbed his wrist, the bubble spread rapidly. Soon enough the dwarf was breathing hard and looking around, his eyes wide as he took in his companions, still trapped, and the small bubble of clear air they were in.

"This is a rescue." Tzedef said, his voice calm, but slightly strained as he kept stomping down the amber much like one would if one were trying to make a path through snow. "Go past me down the tunnel to get out, and I will return with your comrades shortly."

The dwarf looked at him, looked at the tunnel, and visibly decided that questions could wait until after his fellows had been rescued before slipping past Tzedef with a grunt of effort as Tzedef moved forward.

One by one Tzedef freed the other bodyguards, and then, finally, he reached for King Nalimin's wrist.

He wasn't expecting the man to wrench his wrist free as soon as the bubble of air had fully encompassed him, but perhaps he should have. It wasn't likely that a king was particularly familiar with casual touch, after all, and if he was expecting thick dwarven fingers, only to get cool, draconic scales... well.

"This is a rescue." He said, and then, "your priests asked me to retrieve you."

"The priests?" Nalimin repeated, his eyes narrowing and flicking past Tzedef to look down the short passage.

"Perhaps it would be better for me to answer any questions you might have once we are *out* of the amber?" Tzedef suggested, his voice tight.

The scales on the back of his neck were tingling, a feeling that was setting his teeth on edge.

"Right." Nalimin said, and brushed past Tzedef, who hurried after him.

The amber's glow strengthened, and Tzedef watched in alarm as the shattered, scattered, shards of the amber on the stone just a few steps away glowed as well, then evaporated.

And amber closed in all around.

CHAPTER THIRTY-NINE

Escape

Tzedef tensed, waiting for the amber to swamp him. Waiting for darkness to fall, or nothingness to envelope him, or however the stasis exhibited itself to make itself known. Instead, he was left listening to his own harsh, semi-panicked breathing in a closed bubble of amber that was gradually elongating as he sank, and looking at a once again fully engulfed King Nalimin.

Judging from the muffled shouting from outside the amber, the bodyguards weren't happy about this new development, and Tzedef winced. He hadn't had a chance to warn them about the guards, and with all the noise they were making that he could hear even *through* a good five feet of amber, there was no doubt in his mind that the guards would be on them in short order.

Which meant he needed to *move*.

Tzedef scrambled to force steps into the side of the amber, returning to the proper height before 'climbing' forward towards where King Nalimin was and reaching out to seize the back of his coat.

Once again, air bubbled forward to encompass the king, and he jolted forward, pulling his coat out of Tzedef's hand and running face first into the wall of amber. Nalimin had, apparently, been about to start running when he'd seen the amber evaporate, and he hadn't been able to stop in time once he'd realized that he had been fully engulfed.

Nalimin swore viciously, and Tzedef arched one eye-ridge, then carefully pretended not to have heard anything when the king turned around to glare at him.

"What is the meaning of this?"

"I don't know." Tzedef said honestly, "I was simply employed to retrieve you from the amber. This is an unexpected reaction."

It was getting stuffy inside the amber, and Tzedef frowned as Nalimin glanced around.

"The air is getting stale." He said flatly, "How quickly can you get us out."

"Quickly." Tzedef replied, and gestured past the king to where the bodyguards were standing, watching them through the wavery distortion of the amber. "It is only a few feet."

"Good." The king said gruffly, "Then let's get moving."

Tzedef nodded, then clambered out of where he'd been, once again, sinking into the amber, and strode past the king.

Getting out of the amber only took a couple of

minutes, with most of the time spent waiting for the amber to ooze itself out of the way enough for the two of them to squeeze past. By the time the amber parted and let in a blessed rush of cool, cave scented air, they were panting, and, in the dwarf king's case, sweating, and the air they'd been breathing was thick and humid.

Tzedef gasped for clean air, and stumbled forward the last foot or so, only barely keeping himself from collapsing to the floor.

King Nalimin emerged looking much more held together, glancing around with no small amount of irritation as his bodyguards arranged themselves behind and to the sides of him.

"Right. How long has it been?"

"I do not know, your majesty." Tzedef said, reaching down and tucking the useless pick back into the bag before hefting it onto his shoulder. "But, if your majesty pleases, we should leave with all due haste. I believe your priests wish to meet with you in Reyfilton."

"In Reyfilton?" He sounded startled, then scowled suspiciously. "Why?"

"I do not *know*." Tzedef said impatiently, "They claim they were exiled for some reason. Now, if your majesty pleases, we need to *go*."

King Nalimin's scowl deepened, but, after a moment, he made a sharp gesture to his bodyguards and moved to follow Tzedef.

Tzedef was halfway expecting it when they rounded the corner and ran straight into a contingent of guards, all standing at the ready.

In the end, only Tzedef went quietly. The guards were too well armed and armored, he himself was completely unarmed, and though King Nalimin put on all of his royal authority and commanded them to stand down, none of them budged. The bodyguards went down swinging, and King Nalimin himself ended up bludgeoned over the head hard enough to send him down, dizzy and disoriented enough for several of the guards to wrest his sword away from him and fasten thick, iron manacles around his wrists. The same manacles went around Tzedef's wrists, and one by one the bodyguards were arrested as well. Then the six of them were hustled through the tunnels along a path that Tzedef had only briefly explored.

The passage led directly into the dwarven castle, but Tzedef didn't get much opportunity to look around as the guards bundled them swiftly into back hallways and down unused looking staircases until they reached a long hallway with cells on either side. There, they were separated, each of them shoved into a cell of their own, and the doors locked behind them.

The bodyguards, who hadn't stopped shouting the entire time they'd been being rushed down to the dungeon, shouted louder as the guards left, and started bellowing at the tops of their lungs when the door at the end of the hallway shut with a resounding 'thunk'.

"Enough!" Nalimin bellowed, his voice cutting across those of his bodyguards.

The silence that fell *rang*.

And then, into the silence, came a voice that chilled Tzedef's blood.

"It doesn't matter if you shout. There's a silencing spell on the door, they told me."

"Sorecco?" Tzedef rasped incredulously, and scrambled to his feet as best he could with his hands manacled.

"Wait, *Tzedef?*"

"Tzedef is here?" Beech's voice rang through the hallway, "Tzedef, what the *fuck!?* They came and arrested us for colluding with a *revolutionary!* What the hells did you *do?!*"

"They arrested you?" Tzedef asked, and his stomach twisted. That hadn't been part of the plan. He hadn't meant for either Beech or Sorecco to get in trouble. Even Sorecco's involvement with his sleeping spell had been so quiet and small that Tzedef had been honestly sure that no one would notice. "Fuck. Sorecco, Beech, I am so sorry. This was never my intent. You must believe me, this was never part of the plan."

Beech stomped heavily, the sound of horseshoe on stone echoing through the hallway. "That doesn't answer the question! *What did you do!?*"

"I entered the amber and retrieved the dwarven king." Tzedef said simply, and Beech fell into a stunned silence which lasted for all of approximately ten seconds.

"YOU DID WHAT!?"

Tzedef's ears flattened themselves to his head as he

winced.

But it was Sorecco's calm voice that made him cringe.

"All right. So how do we get out?"

"You don't." Nalimin growled. "These cells are impossible to escape. They're physically locked, sealed with magic, and the manacles we're each wearing are magic damping. You won't be able to ca—"

"Uh…" A different voice, one of the bodyguards, Tzedef assumed, interrupted. "Your majesty?"

"What?"

"They didn't search us. They didn't take anything but our weapons."

"Yes? And?" Nalimin demanded impatiently.

"I still have the keys. To the manacles, and the cells."

Silence reigned supreme for several *very* long seconds.

"Well then what are you waiting for!?" Nalimin snapped once the shock had worn off. "Get us out of here!"

"Yessir!" The other dwarf said, and a moment later the sound of heavy manacles hitting the stone floor echoed through the hall.

It took a little more doing for the man to work his arm between the bars of the window on the door, and he ended up having to strip all of his furs and leathers off his upper body to do it, but eventually the key slid into the lock and turned with a soft click.

He re-dressed quickly, and a moment later was working his way through the cells in which his fellows were being held, starting with King Nalimin. It wasn't until he'd released the last of the bodyguards and looked expectantly at the king that Tzedef realized that there was a distinct possibility that he, Sorecco, and Beech wouldn't be released.

But that fear was laid to rest a moment later.

"Release them as well. Obviously something has gone wrong, and they have risked much to come to our aid. It is the least we can do."

"Right." The dwarf carrying the keys nodded, and one by one, released Tzedef and each of his traveling companions.

Beech stomped over to Tzedef immediately, radiating quiet fury as she loomed over him. "You... *you!* You've *ruined* my chances of getting to study the amber! I'm going to be on a *list*, now! They're *never* going to let me within a hundred *yards* of the amber, now! You ruined *everything!*"

Tzedef winced, his ears flattening as he bore up under Beech's verbal assault.

"Why would you—" Her voice cracked, and Tzedef winced again. "Why wouldn't you at least take me *with* you? If you were going to sneak up to see it, why wouldn't you at least bring me along?"

"I could not." He said quietly. "The way had many guard patrols, and was visible from the ground most of the time. I had to use invisibility, and even then I very nearly didn't make it."

"But—!" Beech started, and Nalimin cut her off.

"This is not the time. We have no knowledge of how long it will be before someone comes to check on us. We must leave, *now.*"

"That's great." Sorecco said tersely from over next to the door to his cell. "But I have a problem."

Tzedef glanced over, and his eyes widened slightly at the blood that stained Sorecco's chin, the product of a very obvious split lip that contrasted beautifully with his blooming black eye.

"You do." Tzedef growled. "And they are *about to.*"

"I don't mean *this.*" Sorecco snapped, gesturing at his face, "This is… not fine, but I've had worse. I mean *they took my stick.* And my bell."

Tzedef's teeth gritted.

"Do you require a guide?" He asked, doing his best to keep his voice level, and Sorecco nodded reluctantly then paused, lit up, and scrambled to dig in his pocket.

"Please please please be here, I don't think they took it, but— Yes!" And he pulled out the little brass pigeon, grinning happily.

"Here, Tzedef, hold this for a second."

Mildly bemused, Tzedef walked over and took the bird out of Sorecco's palm, then held still while Sorecco fumbled for his hand, his long, clever fingers dancing across his scales until they found the bird and tapped its head twice.

The bird's head tilted, first this way, then that, and its

wings flipped, resettling themselves close to the fat little body before it fell still again with a little chirp.

"Excellent." Sorecco's grin widened, and he scooped the bird back up into his own palm, and tapped its head once. "Move around, please?"

Tzedef did so, taking a few steps to one side and arching one eye-ridge as the bird turned to face him. Cautiously, Tzedef took a step backwards, and the bird pecked gently at the tip of Sorecco's middle finger.

"You're... There?" Sorecco asked, pointing more or less directly at Tzedef.

"Yes. That's a very well made guide. I'm surprised I haven't seen you use it before."

"I did a few times, back in Vraka. And I used it around Reyfilton, but you were busy. It *is* pretty neat, though. I'll have to go back to Maplemore and thank Maria and Nelthys."

"If we are *quite* done?" Nalimin interrupted, "we need to be gone before they get it into their heads to come check on us. Someone should already have been by, and while I am unsure why no one has, I'm not going to discard favors."

"How are we getting out, though?" Sorecco asked, frowning. "There'll still be guards outside the door, right?"

"That one, yes." Nalimin said grimly. "But not *this* one." He jerked his thumb over his shoulder at the other end of the hallway where a thick, iron banded, wooden door was set into the wall.

"Why would that door remain unguarded?" Tzedef asked, and one of the bodyguards snorted.

"Well, it leads down into the catacombs, don't it? Place is a feckin' maze an all, so no-one can really know how to get round down there. Plus, y'know, there's all kinds of nasties. Word is, the third king was some kinda prodigious necromancer. Knew all kinds of shit that nobody knew where she learned it from, and she never told. She built the catacombs and the Boneyard, and set the dead to guarding the dead so they can rest in peace, right? Grave robbers don't last long round there."

"It's a complicated path," Nalimin admitted, "but the dead are bound to follow the will of the King. Regardless of who sits on the throne, I am still divinely acknowledged as King of Reyfil Mountain. They will obey."

The set of Tzedef's shoulders eased slightly, but Beech pranced anxiously in place.

"Even more underground? Do we have to?"

"Unless you wish to remain here to be remanded back to your cell?" King Nalimin said dryly, and Beech whickered anxiously.

"No. It's- it's fine. I'll come too. Just… does it have to be underground?"

"Technically we're already underground." Sorecco pointed out helpfully, and Beech stomped one back hoof irritably.

"Yes, I *know*, but you don't have to *tell me*!"

"Well then what's the big deal?" Sorecco asked reasonably, and Beech snarled weakly at him.

"The big deal," She says, taking a deep, bracing breath, "is that I doubt those catacombs are built with someone like *me* in mind!"

"It will be fine." Nalimin interrupted impatiently, "now let us *go!*"

Immediately one of the bodyguards, the same dwarf who had, over the course of the last couple of minutes, been gathering up each pair of manacles and relocking the cell doors, stepped forward and slid another key into the plain iron lock. The key was twisted with the grating sound of an unoiled lock, and when he pulled the ring that formed the handle, the door swung open to release the musty scent of bones on a waft of cool, dry, air.

"Let's go." One of the other bodyguards, a dwarf with dirty blond hair and what looked like a wolf pelt slung around his shoulders said, gesturing at the door.

Tzedef stepped forward and peered through the doorway, his eyes automatically adjusting to the darkness beyond and allowing him to see the shallow steps that led down and around a gentle corner.

"How far down is it?"

"A ways." Nalimin said gruffly, and started down the stairs. "Come if you're coming."

The bodyguards follow him, though the red haired key-holder lingered next to the door as Beech took a deep, bracing breath, then followed.

"You'll have to go in front of me." Sorecco said, and Tzedef nodded, then grimaced at himself.

"Yes, I'd assumed as much, or else your guide would

simply point behind you, correct?"

"Yep."

"Right."

Tzedef hesitated for a moment, then murmured a quiet prayer and reached out to brush his fingers against the back of Sorecco's hand.

Saffron light bloomed where they touched, and Sorecco stiffened slightly as his lip scabbed over, then healed, and the bruising around his eye faded.

"Tzedef?"

"A minor healing, only." Tzedef promised quietly. "But if we are to go into the resting place of the dead, I would rather you not have any avenue for infection available."

Sorecco considered that for a moment, then smiled crookedly at him. "Thanks, then."

"Of course." Tzedef said, and turned and started down the stairs. "The stairs are particularly shallow, and quite wide. Be wary."

"Thanks." Sorecco said again, and started cautiously after him.

The door behind them shut, and the entire stairwell was plunged into darkness.

CHAPTER FORTY

Life in the Catacombs

The darkness had only lasted a few seconds before
Beech had muttered a mildly panicked curse about people
with night vision and a small light had bloomed between
her palms. Now, that light was resting on top of her head,
casting a small circle that let her see the next few steps
without ruining the night vision of the people either before
or after her too much. It was, Tzedef thought, a decent
solution, and it seemed to be helping Beech keep her head
about her, which was all to the good.

Sorecco grunted a curse behind him, and Tzedef
hissed as his tail was trodden on.

"Shit, fuck, sorry..." Sorecco muttered, and huffed
an irritated sigh. "This isn't working. The bird works fine
on flat ground, but for stairs... I've almost fallen down
them about six times already. Do you mind if I take your
elbow?"

"I don't." Tzedef said, and paused for a moment,
waiting for Sorecco to get onto the same stair as he was.

It took a bit of finagling, but eventually the two were on the same stair and Sorecco's hand was tucked into the crook of Tzedef's elbow. Carefully, the two of them started down the stairs again, ignoring the impatient huffing of the dwarf behind them.

"So what happened that precipitated you being beaten?" Tzedef asked quietly, and Sorecco snorted.

"I got a bit... mouthy, with the guy who took my stick and my bell. Might've implied that he wanted to use it to replace the one he had up his ass, since mine was of obviously higher quality."

The dwarf behind them snorted, stifling a laugh, and Tzedef carefully smothered his own smile, but let his amusement come clear in his voice.

"Really?"

"Oh yeah." Sorecco grinned, puffing up just a bit with pride. "It was hilarious. Except for the part where he uh... well. Except for the part where my face got all beat up. I really should figure out when to keep my mouth shut, but that's never really been my strong suit. I *like* to talk."

Tzedef chuckled softly. "I had noticed, somehow. Still, perhaps discretion might be the better part of valor?"

Sorecco snorted. "Since when am I valorous? No, I'm a smartass, through and through."

The light ahead of them flickered slightly, and Tzedef peered down to see that the stairwell ended after about another dozen steps, passing through an archway that seemed to be made entirely of bones.

"Nearly there." He informed Sorecco, who nodded.

Tzedef half expected Sorecco to let go of his elbow once they reached the bottom of the stairs, but Sorecco seemed perfectly content to continue using him as a guide, and Tzedef couldn't see a reason to object.

"So now what?" Beech asked, the light bobbing about cheerfully between her ears making her look just the slightest bit ghostly.

Her ears nearly brushed the ceiling, and judging by the way they kept flicking and twitching, she was uncomfortably aware of it.

"Now we leave." King Nalimin said firmly. "You said that the priests were in Reyfilton?"

That last was obviously directed at Tzedef, and he nodded. "Yes. They said they had been exiled from the mountain."

Nalimin frowned. "Exiled? What is the regent *doing...?*"

Beech opened her mouth, and Tzedef caught her eye and shook his head minutely. Now was not the time to tell him that no regency had been set up, and instead there was a new king.

Instead, he simply watched as Nalimin paced a couple of steps away, then back again, thinking.

"Right." He said abruptly, "We're going to the entrance closest to the gate. I want us as far away from this entrance as possible, so that when they do start to look for us, there's no telling where we went."

Tzedef nodded. That made sense. If there was anywhere that the guards would surely check, the only other door out of the dungeon was certainly it.

When the bodyguards fell in around the king Tzedef guided Sorecco to fall in behind them and Beech eagerly joined the group, the faint scent of horse-sweat bringing home how truly stressful this was for her. Tzedef was just grateful that she'd fallen in *behind* Sorecco and himself. There was no way on Chaelu that he wanted to be walking directly behind a nervous centaur, friend or not.

"Keep close." Nalimin instructed as he started to walk away. "The maze likes to play tricks. It won't, since I am here, but if we were to be separated far enough, it might take the opportunity to play some practical jokes."

"What do you mean, practical jokes?" Sorecco asked, and the king sighed, but started to explain as Tzedef examined the walls carefully.

The maze, apparently, was semi-sentient. Brought to 'life' by the will of the mountain's third king, it had been built with the bones of the dwarves who had come before, and, when the third king herself had died, it had simply never *stopped* being something similar to 'alive'.

"No one knows if that was on purpose or not." Nalimin said. "But it listens to whomever is King, and the Guardian Dead keep people from robbing the freshly interred, so it all works out."

Tzedef paused, watching curiously as two pinpoints of ruby light appeared in the eye sockets of a skull in the wall and the jawbone clattered at him.

"Ignore it." Nalimin advised him, pausing as well.

"And don't be alarmed. It won't harm you so long as you do nothing to show hostility or intent to rob the place. At most, it will turn you around. Have you retracing your own footsteps until you grow weary."

"I see…" Tzedef said slowly, and stepped past the skull to continue down the hallway after the king, glancing back once just in time to see a pair of fleshless arms pull themselves out of the wall, then haul the rest of a dwarven skeleton out of the wall and onto the floor. A moment later, it was on its bony feet, and clattering quietly down the hallway away from them.

Here and there, Tzedef caught sight of other skeletons strolling through the hallways, always with bright pricks of ruby light in their eye sockets, but equally always a fair distance away. Never again did he see one as close up as the first one, and he got the distinct impression that the king had somehow ordered them to keep their distance.

It took almost an hour of walking, as best Tzedef could tell, and the walls that they passed went from ivory bones, to dead white bones, and then to rocky walls. The musty, dusty scent of old bones and death faded as the scent of cool mountain air began to filter in. It was obvious that they were getting closer to the exit with every step, which made it all the more concerning when three dwarves in leather aprons barged out of the darkness ahead and ran straight into them.

There was a moment of confusion, and then Tzedef abruptly recognized Ervet and Gharkin, and the king and his bodyguards obviously recognized the elderly woman with them.

"Lady Limnally?" Nalimin sounded surprised as he caught her arms, bracing her as she gasped for breath. "What— Why are you down here? What's wrong?"

"Your Majesty! Don't— don't go up." She wheezed, and the bodyguards traded frowning looks. "You can't— go up. There's guards. Waiting."

"Guards?" Nalimin frowned, "That doesn't make sense. Why would there be guards posted at the entrance to the catacombs? Even if they know that we're gone already- which, granted, is highly likely- setting up guards at the entrance to the catacombs would take much longer than the time we've been down here."

"Would it?" Sorecco asked curiously, and one of the bodyguards, a large dwarf with what looked like fox tails hung as a fringe around his shoulders, shook his head.

"Not with a competent Guardmaster. Give it… mmm, ten minutes before they found us missing. Another ten for that to get up the chain to whoever's in charge now, fifteen to scramble the Guard and get things sorted there… they *could* have guards out at this entrance by this point, if only barely. The question is, how did *you* three get past them? And for that matter, how did you know to come here? How did you know that His Majesty had even been released from the amber?"

Gharkin puffed himself up proudly. "The ways of the god of Reyfil Mountain are not for the uninit—"

Ervet kicked him without looking.

"Jared Stonekeeper told us, Your Majesty. One of

the few remaining loyalists in the castle."

Nalimin gave Gharkin an unimpressed look, then turned his attention to the woman he was still partly supporting. "Lady Limnally?"

"It's true." She said, and let go of his arms, taking a step back and straightening her apron carefully. "But better that I explain somewhere deeper into the catacombs. We aren't safe here."

King Nalimin frowned but glanced around past the priests, and came to a decision.

"Right. Deeper into the catacombs we go. This explanation had better be absolutely spectacular." He paused, then turned to look at Beech, Sorecco, and Tzedef. "You three are free to accompany us, given your apparent involvement. I doubt the guards will be willing to let you go free, regardless."

Sorecco's grip on Tzedef's elbow tightened slightly, but, when Tzedef hummed questioningly at him, he shook his head silently.

"We might as well go, right?" Beech asked, though she looked longingly past where the priests were standing towards the exit. "There's no way we're getting past not only the guards at the exit, but the guards at the checkpoint. Not a chance."

"Checkpoint?" Nalimin asked, then shook his head and turned on his heel, walking back the way they'd come. "Explain later. Come if you're coming."

Every dwarf present hurried after him, and Beech hesitated for a moment longer before trotting after them.

"Is everything alright?" Tzedef kept his voice quiet, and Sorecco grimaced.

"Technically yes? Everything is fine. I'm just... I wish I had my stick. And my bell. One missing is bearable, but it's uncomfortable without either of them."

"I see." Tzedef hummed, and turned to follow the king back down the stone hallway. "I will see if I can do anything to alleviate your discomfort, then."

Sorecco snorted softly, and when Tzedef glanced down at him it was to see him smiling crookedly.

"You already are." His hand squeezed Tzedef's elbow gently, and Tzedef blinked.

"This is the bare minimum that I ought to do." He pointed out. "You were arrested because of me. The loss of your aids is my fault, so it is only fitting that I fill in for them where I can. While I cannot mimic the pure tones of your bell," his voice turned wry, "I can at least perform as a passable facsimile of your stick."

Sorecco snorted again, and the crooked smile turned into a wry grin. "If *this* is what you call a stick, then I'm halfway afraid to see what you think a *tree* is like."

This time the squeeze at his arm was more pointed, and Tzedef paused for a split second, then chuckled, soft and low.

"Fair enough. I suppose I am more than broad enough to not be considered a stick."

Slowly, the walls they passed went from rough stone, to white bones, then to ivory, then to brown; age collecting on the bones in a visible patina. That, more than the increasingly musty scent, told Tzedef exactly how far back in the history of the mountain they were going.

It wasn't until they reached a large 'room', (really a crossroads between several paths) that the king stopped, glanced around, and nodded approvingly.

"This will work."

"This'll work for what?" Beech asked, glancing around as well with a frown on her face.

"Base camp." He said, sounding quite satisfied. "We're deep enough in that I'll have plenty of warning of anyone coming this way, so I'll be able to direct the maze to adjust itself to keep us hidden. Now." He glanced at Tzedef, then Sorecco and Beech. "Introductions are in order, I think."

Tzedef nodded, and then bowed very slightly, pulling Sorecco down with him as well. "A pleasure, Your Majesty. I am Tzedef, a cleric of Hecate, who was entreated by the priesthood of Reyfil Mountain to retrieve you. These are my—"

Nalimin raised one hand, gesturing for him to stop, and Tzedef paused as the king frowned. "Just to be sure… What year is it? How long have I been in amber?"

"It is the year thirty-two ninety-seven." Ervet said promptly, "Your Majesty has been trapped in the amber for a hundred and thirty-six years."

Nalimin grimaced.

"A hundred and thirty-six years… Who has been regent in my stead in that time?"

This time all three of the priests winced.

"What is it?" Nalimin demanded. "What's wrong?"

"Well, Your Majesty, it's like this." Lady Limnally said, and started to explain as carefully as she could.

All in all, Tzedef thought that the king took it rather well. There was no shouting, no pacing, no ranting. All that happened was what little of his face was visible under his beard slowly going pale with anger.

"And the god allowed this?" He asked when Limnally finally finished, his voice forcibly level in a way that didn't quite manage to hide the way it trembled with rage.

Ervet shook his head vigorously, and Gharkin looked offended.

"Of course not." Limnally said calmly, "But unfortunately for us all, there has been a… development. A new god has arrived at the mountain and has ordained Cinnabar king."

Every single dwarf save for the other two priests stopped and stared at the elderly woman.

"A new… what?" Nalimin croaked after a few seconds of dumbfounded silence.

"A new god." Limnally said again. "Cinnabar has been quite adept at spreading his word to the richer denizens of the mountain, and they've taken to it well."

"What sort of god is he?" Nalimin demanded, "How has he swayed my people so easily!?"

"As far as Cinnabar has said, Plutus is a god of

accumulating wealth, and the riches under the earth. She has made several changes to the mountain on his advice that have brought in significant amounts of gold and funneled it nearly straight into the pockets of the people that are directly loyal to her. You can, perhaps, understand why this might appeal to the upper echelons of our society."

King Nalimin looked crestfallen. "And me? What of me? What of my attempts to better the lives of the miners and stoneworkers? The new regulations about mines and the distribution of Liquid Air to those who work them? Was I so quickly forgotten?"

"Not at all!" Ervet hastened to reassure him. "The common folk still remember you quite fondly. There is little love for the new policies that Cinnabar has enacted among them."

"Unfortunately, when we attempted to push back against the new god, Cinnabar exiled our entire priesthood." Limnally said quietly. "Most of our number scattered to the villages within a few days travel of the mountain, including Ervet, Gharkin, and I. Only recently were we told to return to Reyfilton. That someone capable of assisting us would be arriving."

She half turned toward Tzedef, and King Nalimin's eyes snapped over to him. Studying him carefully.

"Introductions." Nalimin said abruptly. "I interrupted you, earlier. You have my apologies."

"It is no trouble, Your Majesty." Tzedef dipped in a shallow bow. "As I said, my name is Tzedef. These are my companions, Sorecco, and Beech."

"I am King Nalimin Reyfil the Second." Nalimin said, and gestured at the four bodyguards. "These are my advisors and guards. Guardmaster Aduni Steelhand, Merchanter Loferek Quicktongue, Orefinder Fellip Stonesinger, and Bookkeeper Westlin Quiverquill."

Tzedef nodded to each of the dwarves as they were introduced in turn.

The Guardmaster was the dwarf with the fox-tail fringe and dark red, nearly brown hair and beard. The Merchanter wore the wolf pelt as though it were a mark of pride. Orefinder Stonesinger, the same dwarf who had told them about the catacombs to begin with, was tall for a dwarf, and dark, with dark hair and gem-bright eyes. It was, however, the Bookkeeper that set the scales on the back of Tzedef's neck to itching.

Oh, to be sure, the man looked harmless enough. He was short, and stocky, and quiet. But his eyes were quick and clever, and Tzedef could feel the Bookkeeper assessing him, Sorecco, and Beech. Searching for flaws in much the same way a jeweler might look for flaws in a gem.

It was a particularly unnerving feeling, but Tzedef had to admit that it wasn't without cause. They were relative unknowns who had shown up out of the blue, in the middle of what seemed like an actual succession crisis. It wasn't exactly the most fortuitous meeting, regardless of the fact that Tzedef had retrieved all of them from the amber. Even being, technically, vouched for by the priests wouldn't be good enough to keep him from scrutiny. Everyone, at this point, was suspect. Including the priests.

"Lady Limnally," Ervet said, taking a pack off his back and setting it down so he could rummage through it, "you should sit. Here."

He withdrew a small wooden stool, just the right size for the high priestess to sit on, and placed it to the side where she would easily be able to watch everyone else.

"Thank you." Limnally said gratefully, sinking down onto the stool with a soft sigh. "Would you boys kindly set up camp? If we're to be staying here, then I'd prefer to be more comfortable."

"Of course, my lady." Ervet said, and glanced over at Gharkin, who took off his own pack and started to rummage through it.

Together, the two of them rapidly set up quite a comfortable camp with things pulled out of their magic bags while the king and his advisors withdrew to the other side of the 'room' to confer in low voices. Tzedef didn't try to listen in, instead turning to Beech and Sorecco.

"Again, you have my apologies. I never intended for this to involve you to this extent."

Beech snorted, a wry twist to her mouth. "What, no swearing this time?"

Tzedef's expression went flat. "A momentary lapse. I can assure you, it shan't happen again."

"I dunno," Sorecco said thoughtfully, a hint of teasing in his voice, "it *was* pretty funny hearing 'fuck' out of you. Maybe you should swear more often."

Tzedef snorted. "I assure you, I have as vulgar a vocabulary as any military medic might have. I simply choose not to use it. There are better ways of expressing displeasure."

Beech snickered at him, then sobered. "Seriously, though. You should have told us. If we'd known there was a risk, we could have taken more precautions. Done things to make sure that if we *were* arrested, we'd have options. As it is, they took our things. Hells, if we're *really* unlucky, they'll have confiscated the cart, too."

Tzedef shook his head. "Not yet, they haven't. My alarm spell has not yet gone off."

She sagged, relieved. "Well that's good, at least. I wasn't really looking forward to trying to get it all back once everything here is sorted out."

Beech glanced over toward the dwarves, then lowered her voice. "We got lucky. I don't know if it's because I'm so damn tall the guards couldn't see past my tits or what, but I've still got my emergency bag."

"Your what?" Sorecco cocked his head, puzzled. "Hang on, I haven't heard of this before, you've got a what now?"

"An emergency bag." Beech told him quietly, and reached down the front of her shirt to pull out a small, palm sized pouch that hung from her neck on a leather thong.

"It's pretty small." She told him, "Barely big enough to get my hand in, but it holds a few things that're supposed to get me back on my feet in an emergency. Some money, a couple of knives, some of Kaz's candies, stuff like that."

"*Huh.*" Sorecco sounded almost offended. "How in the *hells* did I never think of something like that?"

Beech snickered. "Well, you'd need to keep it somewhere where people wouldn't usually think to look, for one."

"Hmmm…" Sorecco's eyes narrowed as he thought, but Tzedef's attention was caught by King Nalimin looking up sharply and going still.

"What is it?" Guardmaster Aduni asked, loudly enough that his voice carried across the small camp to Tzedef. Sorecco and Beech obviously heard it as well, because both of them turned toward the group of dwarves.

"There's a group of guards in the maze." Nalimin said tightly, his eyes distant.

"Searchers?" Aduni asked, and Nalimin nodded.

"I can think of no other reason why such a large group of guards might be in the maze at any time short of the entombment of one of their own. But they carry no litter, and there is a certain determination about them."

"Great." Aduni sighed, and Nalimin's brows furrowed, making him look utterly ferocious as he concentrated.

"I am rearranging the maze. They won't find us here."

"Can you not simply cut this part off from the rest of the maze?" Tzedef asked, walking closer to the dwarves so he wouldn't have to raise his voice.

Nalimin shook his head. "No. Every part of the maze must remain connected to the greater whole. It doesn't allow separations like that."

"Ah."

Nalimin stayed like that for a while, frowning the whole time and occasionally muttering curses against the search party, the maze, Cinnabar, and, Tzedef noted with mild hilarity, Cinnabar's parentage.

There was, apparently, nothing like a coup to estrange one from their family.

CHAPTER FORTY-ONE

Planning

It wasn't until Nalimin dropped onto one of the other stools the priests had dug out of their magic bags, panting and sweating like he'd just run a race in full plate, that Tzedef realized that adjusting the maze on the fly like that must require no small amount of effort.

That was a realization that made him frown. They would have to sleep at some point, and if Cinnabar sent in waves of search parties then King Nalimin would quickly exhaust himself, leaving the rest of them vulnerable. While he wasn't *sure* exactly what fate awaited himself and his companions should they be recaptured, Tzedef wasn't all too keen on finding out. Most countries had only one way of dealing with 'revolutionaries'.

Something occurred to him, and his mouth was open before he could stop it.

"Your Majesty?"

"What?" the word was grunted tiredly, and Tzedef winced, but kept going. In for a copper, in for a plat.

"Is there any way that you could rearrange this area here to only have one entrance?"

"Just the one?" Nalimin looked up at Tzedef, frowning. "How would we escape if they found it? It takes time to convince the maze to change."

"Just the one." Tzedef nodded. "I have an idea as to how it might be defended, but I need two things. First, I need this place to only have one entrance. Second I need— actually no, reverse that. *First* I need to know; do these catacombs run under the entire city?"

"Yes?" Nalimin said cautiously, "Why?"

"Even to the amber?" Tzedef pressed. "Or, ideally, under it, but just close would work, too."

"Yes," Nalimin said, sounding more irritated now. "*Why?*"

Tzedef hesitated. "I have a… contact. In the amber. One who may be able to assist us, so long as I free her from the amber. I have reason to believe that she is a mage of no small power, and it is possible that she may be amicable to making a deal with us."

Nalimin stared at him. "You have a contact. *In* the amber."

"Yes."

"You're mad." Nalimin scoffed, turning away, and Tzedef's eyes narrowed.

"Not at all, *your majesty*. I am a cleric of no small ability myself, and among my gifts lies the ability to send my soul forth to see what my body may not. This woman can do the same, and we met as I was initially searching for you in the amber. We have spoken several times, and I have no reason not to believe her a woman of her word. So long as I free her, she has promised me the magic that I came here seeking, and I believe she may be amicable to assisting us now."

Nalimin huffed disbelievingly, but Bookkeeper Westlin stepped forward.

"Don't go entirely disbelieving him, your maj. There's been tales and tales that people sometimes meet an elven woman in the amber. Never did they speak for longer than a moment or two, but there's whispers she's trapped there for a reason."

Aduni snorted. "Sure, just like we was in there for a reason, kept like a ham in the cold box until whenever we might be needed. Hells, I say if the woman can help, we let her out. It's not like one woman is much of a threat to all of us combined."

Beech shifted in place, looking like she didn't know whether to be offended by that or not.

"It's worth a shot." Ervet said from where he was carefully arranging stones in a circle around another, larger stone, smooth and flat. "If the woman can assist us, then what's the harm? Letting her out puts her in our debt, at the very least, and if she's as powerful as Tzedef seems to think she is, then isn't that to the good?"

Tzedef blinked slowly, keeping his face blank.

"It is, of course, ultimately up to your majesty." He said carefully, "But I truly believe that she will be able to help us."

Nalimin turned back to look at him again, examining Tzedef's face carefully. "You have a plan."

It wasn't a question, but Tzedef nodded anyway. "I do."

"What is it?"

Voice very low, pitched for Nalimin's ears only, Tzedef told him.

Nalimin stared at him. "And you think she can do it?"

"I am almost positive."

Nalimin watched him for a moment longer, an odd, indecisive look on his face, then nodded slowly. "Fine. Have it your way, we'll go and you can retrieve this mystery woman from the amber. However the hells that works for you."

King Nalimin stayed seated until he had finished catching his breath, then stood. "Right, if you're coming to the amber, then you'd best be on your feet and ready. I'm leaving now."

Beech perked up and headed over to him, an eager look on her face.

"I'll sit this one out." Sorecco said from where he'd sat on one of the bedrolls the priests had pulled out of their bags. "If you don't mind."

"That's fine." Tzedef assured him, "I doubt much interesting will be happening, anyway."

"Good." Sorecco grinned at him, "No making tales without me."

"I wouldn't dream of it."

King Nalimin cleared his throat pointedly, and Tzedef glanced over at him, then headed over to join the swiftly growing party.

In the end, everyone except Sorecco and Lady Limnally decided to come, and it was a much larger group than Tzedef had expected that trooped through the bone-filled halls of the catacombs.

"The catacombs don't go right up under the amber," King Nalimin said over his shoulder, "but I think I might be able to convince the maze to shift its bounds just a little. Enough that we can get you into it from beneath. That'll lower the chances of outside interference."

"A sound plan." Tzedef nodded. "What happens if you cannot convince the maze?"

King Nalimin snorted. "Fuck if I know."

"Actually," Gharkin said hesitantly, "wouldn't that be an appropriate time to request a miracle from our god?"

Ervet made a noncommittal humming noise. "Possibly, though it's not typically done to call on him for more than blessing new mines these days…"

"And maybe that's part of the problem that allowed Cinnabar's new god to come waltzing in like he owned the place." Orefinder Fellip snapped, and Ervet winced but nodded, acknowledging the point.

"That's true, it might very well be. Something will likely have to change, and soon."

"We're here." King Nalimin said quietly, and everyone else fell silent as he reached out and placed one large hand on a clear patch of wall. "This is the closest point to the amber. Let's see if the maze can be convinced to shift a bit."

Silence fell, and Tzedef kept his eyes fixed on Nalimin's hand.

Great Lady, please let this work. The prayer was barely a whisper of a thought, reflexive more than anything else, but he felt some of her attention turn his way momentarily, and his eyes widened at the soft feeling of approval that brushed across his mind.

Doing well... My favorite...

Tzedef froze. Dumbfounded. Barely noticing when King Nalimin pulled his hand away from the wall with a frustrated huff and declared that the maze couldn't do it. Unless they dug a new tunnel and connected it to the catacombs themselves, they were on their own.

"Not quite on our own." Ervet said, stepping forward. "Gharkin had a point. We should be able to call on our god to assist here."

"Right." Nalimin said, stepping back out of the way. "The floor is yours, then."

The two priests stepped forward and laid their hands on the stone wall, and closed their eyes.

"Are you okay?" Beech asked quietly, leaning down to speak next to his ear and doing her best not to distract the priests.

Tzedef shook himself out of his stupor. "Yes. I- I'm fine. Everything is fine."

She shot him a slightly skeptical look, but

straightened up, and turned her attention back to the priests.

Tzedef watched them as well, curious to see what their god would do, but still mostly distracted.

He had known on some level that he was Hecate's favored cleric. Hells, he had said as much back in Maplemore, when calling for the judgement of Lucas Miller. But for her to proclaim him her *favorite*... That... He couldn't parse it. Couldn't fathom it. He was no temple priest, doing services for her followers. He was a *cleric*. A wanderer. He stayed in no one place long enough to set down roots, and certainly never stayed long enough to convince anyone of his goddess's qualities. But she had said it. Tzedef had heard her.

Favorite. *Her favorite.*

Pale blue light blooming around the priest's hands dragged Tzedef's attention away from his internal musings, and he watched as the stone there wavered, then rippled, and then, with a soft, grating groan, parted.

Ervet and Gharkin stepped away from the wall, both breathing heavily. Gharkin was visibly sweating, his hands trembling slightly.

"Well done, lad." Ervet clapped Gharkin on the shoulder. "Well done."

"Thank you, sir." Gharkin said, his voice rough, but his spine straightened proudly.

"That should do you." Ervet said, turning towards Tzedef. "It'll take you straight under the amber, deep enough you're not likely to be noticed, and there'll be a flight of stairs at the end that'll take you right up to it."

"Aww…" Beech said quietly from next to him, her ears drooping disappointedly. "I thought we'd get close enough that I could see it too."

"Perfect." Tzedef said quietly. "Thank you, and your god."

He turned to enter the tunnel, which was only a little larger than he was, only to be stopped by the king clearing his throat roughly.

"Just, quick question, here. How d'you plan to breathe? Things got dicey when you were pulling me out of the amber. How d'you plan to deal with that?"

Tzedef blinked at him. "What do you mean? I will not be closing the opening behind me, the air should be fine, should it not?"

Orefinder Fellip groaned loudly. "Gods save us all from—"

He cut off with a loud oof as the Guardmaster elbowed him sharply in the ribs.

"What my *esteemed colleague* was trying to say is that unfortunately, that's not how air in tunnels works. Without ventilation shafts, there's nowhere for any air that flows into the tunnel to go, and so it stagnates. You can suffocate just as well in an open tunnel that's long enough as in a closed bubble."

Tzedef winced. "I see. That is… unfortunate. I do not have anything that might—"

"I have something!" Beech interrupted eagerly,

fishing in her shirt for something. "It's from Kaz! They said that I should definitely try them out if there was a cave in or something, and then come back and let them know how it worked out!"

Out came the little pouch, and Beech opened it and dug inside. "They're here somewhere, hang on… just a… Aha! Got 'em! Here!"

She pulled out her hand, clenched into a fist around something, and held it out to Tzedef.

"Both hands, there's kind of a few of them."

Tzedef blinked, but obediently held out both hands, cupped, under hers, and received a good sized handful of translucent candies.

"Meal lozenges?" He asked, and Beech beamed at him.

"Nope!"

"Then what…?" Tzedef frowned, and Beech giggled.

"They're air lozenges. Kaz said they're good for about ten minutes apiece, unless you're working hard, but they gave me ten of them, so that should be enough for you to find this lady you're looking for, right?"

A hundred minutes of air. Less, probably, since he would be having to climb from the base of the amber to halfway up, so… make that fifty minutes of air. Almost an hour.

"I can make that work." Tzedef nodded, and carefully poured the candies into one palm, then pocketed them. "Thank you, Beech."

"Don't thank me," Beech waved him off with a grin. "Thank Kaz when we get back to Vraka!"

"I will." He nodded, and turned back to the tunnel.

This time no-one stopped him, and he strode carefully into the crack.

The small amount of light filtering into the tunnel from Beech's head light died away quickly, and the tunnel was plunged into the true kind of darkness that can only be found underground. The shades of grey that were his night vision weren't very helpful on stone against stone, but this, however, was something that Tzedef *could* deal with, and with a quietly murmured prayer, he held in his palms a small ball of saffron light. That let him follow the tunnel without bashing his head on the irregular ceiling, or running into any of the small outcroppings along the walls.

The god of Reyfil Mountain may have provided a miracle, but it certainly wasn't a particularly pretty one.

When Tzedef reached the bottom of a set of roughly hewn spiral stairs, and peered upward, he could see a hint of amber glow. It started out dim, but as he marched up the stairs it brightened until he was able to extinguish his own little light.

The stairs terminated abruptly where the amber started, and Tzedef had to slowly work his way up and into it, using whatever force was preventing the amber from touching him to make a small pocket of space around the opening of the stairs. For a long moment he stood there, looking around and bracing himself. Then he took a deep breath, oriented himself on the chunk of castle and started to climb.

It wasn't long before he was running short of breath, and without pausing, Tzedef reached into his pocket and pulled out one of the air lozenges. He was still close enough to the ground that, if it didn't work, he would be able to go back down and get out into fresher air, but he hadn't wanted to waste one on testing it before he needed it.

For a long moment, nothing happened. The lozenge was tasteless on his tongue, though Tzedef could feel it dissolving. Then he went to inhale, and fresh, clean air flowed smoothly into his lungs without ever passing through his nose.

"Oh that is *brilliant*." He murmured appreciatively, and kept climbing with renewed vigor.

Up and up and up he went, slipping another lozenge into his mouth when breathing started to become a major challenge. As he drew closer to the castle he realized that he was going to have to circle around to be able to get in; this side of the castle was an unbroken wall made of huge stone blocks, with no gate or door in sight. So around he circled, climbing steadily until he was at the open side of the castle, and level with the floor Queen Victoria had guided him to.

It was a relief to have solid stone under his feet again when the amber parted to let him step onto the castle's floor, and he glanced around to re-orient himself, then started forward. Door after door after half-open door tempted him with tantalizing glimpses of what lay behind them. Bookcases, and beds, people that must have been servants of some kind or another, trapped in the act of sweeping, or dusting, or laughing, or chatting. One scene he managed to get a glimpse of was a woman with a furious frown on her face, caught in the middle of shaking her finger at another, taller woman. Tzedef couldn't see the second woman's face, but the set of her shoulders seemed unimpressed.

Still, he was on a mission, and he had a limited air supply. He didn't have *time* to investigate every single room he came across, no matter if they were the library or not.

Tzedef followed the faintly familiar corridor until he turned a corner and saw, halfway down the hallway, Queen Victoria's body.

Hurrying was not an option with the amber in the way, but Tzedef gave it a shot anyway, pressing as close to the amber as he could get in an attempt to force it out of the way faster. It was only marginally successful, but marginally was better than nothing, and he was sure that he reached Queen Victoria faster than he otherwise would have. Still, he paused before reaching out to break the last inch of amber between them, glancing around.

"If you are around, you may wish to be in your body when I do this." He warned thin air, "I am not particularly graceful, and I doubt cracking your head on the floor is the awakening you wish to have."

There was no response, but Tzedef hadn't really been expecting one. Still he waited a couple of moments before reaching forward through the amber and touching her wrist.

CHAPTER FORTY-TWO

Retrieving a Queen

She didn't stumble. She wasn't confused. She barely even acknowledged that anything had happened as she finished her step and then stood still, shaking her skirts to straighten them. "Well. That was *thoroughly* unpleasant. Let's never do that again, shall we?"

Tzedef huffed a soft laugh, and then offered her a lozenge. "For when it becomes too hard to breathe." He explained, and she nodded, taking it from him delicately and examining it closely before slipping it into a pocket in her dress.

"I must say," Victoria said glancing around, "This is significantly faster than I had hoped you would free me. Granted, I saw how you freed the dwarven king, but I also saw the arrest afterwards. I was certain that it would delay my release significantly."

"Mmm…" Tzedef hummed around his lozenge. "We escaped, but we have a problem that I believe you may be uniquely suited to solve, Your Majesty."

One delicate, white eyebrow arched over a dark purple eye. "Really now? And what is that?"

"Perhaps I could explain while we move?" Tzedef suggested, and Victoria smiled.

"Very well. This way."

She turned as if to continue walking down the hallway, and Tzedef frowned.

"The exit is this way."

"The exit is, yes," she agreed, half turning back to look at him, "but I assumed you would prefer to retrieve the candle magic now, as opposed to relying on the good will of the dwarves to possibly allow you to retrieve it later."

Tzedef grimaced, but nodded. With how reluctant Ervet had been to even *say* that Tzedef would be allowed to keep the magic, should he find it later, he very much didn't wish to rely on their good will.

"A fair point," he admitted, and stepped towards where Queen Victoria was standing.

She fell in behind him, and Tzedef explained the situation as she directed him down the hall she had been striding along, then around a corner, down some stairs, and deeper into the castle. It wasn't until they reached an ornately carved door decorated with ferns made of glittering amethyst that Tzedef realized where they must be.

"Your Majesty," He said, very carefully, "I thought we were going to a library?"

"We are." Victoria said, sounding highly amused, "My personal library lies through my bedroom. Quickly now, out of the way. It will only open to my hand."

Tzedef sighed heavily and leaned to one side, allowing the relatively tiny woman to slip past him and pull the door open.

Inside was a bedroom, as she'd said. It wasn't, however, over the top, garishly lavish. Instead, it was tastefully decorated in purples and silvers and soft greys that left the room feeling cool and comfortable. Granted, that was all through a haze of amber, so the effect was somewhat lost, but from what he could tell with a brief look around, the room had been designed with comfort first in mind and aesthetics second.

"Over there," Victoria said, "in front of the fireplace."

Tzedef nodded, and moved over to the indicated position. There was a wash of heat as the amber shrank back away from the fire, and Queen Victoria cursed softly, then made a gesture and the fire went out abruptly.

"I had forgotten about that. No need to allow the fire to eat all of our air. Still, that works out just as well. You'll need to step through the fireplace."

Tzedef blinked. "I beg your pardon?"

"My private library is through the fireplace. It's perfectly safe, but you'll need to go first, since the entire thing is full of amber as well."

"Ah." Tzedef said, considering the fireplace. "I see."

After a moment he shrugged and stepped forward, ducking under the lintel and stepping over the ticking remains of the fire. The stone at the back of the fireplace was uncomfortably warm under his hands, but after a moment that ceased to matter as they sank through it.

Bit by bit, Tzedef worked his way through the wall, and when he finally emerged on the other side, it was to look out at a room packed to the brim with books and scrolls from the inside of another fireplace. It took only another moment to make enough space to pull his tail completely through the wall, and no sooner than he had, Victoria stepped through after him, surveying the room with a kind of proprietary pride.

"Right. If you could please start walking along the shelves, I'll be able to gather everything I might need."

Tzedef eyed her, puzzled, but moved to start clearing the closest set of shelves. "Everything you might need?"

"Well, yes." Victoria nodded absently, reaching far deeper than seemed feasible into a pocket on her skirt, then coming out with an empty bag. "I'll need to do a great deal of research. After all, I still need to get my people out of here, and us all and my castle back to where we belong."

"But there will be a path." Tzedef pointed out, and caught the flat look that Queen Victoria gave him out of the corner of his eye.

"If you think for one single second that I am going to venture inside the amber without you present, then you're a fool. And I did not take you for a fool. Nor did I think you were interested in lingering around Reyfil Mountain to allow me to be more leisurely in my selection."

Tzedef blinked at the vehemence in her voice then

winced. Right. If someone happened to cast a spell on the amber while she was inside… and after being trapped for so long… it was a wonder she was as well put together as she currently was. If it had been him, Tzedef was almost sure that he would be a raving mess, but Queen Victoria was moving along a little ways behind him, sweeping armfuls of books off the shelves and into her bag, and being only slightly more careful with the scrolls.

She didn't seem inclined to speak aside from directing him toward specific shelves, and Tzedef was perfectly content to simply walk around the library, examining the spines of the books as he went.

Most of them were marked in a language that he didn't know, the odd angles and swooping curls completely unfamiliar. Still, he didn't take any off the shelves to check the insides- for one, this was Queen Victoria's private library, and she'd said nothing that invited him to peruse. For two, this was Queen Victoria's *private library*. If the woman was half the mage he thought she was, she'd have cursed them to hells and back. He had no wish to see what would happen if anyone other than she touched them.

"Tzedef?"

Tzedef looked up from the dark green leather bound book he was examining the spine of, glancing across the room towards where Queen Victoria was beckoning him over. He'd circumnavigated the room, then walked in a tightening spiral, and now there was only a narrow pillar of amber in the center of the room, and a ceiling of it that was about a foot over his head.

"Yes, your majesty?" He asked, heading over to her.

"Stand here, would you please?"

Tzedef arched one eye ridge, but moved to stand where she'd indicated, a spot directly in front of one of the larger bookcases,

Victoria didn't explain anything, but after a few moments, she reached past him and lifted a plain, brown, leather bound book off the shelf, replacing it with a different, nearly identical volume.

The bookcase slid silently to the side, revealing another room.

This one was completely bare of books, but full of cabinets, shelves, cupboards, and counters.

"In here, please."

"What is this?" Tzedef asked, frowning as he stepped past the bookcase and into the small hollow that his presence had created.

"My smaller workshop. For when I get ideas that need testing right away." Queen Victoria replied calmly, and Tzedef mentally revised his estimation of her potential magical ability up significantly.

"Is there something in particular you need from your workshop?" He asked, glancing around curiously, and Victoria brandished a scroll at him.

"*This* is the candle magic scroll. It has a list of the equipment and supplies that you will need on it, all of which can be found in this room. So. You'll need to go to that cupboard, that storage closet, and those shelves over there."

Tzedef's ears perked up, and he did his best not to

stare at the scroll in her hand.

So close. He was *so. Close.*

But it needed equipment. Supplies. And she was offering to give them to him. So he headed for the indicated spots in the room, and watched as Queen Victoria pulled out blocks of beeswax, bundles of wicks, pots with healthy coatings of wax on the inside already, and an odd leather bundle that seemed rather more heavy than simple leather should be. Everything was tucked into her bag, which seemed no more full than it had at the beginning, and when she was done she nodded, satisfied.

"I think that's just about everything."

"Wonderful. Shall we go, then, your majesty?"

"Yes." She said, and spun on her heel, striding out of the workshop.

The bookcase slid back into place once Tzedef was out of the workshop, and the tail end of Queen Victoria's dress was already slipping through the back wall of the fireplace, making him hurry to catch up.

Tzedef took a moment to look around the mostly emptied library before he stepped through the fireplace wall, then shrugged. If she'd forgotten anything, she could ask him to come with her to retrieve it before he left.

Assuming, of course, that all went well with this ridiculous dwarven coup.

The trip back down through the tunnel was simultaneously easier, and more nerve wracking. Unlike their time in the castle, the air in the tunnel was thick and stuffy, prompting both of them to grab another lozenge, which, luckily, lasted all the way down to the tunnel through the stone beneath the amber.

"So." Victoria said casually as she stepped carefully down the rough tunnel, the soft shine of her pendant providing enough light for both of them to see easily. "You explained the situation. You did *not*, however, explain what you wanted from me."

"The candle magic, obviously." Tzedef said, "But more than that... you are an accomplished mage, correct?"

"Yes."

"There is a particular spell." Tzedef said carefully, keeping his voice quiet. "One that is impossible for adherents to the gods to cast. One that only particularly learned mages *might* know, and if they did, they would do their best to keep others from finding out that they know."

"I see..." Queen Victoria's voice was thoughtful. "And you think I might know this spell? You obviously know *of* it, and you seem to be an accomplished mage in your own right. Is it simply beyond your ability at the moment?"

Tzedef stopped.

"I... No? I am not a mage at all. I am a cleric. I follow the goddess Hecate."

Victoria stopped, turned, and stared at him.

"You what?"

"I am a cleric." Tzedef said slowly, and Victoria looked at him gravely.

"Then we have a problem."

Tzedef tensed, and Queen Victoria scoffed lightly. "Not that kind of problem, do relax. No. The problem is that Candle Magic is an *arcane* working. In its current incarnation, it simply isn't designed to work with the power of the gods."

Tzedef's heart sank. "It... what?"

"You won't be able to use it in its current form." Victoria repeated, and watched him carefully for a long moment before continuing thoughtfully. "However, I promised you the candle magic. One might say that that means I am obligated to ensure that you have a means to *use* it, as well. Tell me about this spell you think I may know, and I will see if it would ease enough of my debt to you, or if I ought to also see about adapting the candle magic."

"To be fair," Tzedef said reasonably, "the spell I hope you know would not be cast at my behest, but for the King of Reyfil Mountain. It would be to him that the debt there would fall."

Queen Victoria hummed thoughtfully, then turned and started walking again, slightly more slowly. "True, but we shall have to see if that's a debt that he is willing to incur. Tell me more."

Tzedef nodded, and started talking.

The rest of the walk passed quickly enough, and by the time they emerged from the crack in the wall, Victoria was nodding thoughtfully.

"Yes, I can see how that would work, and that is

something that is easily within my power to do." She paused, and glanced around at the waiting dwarves, each of whom was a good few inches taller than her, then over at Beech. "You know, they look much larger in person."

That broke some of the tension, and Ervet and Aduni chuckled, grinning at the elven queen.

The Merchanter and the Bookkeeper were standing next to King Nalimin, obviously on guard, and Tzedef recognized the distant look in his eyes as the same look he'd had when he'd been communing with the maze before.

"Is everything alright?" He asked, and Bookkeeper Westlin glanced over at him.

"More search parties. He's moving the base camp closer to here, and getting rid of the extra entrances."

Tzedef hummed, and nodded, and turned to make introductions.

By the time he had finished, so had King Nalimin, and he hustled them all down two corridors and into the camp where Sorecco and Lady Limnally were chatting amicably.

"— so there I was, halfway through my story, and this little shit dumps a washbasin full of snow over my head!" Sorecco said, gesturing expansively as Lady Limnally cackled. "So of course I scream, and now I'm freezing cold, and the other kids, they're laughing, because of course seeing someone get the better of their teacher is hilarious, and my teeth are chattering because it's cold enough to freeze the Storm Queen's tits off. Amarie comes barging out of the kitchen because I'd screamed, and then she gets mad at *me*, like *I'd* done something wrong!"

Tzedef grinned. He'd heard this tale several times since it'd happened, but apparently Sorecco had found a new, appreciative, audience.

"Welcome back, by the way." Sorecco added carelessly, turning towards the entrance they were walking through. "Everything go alright?"

"As well as could be expected." Tzedef said, and then thought for a moment. "Possibly better, actually. Your majesty, this is Sorecco, and Lady Limnally, the high priestess of the god of Reyfil Mountain."

"A pleasure." Queen Victoria said with a nod, and glanced around at the camp, then strode over to where the flat stone was putting off heat. "Right. This will work well. Tzedef? You wish to learn Candle Magic? Come here, I will show it to you as it is now, and then the two of us will work to adjust it for your goddess."

"Right now?" Tzedef asked, surprised. "I would have thought you would wish to rest for a small while, first."

Victoria snorted. "I have been 'resting' for centuries. No, I am done with that. Now is the time to get things *done*. So. Do you wish to learn or not?"

"Yes." Tzedef said firmly, and strode over to the heat-stone.

He watched, lingering a small distance away as she pulled the bag she'd been packing back out of her pocket and removed the equipment she'd taken from the workroom, kneeling next to the heated stone.

"Candle magic is, at its heart, quite simple." She said absently, her voice falling into a lecturing cadence as a block of beeswax lifted into the air and started to break into pieces small enough to fit into the pot she placed on the heating stone.

"First, one must be prepared to make a candle. It will not work with pre-prepared candles."

The wax started to melt, sending the scent of honey and beeswax thick into the air as she pulled out the leather bundle and unrolled it, revealing delicate looking wax carving tools that looked as though they were made of silver.

"You must not pour the whole candle at once, unless your goal is to only have a single long-lasting spell."

Tzedef frowned. "Long lasting? What do you mean? Does the candle not just cast the spells as they should be?"

That jolted Victoria out of her concentration, and she glanced up at him. "Absolutely not. No, that wouldn't be particularly useful, would it? No. What it does is it takes spells that last for only a short time and extends the duration for as long as it takes the candle to burn through that particular layer."

She glanced into the little pot, and swirled it gently by its handle, moving the melting wax around.

"What about spells that just… happen?" Sorecco asked, curious, and Queen Victoria glanced over at him, her purple eyes considering.

"That is where things get a little more complex." She said after a moment. "Yes, spells with no effect duration, such as most healing spells and many offensive spells, will simply go off. They will not have a duration applied to them, nor will they be extended in any other way."

"But...?" Tzedef asked slowly, and she smiled.

"But there's nothing that says that you cannot cast multiple spells on the same layer of the candle. In fact, each layer may be divided concentrically or radially, and, so long as the spell inscription fits within the section, then it's a valid spellform and may be cast as such once the wax holding the inscription melts. Also, there's no set thickness for a layer. So long as it can be properly inscribed on, it will work."

"Oh..." Tzedef breathed, "That is... ingenious."

"It gets better." Victoria said smugly. "Vertical layers, that is, layers that are dipped rather than poured are valid layers as well, so long as the spell is inscribed vertically upon it. This allows even more space for longer inscriptions that might not fit properly into a poured layer, and can still allow for multiple spells to go off at the same time, since the candle can be divided lengthwise just as easily as it can be widthwise. The layers, poured and dipped, may be alternated as well, and the resultant candles can become quite massive."

She glanced into the little pot again, and, deeming the wax melted enough, pulled a mold and a wick out of her bag.

"The pouring isn't necessarily important." She said, carefully arranging everything to her liking and then taking the wax off the stone and tipping the pot to pour some of the beeswax into the mold. "In fact it's easy enough to speed this part along with magic. A touch of ice…"

A cold draft swirled around Tzedef's ankles where he was crouched, and he watched, fascinated, as the wax cooled rapidly, solidifying in streaks from the outside in.

"Now, we simply remove this layer from the mold, trim the wick down since I'm only making a single layered candle to demonstrate, and, using these tools, carve the spell into the wax while almost, but not quite, casting the same spell."

She did so as she spoke, carving symbols that Tzedef didn't recognize into the cool wax in a circle around the wick with rich purple light sparking off her fingertips. When she'd finished, she paused, looking chagrined.

"Is there something wrong?"

"I forgot something." Victoria admitted. "To keep the spellforms from filling in with the next layer, the carvings need to be filled in with another kind of wax. I neglected to bring any from my workroom."

Tzedef winced. "That… we could go back? It would be risky, but we could go back."

"Or," Bookkeeper Westlin drawled, "You could use this. I assume any wax will work?" he added, holding out a stick of bright red sealing wax. "It doesn't need to be consecrated or anything?"

"No, it doesn't need to be special in any way." Victoria said, looking relieved, "Thank you, that will work beautifully."

A snap produced a small flame over her thumb, and she held it close to the end of the sealing wax, letting it drip down into the carvings and cover them completely.

"There. Now, if I were going to do another spell, I would simply carve it into this layer of wax, and then, when it was finished, switch back to the beeswax. Thin layers like this are perfect for one off spells." She said after a few moments. "Now watch."

CHAPTER FORTY-THREE

A War of Two Kings

The wick caught. The sealing wax melted.

As the wax where the inscriptions were carved melted, brightly colored lights started popping into existence around the little room; purples, and blues, and greens, all bobbing merrily in the air and casting odd shadows as they moved.

"Fairy Lights is a reasonably simple spell," Victoria said, sounding pleased, "and the duration is relatively short. This candle should last roughly twice the time as the spell cast ordinarily so you can see for yourself the utility."

"I can already see the utility." Tzedef murmured, glancing around at the lights, then at the candle. "I wonder if it is immune to me?"

Queen Victoria tilted her head. "Immune to you?"

"Yes." Tzedef said, staring into the candle flame contemplatively. "I have... something akin to a curse. Magic items do not work for me. Magic tends to fail when I am around, and no magic cast directly on me, takes. While that last bit has come in handy in the past, it is still more trouble than it is worth. Healing spells and potions, after all, must work directly on the body."

"That sounds like quite a powerful innate ability, especially for one that is constantly active." Victoria observed, and Tzedef's eyes snapped up to hers.

"What?"

She blinked, then looked at him, and realization dawned. "Right, yes. Your people, you call them Gifts, don't you. My apologies, I'd forgotten. Though, I wonder if it's possible for you to suppress it at all, even for a short time. That might let you get around certain limitations."

Tzedef's ears were ringing.

The only thing he could feel was his heart pounding in his chest.

Queen Victoria's lips were moving, but he couldn't hear what she was saying.

Gift.

She thought it was a *Gift*?!

"I don't have a Gift." Tzedef said numbly. "I don't—I've never— *I don't have magic!*"

"Except for when you do." Sorecco said thoughtfully, and his voice cut through the ringing in Tzedef's ears.

"What?"

"Except for when you do." Sorecco repeated patiently. "You even showed Casey and me, remember? Back in Natari, with the magic bag. It worked how many times in a row before failing?"

Tzedef shook his head. "I don't... remember. Several. But that proves nothing! That- it's *always* been like that. If it were a Gift, surely I would be able to control it! Turn it *off* somehow!"

"Not necessarily." Victoria said matter-of-factly. "There are plenty of people out there with uncontrollable innate abilities. There have been plenty of dwarves in the time I was trapped in the amber with innate abilities that they could not control or turn off. I watched many of them. The fact that your innate ability seems to be intermittent is a mark in favor of the idea that it can be suppressed, at least for short periods of time."

Tzedef stared at her, and Queen Victoria met his gaze steadily.

In the end, it was he who broke off, turning away to look down at the candle again before reaching down and picking it up.

Instantly the Fairy Lights, long past their usual lifespan, winked out, leaving Tzedef holding an ordinary candle stub.

He stared at the little flame for a moment longer, then, suddenly furious, he blew it out and tossed the remains of the candle back into the little pot.

"Really?" Victoria looked unimpressed. "With the wick?"

But Tzedef didn't answer her. Instead, he stood up, reached up to the amulet on his chest, and strode away from the group to one of the far corners of the room. It wasn't particularly private, not with so many people around, but it was better than nothing, and if Tzedef didn't get a handle on this right now then… well, he wasn't sure *what* he might do, but he was decently sure it wouldn't be pretty.

The amulet fit into the eye socket of one of the skulls nearest him, and Tzedef propped it there, then sat back to meditate. He wasn't going to bother Hecate with this, but meditation would help get his feet back under him, and he could desperately use a little stability right now.

No one bothered him as he meditated, but even so he found it nearly impossible to clear his mind in the way that usually came so easily to him. Instead of the welcome absence of thought and the peace and calm that came with it, he kept thinking of incidents. Times when something had worked for him. Times when he'd managed to use this water stone or that magic bag, or the other signal flare. Times when, despite how desperately he'd needed something, *anything* to work, it hadn't.

It couldn't be a Gift.

It *couldn't*.

He was a curse. The magicless offspring of two of the most powerful mages in Fernil, born as a sign of the gods' displeasure of their hubris.

But what if? Something whispered in the back of his mind, and Tzedef growled, forcing it away.

It wasn't a Gift. Someone would have noticed before.

He wasn't sure how long it took for him to finally manage to corral his racing thoughts, but several of the dwarves were asleep when he finally opened his eyes again, and Sorecco was curled up as well, leaning against Beech. Tzedef winced when he saw how she'd had to jury-rig a way for herself to sleep by piling the assorted packs and bags of the dwarves up against one of the walls so she could lean her upper body against it. It looked horrifically uncomfortable.

Queen Victoria, however, wasn't asleep, nor was King Nalimin, and Tzedef watched them for a few minutes, observing as the two of them conversed quietly. He couldn't hear what they were saying, but judging from the look on Nalimin's face, it wasn't anything particularly pleasant.

For a moment he considered going over and apologizing for storming off like that. For ruining the candle that Queen Victoria had made as a demonstration despite the lack of any obligation to do so. He had acted like a child being told something he didn't want to hear, and, looking back on it with several hours' distance, he was embarrassed. But she and King Nalimin were deep in conversation, and it would be rude to interrupt.

He watched them for a moment longer, torn, then sighed and stood up, grunting softly as muscles that had frozen in place from long contact with the cold stone of the floor protested vehemently. They protested even louder when he stooped to retrieve his amulet, and Tzedef staggered slightly on his first step towards the camp proper.

The movement, apparently, drew both of the royals' eyes, and Tzedef inclined his head at both of them as he drew closer.

"Your Majesties."

"Tzedef." King Nalimin said, nodding back. "We were just speaking about your idea, and the repercussions of that particular spell being used here."

"Oh?" Tzedef asked, and glanced at Queen Victoria, who was casually sipping on a mug of something that smelled strongly alcoholic.

"Yes." She said. "It turns out that displaying *that* particular talent in this particular place would make me incredibly unpopular, very quickly. We were just discussing the terms of my inevitable banishment."

Tzedef blinked, and Victoria glanced up at him, then laughed at the look on his face.

"Don't worry about it." She advised him. "To be quite honest, if I never see the inside of this mountain again, it would be too soon. As long as I have access to the amber so that I can run experiments on it to try to get my people out, then I won't protest."

Tzedef nodded slowly, then decided to take her advice and not worry about it.

"Have there been any more search parties?" He asked King Nalimin, who nodded.

"Three more." He grumbled, "Idiots, the lot of them. They searched for a good few hours before the maze led them back out."

"Marvelous." Tzedef sighed, and Victoria shrugged.

"It will make it easier to pull this off. The longer it goes without Cinnabar's men bringing us to *her*, the more likely that she will come to *us*."

"True." Nalimin agreed, looking dour. "She always was an impatient child."

"Either way, the likelihood that she will show her face down here within the next day or two is small." Victoria said comfortably. "I give her… a week. One week of ramping up the frequency of the search parties in an attempt to drive you into exhaustion. It will be long enough for her to get frustrated with the perceived incompetence of her men, but not so long that she's completely lost all reason."

Tzedef nodded slowly, then, abruptly, yawned widely, completely caught off guard.

"My apologies. Apparently I am more tired than I thought."

"Sleep, then." Nalimin gestured carelessly over his shoulder at where several empty bedrolls lay next to the heat-stone. "If you are needed, rest assured, you will be woken."

Tzedef nodded, bowed slightly, and bid both rulers good-night.

Victoria's prediction played out almost exactly as she'd said. Over the course of the next few days, the frequency of the search parties increased and King Nalimin needed to spend more and more time communing with the maze; shifting rooms and corridors around so that no one came near enough to smell the beeswax and honey that permeated the air as Queen Victoria and Tzedef made candle after candle.

They were trying to work out how to make the candle magic function when powered by a god rather than by the power of a mortal, and for the most part, it wasn't working particularly well. Candles had melted, refused to melt, burst entirely into flames, *exploded*…

If Tzedef hadn't watched his siblings in the process of learning new spells, he might have been disheartened. As it was, he'd had to apologize profusely to Beech when hot wax from the exploding candle had splattered across the half of the room that included her hindquarters.

She'd been able to clean it off with the same spell she used to get rid of road dust, but she'd still been plenty peeved.

The candle that he'd dropped into the wax pot had still had sealing wax on it, and once the wick had been fished out, Victoria had simply dropped the rest of the stick into the pot. It had turned the pale gold a more rich, reddish orange, which she had said would be used to form alternating layers with the regular beeswax, once they'd solved the problem.

Of course, part of figuring out how to solve the problem was figuring out what the problem *was*, and that part was being remarkably elusive.

"Do you think I channeled too much divinity that time?" Tzedef asked, and Queen Victoria sat back on her heels with a huff.

"I don't see how you could have. That was barely a trickle, and the damn thing still just..."

She huffed again, staring down at the pile of fine wax sand with a sad looking piece of string sticking out of it.

"We've tried you carving the spell you want into the candle. We've tried you carving a prayer into the candle. We've tried you praying over the finished candle. We've tried you praying over the hot wax as it's be poured. You blessing a candle that I've already made didn't do anything at all, which is probably the best result we could expect at this point. What else is there to *try*?"

"Have you dedicated the candle to your goddess as it's being made?" Lady Limnally asked, leaning forward from where she'd been watching their latest attempt. "Or included something that would direct whatever prayer you inscribed on the candle to her?"

Tzedef paused. "I- no. I had assumed that since I was making it, and inscribing the prayer, it would be self evident?"

"Possibly, possibly," Limnally nodded slowly, "but if it isn't, then wouldn't that be just a prayer going out into the aether? Inviting anyone to answer it?"

He frowned thoughtfully, looking down at the pile of wax sand too, then meeting Queen Victoria's eyes. "What do you think?"

She shrugged. "We might as well try it? There's nothing saying that it *wouldn't* work, at the very least, and directing the prayer is probably a good idea. I hadn't thought of the idea that without some kind of mailing address, so to speak, it might fail."

Tzedef nodded slowly, then sighed and reached over to start preparing the next batch of wax.

They poured a narrow taper that looked more like a toy than a candle, and, when it was cool, Tzedef carved Hecate's sigil into it, wrapping the mazelike symbol around the width of the candle. Then they poured another thick layer of wax around the taper and waited for it to cool. This time, the solid wax didn't boil away as he prayed over it. The wick didn't spontaneously combust from the bottom up, nor did the entire thing dissolve into something that was better left hidden deep under the stone. Instead, the carving process proceeded smoothly as Tzedef carved the same prayer he was murmuring around the circumference of the candle- a plea for protection and safety that was similar to the prayer he used to ask for the alarm spell.

When he was done, they sheathed it in another layer of wax, just to keep the carvings from getting mangled by handling, and were left with something that was about the size of his thumb.

"There." Tzedef said, highly satisfied. "We should likely test it, just to ensure the kinks are worked out."

"It's not going to explode again, is it?" Beech asked warily from the other side of the heat stone, and Tzedef glanced over at her.

Being underground for this long had done the centaur no favors. Despite her dark skin she looked wan, and her coat was going dull. She had spent more time huddling closer and closer to the heat stone as the days had progressed, and now, despite being nearly on top of the thing, she was wrapped in a cloak that Gharkin had hesitantly offered her.

"It shouldn't." He said, and she gave him a flat look. "It *shouldn't*." He repeated, and shrugged. "But I won't say that it won't. We won't know until we test it."

"Great..." She sighed, and looked like she would very much like to move away, but couldn't because of the way Sorecco was leaning against her side.

The lack of activity was getting to him, too, and while he'd spent some time regaling Lady Limnally with stories from the last winter, and listened eagerly as she'd shared tales of her childhood and legends of her people, he'd slowly grown more withdrawn and quiet. For the last couple of days, he'd spent most of his time drowsing, leaning against Beech for warmth. Tzedef was honestly worried about the pair of them. Neither were taking this stress particularly well, and he feared what would happen if the plan didn't work as they expected it to.

"We can test it over here." Victoria said, rising gracefully to her feet and beckoning Tzedef over toward the other side of the room.

He rose as well, grunting as his knees protested, and followed her only to stop dead in his tracks as the entire maze shuddered.

"What was that?" Beech demanded sharply, looking around as Sorecco startled fully awake.

King Nalimin, sitting on his bedroll with his

advisors lounging on their own nearby, was sitting bolt
upright.

"That was Cinnabar entering the maze. With a large
group of guards." He said tightly. "It- it's not listening to
me anymore. I can't shift anything. Fuck, this is... why isn't
this working?"

Victoria stared at him for a moment, then groaned
and reached up to massage the bridge of her nose. "Oh that
idiot girl... I told her it would come back to bite someone
in the ass one day."

"What?" Westlin asked, sitting up sharply and
turning to look at her. "What would come back to bite *who*
in the ass?"

"Your king." Victoria said, her voice thick with
sarcasm, "Ennuli the First. She made the maze to listen to
'a divinely appointed king.' Not 'a king appointed by the
god of Reyfil Mountain.' *Any* divinely appointed king. That
makes things both harder, and easier. We won't be able to
rely on the Guardian Dead to act as distractions for any
guards she might bring with her, but she'll be able to find
us without rousing her suspicion as to *why* she can find us
so easily. Tzedef, change of plans. We're field testing your
candle. Over here."

"Field testing it!?" Tzedef was incredulous.

"Yes." Victoria said firmly, striding over to the
center of the camp as the heat stone and various other
things lifted up and out of her way, clearing a space in the
exact center of the room.

Tzedef followed her over, watching the Queen

skeptically. "What exactly do you expect to accomplish with this? Even *if* it works, it's a basic barrier cast from a small candle. It will burn out quickly, won't it?"

"Yes." She said. "And that's the point. We aren't trying to *stop* her. We are trying to *stall* her."

"I know that." Tzedef said impatiently, kneeling to set the candle down and pulling out his little striker. "But even once Cinnabar is taken care of, there will still be the guards."

Victoria shrugged. "You'll need to figure that part out for yourselves. I'm going to be preoccupied."

Tzedef grimaced.

"They're on their way." King Nalimin announced, "Cinnabar can't influence the maze any more than I can at the moment, so they're spreading out in search parties. I can't direct the Guardian Dead to distract or delay them; it's only a matter of time before we're found."

"Right." Ervet said grimly, and he and Gharkin began packing up, with Westlin, Loferek, and Fellip helping to roll up bedrolls and gather the bits and bobs that accumulate around most longer-term camps. Beech scrambled to her feet, and Sorecco stood as well, one hand on her flank.

"What do you need us to do?" Beech said, her legs braced as if she were readying herself for a blow.

Tzedef looked at her for a long moment, and, as though it had never been in question, a decision crystallized in his mind.

"Stand back." He told her. "And do not be afraid."

CHAPTER FORTY-FOUR

Necromancy

Tzedef didn't light the candle right away. Instead, he sat there, waiting for the king's word that the searchers were getting close. Not because of any desire to risk capture, but because the candle was so small it would likely only be good for about fifteen minutes to half an hour at most, and he wanted to be sure that they would get the most possible use out of it.

In the meantime, he fell into a light meditation, reaching for more of his goddess' attention than he usually requested. This would need to be done carefully, but quickly enough that none of Cinnabar's guards would have a chance to react. The less time they had to figure out what was going on, the less bloodshed there would be.

Hecate, queen of the grave, enemies close on those I have sworn to protect. Grant me the assistance of those you have guided before and allow me to direct them as I must. Allow me to prevent meaningless death and allow those who may pass to fall into the final sleep peacefully.

"They're almost here." King Nalimin's voice broke through Tzedef's meditation, and he opened his eyes to see wisps of saffron light drifting off his hands and down the hallway, sinking into the ossuary walls. After a moment, it faded away, and Tzedef nodded to himself, satisfied. He could feel them, now, waiting and ready.

Reaching out with the striker he clicked it next to the wick, then again, until it caught and the candle flared as the beeswax started to melt.

Tzedef held his breath, staring at the tiny candle. This was the moment of truth. If it didn't take, then they were all going to have their work cut out for them.

More wax melted, dripped a little way down the tiny candle, and cooled. And a semi-translucent barrier sprang to life, a hemisphere that encompassed the entirety of the little room, and part of the hallway beyond.

"Well that's pretty." Beech observed, reaching out to poke it gently and pausing only a few centimeters away. "Is that safe? Can I touch it?"

"It's fine." Tzedef assured her absently.

Beech nodded, and prodded the soap-bubble barrier gently.

"It's warm!" she sounded surprised, and Sorecco made an interested noise.

"Really?"

Tzedef smiled crookedly, and turned his attention away from them to walk over to the hallway, his ears perked as he listened hard. Queen Victoria joined him a moment later, and, when he glanced down at her, smiled grimly. "I can hear them. It's almost time."

"Is there anything else you need?" He asked, and she shook her head.

"No. Cinnabar's presence will be enough."

"Good."

They fell silent, and, after a moment, she moved back and out of sight of the hallway. A few seconds later, she started to chant, low and quiet, in a language that set Tzedef's scales to itching.

By that point, Tzedef could hear the approaching guards. Hear the metal against metal sound of armor moving, and footsteps of a fair number of people. He didn't move. Instead he settled himself, readying himself to greet their pursuers.

Only for a touch at his elbow to startle him out of his stance.

"This isn't your fight." King Nalimin told him gravely. "Your assistance has been invaluable, but if I were to allow you alone to face Cinnabar, then could I truly call myself the proper king of Reyfil?"

He shook his head. "We will be the first barrier she faces, aside from your shield. Be prepared to protect yourself, your companions, and my royal counterpart."

That made far too much sense, as little as Tzedef liked it. This was a succession crisis, of a sort, and if outsiders got too visibly involved, then it might cast doubts as to the legitimacy of the king's right to rule, divinely granted or otherwise. Tzedef grimaced, but stepped aside. "As you say, Your Majesty."

Nalimin nodded at him again, and planted himself in the center of the hallway, Aduni on his immediate right, Westlin on his immediate left, Fellip next to Aduni, and Loferek next to Westlin. They made, Tzedef had to admit, a moderately intimidating sight, even without their weapons.

For a moment, he considered standing behind them, lending his silent support. But that would remove the impact that seeing their king standing against them might have on the guards that were approaching, and so he slipped back around the corner. Ervet caught his eye and nodded silently, pressing himself and Gharkin back against the walls, out of sight of the hallway.

The quiet clanking drew closer and closer, and Tzedef's hand twitched, aching for the weight of his mace. He knew the moment the sound passed into audibility for everyone else because Sorecco and the priests stiffened, then pressed back up against the walls even harder. It was pointless, of course, they were already well out of sight of the hall, but the instinct to go for further concealment was one that Tzedef could approve of.

He tensed even further as the footsteps rounded the corner and stuttered, the owners obviously spotting Nalimin and the rest, then slowed down and came to a grumbling, rattling halt.

Light shone down the hallway- not the flickering of torches or candles, but the pure, unwavering light of crystals, casting crisp shadows of the dwarves arrayed in the hallway back into the room.

"You there!" The voice was harsh, "You are wanted for stirring up civil unrest! Place any weapons on the ground and put your hands on your head!"

Nalimin's voice was tight with anger. "I am King Nalimin Reyfil the Second, rightfully ordained king of Reyfil Mountain! Who are you to give orders to your king?"

"King?" Another voice scoffed, female, and throaty, and quite melodically deep. "You are no king. You are a deluded figurehead, acting against the best interests of the mountain and its people!"

Footsteps came closer, slow and measured, and there was a rattling and clanking as guards presumably moved out of the way for whoever was speaking to move through the crowd.

"Cinnabar." Nalimin's voice was a growl, and the woman's retort was sharp.

"*King* Cinnabar! Unlike you, I actually *earned* my place in this mountain!"

"*Horseshit!*" Nalimin snarled, "You were gutter trash when our god chose you as my heir! Everything you have now, you were given on a silver platter!"

"I worked my *ass* off for *everything* I ever got!" Cinnabar shouted back, and Tzedef could almost picture her, red hair gleaming in the light of the crystals, sharp eyes flashing in fury. "The twelve hour study sessions, the pop quizzes on noble houses, the *deportment lessons!* Working my fingers to the *bone* on sums and tax information, and reading until my eyes crossed from the books of the laws of our people? No! No."

Her voice calmed abruptly, turning curt and cold. "No. I *worked* for what I have, and I'll not have anyone saying any different. Not even you, pretender for the throne."

"Pretender—!" Aduni roared, and there was a sound that Tzedef thought might be him taking a step forward.

Cinnabar scoffed derisively. "Captain Melick?"

"Yes your Majesty?"

"Take them."

There was a dull thwump as what sounded like several dwarves strode directly into it the shield, then, from the sound of it, stumbled backwards, swearing viciously.

"You—!" Cinnabar sounded incensed, "You have that mage with you, don't you? Fine! Quintan!"

Someone else moved forward, though Tzedef couldn't get much of an idea of what sort of person they might be until Cinnabar spoke again.

"Bring the shield down!"

Tzedef's eyes widened, and he cast a glance over at Victoria, who was still chanting under her breath. They needed more time! The shield couldn't come down yet! Not until she was ready!

He gritted his teeth, closed his eyes, and stretched out his senses, trailing his attention down the lingering threads of saffron energy. King Nalimin had asked him to leave this to him but Tzedef was, unfortunately, going to have to intervene.

Several things happened in rapid succession.

Bones rattled and scraped as the walls around the guard dwarves came to life, stretching out bony hands and arms to snag weapons and limbs as saffron light flared into life in the eye sockets of the skulls around them.

A higher pitched dwarven voice shouted three words that made the shield ring like a bell.

And Cinnabar shrieked in rage.

"You—! How are you doing this!? The Guardian Dead are deadlocked!"

King Nalimin said nothing, but from Tzedef's multiple points of view, he could see the faint, grim smile on his face as the semi-orderly group of guards dissolved into chaos.

Bit by bit, the skeletons in the walls forced themselves together and pried themselves free, grappling with dwarves over their weapons or, in some cases, simply wrapping the dwarves in bear hugs that pinned their arms to their sides. It was, Tzedef mused, almost sad. The guards had been grouped up in such a way that they wouldn't have been able to use their weapons easily without fouling each other, and in their attempts to be careful not to do so, they'd taken too long to take on the skeletons. Not to mention the fact that swords and spears weren't particularly effective against the bony undead.

He winced as one of his skeletons was pulverized by a mace wielding dwarf who was red with fury, and three more peeled themselves out of the walls, saffron flaring in their eyes.

The shield rang again, and Tzedef's fists clenched. The mage. He had to find the mage. If they brought the shield down too early— There.

A young dwarf, his beard barely long enough for

twin braids, blond and scared looking with Cinnabar looming over him, her hands on his shoulders.

"Bring. It. *Down!*" She roared over the sound of the struggling behind them, and the dwarf, barely more than a teenager, lifted his hands again, pale pink light gathering in his palms.

A group of skeletons descended on them, and the light flickered and died as the boy, the *mage*, Tzedef corrected himself harshly, shrieked in fear.

There are no children in war.

Cinnabar fought.

The mage did not.

And Victoria's eyes opened, blazing with white light as she gestured at Gharkin, who rushed forward to blow out the candle.

The shield fell.

The remaining soldiers rushed toward the king and his men, and the skeletons that Tzedef had held in reserve dog-piled them, not even trying to fight or get their weapons, but simply bearing them down under the sheer weight of numbers.

Queen Victoria strode around the corner, her shadow writhing on the floor in the light of the crystals, and made directly for Cinnabar, who was too busy struggling against the skeletons to notice until the small elven queen was directly in front of her.

One dark hand stretched out and Cinnabar leaned back as best she could, fear bright in her eyes as they flicked from the light bleeding from Victoria's eyes to her hand, then back again. But she couldn't get away. She couldn't escape the implacable grip of the skeletons that had bent her arms up behind her back. She couldn't resist the way they forced her forward until her forehead met Victoria's palm.

Her scream brought a halt to all movement in the hallway.

Cinnabar's eyes were wild when Victoria pulled away, her own eyes back to their usual dark purple.

"You—! *What did you do to me!?*"

"I have severed your link to Plutus." Victoria said calmly, and ignored the horrified gaping from the guards being restrained around her and the way the mage was desperately squirming against the skeleton that held him- trying to get away. "I must admit, I wasn't expecting quite such a deep one. He was empowering you much beyond simply proclaiming you King, wasn't he?"

"You *bitch!*" Cinnabar howled, and her struggles redoubled to the point where she managed to wrest one arm free of the skeleton holding it, reaching for Victoria with clawed fingers. "You have no idea what I've done for this mountain! No idea what I've sacrificed! What I've achieved!"

Queen Victoria skipped nimbly back a couple of steps, neatly avoiding any of the guards and watching Cinnabar with calm, cool, eyes.

"On the contrary." She said flatly. "I know *exactly* what you've done. I've seen the people you've exiled. And executed. And blackmailed and bribed and *tormented.*"

Cinnabar paled sharply, and the skeleton caught her arm again. "L-liar. You're *lying*!"

"Am I?" Victoria asked, and continued without waiting for an answer. "Almi Wainwright. Executed for questioning the new checkpoint and the increasingly relaxed measures that were being put into place to allow 'undesireables' into the mountain. Granted, I can see why you'd have wanted to be rid of the blowhard, but the fact remains that he was executed for questioning your choices. Not particularly well thought out. How long was it before his entire family was exiled, again? Ten years?"

"Liar!" Cinnabar threw herself against the skeletons, struggling madly to get at Victoria, who simply watched her coolly.

"Teekin Chillaxe. Farli Quicktongue."

Loferek made a distressed sound that had Victoria glance over at him for a split second, apology in her eyes.

"Jermy Boardbinder. Yasmin Winterschill. Borli Headbanger."

The list went on and on, delivered in the same flat, unimpressed tone, until King Nalimin stepped forward.

"Enough. All of this will be investigated and, if true, reparations will be made to the families of those... lost."

"Murdered." Victoria said calmly. "Call a spade a spade, Your Majesty."

Nalimin winced, but acknowledged her point with a nod in her direction. "I can't authorize exile or, as might be more appropriate, execution, without granting her the due process that is the right of *every* citizen in the mountain. However in the meantime, I believe we have the perfect place to keep her until her crimes can be fully uncovered."

"Go fuck yourself!" Cinnabar shouted, "I was making this mountain great! I was *helping our people* in a way that you *never* would! I was—!"

She fell abruptly silent, going completely limp, as Victoria whispered a soft phrase and then blew gently in her face.

"What did you do?" Nalimin asked, alarmed.

"Merely a simple sleeping charm. She will wake with no harm done in about eight hours. Now. You were saying about a place to keep her?"

"Yes." King Nalimin said after a moment. "Some place even her most ardent supporters won't be getting her out of without a mutual friend of ours."

Victoria looked at him for a moment, then nodded slowly. "The amber."

"Yes." He said again, and glanced back down the hallway. "Ervet, Gharkin. We will require your assistance to close the passage back up. The rest of you..." He looked down and around at the guards in various states of disarray. Some pinned to the walls by arms and throats and ankles, others restrained in place, and still others simply buried under piles of bones. "Think very carefully about where your loyalties lie, and to whom you've given them.

"Aduni? Lead our guests the the Castle exit and do what you can to retrieve their things for them, then start verifying who among the guard is loyal to Cinnabar directly, and who is loyal to the crown. Westlin? Start looking for records. Anything you can find that would verify what our guest has claimed. Loferek? Check in with the Tradesguilds. I want to know what is going on and how things are doing. Fellip, the same, check with the Stonesingers and the Miner's Guild."

"Yes, Your Majesty." The four dwarves chorused, and bowed in unison before three of them picked their way through the tangle of limbs and bones and immediately split off.

"There will need to be an official ordaining." Limnally said, emerging from the room where they'd all been hiding and walking carefully over to Nalimin. "Or rather, re-ordaining. Just to prove to the people that our god has not yet abandoned us, and that you are, indeed, who you say you are."

Nalimin grunted as the skeletons started to drag their prisoners to either side of the hallway, pinning them to the walls despite any renewed struggles.

Only once they were all pinned did Tzedef cease watching through his minion's eyes and open his own, carefully avoiding looking in Beech and Sorecco's direction.

CHAPTER FORTY-FIVE

Farewells

Limnally caught his eye as he stepped out into the hallway, and beckoned him over as Aduni walked back into the camp room to collect Beech and Sorecco.

"You can release your hold on the dead, now." She murmured to him, and Tzedef glanced over at where the skeletons were still holding the enemy soldie— the *guards*, in place.

"Are you certain?"

"Yes." She nodded. "With Cinnabar's backing gone, control of the maze and the Guardian Dead has reverted to his majesty. It would be for the best if none of Cinnabar's people had a chance to realize that anything was different."

Tzedef nodded as Beech and Sorecco walked past him in Aduni's wake, neither looking at him, and he didn't so much as glance in the direction of the skeletons as he slowly, gradually, released his hold on them.

He could feel something else picking up the slack he was leaving behind, power flowing in to fill the gaps left by the lack of divinity animating them. When he chanced a quick look, he saw that the eye sockets of each skull was lit by ruby colored light rather than the saffron that had indicated his own control.

"Good. Thank you."

"It was no trouble." Tzedef demurred, and Limnally narrowed her eyes up at him.

"It was, and you'll accept my thanks, boy. I know the reputation that necromancers have, and you're a strong one if you're anything. I can tell. That was how many skeletons, and you aren't even breathing hard?"

Tzedef winced.

"It wasn't me?" he tried, "I simply asked Hecate for her assistance in this matter."

Limnally snorted, and beckoned him back toward the camp-room. "Oh, aye, and she just *happened* to choose to assist in this particular way? Pull the other one. No. You knew what you were doing, and you did it well. I'll not ask questions you'd rather not answer, if that's your preference, but I won't have you denying our thanks, nor Orelin's."

Tzedef looked at her blankly. "Who is Orelin?"

Limnally smirked at him, smug as anything as she brought the two of them to a halt just out of earshot of the king, the guards, or the other two priests.

"Orelin is our god. He's told me that you're to receive a blessing from him. A thanks for assisting in this matter. With a king more aligned with him back on the throne, he'll be able to more easily fend off Plutus."

Tzedef stared at Limnally, utterly baffled. "I... see?"

He shook his head. "Actually, no, I don't. I don't understand this at all. I was under the impression that I was working on this at the behest of you priests, not at the behest of the god himself."

She cocked her head, birdlike, to one side. "Is there a difference?"

"Well, yes!" Tzedef exclaimed, only remembering at the last moment to keep his voice down. Then he thought about it for a moment longer and reluctantly conceded. "Actually, no. Not really."

"Then what is there to understand?" Limnally asked practically, and Tzedef scowled at her.

"Why, for one, this god who is well known for the secrecy that surrounds his name, his domains, and essentially everything about him, is allowing you to tell *me* his name!"

"Well I can't very well give you a blessing without you knowing who the blessing is from, can I?" Limnally asked, sounding a little bit cross, "Honestly, it's not that big of a deal. We dwarves, we're a selfish lot, and we wanted to keep our god to ourselves. He's content enough with keeping to this mountain, so the secrecy worked out for both sides. It's not as though you're going to spread it around, are you?"

"I suppose not..." Tzedef allowed, then shook his head and bowed slightly to Limnally. "Thank you, then, for your trust and your god's. I am honored."

"Of course you are." Limnally said, reaching out to pat the back of his hand, and Tzedef suppressed the urge to twitch away. "Now. I can't give you the blessing directly, that would be rude. But Orelin mentioned a statuette?"

Tzedef gave her an odd look. "How is it that the gods keep knowing about that?"

She snorted. "They do talk, you know. It isn't as though they're completely isolated from one another."

Tzedef blinked. "I know that. I just wasn't expecting…"

To be the subject of divine gossip, he didn't say.

"Don't worry about it too much." Limnally said, patting his hand again. "He won't be expecting anything from you. As far as I can tell it's more symbolic than anything else. A little bit of extra luck, that's all."

"Thank you, then." He said again. "The thought is appreciated, though the statuette is likely lost by now. We were not at the inn to pay for the last week, after all."

She winced. "You didn't bring your bag with you?"

"My lady, I was on my way to covertly mine a king out of magical stone. *No*, I did not bring my belongings with me. The only things that were in the bag that was confiscated from me was rented mining equipment."

"Oh. Well that's inconvenient. Smart of you, of course, but inconvenient now. You'll just have to bring the statuette by when you've retrieved your belongings. I doubt Glim will have sold them yet. She usually waits about a month, just in case."

Tzedef arched an eye ridge at her, but Limnally didn't look like she was going to elaborate, simply smiling brightly at him.

"Was there anything else?" Tzedef asked carefully, and Limnally shook her head.

"No. That was all. Just... be sure to keep your assistance under wraps. It is better if the people involved believe it was simply Orelin lending His Majesty more direct assistance."

"Of course." He said, and bowed slightly, watching her turn and wander off towards where Nalimin was still talking quietly with Victoria, before turning and walking the couple of steps over to the center of the room, bending to scoop up the stub of the candle.

It really was just a stub. Even without Gharkin's interference, it likely would have gone out in another few minutes. But it had served its purpose well, and now Tzedef was reasonably sure he had the method for creating the candles down. All that would be required was a few additional tests, just to ensure this first one wasn't a fluke, and he would be able to head back to Fernil.

Movement from the hallway caught his eye, and Tzedef turned in time to see one of the Guardian Dead that were still holding the guards captive release the dwarf it was holding.

"You will come as witness, Captain Melick." Nalimin's voice carried faintly to his ears, and Tzedef thought for a moment, then nodded. It made sense. Having someone who obviously *hadn't* been on their side witness what was going to be done with Cinnabar would help put paid to any rumors that Nalimin had done away with her in secret.

It wouldn't get rid of all the rumors, of course, but it would at least provide some counterpoint to them.

He watched as Nalimin, Victoria, the priests, Melick (being guarded by the same skeleton that had captured him in the first place), and the sleeping form of Cinnabar, still carried by two of the Guardian Dead, headed down the hallway and out of sight.

Absently, his hand tightened around the candle stub, and he strode out of the room, past the shocked silent guards and out into the maze proper.

Only to come face to face with an unimpressed looking Aduni, waiting just around the corner with Sorecco and Beech.

"Took you long enough." He said flatly. "Are you ready now? We've only got so much time before people start getting antsy."

Tzedef blinked. "Yes, I'm ready. My apologies, I was unaware you were waiting for me."

"King said take the guests. You're a guest. Let's go."

"Right..." Tzedef said, and glanced over at Beech, who shifted uncomfortably and glanced away.

He sighed softly, and turned to follow Aduni as he walked away.

Beech summoned her little light again as the walked through the dark hallways and for a time, the four of them strode along in a silence broken only by the sound of their footsteps.

"So." Sorecco said, aiming for casual and missing by a mile. "A necromancer? How long's that been a thing?"

"Since I first swore myself to Hecate." Tzedef said levelly. "I wished for power over death, to better heal my comrades and to prevent them from dying if I could. She granted me... not quite mastery of, but access to the portion of her power mostly associated with the grave."

Beech shuddered gently, and Sorecco elbowed her from where he'd been using her flank as a guide.

"Stop that. It's still Tzedef. He's still our friend."

"Well, yeah..." Beech said reluctantly, "But—"

"No buts." Sorecco said firmly. "It's *Tzedef.* He wouldn't hurt us."

"I know that!" Beech snapped, flicking her tail to smack Sorecco with it. "I just... Necromancy is *wrong!*"

"To you." Sorecco said calmly, and Beech snorted at him.

"I *know,* okay? Just... give me a little time to adjust!"

Sorecco hummed doubtfully, then turned toward Tzedef. "Can I walk on your arm?"

Tzedef blinked at him. "If you like? Though you seem to be doing well enough with Beech's assistance."

"Barely." Sorecco grumbled softly, "This is harder than it probably looks."

"Very well then." Tzedef reached out and slipped his wrist into Sorecco's hand, slowing slightly as Sorecco slid his palm up Tzedef's arm and then around until his hand was tucked neatly into Tzedef's elbow.

They picked up the pace for a couple of steps, catching back up to Aduni and Beech, then fell into step with one another and walked in comfortable silence.

Getting Beech and Sorecco's things was merely a matter of going up through the dungeon again, out the other door, and through a couple of rooms to where the items confiscated from prisoners were kept. Tzedef recognized Sorecco's pack and handed it to him, while Beech's specially made saddlebags were easily retrieved.

Aduni grabbed his own hammer off the weapons rack near the back of the room, and Sorecco's stick-and-bell was there as well, but, although Tzedef looked around, he couldn't see his mace anywhere.

"You left it at the tourism thing, remember?" Sorecco said when Tzedef asked if anyone had seen it.

"I wha—? Oh yes. Right. They required that all weapons be handed over, didn't they…" Tzedef groaned softly. "I shall have to stop back there and ensure that I retrieve it."

"Later, though." Aduni said gruffly, "Right now we're getting you lot out of the mountain as fast as we can. Until word spreads that the king's back, you're all still wanted, probably, and we don't know if or how far Cinnabar spread the word about you."

"Then how're we supposed to get out of the castle?" Beech asked, shifting uneasily on her hooves.

"Leave that to me." Aduni said, and turned to edge past her to the door.

Leaving the castle was surprisingly easy albeit nerve

wracking, but, once they were out, everything proceeded more smoothly than Tzedef had considered possible. They passed through the city unmolested, and when they got to the checkpoint and it looked like the checkpoint guard was about to say something, Aduni pulled a palm-sized crest on a ribbon out of his jacket and showed it to her. From the way her eyes widened and she hustled them through the gate, Tzedef gathered that it was probably best if he didn't ask.

He'd had enough of dwarven politics to last a lifetime, thank you very much.

It was with great relief that they returned to their inn, and, after apologizing profusely to Glim for the sudden lack of payment, paying her back for keeping their items, and piteously (mostly on Sorecco's part) inquiring if their rooms were still open, headed to those same rooms gratefully.

Tzedef didn't even bother to take off his boots. He fell into bed and was asleep before the blanket had even settled fully over him.

The next two weeks were hectic. Reyfil mountain closed completely less than three hours after they'd left the mountain, and it stayed closed for four days. The fifth day, to Tzedef's surprise, when the gates opened again, Limnally herself delivered his mace to him, bringing along the blessing she'd promised and a message that suggested that it was probably better if he didn't try to come into the mountain again any time soon.

This suited Tzedef just fine, and he set about provisioning himself for his next trip.

"I'm going back to Vraka." Beech announced at supper one evening, and Tzedef blinked at her.

"You are? Why?" Sorecco asked incredulously, "Didn't you just get that invitation to come examine the amber as much as you'd like?"

"Yes…" She admitted quietly, and Tzedef's ears perked up.

"But that's wonderful! That's exactly what you wanted, isn't it?"

"It was." She said, staring down at her food. "I just… it's…"

She mumbled something and Tzedef leaned closer, his ears twitching as he tried to hear.

"Come again?" Sorecco said, frowning.

"I don't want to be underground any more." Beech said, "I don't- it was fine before, but now when I go into the mountain all I can feel is the millions of tons of rock, all pressing down on me, and it's *awful*. I hate it. I can't think about anything other than how much I want to be *out*…" She shuddered, and rubbed at her arms, hugging herself.

"It's awful." She repeated, and Tzedef sat back, watching her carefully.

"Are you certain?" He asked, and she nodded, silently miserable. "Very well then. If that is your wish, you can always come back in the future, when the memory is not so fresh. I doubt your invitation to examine the amber is going to expire any time soon."

"You think it'll get better?" Beech asked, perking up a little bit. "Really?"

"I think that you are very determined." Tzedef said firmly, "I doubt you will let *yourself* stop you from pursuing your passions."

Beech grinned a little at that, sheepish, but pleased, and Sorecco nodded slowly.

"Alright, so when're we heading back? Tzedef, I'm counting on you to be a shield. I didn't even manage to get Casey anything shiny to distract her, so she's gonna be in full force."

"Ah." Tzedef said awkwardly, and Sorecco stopped, turning to face him.

"What?"

"I… was not planning on going back to Vraka."

"You what?!" They both cried at once, and Tzedef winced, his ears flattening.

"I thought I made that clear from the outset! Once I found the candle magic, my intent was always to return to Fernil as quickly as possible!"

"Oh." Beech said weakly. "I didn't- that- I didn't realize."

"I don't actually remember you ever saying that." Sorecco said flatly.

"I apologize," Tzedef said, somewhat bewildered, "I could swear that I'd said that, several times at least!"

"Not that I can recall." Sorecco said, then shrugged. "Granted, you spent most of your time preparing with

Beech, so I don't know for sure, but from the sound of it, you probably forgot to tell her, too."

Beech nodded vigorously, and Tzedef grimaced.

"Oh. Well, the both of you have my sincerest apologies, but yes. My plan is to go down to Bacon, and then through there, west towards Precia. The road is almost a straight shot to Wellvish, and the port there is almost guaranteed to have a boat that would get me across the sea to Fernil."

Sorecco frowned. "What were you going to do when I needed to go back, if Beech was staying here?"

"Escort you, obviously." Tzedef said, puzzled that that was even in question. "The road directly west of Vraka leads in roughly the same direction, though it passes through Lindham and—"

"Do *not* go to Lindham!" Beech exclaimed loudly. "Just... *don't*. You don't want to go there. Trust me, okay?"

Tzedef blinked at her, taken aback by her vehemence. "Very well? If you insist. I shall do my best to avoid the place, then."

"Good." Beech said with a firm nod. "Do that. But anyway, leaving. I was thinking about heading out in a few days, honestly. Glim kept the cart in good shape, and all of our things are still there, so aside from picking up some more rations I'm pretty much set."

Sorecco frowned, drumming his fingers on the table as he thought.

"I... can be ready in a couple of days. Like you said, I mostly just need to pick up more rations, but I was going to see about a furred cloak or something, too. It's been getting colder up here, and I don't want to freeze on our way back down."

Tzedef grimaced. That was a point. It *had* been getting colder, and while his coat did a lot to keep him warm, something else to help block the wind wouldn't go amiss.

"How 'bout this." Beech said slowly. "Why don't you travel with us to Bacon? That's about halfway to Vraka, and down south enough that none of us are likely to freeze to death, even if the weather *does* turn nasty. Rain is easier to deal with than snow, after all, and camps are nicer with friends."

Tzedef nodded thoughtfully. Putting his departure off for a few more days wouldn't hurt anything, and he did truly enjoy Sorecco and Beech's company. Having them as traveling companions again would be nice.

"Alright." He said eventually. "We'll do that, then."

So they did.

Procuring a pair of thick cloaks was easy enough, and Beech and Sorecco gathered the supplies they needed (and some they didn't), and a few days after Beech's surprise announcement, they set off.

The trip south was surprisingly smooth. There were no surprise storms, no random hedges in the middle of the road, no bandits or highwaymen... it was simply travel, and that in itself was a pleasant change from the town of Reyfilton.

All too soon, they reached Bacon, and though they stayed in the village's tiny inn together for a couple of days, eventually Tzedef headed out on the road west, heading for Precia.

CHAPTER FORTY-SIX

Epilogue

Day 34,
Month of Life,
Year 3297

Sorecco,

I hope you will excuse the presumption, but of late I find myself wishing for conversation. The road is very lonely without you, or Beech, or Casey, and though it was something I was used to at one point, now I find that the silence wears on me, so I while away the time composing letters to you. It only occurred to me recently that I might write them down so that I could send them. I hope that you may have Casey read yours to you, if that is not too great an imposition.

Since we parted in Bacon, things have become decidedly odd. At one point I found myself being stalked by a pixie, who, when she realized I had seen her, flew away. Either she has become much better at stalking, or she has yet to return, but either way I find myself wondering what her purpose was.

I send this letter from Fort Laketon, and, should you wish to reply, you may address your letter to Anself. That is the next town of note along my route, and from what they tell me here, it also has courier facilities, so I have written ahead and asked that they hold any mail addressed to me there. If you do not wish to correspond, simply do not reply and I will not think to trouble you again.

Hopefully your friend,
Tzedef.

Day 36,

Month of Life,

Year 3297

Casey,

I write to you in the hopes that this letter finds you well. Our trip north went better than expected in some ways, and worse in others. I did manage to find and retrieve the candle magic, but unfortunately we ended up rather entangled in a dwarven succession crisis. All is well, and Sorecco and Beech are on their way back to Vraka as I write this.

As for myself, I am heading to Wellvish, in Precia, so that I might return to Hecate's temple as soon as possible.

Do not worry, both are adequately provisioned, and Beech is quite capable.

As an aside, do you mind if I send letters to Sorecco through you? I do not think you would, which is why there is a letter to him in this bundle, but if you would prefer I not, then I will, of course, abide.

Tzedef

Day 41,

Month of Life,

Year 3297

Dear Tzedef,

What do you MEAN you left them alone!? Anything could happen to them on the road between Bacon and Vraka! You were supposed to come back with them, dammit! I don't care how capable Beech is! I trust YOU! I barely know Beech!!!

(There is a section that has been scribbled out so blackly that nothing underneath it can be read.)

Day 10,

Month of Science

Okay. He's back. He's safe. That's everything I could have asked for, I guess, but you and I are gonna have WORDS the next time I see you, mister! You don't just bait and switch on a girl like that! Besides, how'm I supposed to make sure that YOU'RE safe and sound if you just take off?

Of course I don't mind you sending Sorecco letters through me! I'll read him whatever you send, okay? So you have to write often, just so we know you're doing well.

Sorecco already told you about the apartment, so I'll mostly skip that. It's a really nice place, though! Two whole bedrooms! And a living room! This really is the height of luxury.

I'll write you more later, okay?

Casey

Day 10,

Month of Science,

Year 3297

Dear Tzedef

Don't be stupid! Of course we're friends! And of course I want to write to you, though Casey is already complaining about how sore her wrist is. (He's made me re-write the beginning of this letter three times, now! Of course it's sore!)

Beech and I made it safely back to Vraka, as you can probably tell, and Beech pretended to be my girlfriend when we met up with Casey. Beech tells me that the look on Casey's face was absolutely priceless, and judging from how hard she was laughing, I believe her!

Still, it's nice to be back somewhere I can start to consider home. Oh! I almost forgot to say! Casey bought us a flat! Not rented, *bought*. I'm almost afraid to ask where she got the money, but her job as a bouncer seems to pay really well, and she says that she saved everything she made for the entire time we were gone, so I suppose that makes sense? Still, the place has two bedrooms, which seems like it'd be super expensive. Either way, it's a place to live, and it's already starting to smell like home.

Casey already had my spinning wheel set up for me

when I got here, and I've been working my way through the batts that I was given by the women of Maplemore. I hadn't realized how much I missed doing this, to be honest. Just sitting down to spin after a long day melts any stress away, I highly recommend that you try it, at least once.

Anyway, Casey is complaining about her wrist again, so I suppose I should let her stop writing. I'll definitely write to you again though, so keep the letters coming!

Your friend,

Sorecco

Day 11,

Month of Science,

Year 3297

Dear Tzedef,

Oh, I see how it is! Sorecco and Casey get letters, but nothing at all for poor old Beech? For shame, sir! For shame!

I tease, I tease. I'm not actually upset, though it would have been nice if you'd checked in on me as well!

You'll be happy to know that my letter of permission to examine the amber has started to open a LOT of doors for me! I might even end up with an actual team whenever I decide to head back up there! For now though, I think I want to take the winter and just relax here at home. There's always next summer for another expedition out somewhere to see what kind of cool rocks they have! Hells, I hear the Sand Sea has sand that makes glass that GLOWS! Isn't that neat! I'd love to know how it does that! Maybe if I go out there, I'll find someone who can tell me! Or maybe I'll DISCOVER why! That would be amazing!

Anyway, Kaz wants to know what you think of the candies, and did the air candies work well, and did you want to order any more because they think they can get a delivery made and sent over to Wellvish to meet you there, if you want.

Write me back!

Beech

Day 20,

Month of Science,

Year 3297

Beech,

My sincerest apologies for not including you in my initial batch of letters. I will endeavor to include you in the future.

I am glad to hear that your efforts are paying off and that you are getting the recognition that you deserve after working so hard for it. It only pains me that it seems as though this recognition fully hinged on your ability to gain access to something that has long been considered off limits.

But perhaps that is me being cynical.

Perhaps it truly is just recognition of your own hard work that is finally coming through for you.

I have enclosed a letter for Kaz with this one, detailing the information that they asked for. If you could make sure it gets to them, it would be appreciated. As well, while I would greatly appreciate more of their Candied Consumables, I do not quite trust the mail system with any gold that might be required, so I must respectfully decline their offer.

I hope that your efforts bear all the fruit you desire,

Tzedef

Day 20,

Month of Science,

Year 3297

Sorecco,

Thank you for your letter, and your reassurance. I am pleased that you consider us friends, even though I must return to Fernil.

As I traveled between Fort Laketon and Anself, I found myself thinking more about what Queen Victoria said. About how my lack of magic and inability to use magical items may be a Gift of some sorts, and may be controllable. I do not think she is correct, but something whispers to me 'what if' and I find myself worrying at the thought as though it were a sore tooth.

It is a bothersome thought, and one that I wish had not come up, for I previously found it easier to accept when I only believed my lack to be something imposed on me from an outside source. A curse, or birth defect. To hear that it may be something from within, something that I should be able to learn to control… the thought is maddening. I find myself dwelling on past situations and previous ills that may have been mitigated by the magic that I should have known at that point. The thoughts circle my mind, and refuse to settle until I feel as though I must be half mad.

But enough about my ills. You mentioned spinning. Have you already found customers for your yarn? Or do you spin simply for the joy of it? I do trust you have reached some sort of arrangement with the local Weaver's Guild, for I do not think either you or Casey wish to uproot your lives again.

My next stop will be Tremblinton, and the couriers here in Anself assure me that there is mail services there, so you may address any letters you may choose to write to me there.

Your friend,

Tzedef

Day 30,

Month of Science,

Year 3297

Dear Tzedef,

You don't need to apologize for anything! Like I said, Sorecco came back safely, and that's all I could really ask for, you know? Still, I *am* a little sad that I didn't get to properly say goodbye to you, so you'll have to make sure you come back at some point in the future, okay? After you deliver your candle magic, of course.

My job is going great, thanks for asking! I really like my boss, and it's always fun getting to toss people out on their ears. They never seem to expect it, coming from me.

Inral's trick is REALLY useful for getting knives and bottles out of the hands of drunk people who really shouldn't be handling them! I'm starting to build up quite the collection! I don't know if you'll see her again, but if you do, tell her I say hi and that I hope the feather dye is working out well for her!

Don't run into any trouble you can't get out of!

Casey

Day 2,

Month of Family,

Year 3297

Beech,

I am glad to hear that you have received a teaching position for the coming year. Congratulations are certainly in order, though I do hope that this doesn't mean that you will not be traveling as you seemed to wish to in previous letters. One should always have the opportunity to pursue one's passions, and your passion for your chosen field shines brightly indeed.

Casey tells me that you and Kaz have begun to court, which means that congratulations are in order for that, as well. I hope the two of you will be very happy together. They certainly seemed fond of you when I met them before. Should anything happen, I am always available if you require my assistance with rendering them... well. Out of commission, I suppose one could say.

Tzedef

Day 12,

Month of Family,

Year 3297

Dear Tzedef,

It's good to hear that you made it to Linderwell safely.

After the forest fire incident on your way to Tremblinton, I was worried that something worse would happen.

Granted, a troupe of Brownies intent on robbing you at 'sword' point isn't exactly as safe as I'd've liked, but hearing how you managed to talk them around into becoming your bodyguards for the rest of your trip was HILARIOUS! It's honestly probably for the best that they got bored and left, though. Brownies can be... odd. I heard of one guy who bribed a couple of brownies for years to clean his house, only to one day wake up and find that his whole house had been taken apart and put back together upside down!

I'm not entirely sure that's true, come to think of it. That'd take some pretty powerful magic to do in one night, right? But it's still a funny story, so I won't dismiss it entirely.

This letter will get to you in Wellvish, so when you write back you should tell me what it's like! It's a port city, right? Like Tyona and Natari? But I heard it's also the capital of Precia, so it should be different, too, right?

I hope you aren't planning to try to cross the sea as soon as you get to Wellvish. I heard that the autumn storms are going to be worse this year than last, and only get worse the closer to winter it gets. It worries me. Please, if you can, wait until next summer to make the crossing. I know that getting the candle magic home is important to you, but it isn't worth your life.

Besides, you can't deliver anything if you're dead.

Still, you'll do what you feel you need to, and I shouldn't try to tell you what to do. I just hope you'll be careful, okay? I need you alive to keep telling me tales from around the world.

Always,

Sorecco

Day 13,

Month of Family,

Year 3297

Dear Tzedef,

Something happened today.

I...

I never expected to see him again. Not ever. I don't even know what he was doing here, but he came into my work, drunk as a lord, and started threatening everyone...

Did you know that Inral's trick can be reversed?

You can move stuff away from you, just as easily as you can move it to you.

Rugar is dead, and I...

I don't know what to do.

Everyone tells me it was the right thing to do. My boss is pleased with me for protecting the bar.

I wasn't protecting the bar.

I panicked.

I was scared.

I…

I'll write you more later.

Okay. I'm calmer now. Part of me considered just burning the other letter, but… I feel like you, of all people, would understand. So.

I got another job offer, a couple of days after that. Someone saw me using Inral's trick, and they wanted to know if I was any good at it. I said I was passable, and they asked me a few questions. They called it transposition, which is as good a name as anything, I guess. The job seems alright, and I won't have to quit working at the bar, so I think I'll take it.

Your letters make Sorecco really happy. Thanks for that. He won't tell you, but I think he's been having a hard time at the university. People making things harder on him just because he's not like them.

Idiots.

He's going to be ten times the bard they'll EVER be.

Be safe,

Casey

Day 16,

Month of Family,

Year 3297

Dear Tzedef,

I finally started classes! I've only been to a few so far, but it's been incredible! I'm already learning so much; the teachers are amazing, and the other students are so talented! I'm honestly worried about keeping up, but don't worry! I won't fall behind! I'm going to graduate an accredited bard if it kills me!

(Don't worry, I won't let it kill him.)

I'm in an elocution class, which I wasn't sure I needed until I heard the instructor speak. Her words were like snow, crisp and clear and clean. It was mind boggling. And then she just, on a plat, flipped to speaking like a Permani farmer! Apparently the class is not just to teach people how to speak clearly, but how to pick up any accent they please, to best either blend in with a populace, or to more clearly convey a tale! I can't WAIT to learn this!

There's so many people here, from so many walks of life. I thought it would mostly be nobles and merchantfolk, and there's plenty of those, but there's a surprising number of people like me. Commoners. People who grew up farmers, or herders, or fishers, or forestfolk. And the teachers treat everyone the same!

I can't wait to learn more.

Your good friend,

Sorecco

Day 25,

Month of Family,

Year 3297

Dear Sorecco,

I cannot promise that I will not book passage across the sea until next summer, because I have already done so. My ship leaves in a week, and the captain assures me that the sailing should be relatively smooth. The trip should take about three months, and I will be landing in the port city of Sinlae, in Qifal. You may address future letters there, and I will be sure to read all of them when I arrive.

I am glad that your classes seem to be going well, and that you are eager to learn. Please do not, however, work yourself too hard. Winter is, after all, a dangerous time, and it would pain me greatly to find out that you have fallen ill.

Rest assured- however you do in your classes, no matter where you place in the rankings, or how you do on exams, we, your friends, and your family, are proud of you. You are working hard to accomplish your dream, and that is what matters most.

Your friend,

Tzedef

Day 25,

Month of Family,

Year 3297

Casey,

It is with sorrow that I read your letters, and it is with the humblest of apologies that I write this. If I had managed to track the man down, it would not have been up to you to kill him.

Before you worry, I do not blame you in the slightest. He nearly killed you before. He had proven himself a brute of a man, who would not learn from his own mistakes despite given plentiful opportunities to do so.

You have no doubt heard this from others, but I will reiterate it.

You did the right thing, Casey.

It does not matter that you were scared.

You defended yourself. You defended your co-workers.

You did the right thing, and I do not think less of you.

If you need to, I am always here for you to write to,

and I will do my best to provide a comfortable shoulder on which you can lean.

Tzedef

Day 7,

Month of Night,

Year 3297

Dear Sorecco,

Yes, I have now finally arrived safely in Sinlae. The ship was delayed slightly by several storms, but none of them were particularly bad, nor were we ever in any real danger.

I am more than glad to have solid ground beneath my feet again, however; three months at sea is, as I have thought before, far too long.

As it is now deep winter, the deserts of Qifal are bitterly cold, and I find myself quite put out with the weather. Luckily, my journey to Teskan will take me south and west, and the forests of Jalsemett and Pratopal tend toward milder weather. I have no doubt that that will mean plenty of rain, but rain I can deal with.

I am pleased to hear that your classes are proceeding well, and that your tutor in the art of the lute is working well with you. I do not think that evening meals with wine are typically part of the tutoring experience, but I was tutored by scholars many times my own age as a child, so perhaps things are different when one is roughly the same age as one's teacher.

Nevertheless, your progress is prodigious, and I look forward to hearing you play when next I visit. Next year sometime, perhaps. If, of course, it would not be an imposition.

My next stop will be in the city of Bestiln.

Your friend,

Tzedef

Day 25,

Month of Death,

Year 3298

Dear Sorecco,

Please assure Beech that I have not yet forgotten her.
However, my supply of writing equipment became soaked
by the rain, and so I must rely on what I can purchase from
the couriers to write replies. The prices are quite
exorbitant, and so I must fit all I can in the least space
possible.

If the rain has done anything, it has given me the
resolve I need to begin attempting to suppress my… Gift. If
that truly is what it is.

I am not quite sure how to do so, but the ability to
use magic bags is something that I can no longer overlook
as 'unnecessary.' Not if I am to continue to correspond
with you all regularly.

Casey, while your tales of mischief are entertaining,
I do wonder if you are perhaps growing a touch reckless. I
worry for you. Please, I entreat you, be careful. Even
putting aside the fact that it would destroy Sorecco to lose
you, I myself have a hard time imagining a world without
you in it.

I do not think I will be able to write again until I reach Teskan and can requisition more writing supplies from the temple, so please direct all letters there. It will take me at least a couple of months to arrive, so do not worry if you do not hear from me until the month of Truth.

Yours,

Tzedef

Day 16,

Month of Self,

Year 3298

Dear Sorecco,

As promised, I have arrived safely in Teskan, and, aside from gaining lodgings at the temple and handing over the Candle Magic, the first thing I did was retrieve the letters left for me at the courier's office.

I did not expect such a pile, but it is heartening to know that I was thought of through those cold months.

I am equally glad that this last winter seemed to be nowhere near as bad as the winter before. That thought had worried me a great deal, and I must admit that I tried to get to Teskan all the quicker, just to reassure myself that all was well.

Spring will be dawning soon, and with it, planting season. I assume that your classes will be letting out around then, so that those with duties at home may see to them? What do you plan to do? Will you travel? Or do you plan to spend more time with your tutor? I recall you saying in one of your letters that he hailed from the lake village not far from the city.

Teskan, too, is near a lake, though to be honest,

calling the Lekato Sea a lake is doing it a grand disservice. Luckily, the temple is on the other side of the city from the docks, because to tell the truth, I am not overly fond of the smell of fish.

The high priest at the temple was overjoyed to receive the candle magic, and I was highly praised for completing the quest. There was even talk of promoting me to a senior position in the temple, but I declined. The static life of a priest is not for me; I prefer to wander as I may, and do what good I can in the world along the way. Hecate, at least, seems to understand that, and granted my petition to remain free of temple life.

I will be in the city of Amri, next.

Tzedef

Day 33,

Month of Peace,

Year 3298

Dear Sorecco,

While I do not think it is my place to intervene in the arguments between Casey and yourself, I also, in this case, think you may not be being entirely fair to Casey.

It is not her fault that your tutor turned out to be a philanderer, nor is it her fault for pointing it out. Would you rather have remained ignorant until much later? Or know now, when you could cut ties with him without ruining your potential grades? As it is, this provides you ample opportunity to find another tutor. One who is, perhaps, more professional?

Still, as I said, I do not wish to be seen as taking sides. I only wish for your continued happiness and well-being. You have worked too hard for your dreams to be dashed due to one man.

You are an incredible person, Sorecco, and I know you have what it takes to succeed. If you disregard anything else I say in this letter, do not disregard this- I believe in your ability. I know you can do this.

I will be wandering through several small towns in

the near future, but I believe the next place with mail service will be Rilton.

Always,

Tzedef

Day 3,

Month of Day,

Year 3298

Dear Sorecco,

Please convey my well wishes to Casey- It is my hope that she has recovered well, and that all has returned to rights.

Yes Casey, I know you are reading this to Sorecco, but it is polite to address the addressee, rather than the one doing the reading.

As we approach the summer solstice, I cannot help but wonder what sort of festivals Vraka and the surrounding towns must put on. Here, things are relatively segregated, with each town holding their own celebrations. There, I wonder if it is more like the festival I witnessed in Natari, with people coming from all around to celebrate together.

If you can, will you visit the festival for me, and write to tell me about it? I find myself missing both of your company more often, now, though I feel as though I should have long since re-accustomed myself to traveling alone. Hearing about the fun you will have at a festival may help things feel not quite so alone.

There is not much to say, recently. Things have been relatively quiet, with only the occasional farming accident to heal. I have spent much of my time traveling around the south of the continent, since to return to Yaelin requires me passing through Tremaine, and, for a multitude of reasons, that is not the best idea for me. Luckily, the south is quite a big area, and there is much for me to explore.

I will write again when I have something interesting to report.

Yours,

Tzedef

Day 42,

Month of Science,

Year 3298

Dear Sorecco and Casey,

Please accept my fullest apologies for not writing for so long. The last two months have been remarkably empty, and so I have, in my boredom, begun to circle back around towards Teskan. I believe that I may spend the winter at the temple, and then, next spring, return to Malfeir and make my way to Vraka. I hope this plan meets with both of your approval?

You may, of course, tell me to take my plan and shove it, and I will not think to trouble you again. Letters are, after all, little substitute for the presence of a friend, and I would not blame you were you to feel as though we have grown distant.

I will write to you again soon, I promise,

Please address your next letters to Janston

Tzedef

Day 11,

Month of Law,

Year 3298

Dear Sorecco,

Very well! There is no need to shout! I will take it as
a given that I am welcome in your home, then, and will plan
accordingly. (I will, of course, send you a letter before I set
sail, so that you are not taken entirely unaware by me
simply showing up.)

Unfortunately, something else has come up, and
while I do not think it will interfere with my visiting next
year, it is something that rather urgently needs addressing.

On my way back to Teskan, I have begun hearing
rumors of people going to Teskan on trips, delivering food
for market, or going to buy odds or ends, and returning
changed. They say that they go there, and return with a
newfound god, even if they had previously dedicated
themselves to a different god. I have not heard of any
violence perpetrated by these changed people, or on them,
but it makes the scales on the back of my neck prickle, and
I do not like where I fear this is heading.

With that said, I am returning to Teskan as quickly
as possible to assure myself that Hecate's adherents are
well and unaffected, and, if possible, to get to the bottom of

this.

I remain, as always, your friend,

Tzedef

Day 5,

Month of Emotion,

Year 3298

Dear Tzedef,

That sounds worrying. I don't know what's going on in Teskan, but that really doesn't sound good. Please be careful?

What am I saying. I know you will be. You're always careful. I'm sure everything is fine, and this is just going to be a matter of people not approving of a newly formed god. It'll be fine.

You'll be fine.

You're a tough guy, after all!

Things are going alright over here! I did what you suggested, and found a new tutor. I'm kinda mad that it took so long, we're already halfway through the school year, but Emelia is really good, and she's introduced me to an instrument similar to a lute called a mandolin. I think I prefer the lute, honestly, I like the tonality better, but Emelia is sure that learning the mandolin as well can only help me develop my ear.

It's weird, but the more I learn, the easier I find my Gift coming to me, and the more depth I can perceive with it. I feel as though I'm getting more information than I should be, if that makes any sense? I don't know. It's hard to explain. Still, it seems to be helping in some of my classes.

Master Eldrin has been talking about an assignment that we're supposed to be getting officially at the close of the school year, for spring. Something about unearthing the history and lore of a magical item. People are already scouring the pawn and junk shops, since rumor has it if you bring him something cheap or common he fails you on the spot. I was thinking I might do my project on my little bird. I haven't heard of anything else like it, after all, which means it must be pretty unique. I know that'll make it harder to figure out, but I think it'll be worth it! Maybe I'll even impress him!

Let me know how everything goes, okay?

Yours,

Sorecco

Letter Undeliverable

Day 31,

Month of Emotion,

Year 3298

Dear Tzedef,

I know that it was probably just a delivery error or something, but my last letter was returned to me, so I thought I'd try sending it again, with this note. Write me back when you get this, okay? Casey says you're probably fine, but I can't shake the feeling that something is wrong.

Your friend,

Sorecco

Letter Undeliverable

Day 15,

Month of Night

Year 3298

Tzedef? Is everything okay? I know we've gone longer without hearing from you, but this is getting worrisome.

Sorecco

Letter Undeliverable

Day 15,

Month of Night,

Year 3298

    Tzedef, this isn't funny. Sorecco's starting to freak out, and I'm getting worried too. Write us back, even just to tell us to fuck off, or I'm going to start having to call in whatever favors I can so we can find you. I swear to my fifth grandfather, if you're just avoiding us for some reason I'm going to tear you a new asshole.

Casey

Letter Undeliverable

Day 1,

Month of Death,

Year 3299

Okay, we've officially passed concerned and gone straight to pissed off. Sorecco is frantic. Where the hell are you that the letters are being returned marked undeliverable!? Fuck, at this rate Sorecco's going to leave school and head for Tyona to try to catch a ship across the sea to look for you. I'm only partly exaggerating, by the way. You'd better be hurting, and hurting bad, or I'm going to kick your ass for making him worry like this.

Casey

Letter Undeliverable

www.ingramcontent.com/pod-product-compliance
Lightning Source LLC
Chambersburg PA
CBHW030737030726
47497CB00001B/21